A restored family, a renewed hope...

a new
promise

A restored family, a renewed hope...

a new
promise

julie eller

TATE PUBLISHING & *Enterprises*

Published by Tate Publishing & Enterprises, LLC
127 E. Trade Center Terrace | Mustang, Oklahoma 73064 USA
1.888.361.9473 | www.tatepublishing.com

Tate Publishing is committed to excellence in the publishing industry. The company reflects the philosophy established by the founders, based on Psalms 68:11,
"The Lord gave the word and great was the company of those who published it."

Book design copyright © 2007 by Tate Publishing, LLC. All rights reserved.
Cover design by Melissa M. Griggs
Interior design by Lindsay B. Behrens

Published in the United States of America

ISBN: 978-1-60247-482-6
07/06.11

Dedication

This book is dedicated to my precious Lord, giver of all good things. It is my heartfelt desire that You will use this book to Your glory, to further Your kingdom, and to encourage those who are struggling with difficult life circumstances. May Your steadfast love be experienced by each person seeking You, and may they experience Your Holy presence and peace when all seems hopeless.

> May the words of my mouth and the meditation of my heart be pleasing in Your sight, O Lord, my Rock and my Redeemer.
>
> Psalms 19:14, NIV

Acknowledgments

First and foremost, thanks to my Heavenly Father, for inspiring this story and for opening the doors that led to its publication. You are an awesome God, and the writing of this book was an incredible journey in grace and submission to Your calling. I desire nothing more than to write the stories You inspire for the rest of my life.

A big thank-you to Dr. Ali Samii, University Of Washington and Harborview Medical Center Neurology Service/Movements Disorders Clinic. Thank you for carving out a precious hour of your day to meet with me three years ago. Your insights were invaluable. I have no doubt that you are a blessing to the patients and families who seek your expertise.

Thank you, Mary for doing my "first read." We go way back, girl, and I cherish the memories. You are an amazing woman of faith, a powerful prayer warrior, and friend without equal. How I'd love to have the chance to do one more trail ride with you before all we're capable of riding are rocking chairs!

Thank you to my husband, Mike, our sons, Bill and Chris, Mom, Chet, Bill and Judy, and sisters/brothers-in-law for your support and encouragement. Know how precious each of you are to me. I am truly blessed by your presence in my life.

Many thanks to everyone at Tate for your belief in me and your enthusiasm for this book. May the Lord bless you richly as you follow His vision for your ministry.

Thanks, Cherie, for your friendship and support through this process. It's my prayer that the Lord will continue to use you to reach those in need of comfort and encouragement.

Thank you to readers who have spent their hard-earned dollars to read this story. May you find it a source of encouragement and hope, and a reminder that our Lord watches over each of us faithfully. You are not alone.

Prologue

The headlights cut through the summer night, approaching the darkened brick building at a steady forty miles per hour, illuminating the shrubbery and reflecting their light in the darkened windows. A 1992 Chevy truck cut across the sidewalk onto the manicured lawn, stereo blaring, sinking deep ruts into the dew-kissed grass.

"Turn down the freakin' radio, Dwight!"

"Gonna make me?"

A third voice hissed, "Will you idiots shut up? Come on, Parnell, do your thing, and let's get out of here!"

"Hold on." Swinging his denim-clad legs down from the truck bed, a dark-eyed youth uncapped a flask of Black Velvet, took a long pull, gained his feet awkwardly, and saluted the window directly ahead.

"How's it going, Mom, huh? Still hanging in, I guess."

Wasn't that the truth. Hanging around in this joint almost a year and you couldn't prove it by her. Lying in her bed, right through that window. If he wanted to, he could probably even see her. All he had to do was walk right up there, stick his head over the sill, and look in. If he wanted to, which was a definite no-way. Lying there with a tube down her throat to breathe for her and a tube in her stomach to feed her. That wasn't any way to live. Course, it wasn't living, was it? It wasn't living if a person couldn't see a new day beginning or talk to the ones they loved, or even eat a meal, for cryin' out loud! When his time came...well, *his* time wasn't going to come. That decision had already been made; no way was he sticking around for *this* kind of exit.

"Come on, Parnell, let's get out of here!"

"Will you *chill,* Dwight!"

"Yeah, show some respect, Dwight."

Snickers and a loud, drunken belch overrode the music that fairly rocked the pickup truck and vibrated the ground it stood on.

Removing the cap, he tipped the bottle to his lips again, then wiping his mouth with the back of his hand, took aim with an unsteady arm and let the bottle fly, arcing in slow motion, making contact with the narrow glass window with a loud crash. Behind him, a chorus of voices erupted in dismay.

"What are you *doing,* Ty!"

"Come on, man, let's go!"

Body swaying, he blinked as lights flooded the grassy area, hearing the lone siren approaching in the distance.

"Whaddya think of that, Mom? You awake *now?*"

"Come *on,* Parnell, move!"

Great idea, if only he could get his legs to cooperate. Feeling the Velvet drape his senses like a snug blanket, he heard the grinding of gears and smelled the exhaust as the pickup roared across the grass, tires thumping loudly as they made the drop from curb to street, then heard the squeal as rubber grabbed pavement in a frantic race against time.

The county patrol vehicle, lights flashing but siren thankfully silenced, pulled up on the street, two deputies exiting the cab of the green and white Explorer.

"Put your hands where we can see them, son."

A numbing darkness approaching on fluttering wings, Ty muttered, "I'm not your son," dropped to his knees and then face-first onto the grass, the hovering darkness relentlessly taking possession.

Chapter 1

"You're about at the end of your assets, Scott, but I guess you already knew that or we wouldn't be talking."

The attorney's words ringing through his mind, Scott Parnell made his way toward home after an hour's worth of bad news on a beautiful June morning. Exiting the highway that left Wenatchee, Washington, in his rearview mirror, he made his way toward Blewitt Pass, waiting for the tension to lessen as he made the climb in elevation toward the small town of Shuksan, and home.

It promised to be another flawless June day, which meant good haying, both swathing the uncut alfalfa as well as drying the grass that lay waiting for the baler to move down the rows, turning the mound of loose alfalfa into snugly tied bales. If not for this unavoidable trip to consult with his attorney, he'd have been in the field a couple of hours ago. As it was, he'd lost the better part of the morning at the time of year when every hour counted, but it couldn't be helped. After delaying longer than he should have, he'd finally made the call, and now he had the answers he'd feared.

"Washington is a no-fault divorce state, Scott, which means Rachel won't need an attorney. In most cases, you wouldn't need legal advice, either, but we both know this isn't an ordinary case. I would recommend that you obtain a notarized statement from Rachel's primary physician, stating her condition, to present to the court, and also documentation of the costs associated with her care facility. But, Scott, you need to make a decision soon. I know how difficult this must be for you, but it's my job to advise you of your options, and this is where the rubber meets the road, my friend."

Needing air, Scott cranked the window open and breathed deeply of the rich summer air. The comforting aroma of freshly mown hay with a hint of manure wafted into the cab, and he allowed these familiar smells to distract him from his thoughts. For a moment, he'd felt as though he were suffocating, replaying the attorney's words in his mind. The prospect of having this conversation with any other attorney was nearly beyond imagining, but this was Peter, and they'd grown up together; splashing in the shallow waters of the Icicle River as kids, casting their fishing lines into chilly alpine lakes on lazy summer evenings, and ice-fishing on bitter-cold winter days. Then later, through high school, when their days were no longer lazy during summertime, bucking hay bales and driving trucks filled with wheat to the storage elevators. They'd been as close as brothers in those days, and Scott had some great memories of the days before Peter's path had led him from the quiet mountain town to Central Washington University in Ellensburg, and then to Gonzaga Law in Spokane. His friend had chosen to hang his shingle in Wenatchee after passing the bar, preferring to return to a more rural area, though his education and talents could have taken him to far broader fields, and certainly greater financial opportunity. But, as Peter was fond of saying, "Money ain't everything, bubba." Scott shared those same sentiments and respected his friend for his spirit of humility and service in providing legal services to those who struggled financially and otherwise. Peter had a reputation for willingness to represent those struggling in abusive marriages and those with limited financial resources.

It humbled and pained Scott that he numbered among these, as far as the financial piece of it. He and Rach had had none of the other issues Peter routinely dealt with; their marriage had been one of mutual trust and respect. But those days were gone forever, and now they existed only in his memory and in the kids' memories. It was impossible to know if Rachel possessed conscious thought at any level; he'd been advised that it was unlikely. No, these days Rach existed only in the most basic biological sense, with none of the essence of her very *Rachel-ness* remaining. There were no magic potions or new treatments coming down the pike, no new wonder drugs still in clinical trials, and no hope for recovery.

In the dark hours of the night, he sometimes wondered what had happened to his life, wishing himself back ten years, or longer, to the days when they'd been just another young couple raising their babies and forging their paths toward the future, but as his mother had often remarked during his childhood, when he'd wished aloud for something beyond their means, "If wishes were horses, son, we'd all ride."

"We'd all ride," Scott mused, eyes drawn to the passing landscape. The only ride Rachel would be taking would be a short trip in Bill Palmer's special Cadillac to the quiet cemetery at the hilltop overlooking Shuksan. The ride she'd have taken weeks ago if he'd respected her wishes.

The weekly visits he made on Sunday afternoons, dressed in his cleanest jeans and shirts that sported uncomfortably tight collars and trading his John Deere cap for a black Stetson, were more for Tawnya than for himself anymore. Chattering away to her prostrate mother, sharing stories of her prize rabbits and new kittens, recounting highlights of the school week, Tawnya accepted the mechanisms that kept her mother's body functioning. She was a favorite of the nurses, bringing homemade cards and drawings and seeking the comfort of feminine contact much like a bee searches a flower for pollen. And why wouldn't she; what twelve-year-old girl didn't need a mother to help her make the transition from childhood to womanhood? Problem was, when these women went home at the end of their shifts, they had their own daughters waiting for them, and Tawnya was left with the promise of Sunday afternoons in her mother's silent and unresponsive company.

He hoped Rachel was no longer aware of the fact that Ty's shadow had never crossed the threshold of the nursing home's entrance. It had been all he could do to get Ty in the truck on Christmas Eve, and then once in the parking lot, he'd refused to enter the building. Weary of fighting, Scott had taken the path of least resistance and stopped trying, and now it was just he and Tawnya each Sunday.

Dropping speed to an even twenty-five, he made his way through town, unconsciously slowing, as he always did, as he approached Fircrest Manor, where Rachel resided in that shadowy world somewhere between life and death. Someone had sure done a number on the front lawn, Scott noted, peering closely at the damaged sod. Kids, probably, tanked up and without one rational thought between a half-dozen guys. His foot hit the brake hard, noting that the window in Rachel's room was boarded up. He debated making a quick stop but then decided that if Rachel had been affected, Fircrest would have called. As far as late night phone calls went, whether it involved Ty or Rachel, no news was definitely good news.

Accelerating again, he made his way through the quiet streets. Coming to the other end of town, he glanced casually at the Kittitas County Sheriff's Department and froze. A red and silver Chevy truck with enormous tires was parked in the lot, mud-flecked and sporting a Shuksan Bears bumper sticker. Ty's truck. Turning into the parking lot, Scott pulled his own pickup to a stop next to Ty's, threw the door open, and dropped his feet to the asphalt, wincing as he worked the stiffness out of his protesting joints. Noting the collection of beer cans and cigarette butts littering the bed of Ty's truck, he drew a deep breath and turned resolutely to the building's entrance.

The dispatcher, an older woman dressed in a blinding lime green blouse, glanced up, greeting him politely.

"May I help you?"

"Yes, ma'am, my son's truck's parked out front, the 'ninety-two Chevy. I guess I'm wondering if he's here?"

"Would that be Tyler Parnell?"

Heart sinking, he replied, "Yes, ma'am."

The woman rose from her chair, revealing a matching pair of green slacks.

"If you'll just have a seat for a minute, I'll notify Sheriff Clark that you're here. Would you like a cup of coffee?"

Declining, Scott sank into a plastic chair. Had Ty's truck been parked in the yard when he'd left for Wenatchee at six-thirty? He hadn't paid any attention, which didn't say much for his parental observational skills. Sure, his mind had been filled with the upcoming meeting with Peter, but that didn't excuse him from his basic responsibilities. Rubbing his eyes, feeling a headache building, he leaned his head back against the wall, willing the pressure behind his temples to dissipate.

"Scott?"

Scott opened his eyes, wincing as the glare of fluorescent lighting teased the aching behind his right eye into a full symphony. Rising to his feet, he met the other man's extended hand with his own.

"How're you doing, Jim?"

"Not bad, Scott, and yourself?"

Shrugging, he said, "Oh, keeping busy, you know, up to my elbows in haying right now. But I guess I've got another problem at the moment, don't I?"

With a wry grin, Jim shook his head. "Your words, my friend, not mine."

"So what's going on?"

"Well, that's where we're kinda fuzzy. We had a call from Fircrest about twelve-thirty this morning, disturbance of the peace. Bunch of kids out front in a truck, whooping it up, just making a lot of noise at first, but then somebody threw a bottle, busted a window out."

The light dawned.

"Rachel's window."

"Evidently. Anyway, by the time we got there, the truck was gone, and Ty was standing out front. Got there just in time to see him pass out. Now, he's fine, Scott. I've kept an eye on him through the night, and he's awake now. Doesn't have the best head, mind, but he is awake. Want to come on back?"

"Not really, but I'll follow you."

Following the deputy through a set of double doors, Scott let out a low whistle.

"You've got a regular Motel 6 here, Jim; you leave the lights on for 'em."

"Yeah, and if you're in the mood for lace curtains and blueberry muffins, this ain't the place for you."

"Wouldn't be even if there were muffins."

Stopping before the third cell, Jim pushed the unlocked door open.

"Rise and shine, Ty. Somebody here to see you."

The figure on the cot lay silent for a long moment, then slowly rolled to a sit. Casting a glance at the door, upon seeing his father, he groaned, dropping back to the mattress.

"Come on out of there, Ty. Let's talk in my office."

Scott stepped aside to allow his son to pass through the cell door. At the moment, he couldn't have uttered a word if his life depended on it. The sight of his son through bars, unlocked though they may have been, was something he could have lived a lifetime without. The boy wouldn't even look him in the eye, which he guessed shouldn't be a surprise.

Following Jim and Ty through the lobby into a small office, Scott sat in the chair Jim indicated with a wave of his hand.

"How you feeling by now, Ty?"

Casting a sullen glance at the deputy, Ty replied, "Just dandy."

Leaning back in his chair, ignoring the ominous squeaks of protest emanating from the hydraulic mechanism, Jim eyed the youth sprawling in the chair across the desk. Shifting heavily onto his left hip, he reached into his right pants pocket, produced a key ring, and tossed it onto the desk. Watching the boy's eyes flicker for an instant, he continued, "Thought you might recognize these. Your truck's out front; somebody dropped it by a few hours ago. Interesting that they knew right where to find you, don't you think?"

Not deigning to reply, Ty shrugged his shoulders.

Glancing at Scott, Jim straightened in his chair and steepled his fingers on the desk.

"What happened over at Fircrest last night?"

Eyes still on the key ring, Ty replied, "Don't remember."

"I'd personally prefer not to play games this early in the morning, so let's cut to the chase, Tyler. Tell me a story. Tell me how somebody gets it in their head to vandalize a nursing home in the middle of the night, scare a bunch of elderly people out of their wits, and end up passing out while your buddies leave you hung out to dry."

Ty flashed a resentful glare.

"That's not what happened."

Scott broke into the conversation, "Then let's hear what did happen, Ty, and I mean now."

Turning a baleful eye toward his father, stifling a yawn, Ty shrugged his shoulders again.

"Nothin' to tell."

Silence hung in the air for a few moments, then Jim spoke, "Fircrest isn't going to press charges. This time. But you'd better think twice before you pay a midnight visit to your mother again. You hear me, son? We all know about your mom, Ty, and people are willing to cut you a little slack. But only a little, and just this once, you understand?"

"Whatever."

Observing the boy for a long moment, Jim straightened in his chair, springs protesting once again.

"Go on with your dad now, you're free to go."

Scott reached deftly across the desk, snagging the key ring as Ty reached his arm in the same direction.

"Not a chance, Tyler. Go wait in the truck. *My* truck."

The men stood silently as Ty brushed past his father through the office door.

"Thanks, Jim. I appreciate it."

"Nothing to thank me for, Scott. I didn't call you after we brought him in because there wasn't anything more to do at that point and I figured if I didn't see you this morning, I'd give you a call. I didn't think you needed to lose a night's sleep over this."

"I appreciate it, Jim. I'm sorry about this, sorrier than I can tell you."

"Not your fault, old man. I wish I had some words of wisdom for you. I know he's going through a lot right now, but I also know the road he's traveling leads straight into the juvenile system, and I don't want to see that happen, Scott. Let me know if there's anything we can do for you, Susie and me, okay?"

"Thanks, Jim. Tell her hi for me."

"Will do. Hang in there, buddy."

Lifting a hand in farewell, Scott left the office, nodding to the dispatcher on the way out. Exiting the building into bright sunlight, he glanced at his watch. Ten-thirty. Sighing, he stood for a moment, hands on hips, watching his son, who sat with head leaned back against the seat, eyes closed against the brightness of the morning sun.

Pulling the driver's door open, he looked across the seat at his son. Seating himself behind the wheel, he held the boy's gaze briefly, then inserted the key into the ignition and fired the engine. Shifting to look over his shoulder, he backed the truck around and turned to re-enter the town.

"Why can't I drive my truck home?"

"We're not going home."

Silence.

"Then where are we going?"

Tipping a quick glance, Scott let his eyes pass over the tousled hair, seeing the pallor beneath the tan.

"Right now we're going to Fircrest, and you're going to take your lumps like a man."

Ty slumped lower in the seat, groaning.

"Can't I do it tomorrow when I feel better?"

"'Fraid not, Tyler. We've already lost half a day; it's not gonna happen again tomorrow. No way we're letting the day go by without dealing with this."

Pulling into the visitor parking area, Scott shifted into park and stepped out onto the pavement. Tyler sat still as a stone in the passenger seat, a mulish expression on his face. Rounding the truck and throwing open the passenger door, he barked, "Now, mister."

"All right, get off my butt."

"You've not even begun to feel me on it at this point."

Ty muttered something under his breath.

Scott demanded, "What was that?"

"Drop dead."

Eye to eye, father and son stood at the wide glass entrance, doors automatically swept open at the pressure of their feet on the sensors. Aware of the aide seated at the nurse's station, Scott spoke between gritted teeth, "After you."

Flanking Ty's left shoulder, Scott spoke to the aide, "Good morning. Is Mrs. Westin available?"

Smiling, the woman asked, "May I say who would like to speak with her?"

"Scott and Tyler Parnell."

"Oh." Smile fading, the woman's friendly manner was replaced by a business-like demeanor and she replied, "If you'll have a seat in the waiting area, I'll see if Mrs. Westin is available."

Dropping into another seat in another waiting room, Scott

looked about the silent lobby. Tasteful prints of mountain meadows and cerulean blue lakes hung on the walls, and a tall vase of silk flowers stood on a table. As many times as he'd come through these doors, this was the first time he'd sat in these chairs. Instead, four times a month his feet carried him through this lobby, down the main hall to the third door on the left, to witness the silent, ongoing physical deterioration of a wife and mother who had never intended to reach this point.

He himself had allowed Rachel to arrive at the state in which she lay suspended and unaware of the world around her, ignoring not only the conversations that had taken place in earlier years but also the signed document bearing her spidery signature, signed by a hand made unsteady by the jerking movements that had wracked her body. A living will. A piece of paper that bespoke her wishes to spare her family the emotional and financial burden of these unknowing, unfeeling mornings, noons, and nights that bled one into the next, relentless and unending.

"Promise me, Scott, that when the time comes for the ventilator that you won't let them do it. Just let me go."

Just let her go. As if the words could make the action easier to accept. She'd moved beyond knowing the difference about anything in her world eight months ago, and, contrary to her wishes, he'd been unable to watch as she struggled to draw air into lungs inhibited by a body frozen into paralysis. So, a promise made had been a promise he'd been unable to carry through, for the kids' sakes as well as his own, he'd argued with himself. Now, though, he was forced to re-examine his motives in light of Ty's behavior last night and ask himself a difficult question: How much harder was it on the kids to have Rachel "alive"?

And now for the real clincher. How was he expected to make the decision to "pull the plug," discontinuing the feeding tubes and respirator, knowing he was escorting her through death's door, which had swung open in invitation ten years ago when Huntington's disease had tightened its painful grip on Rachel's body.

Knowing Rachel's expressed wishes, how could he hold on to the decision not to?

Ventilator settings, feeding tubes that needed replacing every so often to prevent infection or blockage, urinary catheters, sponge baths, and bedsores.

She'd be appalled if she could see herself and, he knew, miserably disappointed in him, but how was he supposed to make the decision that would end the body's struggle for survival and allow the soul to be at peace?

He'd believed in God's promise of eternal life, believed that He'd prepared a place for Rach in that special place where there was no sickness or pain, just as he knew without a doubt that Rachel had been ready to join her Heavenly Father months ago. The sticking point was himself, and he struggled with the enormity of the responsibility he held as Rachel's husband. So he held on, and Rachel held on, but what was he holding on to, and for whose benefit?

Half an hour later, he and Ty walked back out the sliding glass doors, their mission complete. Ty had grudgingly expressed remorse for his actions and had agreed to repay the cost of replacing the window he'd broken, as well as to replace two sprinkler heads destroyed under the tires of his truck. Now, back at the sheriff's department, Scott shifted into park, handed Ty his keys, and said, "Go home. Get some rest."

"What about the baling?"

"You're in no shape to be running equipment. Get yourself and your truck cleaned up and turn on the irrigation in the alfalfa."

Not meeting his father's gaze, Ty nodded. Scott folded his arms across his chest, leaned a hip against the truck, and said, "I want you to think about what happened last night and also why it happened, Ty. 'Cause I can't quite believe you ended up at Fircrest on accident. And your mom's window didn't get broken out on accident. I know you're angry, son, and I understand. I really do. But it's not your mother's fault, and I won't have you behaving like it is, got it?"

"Yeah."

Shifting into gear, "Okay, I need to get going. I'll see you tonight."

He watched his son pull out of the parking lot and turn toward home, feeling inadequate and helpless in the face of the Tyler's rebellion. Jim had hit the nail on the head; his son was headed down a dangerous path and either didn't see it or didn't care. Either way, the path was a treacherous one, and the view at the end of the trail wouldn't be worth the trip. They could surely use a miracle about now, but Scott wasn't holding his breath on that one. It was pretty obvious that they were on their own.

Chapter 2

The process of haying had come a long way from the early days the Parnells had farmed the valley he called home. Back then, haying was a backbreaking chore that required a team of horses pulling a hay wagon and strong men swinging scythes and pitchforks under the summer sun, always keeping a keen eye out for rattlesnakes. Sitting in the air-conditioned cab of his Massey-Ferguson swather, Scott could listen to the farm report on the AM/FM radio or, after hearing market prices for soybeans in the Midwest or price per pound for weaner hogs, could plug a cassette tape into the slot below the radio dial. He enjoyed haying, which was a good thing, as he made a living doing custom haying and harvest, keeping him busy from May through September. There was nothing like the sweet perfume of freshly mown alfalfa on a warm summer morning.

The first cutting of hay, which was usually a faster process because the grass was still a little thin coming off winter, happened in late May. The second cutting could usually be counted on being ready around the middle of July and the final cutting in September, right after wheat harvest. With Ty back in school and unavailable to run the baler, third cutting was always fraught with the worry that the weather wouldn't hold or that equipment breakdown would delay the completion of wheat harvest.

He had a good clientele built up, had done work for the same farmers for fifteen years, adding new clients occasionally, some as far as fifty miles away. This particular job, the Reardan's, was one of his favorites; close to home and in a beautiful setting with the jagged granite peaks of the Stewart Mountain range visible while making the pass over the southwest end of the meadow.

Used to be he'd had his own land to tend as well as the custom jobs, but this year, now that the last two hundred-acre parcel was gone, he no longer had to take into consideration how many jobs he could handle on top of his own spread. No, those days were gone for good and except for the ten acres the house and barn stood on, all that remained of the home place, he had no responsibilities or ties to the land that had been passed down five generations. Land that he'd relinquished with sorrow and guilt but the price of which had enabled Rachel to receive quality nursing care. Only when he looked at his children did he feel a pang of regret that this generation would mark the end of the tradition begun over one hundred years ago, when the grandparents of his parents had settled and cleared this land acre by back-breaking acre. There had been eight hundred acres, fine land that had nurtured livestock and grown seed crops, now whittled away to a little over ten acres.

In the foothills of the east slopes of the Cascade mountain range, the Shuksan area was blessed with fertile soil, abundant water in lakes and streams, and dotted with Ponderosa pines and Douglas fir. Fields of golden wheat lay fringed with forest and offered spectacular views of the Cascades. Range cattle grazed under the blue sky, and nearly every ranch boasted a horse trailer; kids growing up here were avid horseback riders, both for work and for pleasure.

Finishing the final sweep that completed the actual mowing of the hay, Scott brought the swather out of the field onto the frontage road, making his way slowly to the large pole building across the yard from the Reardan's house. Bringing the swather to an idle, then switching the engine off, Scott reached for his empty lunch box, wiped his face with a threadbare blue towel, and exited the cab. Dropping to the ground, he grimaced as his legs, stiff from sitting for several hours, became accustomed to the sudden shock of holding him upright. He wouldn't see forty again, and his body delighted in rubbing his nose in this little detail. Rolling his shoulders and neck from side to side, he checked his watch, debating whether or not to make a couple of passes with the baler. Five o'clock, which left him plenty of daylight. Time being money, there was no question that he could get a good couple of hours of baling in before the evening dew set in, ending the process for another day.

Timing was everything for this part of the haying process; baling damp hay that hadn't been allowed to cure in the sun until completely dry, or had been saturated with rain, was asking for trouble. Mold, unhealthy and dangerous for livestock and, strangely enough, fire. There had been several barn fires over the years, resulting in the total loss of the buildings and contents, even livestock. Hay that had been insufficiently cured before baling emitted a gas that was highly unstable, leading to spontaneous combustion, so it didn't pay to be in too big a hurry for this part of haying. Depending on how large the area he was haying, before Ty was old enough to operate the baler, he'd finish cutting a job, go to the next and finish cutting there, then return to the first to do the baling. Working in a systematic fashion of rotating through his clients, he'd managed pretty well. Now, with Ty on his third summer of running the baler, it had taken some of the pressure off himself, allowing him to add to his client list, augmenting his income. He didn't like to think about how he was going to manage when the day came that his son wasn't here to help keep things running smoothly, or how he was going to buck all those bales from field to truck, then from truck to hay shed by himself again; his body continuing to remind him that he wasn't twenty any longer.

Ty. And Peter. What a morning it had been.

Keeping an eye on the neat rows of downed hay, Scott slowly made his way down one row after another, the large machine giving birth to tidy bales tied with baling twine. He always felt a deep satisfaction during this part of a job; seeing the end result and experiencing gratitude for nature's beneficence.

Rachel. And Tawnya. Worries that rode shotgun more days than not and were never far from his thoughts.

One of the things he missed the most was the luxury of knowing at the end of a day spent haying or harvesting wheat that upon his return home, dirty, hot, and tired, there would be a hot meal waiting, a cool shower with freshly laundered towels and clean clothes waiting in the drawers. Of course, it had been several years since he'd actually experienced this luxury, but there wasn't anything wrong with his memory.

It had been three years since Rachel had been able to cook. Unable to function safely in the kitchen because the uncontrollable jerking body movements made it unsafe for her to operate burners or handle knives, under considerable duress she'd hung up her apron for good. There had been several minor burns and spills of hot liquids, but the incident that had brought an end to the denial under which Scott himself had been laboring, had involved a boning knife and Rachel's left hand. Tawyna had been helping her mother prepare stew on a winter afternoon, chopping vegetables while Rachel had diced the meat.

With a child's eagerness to please and an insight that belied her tender years, Tawnya had ensconced herself in the kitchen during meal preparations months before, when Rachel began having increasing difficulty performing routine tasks. Tawyna had absorbed practical knowledge and food safety tips, soaking up her mother's instructions like a sponge, seeming to understand that it was vital that she do so at this time.

On that winter afternoon, snow swirling outside the windows, Tawyna had worked alongside her mother in the cozy kitchen, pausing to peer through the window on the oven's door at the chocolate cake baking inside. Across the kitchen, she had heard her mother's dismayed cry along with the simultaneous clatter of a knife falling to the floor and turned to see a gash in Rachel's left hand, blood spraying the counter. Screaming for her father, Tawnya had stood frozen in place, watching her mother's blood saturate the counter, run down the side of the cupboards, and pool on the linoleum. Scott and Ty had arrived from different ends of the house, each through a separate door, and while Scott's feet had skidded to a dead halt at the scene unfolding before him, Ty had had the presence of mind to grab a thick towel, wrap his mother's hand, and apply pressure above the laceration. A frantic trip to the tiny local hospital's emergency room on an icy road had ensued, Tyler continuing to hold pressure to his mother's hand. After cleaning and numbing the area, inserting twenty-three stitches in three layers of tissue, and administration of a tetanus booster, Dr. Morgan had taken Scott aside.

"I understand that this was a kitchen injury. I must say that I'm amazed that something like this hasn't happened months ago. She simply mustn't be allowed to prepare meals, Mr. Parnell. I'm sorry, but that's as clear as I can make it."

Before Rachel had been discharged, the doctor had had a similar conversation with her. Limbs more active than usual because of her agitation, Rachel had wept, pleading for a prescription that would help her maintain her independence for just a while longer, which had been deferred to consultation with her neurologist. They had been advised that she not attempt to climb stairs any longer due to the risk of unsteadiness and falling. She was also to bathe or shower only with an aide, with falls again being the concern. The doctor had informed Scott bluntly that his wife was in the late middle stages of Huntington's disease, moving rapidly toward the day when she'd be dependent on total care, unable to feed herself, unable to move her body at will, and unable to communicate.

They'd known the diagnosis, of course, had known for two years at that point, but denial was a common occurrence in both patients and families, or so they'd been told by three neurologists and compassionate strangers at Huntington's support groups. Rachel had been experiencing vague symptoms for the past six years, which she had tried to withhold from her husband and children. The symptom complex had begun when she was thirty-one, with a segue from her normally placid, calm demeanor into bouts of moodiness and depression, occasionally lashing out in unexpected outbursts of temper. This progressed into a period of exaggerated sexual appetite, which left Scott torn between enjoyment of the eagerness of Rachel's responses and a vague disquiet at the changes in his wife's personality.

Returning to the fragrant summer evening, Scott sat numbly in the cab of the baler, amazed to see that seven o'clock had come and gone; dusk was falling and crickets were chirping. He'd gotten quite a bit more done than he'd expected, which was always good. Work had been his focus over the past few years, keeping his mind and body occupied as well as keeping the money rolling in, for there wasn't ever enough money these days. Inpatient care was morbidly expensive, and he'd finally sold off the last of his land. Fircrest was paid up through October; what he'd do then was a nauseating fist in his stomach. His desperation had led him to his friend, who had broached the possibility of divorce. If, no longer financially responsible for Rachel, the State Of Washington picking up the tab for her care, he'd be spared the agony of making the decision to remove life support.

The money wasn't there, that was the bottom line. He supposed he could go down to the bank and take out a home equity line of credit on the house, buy himself, and Rachel, some time, but what then? A monthly payment on the house that his parents had owned free and clear when they'd passed the property on to him? It just didn't sit right. That, and the fact that he'd be worse off financially than he was now, having to worry about a mortgage payment on top of everything else.

But it was Rachel, and what else could he do? Bring her home? Expect the kids to change her diapers, turn her every couple of hours so that she wasn't as likely to develop bed sores or pneumonia, and monitor IV sites for infection or blockage? No way was he going to allow that happen. He'd thought about Catherine, but dismissed this as quickly as he'd considered it; a seventy-five-year-old woman had no business nursing a completely dependent grown woman, even if it was her daughter. She simply didn't have the stamina.

Regardless of how he weighed his options, turned the possibilities over in his mind, he ended up in the same place every time.

He couldn't afford to pay Fircrest, and he couldn't afford not to. *"Just let me go, Scott. Promise me!"*

If he still believed that it would do any good, he'd pray, but he'd given up on that quite awhile ago. The prayers of supplication, of desperation and, in the end, of anger and accusation, all seemed to have gone unnoticed. It was pretty clear that whatever God was doing these days, He was doing it in someone else's life, someone more deserving of His attention than Scott himself.

Nope. Prayer was for those who still had some hope left, not for those who no longer believed anyone was on the receiving end. He'd save God the trouble of being bothered while He went about the obviously more important business of helping others and just do his level-best to deal with his problems on his own. If his best hadn't been enough, then he'd just have to step up his efforts. When there was a will, there was a way, right? My will, my way. When it came right down to it, what else was there?

He turned toward home, a vast emptiness filling him completely.

Chapter 3

*H*e always enjoyed washing his truck, washing the mud away in brownish-yellow suds, leaving the paint clean and shining. Flipping the valve on the hose, Ty moved slowly from front to back, sending water sheeting across the hood and cascading down to the gravel. Unable to resist, he placed a thumb over the end, pointed the hose at Skip, and removed his thumb, sending a jet of water toward the dog. Shaking himself vigorously, Skip approached with a grin; this was their routine and one they each enjoyed, although it was a toss-up who would be drenched more thoroughly by the time the water had been turned off. Sending another spray of water toward the dog, Ty grinned as Skip disappeared around the bed of the truck, only to reappear a moment later, eyes alight and asking for more. Accommodating him, Ty groaned, "No, Skip!" as the dog moved into a mighty whole body shake, sending droplets of water every direction. Tennis shoes soaked through, Ty made his way on squishy feet to the spigot, turning off the water.

"Fun's over, bud."

Yep, that was for sure. Last night had been fun, up until the guys had ditched him in front of Fircrest and taken off in his truck. He still couldn't believe they'd actually bailed on him. He wished he could remember how he'd come to be there; his memory was strangely fuzzy on certain points. Deputy Clark said he'd passed out, which he knew had to be a load of garbage because he never passed out, it was the stuff of legend among his buddies. He'd also said that Ty had thrown a bottle through Mom's window; apparently somebody inside the building had reported to the dispatcher that she'd seen him do it. Well, Jim Clark and his old man had grown up together, kicked up their own ruckus in high school, and were still thick as thieves, so it stood to reason that he'd kiss up to Dad.

What was the big deal about a little Black Velvet, anyway? The way his dad had looked at him at the jail, you'd think he'd taken the scissors to his mother's pictures or something. He'd never known his father to be a hypocrite, and he'd heard stories about some of his shenanigans when he'd been in high school, so it wasn't like *he'd* been so lily-white himself.

But maybe the fuzzy memory was something else entirely. Perhaps it was That Which We Never Speak Of, the dark cloud that seemed to hover over himself, his father, and sister as though they would never again break through to the sun's warmth.

They never spoke of Mom's illness, and the uncertainty of the legacy of Huntington's that may or may not have been bequeathed to Tawnya and he before they'd even been born. On a scale of one to ten, with ten being the worst thing he could imagine, this uncertainty came in at about seventy-seven. Even worse, there wasn't anyone he could talk to about the situation; Dad had an invisible mask that dropped over his features whenever he'd broached the topic, and Ty had learned to not even go there. Aside from a few conversations he'd had with Dwight, it was unthinkable to show this kind of vulnerability to his friends, and Tawnya was just a kid. So, he didn't talk about it. But he'd stumbled across something that *did* help.

As long as the liquor store stocked Velvet, he had no worries. It was only when reality crossed his path that he suffered the anxiety of his situation. Was it any wonder that he preferred stumbling around drunk to being sober?

Because I'm sick like Mom, that's why. I'm gonna end up out of my mind and staggering like I'm drunk even when I'm not, walking that way every day, until I can't walk at all.

He reminded himself that until he was tested, he shouldn't borrow trouble, that he had a fifty-fifty chance of testing negative for the Huntington's gene that was passed seemingly randomly from generation to generation. He hadn't fully understood the ramifications of the disease process in relation to Tawnya and himself until he was fourteen, when Mom's symptoms had taken an erratic downturn. He'd sat in a sterile office with his parents and a genetic counselor, who had shown him diagrams and explained in words an adolescent could understand that Huntington's was a debilitating degeneration of the brain and central nervous system. He'd discovered that day that he could undergo genetic testing if he so desired, to know one way or the other whether he faced the same devastating deterioration of body and mind, but that he'd have to wait until he was eighteen to do so. The guy might as well have said he'd have to wait ten years rather than nearly four; a lifetime to a fourteen-year-old who lived every day with a mother who could no longer cook, descend the stairs to the basement to do laundry, drive her children to school events, or remember half of what was said to her.

Well, he'd survived three years since that horrible session at the University of Washington Medical Center's Genetics Clinic. In four months he'd be eighteen, and the day after he planned to be rolling up his sleeve for the needle. One way or the other, good news or bad, he needed to know. It was hard enough trying to keep his grades up to graduate high school, much less look on to college; what earthly good would a college education do someone who was just going to turn into a vegetable anyway?

Tears burned his nose, stinging his eyes and cranking his temper up a notch. At this rate, he'd turn into such a girl that he'd be in playing Barbie with his sister. As if on cue, Tawnya appeared at the front door. Wearing one of her father's thin undershirts over jean shorts cut high over chubby thighs, she leaned down to absently scratch a mosquito bite on the side of her right calf.

"Ty?"

"What?"

"What are you doing here?"

"Washing the truck, what's it look like?

His sister reminded him of a yearling heifer, Ty thought uncharitably. Gawky and ungainly, she was about as graceful as a bull in a china cabinet and every bit as charming. It wasn't her fault that her clothes looked like something a sixty-year-old woman would wear, considering Grandma was the one buying them, but it surely wouldn't kill her to wash her hair more than once a month. And, Ty noted with frank embarrassment, his sister needed a bra. His sister needed quite a bit more than some personal hygiene tips and a brassiere, though. Ty himself was running low on socks and under-wear; it didn't help that Dad raided his sock drawer regularly. Mom would have curled up and died if she could see her family's shabby appearance.

Dad just didn't seem to have a clue.

Tawnya's voice broke into his reverie, "No, I mean, what are you doing at home instead of working with Dad?"

"None of your business."

"Where are you going?"

"Turn the irrigation on the alfalfa." Turning the key and firing the engine, upon lifting his gaze, he grunted in exasperation. Tawyna stood in front of the truck, stubbornly fixed in place.

"Come on, Tawnya, move it!"

"I wanna come."

With a longsuffering sigh, Ty reached across, threw open the pas-senger door, and said, "Come on, then."

Climbing into the cab, Tawnya wrinkled her nose and kicked a crumpled Alpine Burger bag aside.

"You're such a pig. Want me to go get a garbage bag?"

"No."

"Be a slob, then."

Checking his watch, Ty queried, "What's for supper?"

"I told Dad I was making spaghetti, but we don't have any ham-burger in the freezer, so we're having scrambled eggs and waffles."

"You know the old man hates that, Tawnya. 'A man wants to eat a real meal when he sits down to supper,' remember?"

"Well, I can't help it, Ty. Grandma hasn't come to take me gro-cery shopping, and we're almost out of everything. I took the last loaf of bread out of the freezer this morning."

The stupid water could run a while longer this time. This was a good excuse to go into town, drop Tawnya off at the grocery store, and give him a chance to try to run Dwight to ground, find out what had actually happened last night.

"Let's go change clothes and then we'll go into town, Tawn. I'll drop you off at the store and then come back and pick you up."

Following Ty up the stairs, Tawnya hurriedly made her way up the stairs to her room, removing and folding her clothes neatly.

Digging her favorite pair of jeans out of the dresser, she struggled to pull them over her hips and dropped flat onto her back on the bed, forcing the zipper closed. This was progress, then; a couple of weeks ago she hadn't even been able to bring the edges together, so it was working, miserable as it was.

And to think that when she was a little kid, she'd hated it when she was sick to her stomach. Now, it was just something she did every day. What went down soon came back up. Not her favorite moments of the day, but who could argue with success?

She crossed to the closet, pulled out a blue and green plaid blouse, and slipped it over her shoulders and dealt with the buttons. Examining her reflection in the mirror, she quickly pulled a brush through her hair, wincing as the brush made contact with the snarl of tangles that hung at the nape of her neck. A round face with brown eyes looked back at her. A smattering of pimples dotted her chin, cheeks, and forehead. Before school had let out for summer, she'd had a flare of inspiration. She'd discovered Mom's old makeup in Dad's bathroom cabinet and removed the whole kit and caboodle into her bedroom one day, experimenting until she thought she'd had the knack of applying eye shadow and mascara correctly. Discovering the magic of both liquid and powder foundation, grown tacky with age, she'd buried those blemishes under a smooth coat of makeup, much like spreading Miracle Whip onto a slice of bread.

She'd been so excited, she could hardly wait for school the next morning; maybe now she'd fit in again with the girls who'd been her friends in grade school but who now seemed so much more mature. Between classes and at lunch, there was always a cluster of girls in front of the mirrors in the bathroom, freshening lip gloss and fluffing their hair. It all seemed a bit silly to Tawnya; everybody knew they had gym right after lunch. They'd just get sweaty and all their efforts would be ruined.

But she'd hung back, uninvited into the intimate circle of former friends now evolving into sophisticated teens; several already had had their thirteenth birthday. Some of them even had their periods. Not that she was jealous, of course.

The other girls, Kendra and Kara, Crystal and Ariel, had slumber parties every few weeks, invitations desperately coveted by any girl unlucky or unpopular enough to be excluded. Most Mondays after these sleepovers there could be overheard giggling reports of the hostess' mother applying beauty mud baths to rapt adolescent faces, of midnight feasts of pizza and brownies or ice cream sundaes and later, under cover of darkness, whispered tales of how it really felt to be kissed by a boy. Yes, those sleepovers were the epitome of social success in the complicated universe that was the seventh grade.

Tawyna had never been invited.

Now, standing in front of the round mirror hanging over the sink, the memory of her excited foray to school the day after she'd discovered her mother's makeup brought an embarrassed flush to her cheeks. She'd so carefully applied the sky blue eye shadow to her lids, struggled with the mysteries of mascara application, and had noted with great satisfaction that there wasn't a single pimple to be seen anywhere on her face. She'd skulked down the stairs and out the front door—anxious to avoid Daddy, who still thought she was about eight years old—just as the school bus rumbled into the yard. She'd figured the bus driver's raised and hastily lowered brows was just surprise that little Tawnya was old enough to wear makeup. Feeling smugly confident and amazingly grown up, her illusions and self-confidence were smashed to glittering shards long before the aroma of the cafeteria's Tuesday offering of beefaroni had wafted through Shuksan Middle School.

Blithely enjoying the fact that the other students had noticed the overnight transformation, first and second periods had passed in a glow of well-being. With the delicious anticipation of, for the very first time, freshening her own makeup, finally absorbed into the exclusive clique of girls who congregated before those hallowed mirrors, Tawyna pushed open the bathroom door.

"...even believe that she'd have the nerve to show up looking like that? I thought I was gonna bust out laughing when I saw her."

"What about that blush? She looks like she belongs in the circus!"

"She *does* belong in the circus."

Laughter rang through the room, echoing off the tile walls.

"And did you see how pleased she is with herself? Like she has no clue what a joke she is. If it were me, I'd worry more about those nasty teeth than makeup."

"Yeah, and it would sure be horrible if half-*Ton*-ya missed a meal!"

Somehow she'd known they were talking about her. Tawnya felt color rise in her cheeks, and her stomach cramped tightly. Clutching her purse tightly, she must have made a sound because each member of the group turned to see her standing in the door. A split second seeming to last an eternity; with a choking sob, she turned and fled on unusually agile feet down the crowded hall, past the administrative offices, and finally through the front door to fresh air and sunshine. Running until she had a painful stitch in her side, she bent forward, rubbing fists over teary eyes. Dropping wearily onto someone's lawn, she reviewed her options. No way she could return to school today; the thought of facing the fresh humiliation of the ridicule of her "friends" brought a fresh wave of tears to her swollen eyes. So, that left only one alternative.

Grandma.

She'd appeared on Grandma's front porch at 10:30 that morning, rung the doorbell, and waited, needing a tissue desperately. The door had swung open, and Grandma had appeared, taken by surprise.

"Tawnya, what on earth are you doing here? Come inside."

Following Grandma into the spotless kitchen, she'd made a bee-line to the roll of paper towels hanging above the garbage can, blew her nose vigorously, and dabbed at her eyes.

"Come and sit down, honey. Tell Grandma what's going on. What on earth do you have on your face?"

She'd sat with Grandma and the whole miserable story had come out, how she'd practiced so hard last night and woke up especially early this morning so she'd have time to get it perfect, how she'd been so proud of her appearance, and finally the excruciatingly painful scene in the bathroom and her resulting flight from the school.

"I'm so embarrassed, Grandma. I don't think I can ever go back there."

"I should think you'd be embarrassed, Tawnya; you're much too young to wear makeup. What on earth were you thinking? Well, it's done now and tomorrow's another day. Go on into the bathroom and clean that mess off your face, you'll feel better then. We'll have a little lunch and then I'll drive you home."

Sitting mutely, Grandma watching her closely, Tawnya hadn't bothered to correct her misconception, that the girls' scorn hadn't been because she was wearing makeup, but rather that she didn't know how to apply it correctly or, apparently, have the right makeup to begin with. Grandma wouldn't believe her, anyway. She was really old-fashioned; she didn't even wear pants!

She'd gone into the bathroom, filled the sink with warm water, and scrubbed her face clean, soaping and rinsing repeatedly. The pimples were back in full bloom, but at least the horrible black rings around her eyes from smeared mascara were gone. When she'd re-entered the kitchen, Grandma was on the phone talking to the lady in the office at school, explaining that Tawnya wasn't feeling well and would be back tomorrow. She'd given Tawnya a hug and then, true to her promise, had fixed her favorite deviled ham sandwiches, cut into fancy shapes with the crusts removed, just like they would at a proper tea party. She'd set their plates onto the little picnic table on the back patio near the climbing roses. After mixing some lemonade in a frosty pitcher, preparing a plate of sliced cucumbers and tomatoes and some sweet rolls hastily defrosted in the microwave, they'd eaten their lunch in the sunshine.

She knew Grandma loved her, and she loved Grandma, as well. When she was younger, they'd been really close, but for the last year or two, for some reason Grandma was becoming more critical of Tawnya. It was as if the older Tawnya became, the less Grandma approved of her. It was puzzling, because to her own mind, she hadn't changed; she didn't know what bothered Grandma so much about the fact that she'd be a teenager in three months.

Putting this worry from her mind, Tawnya's thoughts returned to this morning when Daddy was getting ready to go. He'd asked if she'd wanted to go along to spend the day with Ariel. He didn't know about the makeup fiasco or that Ariel was the shining star around whom the other untouchables orbited, hoping to reflect some of her radiance, and following her lead in the tormenting of lesser creatures like herself.

She'd sooner be smeared in honey and left for the ants than spend the day with Ariel Reardan.

Sometimes Daddy was as dense as a brick wall. He seemed to think that just because you were in the same grade with someone, you were automatically friends. When was the last time she'd had any friends to spend the day, much less the night? Of course, now she didn't have any friends to invite anyway.

The screen door banged shut, and the warning from below broke the silence, "I'm leaving in two minutes whether you're down here or not!"

Sighing, she switched off the bathroom light, retrieved her purse, and hurried down the staircase. Maybe they'd have some strawberry ice cream at Harvest Foods, the really creamy kind that had big chunks of berry in it. She'd use some of her allowance to buy some Hershey bars, the ones with almonds. Who cared whether or not they caused pimples or how many calories they contained?

A girl had to have something to look forward to.

Chapter 4

*C*eleste Malloy entered the Capital One Building, shaking raindrops from her umbrella, brushed the lapels of her silk jacket, and stepped into the waiting elevator. A June day in Seattle was often a rainy day, and today was no exception.

Thanking the occupants already in the elevator for holding it for her, she exchanged greetings with a financial analyst who worked a floor up from the firm. Setting her briefcase onto the floor, she noted that the button for her floor, forty-seven, was already illuminated. Leaning against the railing, she settled in to await the ascent into the clouds. The third passenger, a man in his late thirties with carefully coiffed blond hair ran a quick audit of Celeste's black pumps, long expanse of stockinged leg, and black skirt that skimmed an inch above her knees, meeting her eyes as he continued his appraisal. Flashing what he doubtless considered a winning smile, he exuded "lady-killer," confident in his charms.

"How'd you like to blow the morning off and spend it doing something more stimulating than taking minutes for the boss?"

Bracing herself as the elevator stopped on the twenty-third floor, doors opening to an empty hallway, Celeste regarded him coolly.

"Are you speaking to me?"

"And smart too. My lucky day. Yeah, sugar, I'm talking to you. For you, I'd ride right back down this elevator instead of spending the morning with some accountant broad."

Already fearing she knew the answer, Celeste asked, "Some accountant broad, hmm? Who are you scheduled to see?"

"Some woman my father set me up to meet," he replied, digging in his pocket for a card. "Here it is, Celeste Malloy. Some wrinkled old bat, probably. Anyway, what do you say, honey?"

"I have quite a full morning, thank you."

Celeste bent to retrieve her briefcase as the elevator stopped at the forty-seventh floor. As the door swept open, she preceded her client through the doors and into the reception area.

"Someone will be with you momentarily." Without a backward glance, Celeste continued through the open room into the hallway that led to her office. Gloria, the frighteningly efficient office manager, greeted her by name. From the corner of her eye, Celeste had the briefest impression of the man's double-take and smiled to herself as she continued into the hallway that led to her office.

Upon checking in with the reception desk, the client had casually—too casually—inquired, "Would that be the Celeste Malloy I'm scheduled to see this morning?"

"Yes, that was she. I'm sure it'll only be a few minutes until she's ready to speak with you."

"She's a good accountant?"

"Oh, yes, she's one of our rising stars, a candidate for full partnership soon. You'll be in very good hands."

"Terrific."

The client seated himself across from the aquarium with a heavy sigh, staring glumly into the depths of the crystalline water.

In her office, Celeste disposed of her jacket, checked her voice mail, and jotted a quick note to herself, "Lunch with Analiese, noon." Setting her briefcase on the desk, she removed the file she'd reviewed at home over the weekend.

Spencer Beckwith was the thirty-nine-year-old silver-spoon-fed offspring of an influential King County Superior Court judge and wealthy socialite wife, in and out of rehab several times, with two failed business ventures, three failed marriages, and more debt than he could shake a stick at. The financial ax posed over his irrepressible and irresponsible neck at this juncture, however, was held in the steely grip of the Internal Revenue Service, to the tune of a quarter million dollars in unpaid back taxes and penalties. His Honor had faithfully arrived on the scene with bailing bucket and mop several times over the years but apparently had reached both his financial and emotional endurance point and had finally called his good buddy, Jefferson Biddle, senior partner of Biddle, Barton, Sutton and Swales, Certified Public Accountants.

"I have a client I'd like you to take over, Celeste. His father's an old friend of mine, and I'd like you to handle this one. Judge Beckwith would be very grateful."

Never one to walk away from a challenge, Celeste had acquiesced. In the thirteen years she'd been a practicing accountant, she'd seen just about every financial crisis imaginable and relished the prospect of rolling up her figurative sleeves, burying herself deep in the Washington state tax journals, and picking the brain of the resident tax attorney.

Pulling her mind back to her client, Celeste repositioned the two-inch thick folder a fraction of an inch, then extended a cultured raspberry nail to the intercom.

"Sheri, I'm ready for Mr. Beckwith."

"We'll be right there, Celeste."

Settling herself into her chair, she pulled open the top drawer, gave her face and hair a quick once-over in the small hand mirror and slid the drawer shut as the knock sounded at the door.

"Come in." Rising to her feet, Celeste circled the desk to officially meet her client, hand extended in greeting.

"Mr. Beckwith, good morning. I'm Celeste Malloy. Would you like coffee? Sheri, would you…"

"Absolutely. Cream or sugar, Mr. Beckwith?"

"Both. Please."

The other woman exited silently, closing the door behind her.

"Please, won't you have a seat?" Celeste eased herself into her chair and met his gaze steadily.

Lowering himself uneasily to the edge of the chair Celeste had indicated with discomfiture, her client stammered, "Ms. Malloy, I want to, uh, need to apologize for that thing in the elevator; I had no idea…anyway, I'm sorry."

Smiling pleasantly, Celeste replied, "That's quite all right, Mr. Beckwith. I'm certain that any number of women would be flattered to receive an indecent proposal at eight-fifteen in the morning."

"But you aren't one of those women."

"I can see that we understand each other perfectly, Mr. Beckwith. Let's just put it behind us, shall we?"

"Uh, yeah, with pleasure."

Knocking discreetly, Sheri entered quietly, served the coffee and excused herself.

"Very well, Mr. Beckwith, shall we begin? I've had the opportunity to review your financials. I suppose the first thing I need to clarify is that it has, indeed, been two years since you've paid quarterly estimated taxes?"

Entering the break room nearly three hours later, Celeste drew a paper cup of cold water from the dispenser. Drinking it down in one shot, she closed her eyes in appreciation; her throat was dry and scratchy after her morning consultation. Moving to stand by the window, she examined the sky. Nothing but heavy, gray clouds, with more predicted to roll in from the Pacific, bringing rain off and on through the rest of the week.

On days like this, she wanted only to curl up in her sweats, pull a blanket over her head, and sleep. She'd called Seattle home for seventeen years now and had spent the first eighteen on the "dry" side of the mountains. If there was anything about Shuksan that beckoned to her, it was the memory of hot summer days and clear, starry nights. When she took the infrequent stroll down memory lane, the occasions that leapt from the darkest corners of her mind were the carefree days of summer, cannon-balling off Catfish Charlie's rock into the sparkling blue water of Carrot Lake. As far as she knew, no one really knew how the lake had gotten its name. She and Rachel had spent lazy summer afternoons poking around the lake, searching for the wild carrots they knew must have gone to seed. Other than the occasional beer can and rusted fishing lures, they usually rode back to town on their ten-speeds, pink handlebar baskets devoid of treasure.

Everybody knew about Catfish Charlie, though. He'd lived in a shack out near a huge promontory that overhung the east bank of the lake. He had pretty much been a hermit and kept to himself except every so often when he'd show up in Shuksan, driving his ancient motorcycle with sidecar, a relic from the World War II era. Spewing clouds of black exhaust, sputtering engine blasting the eardrums of all within city limits, Charlie's appearance in town meant two things; there was fresh lake trout to be had, and the Oasis Tavern would need to be hosed down after closing that night. Charlie was known for many things; his personal hygiene wasn't numbered among these.

Charlie had had another interesting mode of transportation at his disposal; an eccentric old boat he'd jury-rigged together from the fuel tanks of an old Cessna. Cut into half lengthwise, he'd welded the tanks together side to side, added floats to front and rear, and attached a couple of splintery wood planks for seats. A pair of mismatched paddles completed the aquatic ensemble. Despite wagers to the contrary, it had proven seaworthy and not just under its builder's command, either. Celeste had been the first, other than Charlie himself, to captain his prize vessel, and she'd walked tall and proud the summer of her fourteenth year, the only one, boy *or* girl, brave enough to take the dare to untie Charlie's eccentric vessel from the rickety dock, step into the rocking belly, and plant her rump onto the rough seat.

The dare had been to row out to the middle of the lake, where Charlie was sure to notice his boat from the vantage point of the rocking chair positioned on the sagging front porch, continue on to the opposite bank, leave the boat, and make her escape with the rest of the gang. She'd managed to get away from the dock and, after a few false starts, gotten the feel of the oars and, peering backward over her shoulder, rowed strenuously out into the depths. A roar of outrage split the quiet afternoon, and Celeste watched, pulse pounding, as Charlie disappeared into his cabin, reappearing with his shotgun. He'd actually fired into the air twice before Celeste had the presence of mind to abandon ship, catapulting over the side with an unceremonious splash, shot pellets peppering her skin. She'd swam for what had seemed like miles, intent on reaching the opposite bank, and only when she dragged herself onto the grassy bank did she realize that she'd lost Rachel's birthstone bracelet in her undignified leap overboard.

To this day, Celeste wondered why she'd been so set on liberating that bracelet right from under Rach's nose. It wasn't that it was an expensive piece of jewelry, nor did she care that the golden topaz

November birthstone wasn't her own, but she'd cared a great deal about the statement that her appropriation of the bracelet would make to her sister and her mother.

They'd taken notice when she'd arrived home on her bike that day, soaked from head to sneakers and with the color of high adventure in her cheeks. Distracted from their afternoon project of canning peaches, they'd come outside to cluck over her appearance like a couple of broody hens. Later that night, after the chafing ride home on the banana seat of her purple Stingray bicycle, the slivers that had worked their way from Charlie's miserable shipboard seating accommodations through Celeste's Levi cut-offs were causing the tender skin of her bottom to welt painfully. Discovering firsthand that it is an anatomic impossibility to remove splinters from one's own backside, she'd finally beseeched Rachel to put an end to her misery. They'd spent an uncomfortable hour in the bathroom, Celeste draped ignominiously over the edge of the tub, all thoughts of dignity and modesty evaporating as rapidly as the odor of the isopropyl alcohol, and stinging her pride as surely as the alcohol stung her lacerated skin. Armed with needle and tweezers, Rach had performed splinterectomy, scolding and digging for information as diligently as she'd dug for slivers.

Well, she'd wanted to know, and Celeste had obliged her, including admitting to the loss of the bracelet that lay somewhere on the rocky bottom of Carrot Lake. It was probably still there to this day, even though Charlie, the sidecar motorcycle, and boat were long gone.

The entire county had been stunned to discover that Charlie had been quite a wealthy old coot. An important-looking entourage in a rented Lincoln Town Car had appeared in town shortly after his death during Celeste's college years. Apparently, Charlie had hailed from Chicago, from whence he had fled three decades earlier, leaving behind a loving but bewildered family in a crenellated mansion on the shores of Lake Michigan. He'd simply traded one lake for another and had lived to bear out the truism that one man's shack was another man's castle.

You just never knew about people. The longer she practiced accounting, the more she pondered human nature; how a person dealt with his financial affairs was often strangely out of character with the rest of the person they appeared to be. Mother, for example, still working at seventy-four, selling auto, home, and crop insurance out of her home. To this day, Mother rarely sat down to a meal without the phone ringing with yet another frantic customer on the other end, complaining about the escalating cost of premiums or reporting that Junior had had *another* fender-bender.

Mother wouldn't ever retire, because to do so would be to admit that she was no longer useful. And to a lifetime devotee to the institution of caretaking, there existed no fate so dismal as not being productive, of not being *needed* any longer.

"Penny for your thoughts." Turning from the window, Celeste smiled at her friend.

"And you'd probably be overpaying. How's it going, Ana?"

Skin the color of caramel with a short-cropped cap of hair, Ana was a stunningly beautiful woman. Warm and genuine, she radiated kindness and good humor and had a low, melodious laugh that poured over a person like slow, warm molasses.

"Well, it's Monday, you know. Ready for lunch?"

"It isn't noon yet, is it? I've only been in here a couple of minutes."

Analiese shook her head. "Try half an hour, sugar."

Half an hour? "I can't believe it."

"Better watch yourself, Mizz Malloy; word's gonna get out that you're a mere mortal just like the rest of us around here; either that, or maybe you're in love."

"It'd be news to me too."

Ana chuckled, "And here I was sure I'd heard someone singing, 'Someday My Prince Will Come.'"

"Either your hearing's going or you'd better keep an eye open for him yourself. Now, are we doing lunch or are you just going to keep giving me grief?"

"I'd actually kinda figured on both, girlfriend."

Seated in a booth in the deli on the second floor, Celeste laid her menu at the edge of the table, spread her napkin across her lap, and fussed with her water glass, removing the paper cover from the straw and wiping condensation from the table where the glass had been placed by the harried waitress.

Observing this exacting routine, Analiese observed, "You're acting like a little old lady; a place for everything and everything in it's place."

"We old maids have our routines too. So, why don't you jump off my case and tell me what's going on with that gorgeous young thing you're living with?"

"You do not want to know, my friend; take my word for it."

"Keeping you hopping, is she?"

Pouring a packet of sugar into her tea, Analiese shook her head ruefully. "You don't know the half of it."

Settling her spine against the cushions, Celeste ordered, "Spill."

"Well, for starters, we're into menstruation and mood swings, still want to hear more?"

"Spare no detail."

"Okay. Did I tell you Tori and her friends from her youth group have been doing volunteer work at the teen shelter down on Pine?"

"Three hots and a cot for runaways and street kids, right?"

"That's it. Well, the youth pastor had challenged the kids to donate a few hours every week to the shelter, to kind of broaden their world view, you know? Give them a glimpse beyond their own front door, right?"

"Right."

"Well, Tori really got into it, you know, became 'invested' in these kids and would come home and tell me stories about their lives, about how a lot of them had been on the street since they were eleven, some of them have tested HIV-positive at thirteen, Celeste. It's enough to make me want to cry. But Tori, she's able to 'see' their world, I guess, because she's their age and can relate to them, at least on some level. So, she'd gotten really close to one girl, Dacia, who's fourteen and has been in and out of there for two years. She's been lucky, has tested negative up until two weeks ago. It just broke Tori's heart. She came home that night, crying like her heart was breaking and asking me how she could be more upset about this girl testing positive for HIV than Dacia herself. She must've asked herself the same question, because she answered it for herself right then and there; she said the girl who'd been Dacia was already dead and that there were ways of dying inside while your body just kept right on going. I tell you, Celeste, I had goosebumps when she said that. I'm worried about her. I mean, I think it's a good thing that she's involved in a ministry, but she's so enmeshed in it. It's such a harsh thing for her to be exposed to. I really don't know how to handle the situation anymore."

"I'm assuming you've brought the situation to the Lord in prayer?"

Ana nodded. "Oh, yes. Tori and I have prayed together too. I'm really struggling with the Lord's will in this, Celeste. I know that I need to step back and allow Him to work in her life, in His way and in His time, but it's hard to know when I need to follow my own instincts and when I just need to get out of His way and trust Him to protect her."

"I think those are the issues every parent faces, Ana, and I do think that sometimes parents can be too protective of kids, for all the right reasons. We don't know how the Lord is planning to use Tori in His service, but I believe that He is working in her life right now, and, hard as it may be, we need to trust that He knows what He's doing."

"In other words, 'hands-off?'"

"Not so much hands-off as placing her in the Lord's hands and trusting Him to protect her."

Ana sighed. "It's hard, girl. Really hard. I'll admit that I've tried to shelter her maybe more than I should, but it's a rough world, and I don't want her to lose her innocence too soon. And when I say innocence, I'm not talking about virginity. I know where she stands on *that* issue."

"She made the commitment, didn't she?"

"Yes, the 'True Love Waits' commitment. I'm really proud of her. She has such faith, Celeste. Sometimes I forget she's only fourteen." Ana smiled a thank-you at the waitress, then crumbled a cracker into her soup. "Sometimes I think maybe I should get her out of the city, find a nice, quiet little place that's more wholesome. But then there's the problem of finding a job that pays enough to support us."

Pushing a piece of lettuce around with her fork, Celeste speared a crouton.

"There are problems in small towns too, Ana, just on a smaller scale."

"I know. Remember, I'm a small town girl myself."

Analiese was a transplant from Mississippi Delta country by way of Stanford Business School, where she'd received a full academic scholarship, then returned to grad school to complete a law degree after passing the CPA. She'd come to Biddle, Barton, Sutton & Swales ten years ago, the single mother of a darling three-year-old. Married briefly in law school, she was raising her daughter alone. As she'd told Celeste, her husband had "looked good on paper, so to speak. Unfortunately, he wasn't the person I thought he was, but I wouldn't have Tori otherwise, and I'll never be sorry for that."

The women had bonded quickly for all that, on the surface, it appeared that they had little in common. They discovered that they shared a similar value system, as well as a strong faith in God, and had "adopted" each other early on. Celeste had watched Tori grow from a precocious toddler into a lovely young lady and had been Ana's confidant and prayer partner over the years.

Ana remarked, "It's times like this that I almost wish I had someone to help ground me, you know, balance the parenting thing out."

"If you want my opinion, Ana, you're doing a great job, and I don't think you'd make the tough calls any differently if there was a father figure involved. If the Lord has that sort of plan for you, and for Tori, then it'll happen when the time's right."

"I don't know, Celeste. It would have to be somebody awfully special at this stage in our lives."

Preparing for bed that night, Celeste recalled her friend's remark. *Somebody awfully special.* Perhaps the Lord did have someone for Ana. If He did, she had no doubt that he'd come onto the scene in due time. For herself, she was beginning to question whether marriage and family were a part of God's plan for her life, no matter how deeply she may desire these things. She did desire marriage and a family, so much so that the wanting sometimes brought tears to her eyes during her nightly prayers.

But, like Ana, her own standards were high. She'd pretty much given up on dating altogether; one disastrous date after another had finally left her cold to the prospect. She wasn't interested in meeting someone over drinks, was weary of seemingly innocent dinner invitations in which well-intentioned friends would ambush her with a single guy they'd managed to round up. She'd taken a chance on a web-business linking Christian singles, but had discovered that most of the men linked to the site were at least five years younger than she, if not fifteen to twenty years older. The few men who attended the Thursday night Bible study that she and Ana participated in were already married.

Finding Mr. Right hadn't been a single-minded focus over the years. She'd worked hard to establish herself professionally and figured that when the Lord's timing was perfect, He would bring her future husband into her life. She was now thirty-five and still waiting, but beginning to reconcile herself to the possibility that it just wasn't going to happen.

It wasn't as though she hadn't met some nice men over the years, even had a few repeat dates from time to time, but had been surprised and saddened to realize that even guys who claimed to follow Christ's path had certain expectations that she wasn't prepared to meet. While, for the most part, they had expressed respect for her commitment to purity, they'd never called and asked to see her again, either. The straw that had broken the camel's back was the last man she'd met for coffee after several weeks of e-mailing and telephone conversations. They'd dated for several weeks, and she'd begun to think that maybe, just maybe, this was finally the *one*. The wake-up call had arrived like a splash of cold water in the face when, after she'd invited him to her home, cooked dinner for him, he'd honestly believed he was entitled to a more intimate conclusion to the evening than she was prepared to give. When persuasion hadn't worked, he'd told her he loved her, fully expecting this to overcome her resistance. While a part of her longed to hear those words, in that moment she'd seen him clearly and known that this man would never truly respect her, would never truly love her. The words he'd flung at her as she showed him the door had stung like tiny stones striking her heart, and she wondered how she could have possibly been so wrong about him.

You don't actually expect to find somebody who agrees to no sex before the wedding, do you? What planet did you come from, anyway?

The next day, she'd cancelled her membership to the dating service.

After that experience, she'd ceased to actively search for The One, had moved ahead with her life, trusting that in the Lord's time she would hear Him say, "This is the one I have created just for you, Celeste."

Now she'd come to a place in her life in which she'd begun to examine her direction, career-wise and personally. She was on track at work with promotion to partnership looking good within a year. She'd worked long and hard to get to this level, with many weekends spent working at home after fifty to sixty-hour workweeks in the office. The demands of the job had cut into her time such that she hadn't even been home for several months, and her conscience was prodding her to take a weekend, leave work at the office, and spend some time with her mother, niece, and nephew back in Shuksan.

Rachel's daughter, Tawnya, was just about the same age as Tori, if she remembered correctly. Moving to her dresser, she picked up the framed photograph of herself with Rachel's family, taken several Christmases ago. With a critical eye, she examined her sister and herself, seated side-by-side on the sofa. A person would never know they were sisters, which, of course, by birth, they weren't. Rachel was a delicate brunette with dark eyes and a mass of curly dark hair. Celeste herself had stood a head taller than her sister, a palomino's mane of thick blonde hair spilling to the middle of her back.

Still holding the picture in her hand, she lay on the bed, staring at the faces of her sister and family, thoughts jumbled and confused. It was extremely painful to think about Rachel at all these days, and most of the time it was easier to simply put her situation out of her mind. Thinking about her conversation with Analiese, she suddenly wondered how Tawnya was holding up after so many months without her mother's presence in her young life. How would she herself have handled a similar situation when she had been twelve or thirteen?

The last time Celeste had seen her sister, she'd still been at home, living in the hospital bed that had been moved into the downstairs guest bedroom. Somehow Celeste hadn't understood the severity of Rach's condition, had been unaware of the degree to which her illness had whittled her already delicate body into nothing more than a small mound under the blankets. Trying to cover her shock, she'd tried to speak with Rachel, and knew by watching her sister's eyes that she had recognized her, for a while, anyway. Soon, however, Rachel's awareness had drifted away, and she had retreated into that place in her mind where no one could follow. Overriding the sorrow of witnessing Rachel's dramatic decline was guilt; she'd allowed the demands of her job to keep her away until it was too late to make up for the lost years.

She'd carry that ache with her for the rest of her life.

There wasn't anything more she could do for Rachel, but perhaps there was something she could do for Rachel's children. It was true that she hadn't been as involved with the kids' lives over the years as she'd have like to have been, but maybe it wasn't too late.

She'd go this weekend, leave straight from work Friday night and spend a couple of days out at the farm. She'd clean the fridge, do some laundry, and maybe mop the floors, whatever needed to be done. Of course, this meant she'd run into Scott at some point, but that couldn't be helped. Rachel and Scott had begun dating in high school and had been married shortly after Rach's graduation, and Celeste had known him for years. He was a nice guy, a great husband and father, and he'd loved Rachel to distraction. In the years since Rach's diagnosis, the man she'd known since her childhood had slowly become a stranger. He'd always been a quiet, introspective guy, but the intervening years, the stress of Rachel's illness, had drawn him deeper into himself. He was pleasant enough, but it was as though his pain had transformed him into a hurting, hollow man who existed in a state of bitterness and blame.

She was fresh out of ideas when it came to offering support or assistance; he'd made it exceedingly clear that he was just fine, the kids were just fine, and that she didn't need to worry on their accounts.

Except they weren't fine, and therein lie the dilemma. To what degree was it possible to involve herself in their lives when she was being held at arms' length? In what ways could she help Ty and Tawnya without stepping on Scott's toes? She'd upheld the situation in prayer for months, but other than the growing certainty that the time to act was *now,* she had no further insights.

She knelt beside her bed and spoke to her Father in heaven, thanking Him for His grace and laying her concerns at His feet. "Show me what You would have me do, Lord. I want so badly to help in any way I can." Finally, at peace, she rose from her knees and prepared for bed. Although her bed was empty save for herself, she'd never entered it lonely.

Blessed be Your name, Lord, my comfort and defender. Blessed be Your glorious name…

Heart filled with praise, she slipped into sleep.

Chapter 5

The kitchen was finally clean. Folding the dish towel neatly, Catherine cast a glance about the room, making sure there was nothing she'd overlooked. The white Formica counters gleamed, everything was in its place. Satisfied, she checked her watch; just enough time to change blouses and drive to the church. Thursday morning was quilting in the church basement with the auxiliary ladies, and she hadn't missed a session in fifteen years. Not even the week Ed passed away. Some of the women hadn't understood how she could appear with sewing bag in tow one day after burying her husband, but Catherine knew that work was the best cure for what ailed a person. Why, there was scarcely a day when she didn't have something planned, whether it was an insurance consultation or simply shampooing and setting hair over at Fircrest on Monday afternoons. There was Bible study Wednesday nights, quilting Thursday morning, choir practice Thursday nights and church Sunday morning, of course. Sunday afternoons she went on over to Fircrest to visit Rachel after putting a roast or ham into the oven to bake. Scott and the kids always came to Sunday dinner after visiting Rachel. Tuesday afternoons Tawnya usually stopped by after school and Catherine took her over to Harvest Foods grocery shopping. That girl was a good little shopper, had her list already made and coupons clipped and ready. Catherine had groomed her over the last two years, and now she could budget and plan meals for the week just like a little mother.

She was proud of Tawnya; she'd had to grow up quickly with her mother's situation, but Catherine dismissed the suggestion that Tawnya was expected to carry too much responsibility for her age.

When the ladies at church had attempted to broach the subject with Catherine, she'd tartly reminded them that in their grandmothers' time, girls were often married by fourteen and certainly responsible for household chores much earlier than that.

"But things are different now, Catherine. And Tawnya's so quiet, she always seems so sad. She doesn't appear to have much to do with the other girls. She needs a chance to just be a child a little longer."

Well, there wasn't anything Catherine could do about Tawnya's growing up, but she could help be sure her granddaughter's time was spent productively, learning homemaking skills and limiting her exposure to the television. All of the ladies agreed that it was such a shame about poor Rachel; that a young wife and mother should be struck down with a horrible disease, leaving her family to struggle along as best they could. But, they agreed, it was a blessing that Rachel couldn't see the hole her absence had created in her husband and children's lives. She'd have suffered the worse for the knowledge.

No one could possibly know what a crushing blow it had been to Catherine to lose her special little girl, her gift from God when she believed she'd be forever childless. When she and Ed had married, they'd agreed that they wanted a large family, at least four children, and had waited through the first months of their marriage for the good news of a pregnancy. But the months had turned into a year, then two, five, and finally ten. In those days, there wasn't any such thing as infertility workup. In those days, when these things were discussed, it was in the context of whose "fault" it was they couldn't start a family.

She and Ed had prayed every night, prayed that God would see fit to bless them with just one baby. Catherine still remembered the hope that had lived month after month, that maybe this time she was really pregnant, then the crushing disappointment, months turning into years.

Finally, the summer Catherine was thirty-three and Ed forty, after having resigned themselves to being childless, a miracle had occurred. Pastor Clark had knocked on their door one evening after supper, bringing news that had changed their lives. A minister friend in Spokane had a young woman in his congregation pregnant out of wedlock. She'd come to her minister in secrecy, having made arrangements to go away until after the baby was born, so as not to embarrass her family. She was said to be a fine young woman who had just been caught in an unfortunate situation; were Ed and Catherine interested in adoption?

They'd talked long into the night and for the next week. Ed was reluctant, had kept saying that he wanted his *own* child, but Catherine had known better, had known from the start that God had brought the knowledge of this young woman to them, making it possible that they could be parents after so many years. In the end, Ed had agreed, and as soon as he'd seen that precious little girl, all of his reservations had disappeared like smoke in the wind. They'd raised their little daughter and enjoyed every moment of the experience. She was the most beautiful little girl in Shuksan, curly dark brown hair that her mother had adorned with fancy ribbons and barrettes and expressive dark eyes. She'd been a constant source of delight, proving to be very musical, beginning piano lessons in kindergarten. By the time she was in high school, she was accompanying the church choir and also directing the children's choir, which she'd continued until she became too ill to do so.

Yes, Catherine thought once again, *Rachel had been a joy from the beginning.* She had been her best friend, really. She couldn't remember a time that they hadn't worked together in the garden and kitchen, canning vegetables and fruit in the summer, or working on their sewing projects on bitter winter afternoons. She'd never even contemplated the possibility of a future without her Rachel, but God had had other plans.

She agonized in the deepest valley of her soul, knowing that she was being punished. She'd spent some of the darkest hours of her life on her knees, begging God that her sin be made known to her, that Rachel might be made whole again. *Take me, God,* she'd pleaded, *not my Rachel,* knowing full well that she shouldn't attempt to bargain with Him or question His will.

Rachel lay in dark silence, kept alive by the machines that performed her basic bodily functions for her, but Catherine hadn't given up, would never give up. There wasn't anything the Lord couldn't do, no miracle impossible under His hand. She prayed all the harder these days, because she sensed that time was running out, that Rachel's tenuous hold on life was weakening. Holding firmly to her faith in God's almighty power, she'd urged Scott to exercise any and all means available to maintain Rachel's life.

Standing at the kitchen sink, Catherine pulled her thoughts together once more, horrified to see that it was ten minutes to ten; she'd be late to quilting! Sewing bag in hand, Catherine gathered her purse and keys. If she didn't get hung up at the railroad tracks, she should just make it to the church just in time. She hoped someone remembered to bring refreshments this week; she dearly loved those chocolate doughnuts with chocolate icing. Oh, and those wonderful carrot cake bars with the cream cheese frosting.

The ladies would pray today during their time together. They'd pray for Rachel, that the hand of healing would be laid upon her. Surely one day soon the Lord would reward their faith and restore Rachel to full health.

Good humor restored, she closed the door behind her, then hurried down the sidewalk.

Chapter 6

The week had flown by in a haze of client meetings, long sessions researching taxation laws, and preparing for Spencer Beckwith's court hearing. As his accountant, Celeste was working closely with his attorney, with whom she would present documentation of her client's good faith proposal to repay the IRS. He'd put his house on the market and, with a little luck, would be able to retire the debt. Of course, he'd have to pay capital gains on the sale of his home, a sharp little twinge of inescapable irony.

Last night she'd done a flurry of laundry, packed her bag for the weekend, and left the office at five p.m., fighting the snarl of rush-hour traffic out of the Seattle metro area. Finally turning onto eastbound Interstate 90, she crossed the floating bridge across Mercer Island, past Issaquah, and finally past the outlying homes and businesses, into the trees.

Leaving civilization behind, she began the steady climb that would take her over Snoqualmie Pass and lead her eventually to the exit that would bring her squarely face to face with her roots. Shuksan. A quiet town with a population of about two thousand, including outlying ranches, you had a good chance of seeing locals wearing cowboy boots and Montana Silversmith buckles won in rodeo events for calf roping and bull riding. The Junior Rodeo program was thriving, with not just boys involved. Girls participated in barrel racing, pole bending, and some even participated in calf roping.

The summer evening beckoned; Celeste touched a button and opened the sun roof. One hand on the wheel, she reached back and removed the pins holding her hair in its office chignon and shook her head, sending long golden strands loose into the breeze. Simply letting her hair down was a release of tension; nothing seemed to announce the end of the workday the way this small gesture did. Now, leaning her head and shoulders back against the leather seat, she cleared her mind of the events of the week and breathed deeply of the fresh mountain air; pine, grass, even the damp scent of bark and mulch from the forest floor.

There was nothing like summer in the mountains. The drive itself was spectacular this evening; the descending sun bathing the mountain meadows to the side of the highway in its golden light. Green everywhere; the deep green of the field grass, darker green of the trees, and a green so dense to be nearly black when looking at the ridges and slopes set back further from the road. Sunlight shimmered on water; the Snoqualmie River and Lake Kachess. A slight breeze kissed the long grass, sending it into a graceful dance. Overhead, Celeste noted to her delight that there were patches of blue sky; she seemed to have left the dark rain clouds behind her. She was ready for some sunshine.

Absently working her foot out of a navy pump, she planted her stockinged foot onto the gas pedal, sighing in relief as she wiggled her toes in the fresh air. Dropping down the incline that led into the Shuksan city limits, Celeste glanced at her watch. At some point, the sun had dropped behind the peaks behind her, and the air was taking on the feel of approaching night. Slowing to thirty miles per hour, she cruised down Main Street, deserted except for a group of kids hanging around the entrance to the grocery store and the usual full parking lot at Alpine Burger. The other businesses were dark, having closed down for the night, or the weekend, depending upon their professions.

Nothing ever seemed to change around Shuksan.

A few short blocks later, she was parked at the curb in front of her childhood home. In the moments before she faced her mother, she offered up a heartfelt prayer for patience and for the capacity to love her mother the way she wanted to, the way she *should*. Searching for the anticipation she would have liked to experience upon returning home, she felt only the inevitable sinking feeling in her stomach and the sense of emotional vulnerability that never seemed to dissipate, no matter how many birthdays she'd celebrated.

"Mother, where's the crystal vase/silver candlesticks/lace tablecloth I gave you?"

"Oh, I donated it at the church rummage sale; it brought a good price. Now, Celeste, don't look at me like that; I'm not one to put on airs. What would I do with something that fancy?"

"But I picked it out just for you, Mom. I wanted you to have something pretty."

"Pretty expensive is what it is. Always showing off your money, aren't you, Celeste? Well, if you want to spend money, you can make a donation to the church. We're raising money to repair the roof/furnace/kitchen, and they need it more than I do."

Tucking away the hurtful memories, Celeste slipped her right foot back into the pump, removed the keys from the ignition and grabbed her purse. As she made her way to the open trunk, the front door swung open, spilling a crescent of light onto the front porch.

"You're here."

Forcing a pleasant smile to her lips, Celeste met her mother in the middle of the sidewalk, embracing the older woman.

"It's good to see you, Mom."

"Well, bring your bag in so we can close the door, the bugs are already bad tonight."

Celeste returned to the car, closed the trunk, and activated the lock/alarm system. Hefting her bags, she followed Catherine into the house.

"You don't have to lock your car here, Celeste. I'm sure no one will bother it."

"I know, Mother, it's just force of habit, that's all."

"I don't know how you can live in that city; do you know what the rate of car prowl and outright vehicle theft is in Seattle? Horrible! The insurance company doesn't have any choice but to raise premiums. Well, anyway, you didn't drive all this way to hear me spout statistics, I'm sure. Would you like something to eat?"

"Something light, Mom, if you have anything."

"Light, you mean that vegetarian stuff?" Catherine switched on the kitchen light, revealing the same aged counters, cupboards, and linoleum that had been installed when the house had been built in the 1940s.

"No, Mom, really, just some fruit if you have any, and maybe some tea or anything cold. Please don't go to any trouble."

"Oh, it's no trouble, let me just look here. I have some nice left-over pork roast, how about a sandwich? Or I could open a can of deviled ham."

Ugh. "No, really, Mom, I'm not that hungry. Just an apple would be fine." Pork roast. Deviled ham, probably swimming in mayonnaise! Might as well stick a spoon into a can of lard and ladle it right onto her plate.

"Mom, I'm just going to run my bags upstairs, I'll be right back." Escaping for a moment, she blew out a deep breath. Climbing the stairs, she reached the landing and humped her bags down the hall to her old room. The same double bed stood in its same spot before the window. The walls were still the same pale green, ceiling sloping steeply on the far side of the room under the pitch of the roof. Her room, her refuge of sanity where she'd retreated to lose herself in books and music. Letting her eyes roam the familiar room, she finally felt it; the elbow's nudge of nostalgia. Crossing to the closet, she pulled the door open and checked the floor; yes, the boxes were here. She promised herself that she'd go through them later, after spending some time with Mother, and eating her apple, a wonderfully satisfying meal after a lunch of chicken pita sandwich and a protein bar eaten at her desk nine hours ago. Well, her days of eating pork or anything that required mayonnaise to render it edible were long past.

She changed from her business suit into her favorite sweat pants and a baggy T-shirt, then brushed her wind-blown hair. Finally, having exhausted all reasonable delaying tactics, she ordered herself to get downstairs and visit with Mother.

"Lord, help me to be patient. Help me to be kind, no matter how frustrated I feel."

Snapping the light off as she left the room, stood at the head of the stairs, and inhaled a great breath, then ran lightly downstairs.

Catherine was finishing setting food on the table as Celeste appeared at the doorway. "Mom, really, you didn't have to go to all this trouble."

"It's no trouble, just a few things I had in the fridge."

Seating herself at the table, Celeste beheld the offering spread across the table. A small container of macaroni and cheese, a bowl of sliced cucumbers in vinegar and sugar, and half of a pork roast sandwich laying on her plate. A pitcher of tea sat in the center of the table, and a single Red Delicious apple sat next to the ice-filled glass.

"Thanks, Mom." How was she going to choke that sandwich down with Mother sitting two feet away, monitoring every bite she took? Resigned, Celeste spread the napkin over her lap, added macaroni and cucumbers to her plate, closed her eyes mentally, then picked up the sandwich and took a tiny bite. Was there anything nastier than cold pork roast with its layer of grease the color and consistency of dried Elmer's glue? Hoping to distract herself as much as her mother, she questioned, "How's Rachel, Mom?"

"Oh, failing, I think, Celeste, much as I hate to admit it."

Pulling her thoughts back to the present, she forced her attention to her mother's words. "Miracles happen, Celeste. I pray every day for a miracle for Rachel."

"I know, Mom, but sometimes we have to accept that no matter how much we pray, that…I'm sorry. It's just that, well, Rachel's not going to get better, Mom."

"So now you presume to know God's plan for your sister?"

"No, of course not, Mom, but I think we need to be realistic and accept that His will supercedes our desires."

Eyes dry, great sadness on her face, Catherine rose from the table. "If you're finished, I'll clear the food away." With brisk movements, she reached for the bowl of cucumbers, her daughter's hand staying hers.

"Mom."

Refusing to meet her daughter's gaze, Catherine pulled away, picking up the conversational ball and skirting the painful issue of Rachel's plight. "What are your plans for tomorrow?"

"I thought I'd go out to the farm in the morning, help around the house a little, maybe do some laundry and clean bathrooms, something that needs help catching up on. Then, in the afternoon, I'd like to go over to Fircrest and visit Rach. I know she can't speak, but I want to see her anyway. After that, I thought I'd take Tawnya out for a drive, buy her an ice cream cone, spend a little time with her. I know I haven't been very involved with the kids, but I'd like to change that."

"For heavens' sakes, don't be buying her ice cream! That girl has gained so much weight, I don't know what she's thinking! And Tyler, well, he's completely out of control, and Scott just turns a blind eye to it."

"It can't be easy for any of them, Mom."

"Well, of course it's not easy, but a person can't just *give up,* after all!"

Celeste sighed and changed tactics. "Let's plan to run out there in the morning and then we can bring Tawnya back into town for lunch. Any suggestions?"

Frowning, Catherine mused, "Why, I suppose there's Clifford's, but I've heard the food has really slipped there."

"What about the Hay Wagon? They're still around, aren't they?"

"Well, yes, but expensive!"

"That's okay, Mom. Let me treat you to lunch. I never get the chance. Okay? Please? Now I think I'll head up to bed. Sleep well, I'll see you in the morning." Leaning to embrace her mother, she felt the other woman's spine, stiff as a poker, arms holding her just far enough a distance from herself to send the message, "I'm uncomfortable around you." Sighing, she murmured, "Goodnight, Mom."

"Goodnight, dear."

Wearily climbing the narrow staircase, Celeste had but one objective; the old iron-springed bed that squeaked loudly at the slightest movement. She closed the door behind her, crossed to the bed and sat wearily, shoulders slumped. The long day and the stress of her homecoming had drained the last of her energy, both physical and emotional. Suddenly feeling stifled, longing for some air, Celeste struggled with the window, finally forcing it upward. Inhaling a deep breath of fresh air, she offered a prayer of thanks for safe travel, and for her mother, that her bitterness be set aside and God's comfort would envelop her spirit.

Easing into bed, she snapped off the nightlight and burrowed herself into the blankets. Tomorrow would be better, because then she'd be able to do something tangible for her niece and nephew, even for Scott, although that wasn't her primary motivation.

Below, in the bedroom she'd shared with her husband for over twenty years, Catherine prepared for the night. After prayers, she rose from her knees and gratefully entered her bed. Tired as she was, she was unable to sleep. Unable to find a comfortable position, she tossed from one side to the other, hearing the unfamiliar sound of springs creaking in the room upstairs. It had been more than a year since her youngest daughter had been home. Why had she come at this time, this daughter who, by word and actions, made it clear in so many ways that she was ashamed of her humble origins and had taken great pains to recreate herself into a sophisticated and wealthy woman? Lying cocooned in blankets, Catherine remembered the last time she'd visited Seattle and had spent the night with her daughter in the lovely condominium. It had been last summer, when she'd had an insurance convention at one of the area hotels, and Celeste had promptly invited her to spend the night. She hadn't yet seen her daughter's new home, purchased after she'd sold her first condo at a great profit, making it possible to afford a large down payment on this one. Why, Celeste had told her that she could have paid the condo off entirely between the proceeds from her old place and liquidating some of her investments, but needed a mortgage for tax benefit.

Catherine hadn't known what to expect when she'd arrived at her daughter's home, but she hadn't expected what she'd seen. Near the north end of Lake Washington, not too far from where the sailboats docked at the North End Marina, the condo faced east, looking across to the opposite side of the lake with its million dollar homes climbing the Kenmore Hills. Beyond this lay a spectacular view of the Cascades, snow-capped even in June. The condo was fifteen hundred square feet, with two bedrooms, a gourmet kitchen, and entertainment-sized formal dining area. A white marble gas fireplace centered the living room and through the sliding glass door laid a large terrace with sunken hot tub. Celeste had served dinner on the round glass-topped table on the terrace that evening. They'd watched the light fade from the sky while the lake's surface became as dark as sapphire as lights slowly began to twinkle from Kenmore Hills.

In her solitary bed, Catherine experienced a wave of envy so intense it brought tears to her eyes. Celeste would never know what it was to be seventy-five years old and worrying about her financial future; her daughter would never have any of these worries. Even if she never married, and it was beginning to look as though she wouldn't, she'd still be financially independent.

In her heart, Catherine acknowledged that it was wrong to harbor such resentment toward her daughter, but it was just so unfair! How could God allow one child to endure such hardship while blessing the other so? How could He put Rachel's children, Rachel's husband, through this misery, while Celeste carried blithely on with her life, without a care in the world?

Scripture promised that what she sewed in tears, she'd reap in joy. There had been little enough joy in her life since Rachel had been diagnosed with Huntington's, but on the day that Rachel stood before them whole and healthy once again, there would be joy beyond measure.

Comforted in His promise, she slept.

Chapter 7

"Aunt Celeste!" Tawnya burst through the front door shortly after nine-thirty on a sparkling Saturday morning, waiting impatiently for her aunt to extricate herself from her car.

After embracing her niece, Celeste held her at arm's length, examining her. "Oh, it's so good to see you, Tawnya. And look at you! You've grown a foot since I saw you last."

"Hello, dear."

Moving to give her grandmother a quick hug, the girl greeted the older woman. "Hi, Grandma. Well, come inside, okay?"

As they entered the old farmhouse, Celeste saw that her mother had spoken the truth; the place was shipshape, and the odor of Pine-Sol wafted from the direction of kitchen and bathroom.

"Tawnya, is there anything I can do to help you? Clean the oven or the refrigerator, anything?"

"No, thanks, Aunt Celeste. I get the housecleaning done early on Saturdays so I have the rest of the day to do other stuff."

She even sounded like her mother and grandmother, Celeste thought in amazement. She herself was more of a sporadic housekeeper, could go for several weeks without thinking about vacuuming or cleaning out the refrigerator, until the urge would suddenly take hold and she'd spend the better part of a day scurrying around like a madwoman on a cleaning frenzy. Not the way she'd been raised, no indeed.

"In that case, come here and sit down, tell me about your life. You're going to be in eighth grade this fall?"

"Yes."

"Does Mrs. Abbott still teach eighth grade?"

"Yeah."

"Seriously? She was about a hundred and five years old when *I* was in eighth grade! So, tell me what you do for fun."

Tawnya hesitated for a moment, eyes seeking her grandmother's. "Well, I ride Shadow, and I like to read. I'd really like to take piano lessons, but maybe now isn't the best time. And I have my rabbits; I'm going to enter them in the fair again this year. I won a blue ribbon last year for my summer litter."

"What about friends, dances, that kind of thing?"

Dropping her eyes, Tawnya said, "No," almost shyly, shaking her head in denial.

"Well, for land's sake, Celeste, she's only twelve years old. She isn't old enough to be thinking about dances and all that nonsense yet."

"Oh, Grandma, there're dances at my school a lot, I just never go."

"That's a good girl, Grandma's proud of you."

As silence fell, Celeste sensed the tension in the room; there was some sort of uncomfortable power struggle gathering its life breath between the older woman and the young girl. Something familiar enough to raise the tiny hairs on the back of Celeste's arms.

Forcing unpleasant memories from her mind, Celeste searched desperately for a distraction. "How about we go to lunch in town before we visit your mom? We'll do the Hay Wagon, my treat. What do you say, Mom?"

"Well, I...I suppose that would be all right."

"Great. So, Tawnya, are you sure there isn't anything I can do to help you? Put a load of laundry in, anything?"

"No, thanks anyway, Aunt Celeste. I got up really early so I'd be done by the time you got here."

"What a great kid you are." Celeste smiled warmly at her niece. "Well, what do you say we head into town, check out some of the shops, and blow some money before lunch?"

"I need to change clothes first, okay? I'll hurry."

"Take your time, Tawnya."

As her niece pounded up the staircase, Celeste turned to her mother. "Thank you, Mother."

"For what?"

"For agreeing to go out to lunch and having a girls' day out. I think Tawnya really needs some 'girl time.'"

Shaking her head, Catherine replied, "I still don't see why we need to eat lunch out when I have plenty of food at home. It just seems like it'll teach her to be wasteful of food and money. Now, I'm going to run out back and check the roses for aphids while she changes clothes."

Celeste shook her head. Mother lived in a totally different world, and she was beginning to believe that she'd never be able to cross the bridge to that world. Who'd have thought a twenty-dollar lunch would cause such a disturbance in Mother's comfort zone?

At loose ends, she sat alone in the living room, gaze falling on the old upright piano in one corner. Finally, she went to the bench, sat, and slowly lifted the cover from the keys. Hands in lap, she reached a tentative hand, hearing the notes float into the summer morning. She'd wanted nothing more than to learn piano when she was Tawnya's age, and thanks to Mrs. Bateham, she'd learned the rudiments. Mrs. Bateham had been the music teacher and had given private lessons. She'd come across Celeste longingly stroking the keys after school in the band room one afternoon after the final bell had rung. *Would you like to learn piano,* she'd asked, eyes kind and warm. *How about a trade, then? If you'll mow my lawn every week, I'll give you a lesson afterward. Thursday afternoons, at my house, four-thirty.*

And so it had begun and had continued until Celeste was a sophomore, when her interests had moved in another direction and that interlude in her life had ended. She owed Mrs. Bateham a great deal, which she'd come to realize only in later years. The woman who'd supplemented her income by teaching privately had had enough insight to intuitively understand that there was room for only one star in the Malloy household and had cared enough to become involved anyway.

Removing a sheaf of sheet music from under the lid of the piano bench, she thumbed through the pages, finally stopping at the theme song from "You Light Up My Life." Grinning, she lay the others aside and positioned the music on the rack. Flexing her fingers, she ran through a series of scales, wincing at the sour notes, then began the introduction.

In her room, Tawnya was digging frantically through her dresser drawers when the first notes drifted up the stairs. Aunt Celeste could play the piano? She'd never known that, but then there were many things she didn't know about Aunt Celeste. She was really nice and so beautiful. She had such gorgeous blonde hair, and her nails were incredible. She always had the coolest clothes too. Today she was wearing a blue and yellow skirt of some kind of crinkly material that came to about mid-calf with a yellow T-shirt tucked into the waistband and a pair of strappy sandals that showed off her polished toenails. She had dangly blue topaz earrings that matched her eyes, with another blue topaz encircled with diamonds on a gold chain around her neck. When she'd gotten out of her little red car, hooking her sunglasses onto the front of her shirt, she'd looked like a movie star.

She hoped some of the girls would see them in town today; no one had an aunt as beautiful as Aunt Celeste. She could wear a gunny sack and still look like a model.

Which brought her back to the problem at hand; what to wear. It was too hot for jeans, Grandma didn't like her to wear shorts to town for whatever reason, and if she showed up in town in one of her church dresses on Saturday, she'd really look stupid. A wave of self-pity engulfed her, bringing hot tears to her eyes.

Slumping on the bed, she let the tears come, stinging her eyes and nose. At the knock, she hurriedly wiped the tears from her cheeks, "Who is it?"

"Just me, kiddo. Thought I'd give the piano a break and come pester you for a while, okay?"

"Just a second, Aunt Celeste."

Waiting, Celeste heard the unmistakable sound of her niece blowing her nose, then footsteps before the door opened. Observing the red eyes and swollen face, Celeste floundered for a moment. How did one deal with tears in a girl this age—did they prefer that a person pretend not to notice? Going with instinct, she raised a hand to Tawnya's cheek, brushing away a tear.

"I know I haven't played for awhile, but please don't tell me my rendition of 'You Light Up My Life' reduced you to tears."

A watery chuckle escaped, "No."

"Okay, then, I'll ask straight out; what's wrong, Tawn? Can I help?"

Shaking her head, brushing at the tears that continued to leak from her eyes, Tawnya replied, "I don't have anything decent to wear. All of my clothes look like either Grandma or a nine-year-old should be wearing them. I love the jeans you sent me for my birthday, but it's so hot out. Grandma'll have a fit if I come down in shorts when we're going to town, and I'm not going to wear one of my church dresses. I'd rather stay home!"

What in the world was wrong with Scott? Compassion and frustration struggling for dominance, she kept her voice deliberately light. "This is a definite problem, my dear, but one that can easily be remedied. Tell you what, let's run by Rumleys before lunch. Do they still have a pretty good selection of clothes? Well, we'll get you duded up right, my treat. And I'll bring Grandma into the loop about wearing your shorts into town, how about it?"

Fresh tears brimming, Tawnya nodded. Sliding an arm around the girl's shoulder, Celeste drew her close. "It's okay, hon. Why don't you go wash your face, get yourself together. I'll go down and bring Grandma up to speed. Okay?" Tawnya nodded wordlessly. "All right. See you in a few minutes."

Letting herself into the hallway, Celeste closed the door behind her and stood for a moment. It wouldn't do to let Mother see that she was upset; it was going to require subtlety to pull this off. Taking a deep breath, she descended the stairs, announcing, "She'll be right down. We've revised the plan a little, Mother; we're going to stop in at Rumleys on our way to lunch so Tawnya can pick out a pair of jeans and a shirt or two. I told her I was sure you wouldn't mind."

Surprise registered on the older woman's face, "But she has a closet full of clothes, Celeste, why does she need something new?"

"Apparently she's outgrowing things, and since I'm here now, we'll just pretend we're getting a jump on back-to-school shopping. I'd like to do this for her, Mom. The other thing is that she's going to have to wear her shorts into town because she doesn't have any pants that fit, but she'll wear her new things afterward, okay?"

"Well, I suppose so. But I don't know what you're going to find for her in Rumleys; they seem to think that girls are all a size five. I haven't had any luck in there for a couple of years."

"Well, we'll just have to see what they have. Maybe we'll get lucky and they'll have some new stock in."

The drive to town passed uneventfully and soon they were inspecting racks of shirts. A large section of wall was shelved and contained a variety of jeans, Levis, Wranglers, even Guess. Celeste kept her distance, poking through the racks and watching her niece as she looked through the merchandise. From twenty paces or standing near her, there could be no denying that Tawnya was ready, past ready, for a bra. She wrestled with herself for long moments; whether to get involved in something as personal as a girl's first bra, coming rapidly to the conclusion that if not she, then who? Obviously Mother didn't have eyes in her head and was stubbornly clinging to the notion that Tawnya was still a little girl. Remembering her own experiences at a similar age, the decision was made; surely it would be less embarrassing for Tawnya if Celeste stepped in than if it were left to Mother. With this in mind, she beheld her niece with an assessing eye, then headed directly for the lingerie section. Perusing training bras, she decided that this wasn't going to be as easy as it looked. After approaching the clerk with her dilemma, she waited while the woman studied the girl, then nodded decisively, selecting three boxes from a rack.

"These are the most popular styles for young girls, adjustable straps and plenty of room to grow."

After thanking her, Celeste took the boxes and met Tawnya at the dressing room.

"Aunt Celeste, I found two pair of jeans that fit. And here are two shirts, too. Do you want to see them?"

"Sure, but first, can I talk to you inside for a minute?"

"Sure."

Closing the door behind them, Celeste produced the boxes. "How would you feel about checking these out?" At Tawnya's vivid blush, she continued, "I'm not trying to embarrass you, hon, but it's time to bite the bullet and strap yourself in."

Snickering, Tawnya examined the boxes. "These aren't as sexy as the Victoria's Secret bras they have on TV."

"I don't think they have training bras by Victoria's Secret, kiddo. Sorry."

A short time later, the women walked out of the store with both pair of jeans, three shirts, and two brassieres, plus several pair of socks for Tawnya and, at her shy request, several pairs for her father and brother as well.

"I'll pay you back, Aunt Celeste, for everything."

Tugging a lock of hair between Tawnya's shoulder blades, Celeste replied, "No, you certainly will not and that's final. Consider this your first round of school shopping. Now, how about lunch?"

They'd had an enjoyable lunch at the Hay Wagon; Tawnya and Catherine visiting the smorgasbord. Celeste settled for a dinner salad and a large glass of ice water with a lemon wedge. Looking about, she recognized a familiar face coming out of the kitchen.

"Mom, is that Connie Ripley, back cleaning tables?"

Craning her head to look, Catherine replied, "Yes, I believe it is. I didn't know she worked here. The last I knew she was working over at the gas station, there's that mini-mart there now, you know."

"I'll be right back, I want to say hi."

Making her way across the room, she revisited memories of the vivacious redhead with the amazing belly laugh who had driven a refurbished hearse and attended Sunday school and youth group activities with Celeste. Going steady with Darrell Ripley since seventh grade, she'd married him three weeks after graduation and had produced four (or was it five?) children over the years.

Celeste approached on silent feet. "Hey, you."

Whirling, Connie's eyes widened and on a laugh, tossed the soiled dishrag onto the table and gave Celeste a quick hug. "Celeste, my gosh, it's great to see you! How long are you in town?"

"Just for the weekend."

"I'm so sorry about Rachel; I think about you a lot but aren't any good at letter-writing, you know how it is."

"Yes, I do. Connie, I don't want to get you into trouble so I'll take off, but it's so good to see you. Can I give you a call tonight? There's something I want to run by you."

"Yeah, I'll be around. Here," scribbling a number on a napkin, which she thrust at Celeste, "gotta run, but call, okay?"

"Count on it."

Watching her friend disappear through a door that presumably led to the kitchen, Celeste drew a deep breath, then wound her way back to where her mother and niece waited. Just seeing Connie released a horde of old memories. The day after eighth grade graduation, she'd spent the night with Connie, one of the girls her mother approved of. They'd gone "swimming" at ten p.m. in the large round horse trough that Connie's father had set up as a pool in the backyard, and Celeste had reveled in the freedom of splashing about under the night sky, lying on her back and counting stars. They'd attended church camp together, completed Confirmation classes side by side, and double-dated for Senior Prom. Why had she fallen out of contact with her old friend? Her friendship with Connie was yet another casualty of her career-driven life, and she promised herself that from now on, she'd do better.

After lunch, they'd driven to Fircrest, and Celeste had come away with a pain in her heart that she knew would lodge there for the rest of her life. Catherine and Tawnya had walked blithely through the door, accepting the sight that lay before them visit after visit. The first impression that registered through Celeste's mind was the sound of the ventilator, a hissing, pumping entity that dominated the silent room. As she watched Tawnya greet her mother, kissing her on the forehead, helpless tears blurred Celeste's eyes. The tiny, diminished person lying unmoving in the sterile bed wasn't the sister with whom she'd shared a complex relationship until it was too late to redefine and move beyond the lines they'd each retreated behind.

"Come in, Aunt Celeste. Mom, Aunt Celeste is here. Grandma's here too."

The distance between the door and the bedside were the most difficult steps Celeste had taken in her life. It was Rachel, but it wasn't; the thick curly hair was cut short to her scalp and the shapely brows she'd maintained so diligently were bushy and overgrown. Her limbs had begun to curl and contort, pulling her body into the fetal position; the body's instinctual return to the pose in which it had spent its formative months safely in the womb.

With a voice she scarcely recognized as her own, she spoke quietly, "Hi, Rach," a choking pain lodging in her throat. Turning away from the bed, she averted her eyes and struggled against the tears that came despite her best intentions.

"It's okay, Aunt Celeste; she doesn't hurt anywhere, does she, Grandma? And she can hear us talking, right?"

"I don't know, honey, but we talk to her anyway. Hello, sweetheart, how's my girl today?"

Celeste endured the remainder of the visit in a numbing wave of pain and guilt, engulfed with pity for the young wife and mother who lay beyond reach of those who loved her most. *Why not me,* she asked God silently, *with no children or husband to leave behind, instead of a gentle, caring woman who'd devoted her life to service to God and family?*

The mood was subdued as the women returned to the car an hour later. Pulling her sunglasses from the visor, Celeste slid them over her eyes, thankful to shield her swollen eyes from the brightness of the sun. Taking a deep breath, she put the car into gear, making an effort to add a cheery note to her voice.

"Does anybody mind if we stop at the drugstore before we leave town?"

Once in the old building that hadn't changed appreciably in the last forty years, the women each went their own way, Catherine to visit with the pharmacist, Celeste making her purchases discreetly.

Tawnya stood before the row of candy bars, taking a mental tally of the money in her possession. Five dollars. Enough for three candy bars, with change to spare. She carried her selections to the counter and dug through her purse for the money, keeping an eye peeled for Grandma, who would have a fit if she saw her frittering her money away on junk. To her chagrin, Grandma was bearing down on her, and Mrs. Sterling was slow as next Christmas ringing her purchases up. Grandma's voice was loud enough to carry through the entire building, and Tawnya felt her cheeks growing red, even as tears filled her eyes.

"Tawnya Rose Parnell, you put that candy back this minute.

No, Evelyn, don't ring them up. For crying out loud, young lady, your aunt just had to buy you new clothes because you're too fat for your old ones, and here you are, buying more candy! What are you thinking?"

Face a mottled scarlet, voice quavering with humiliation and tears, Tawnya cried, "It's my allowance, Grandma! I can buy whatever I want!"

Catherine extended her hand. "Give it to me, this minute."

Tawnya stood in mute devastation, tears streaking her cheeks, then threw the wadded dollar bills on the counter and ran toward the door, making her escape. Exiting the building, she fled to the corner of the brick structure, flattened her back to the window, and allowed the tears to fall unobstructed. What was the big deal about buying some candy bars with her allowance? How could Grandma embarrass her like that, in public? And to demand that she hand over her allowance to boot! She glanced up and down the street, assuring herself that she was alone and that no one had witnessed her shame.

The tinkling of the bell on the front door broke through the silence. Grandma and Aunt Celeste. Just great. She didn't trust herself to be around Grandma right now, but had no other way home.

Celeste had witnessed the drama, aghast at her mother's tactics, and had quickly paid for her items and escorted Catherine from the store. "Mom, get in the car. I'm going to take you home. Tawnya, hon, hang out for about ten minutes, I'll be right back. I'm going to run Grandma home, then I'll come pick you up and take you home, okay?"

"Whatever."

Celeste paused, looking her niece square in the eye. "You aren't going to ditch me, are you?"

"No."

"Okay, see you in a few."

The tension in the car on the way back to Catherine's was a palpable, living entity. Unable to bear the silence, Catherine exclaimed, "Why you're pampering that girl is beyond me! We should be taking her straight home instead of getting rid of me so you can pander to her whims."

Celeste gripped the steering wheel and prayed for forbearance. "I don't want to fight about this, Mother. But you shouldn't have embarrassed her in the store that way. And to demand that she hand over her allowance! Mom, that's just wrong!"

Rampant with sarcasm, Catherine retorted, "Yes, I forgot that you're the expert on parenting, with your fancy condominium and fancy job and no ring on your finger!"

Blinking back hot tears at her mother's biting tone and scathing words, "I don't have to be a mother to see how much pain that girl is in, Mother. Keep going this way and you'll lose her!"

"Yes, I suppose she'll run off to the big city and forget all about her family, just like someone else I could mention."

It was useless. Celeste shook her head and held her tongue. Pulling up to the curb in front of her mother's house, she waited until Catherine had extracted herself from the car, then said, "I'll see you tonight, Mother." The passenger door slammed shut and her mother, spine rigid, made her way toward the front door. Celeste pulled back into the street and returned to the drugstore, leaning over to open the door for her niece. "Hop in."

Tawnya settled herself in the seat, "hands-off" written all over her countenance. After three blocks, in a belligerent tone, she queried, "Aren't you going to get all over my case too?"

Focusing on the road, Celeste shook her head. "No."

"Why not?"

"Because I don't think it would serve any purpose other than make you feel worse than you already do."

Tawnya muttered, "I hate her."

"No, you don't. You're hurt and embarrassed, and you have every right to be."

Tawnya shot a surprised glance toward her aunt. "You're not going to tell me how I'm being disrespectful and how fat and disgusting I am?"

"No, because you're not fat and disgusting. As far as the disrespect issue goes, it's easy to let our anger get the best of us sometimes. Ideally, you'd apologize to Grandma next time you see her, and she would reciprocate, but I wouldn't count on that. You don't have any control over someone else's actions, only your own. Right? I think all you can do at this point is to ask the Lord's help in coming to the place where you can forgive Grandma, and then ask Grandma for her forgiveness. It's all part of the same cycle, and it all starts with Him, Tawn. He forgave us first and wants us to do the same to those who hurt us, even if we need to ask Him for help to do it. In fact, He *wants* us to ask for that help."

Tawyna shook her head. "It won't do any good. I'll just get mad again next time she does something and then I'll be right back in the same place, having to ask forgiveness again."

"And He knows that. That's the way we're wired, hon, every single one of us. Because we're not perfect people. When something happens, when someone does or says something to hurt us, that's our natural reaction. But we have to remember that we hurt God by our words and actions too. If we come before Him and ask forgiveness, He gives that forgiveness and wants us to do the same for the people who hurt us. He's our perfect example of grace and compassion. Not that it's easy, it seldom is. But I know, for myself, that I feel so much better, cleaned out somehow, when I've let go of anger."

They rode in silence for a distance, then Celeste spoke again. "Tawn...I *am* concerned about you, and not because I think you're fat. I'm concerned that you have such a low opinion of yourself. That bothers me."

"I'm fine. Don't worry about me.

"But I do. I worry because I see a young woman who's in a lot of pain and because I love her and want her to be happy."

"I'd be plenty happy if everybody would just leave me alone!"

Lord, please give me the right words...I'm really struggling here! Help me to express to this girl how much You love her, and how much I love her.

Pulling off the main road, Celeste turned off the engine and faced her niece. "Tawyna...will you pray with me? Please?"

"Pray if you want, I don't care."

Celeste reached a hand across the seat, palm up, in invitation. After a brief hesitation, Tawnya placed her hand in Celeste's. Bowing her head, Celeste prayed aloud.

"Heavenly Father, we come before You this afternoon asking that You will lay Your hand of comfort and healing upon Tawnya. Lord, we know that You see deep into our hearts. You know our hurts and disappointments. We know You love us and that You are there and hear our prayers. Father, I ask that You will be very close to Tawnya and keep her in that safe place that You promise in Scripture, where she will find comfort in You. Lord, help her to see that she is loved, completely and without reservation. Thank You, Father. In Jesus' name. Amen."

Eyes still closed, she squeezed the hand in her own. "There isn't anything that we can't take to the Lord and lay at His feet, Tawn. Anything and everything, no matter how small or large. Remember that, okay?"

They shared a quiet moment, then Celeste stretched. "Well. Guess I'd better get you home. Do you have anything planned for supper tonight?"

"No. I was supposed to stop at the store and get something but…"

"No problem, we'll just run back into town. How about you take a night off and let Auntie Celeste try her hand in the kitchen? What sounds good? Chicken breasts? Burgers? You're calling the shots, kiddo."

"Doesn't matter to me. But I can help, if you want."

"Sure, that'd be great. Hey, suppose your dad and brother are up for tofu burgers?"

"You've got to be kidding! He'd feed them to the dog and eat a bowl of cereal instead."

With a mock sigh, Celeste replied, "Kinda what I figured. Well, I suppose we can find *something* to feed them, anyway."

Tongue in cheek, Tawnya volunteered, "I vote for eggplant Parmesan."

"A girl after my own heart. I'll show you the finer points of eggplant selection—you can surprise them sometime when I'm not around."

"Oh, they'd be surprised all right."

"You're a good kid, you know that?"

"You're just buttering me up, trying to get me to eat tofu."

"Figured that out, did you? Well, I guess just this once I can let you off the hook. So, what'll it be? What's your favorite?"

"Lasagna. Lots of cheese. And garlic bread. And fudge cake for dessert, with ice cream."

"You're killing me, girl! Okay. Throw in a green salad and you've got a deal."

"Okay."

"Lots of fruits and veggies, kiddo. Fills you up without a lot of calories."

Shopping trip behind them, they put supper together, enjoying their time together, then Celeste pleaded exhaustion and fled, before her brother-in-law came in from the field. She'd deal with him tomorrow, after she'd had a chance to gather her thoughts and plot her strategy.

Mother waited at home, probably loaded for bear and aiming both barrels in her direction.

No wonder she hadn't been home sooner; she was absolutely whipped, physically and emotionally.

But she felt better about her niece, and that was something, and when the rest of her concerns had been addressed, she'd feel better yet.

This must be what Ana experienced in her role as mother; the worries never really abated. Ana's philosophy was "one day at a time, and lots of prayer."

Celeste's last thought before sleep was that St. Paul must have been speaking to mothers, in particular, when he exhorted believers to "pray without ceasing." Only one day and she was already whirling with fatigue and second-guessing herself; words she'd spoken, attitudes portrayed, and faith demonstrated. Maybe the Lord knew motherhood was too much for her temperament and that was why she was still single and childless.

Maybe her role was to be a more active participant in the lives of her sister's children. This was something she could do. Maybe after a good night's sleep, she'd feel less like a wet mop and more like a role model.

"Help me, Lord, to accomplish the things You would have me do, in Tawnya and Tyler's lives. And Scott's, if that's Your will. Thank You, Lord. Amen.

Chapter 8

*I*f anyone had told Scott that he'd spend an hour with his sister-in-law, listening to her proposals for the care and feeding of his family, he'd have assumed there was another Malloy sister tucked away somewhere, a deep, dark family secret only now unveiled. He was still thunderstruck by the fact that sophisticated Celeste, an absentee aunt if ever there had been one, had armed herself with the cold, hard truth and entered the coliseum to face down the lion. The memory still stung. The points she'd brought up were valid, which hadn't necessarily made them any easier to digest. She hadn't come right out and told him he was a poor father, but she had delineated his oversights in a matter-of-fact way that left little room for argument but just enough wiggle-room to squirm about in discomfort. There were three major points, if his grasp of the conversation was accurate.

First and foremost, it was Celeste's opinion that he had unrealistic expectations of his daughter; at age twelve, she shouldn't be expected, nor allowed, to step into her mother's shoes as far as maintaining home and hearth and garden as well. Without raising her voice or saying anything directly accusatory, she'd painted a disturbing picture of a girl who was socially isolated, had very low self-esteem, and had some personal and emotional needs that weren't being addressed.

Overweight? Tawnya? Sure, she was a little chunky, but she'd snap out of it in a couple of years, when she started caring more about her appearance. In the meantime, let her eat what she wanted.

Those were two of Celeste's allegations. Recalling the conversation, Scott's cheeks burned with embarrassment; no, he hadn't had either of the kids to the dentist for a couple of years. No, there wasn't any particular reason, it just had turned out that way what with Rachel needing constant care and their never having an extra penny. "Okay, I dropped the ball," he'd admitted, throat tight with shame, which had easily morphed into anger, which he'd directed her way. She'd eyed him silently as he'd explained the situation in a clipped voice, it was all he could do to pay for his wife's care and keep the kids fed; some things had had to be put on the back burner, but he was doing the best he could.

But she was right; he owed his kids the basics, like visits to the dentist, optometrist, and even dermatologist. He was vaguely ashamed when he thought about the last one; he'd seen the pimples and figured she'd grow out of them, the way Ty had, the way himself had. It was different for girls, Celeste had informed him, because their whole hormonal construct was different and besides, it was a far more sensitive issue for girls at this age than for guys. He'd taken a good hard look at his daughter, then, and had finally truly seen her. It wasn't just pimples dotting her skin but deep, angry-appearing blemishes, accompanied by a smattering of blackheads and some pitted craters from acne scars already.

Celeste was right. Where had he been hiding the last year?

And her teeth; when had she grown another row of teeth in the gum line above her permanent teeth? Poor kid, even *those* weren't anything to write home about. He'd known Rachel had had braces, had seen school pictures from her childhood and had marveled at the difference in her smile before and after, but hadn't given a thought to the possibility that Tawnya may have inherited some of her mom's genetic predisposition to bad teeth.

One more strike against him. He'd made a point of surreptitiously checking out Ty's teeth afterward; thankfully, they looked fine, although surely he could stand a visit to the dentist regardless. They had no dental coverage, though, and while his pocketbook could stand a couple of visits for routine cleaning and so forth, he knew for a certainty that orthodontia was well out of reach.

This is why denial is preferable to the harsh realities of life, he mused. Once a person had accepted the reality of something, it made it much harder to scuttle back into that dank hole of denial. The only way his daughter's situation would fail to dominate his conscious-ness now that he'd been dragged kicking and screaming into the light was if someone came at him with a hammer and chisel and dug it out manually.

But Celeste hadn't enlightened him to the unacceptability of the present state of affairs only to back away and leave him to muck along by himself but had presented her simple, well-thought-out proposals, and the leaking life raft of his overwhelmed fatherhood had been effectively blown out of the water. A housekeeper, specifi-cally Connie Ripley, would come twice a week to clean the house, do some laundry, and prepare some meals that could be frozen and reheated.

Piano lessons for his daughter; he hadn't even known she was interested in playing. She'd overridden his protests of his inability to afford these small luxuries by informing him that these things were her way of doing something for her sister and for the kids; she'd been uninvolved for too long and knew of no way to provide assistance than some organizational details and the financing thereof.

Then for the absolute whopper. "I'd like your permission to get both of the kids into the dentist here and after any fillings or what-ever needs to be done, I'd like to schedule Tawnya with an orthodon-tist in Seattle for a consultation. And with a dermatologist as well. Yes, I realize you don't have dental coverage, Scott; it's all right, this is something I want to do. I'd do the same for my child; please let me do this for Rachel's. Because the money is such a small thing when you consider the difference this will make in her self-esteem. So, do I have your permission to get things set up so that she can have the braces on before school starts?"

What could he say? Presented with the undisputable facts, emo-tions a jumble, and stumbling over his words, he'd accepted with grace and humility. If there remained a slow burn of humiliation that he'd dropped the parental ball to the extent that Celeste, of all people, would not only notice but confront him with it, then he'd just have to chalk it up and douse the embers. And he *was* grateful for being provided such seemingly easy solutions to the problems, even if he'd been blind to those problems beforehand.

Now, settling himself in the porch swing, watching the stars twinkling beyond the roof of the porch, he "spoke" to his wife, something he often did. It somehow comforted him to maintain a connection with Rachel, however one-sided it may be.

"Rach, I'm so glad you can't see what's happened to our family, to your children. You wouldn't believe Celeste, either; she's really stepped up to the plate. I'm grateful to her, Rach, but I still just don't really like the woman, you know? She's so in *control,* I guess, puts her head to a problem, comes up with a solution, and moves on it, like, bam! I know, she has a whole different life than we do, I guess she's just so *different* from you, Rach. I miss you so much."

Distracted by the plaintive whining and the warm weight of the dog's head on his knee, Scott scratched Skip behind the furry ears. Mind wandering, once again he "saw" his sister-in-law as she'd stood before him earlier that day. After eating dinner at Catherine's, a Sunday tradition from which he wished he knew how to gracefully extricate he and the kids, at least a couple of times a month, Celeste had asked to speak with him privately. The kids had disappeared down the street, and Catherine had been occupied with cleaning up the kitchen. They'd exited through the kitchen door to the backyard and sat at the picnic table in the shade of the big sycamore tree.

He'd forgotten how tall she was; she looked him square in the eye without even wearing heels. Rachel was petite; her head had reached his shoulder and he was accustomed to tipping his head downward when speaking to most women, so it was kind of disconcerting to meet those vibrant blue eyes on the level. Everything was different, the room felt different, even the air was different when Celeste was around, for some reason. Whatever it was, she exuded a calm confidence in herself, spoke in a modulated voice, and carried herself in a manner that stated, "I know exactly who I am and am content with that person."

Well, why shouldn't she be? She was just as beautiful today as she had been when he'd married her sister, though she hadn't yet reached the zenith of her beauty, but she was certainly in full bloom now. She'd been wearing a classy linen jacket with matching slacks and coordinated blouse beneath, kind of a light khaki color, with lace accents on collar and blouse, sleeves pushed up to her elbows, revealing slim forearms, the left sporting a narrow diamond tennis bracelet. Her hair had been pulled into a sleek French braid, accentuating her cheekbones and showcasing blue, blue eyes under tawny brows. Tall and slender, she moved with an innate grace that reminded him of a fine Palomino mare he'd seen in a parade many years ago.

He'd been astonished to realize that he found her attractive, even comparing her to Rachel, which had brought him to his senses like a bucket of water to the face.

Get a grip! She's your sister-in-law, for crying out loud! And what are you doing, comparing her to Rachel, anyway? Of course she's beautiful, that's not exactly a news flash."

Still, he had a hard time pulling his thoughts away from the woman he'd known since her preteen days and had watched grow from a daredevil tomboy into the stylish, beautiful woman she'd become.

He'd liked her better before independence and sophistication had molded her into someone he no longer knew, living a life he couldn't comprehend. But there was no question that her heart was in the right place, much as it galled him to admit it. And, much as it may sting his pride, he knew that he would accept the help she offered, for the sake of the kids. Sometimes pride had to take a backseat to doing what needed to be done in someone else's best interests.

Sometimes it was possible to actually love someone too much to really see what was in their best interests. It was natural to want to protect those in our care, insulate them from life's painful realities and from any potential sources of heartache. Call it having blinders on, call it denial, put whatever name you want on it, the end result was the same; a person's best intentions often ended up serving himself rather than the other person. Wasn't it human nature to assume we knew what was best for those we loved?

Wasn't Rachel was a perfect example of this? Wasn't the fact that she was still living, despite her expressed wishes, a result of his assuming he knew what was best for Rach, for himself, and for the kids?

Well, he did the best he could, whether it was for Rach or the kids; that's all he could do. Who else was going to make these tough decisions? God? If it was His will that Rach die, then why hadn't she simply passed during one of the bouts of infection that she frequently suffered, whether urinary tract infections from the catheter, bronchitis and pneumonia from lying flat on her back, or infection from the bed sores? No, God obviously wasn't ready for Rach, or she'd already be gone. Either that, or He just wanted to torture Scott with his helplessness to deal with the situation.

In the end, it all came down to rest on his shoulders. And that was fine, he preferred it this way. Knowing you were on your own was somehow liberating; you knew where you stood and didn't need to waste your time thinking Someone Else was in charge. And if he didn't like the options available to him, well, that was just life. Nobody ever promised it would be easy, after all.

He rose stiffly from the swing and crossed the porch to the screen door and entered the house. His mother's vintage grandfather clock struck nine o'clock. Celeste would probably be getting home soon, back to her life, farther from Shuksan than merely road miles. He still couldn't quite understand why she wanted to do these things for Tawnya; it wasn't as though his daughter had done anything to deserve her aunt's generosity. In his experience, when something good came his way, there was usually a string or two attached.

Not this time, though. If he happened to come across a string, he knew how to snip through it. Someday even the heartstrings that still reached from his heart to Rachel's would be severed. Nothing survived unscathed, even those things that he held dearest. Especially the most precious things. Perhaps the trick was learning to distance himself from feeling strongly about anyone, even the kids. Perhaps that was the best protection he could offer all of them, the gift of complacency.

If he didn't allow himself to really love the kids, then maybe God would leave them alone. Maybe He'd be satisfied with having taken their mother and wouldn't interfere with his family again, if He saw that Scott was immune to further hurt. That was going to be the catch, though, because he did love the kids and couldn't imagine the time that he'd be able to close that part of himself off, even if his vulnerability left all of them open to further interference from God.

"Stay away from us, God, do You hear me? You've already done enough here. Just leave us alone."

Even as the words left his heart, he remembered that he no longer prayed. Just a temporary lapse, the sort of involuntary prayer that escaped a person hoping to make the traffic light before it turned, or that a check would arrive in the mail when the bank balance was low. Reflex, really, not expecting anyone to actually hear or care.

"If You're listening, God, then you know I mean it. We don't need any more of Your kind of love and caring. We've had enough to last us a lifetime."

As he tossed in his bed, he acknowledged that he couldn't have completely given up on God if he kept talking to Him. Okay, fine, he'd concede that He was there. The problem, of course, was that no matter how desperate and heartfelt his prayers had been, there was only silence on the other end. A good father didn't just shut his children out and ignore their needs, their pleas for help. A good father made himself available to his children and guided them through their problems with wisdom and love.

"So what does that say about your shutting the kids out for the last couple of years, pretending everything's fine? Aren't you guilty of the same thing you're blaming God for?"

He lay in the darkness, uncomfortable with the parallel he'd drawn but unwilling to examine it more thoroughly. Snapping on the nightlight, he dug through the stack of magazines on the nightstand and drew out the new issue of *Practical Farming*. With any luck, he'd doze off reading.

With any luck, he'd wake up and the last seven years would have all been an incredibly bad dream, the sun would be shining on Rach's hair, spread across her pillow, and the world would be a friendly place once more.

When he did finally drift into sleep, his dreams were filled with images of Rachel and the younger sister who'd been such a part of their younger lives, who'd drifted away as the years had passed. In his dreams, they were seventeen and ten, respectively, and life was once again filled with promise.

Even in deepest sleep, he knew that the morning would bring reality once again. He pushed consciousness away and held tightly to his dreams and the life he'd lost.

Chapter 9

Driving into the glow of the setting sun, Celeste crossed the miles that led back to her life; the bustling city and the calm quiet of her office. She was exhausted; it seemed that dealing with kids' problems, even from a safe distance, was even more taxing than she'd realized. She had a better understanding now of the sentiments expressed by women in her office who were mothers, remarks to the effect that they were glad to come back to work on Monday morning, if only for some peace and quiet.

She thought she might possibly have an inkling as to what they were talking about after the weekend. Not that it had been all that demanding really, just emotionally taxing, which she'd discovered could be even more draining than hard physical labor. She had her work cut out for her this week; scheduling dental appointments for Tawnya and Tyler back home, then coordinating an orthodontic consultation here in Seattle, and finally scheduling a dermatology consultation at the same time her niece was in town. Then, there was the issue of physically having Tawnya here; she'd obviously have to both pick her up and return her. Well, she could stay a week and they'd do some fun things, do some real school shopping and maybe urge her into a styling salon to do something with that hair. Inspiration struck, and she remembered that Tori was about Tawnya's age; maybe she could get them together and see how they got along together; take them out for pizza and roller-skating, maybe. Did kids their age still roller-skate? If not, perhaps a movie.

Satisfied with her plans, her mind drifted to her nephew. What a good-looking kid, all shoulders and muscle, flashing dark eyes and, she had discerned, a healthy dose of attitude. He hadn't spoken but maybe ten words to her, and those about her car. Well, what seventeen-year-old boy didn't appreciate a powerful engine under a cherry red exterior? It was obvious he'd been dying to drive it but hadn't asked. Which was probably a very good thing because no one drove the Beamer but Celeste herself. There was something about Ty that bothered her, though, but she couldn't quite put her finger on it. Just an elusive feeling, maybe the way she felt him watching her when he thought her attention was elsewhere.

Well, what could she expect? Tyler didn't know her, really. It was only natural that he'd hold back until he'd come to know her better.

And then there was Scott. He'd aged in the last year or so, his hair had a lot more gray, but it was the kind of silvery gray that looks so distinguished on guys, especially with his youthful face. He really did have a nice smile; he was one of those people who looked about average until they smiled, and then their whole face just lit up. She hoped he'd get himself to the dentist eventually; it would be a shame to waste that smile. Not that it had been all that evident in the time they'd spent together, but then he hadn't had much to smile about for a very long time now.

As the evening air cooled, she turned her face to the sun roof, trying to capture the essence of the mountain air before she descended into urbanity once again. Dusk was turning the western sky a deep peachy-amethyst color. That was one drawback of her condo; she had eastern exposure and wasn't able to watch the sunsets, but there were some beautiful mornings out on the lake. On summer weekends, the lake was alive with boats; sailboats with their colorful sails, fishing boats, ski boats and, of course, the inevitable jet skis. She loved to sit on her balcony with a cool drink in hand, watching the activity on the water and feeling the cool breeze on her face. Sometimes, though, it seemed a shame that the pristine beauty of the lake was marred by the seemingly endless water traffic and the sea planes that landed near her condo and taxied to dock at the terminal at the north end of the lake.

Imagine how it would be to live out on Carrot Lake, surrounded by quiet and the sounds of nature. A log house nestled right at the edge of the woods on the east bank, where a person could watch the sunsets exploding into color and turning the lake's surface into nature's mirror. Of course, she had no idea who even owned the land anymore, although that could easily be looked up through the county clerk's office. The land couldn't be all that expensive, could it? She could always make a phone call or two.

And then what? What possible reason could she have to want to buy that land when her life was here? And let's not forget that Mother is a short three miles down the road; when she'd escaped to college, she'd vowed to never live within a hundred miles of her mother again!

Pulling into her parking place at the rear of her building, she wearily lugged her bag to the elevator and punched the button. Inserting the key into the lock, she entered her home, disarmed the security system, and dropped the bag beside the door. The place was stuffy after being closed up for three days, and she opened the sliding glass door that opened to her balcony, opening the small kitchen window as well. The other windows had security locks that allowed them to be opened only a crack. Her bedroom felt like a tomb, airless and hot. Unpacking her bag, she thought of her old room back at Mother's, how the cool night air had caressed her skin, curtains billowing gently in the breeze. She reminded herself that no one was liable to put forth the effort to break into a second story window back home; she didn't have the luxury of taking her safety for granted here in the city.

After changing into sweats and tee-shirt, she stopped in the kitchen for a glass of ice water, then carried it through the slider to the table outside. Setting the glass absently on the table, she moved silently to the balcony's waist-high stone enclosure, resting her elbows on the surface. A couple of lights bobbed gently on the water; more than one person was sleeping in their cabin cruiser. The night was quiet, city-quiet; no sirens at the moment, just the background traffic noise and the sounds of stereos and television sets from neighboring units. But there were no crickets or frogs singing. How could she have forgotten the frogs?

Draining her water glass, she deposited it in the kitchen sink, double-checked the locks, and finally pulled the blankets back on her bed. Pensive mood still lingering, she wondered how Scott dealt with the loneliness and loss of intimacy in his life after years of a happy marriage. Lying in the dark, she recalled family gatherings during the days when Rachel had still been healthy. He'd never been an overly demonstrative guy, but there'd been no doubt in Celeste's mind that he was firmly committed to his Rachel and that his marriage vows were sacrosanct.

Tired, but unable to relax, she pounded her pillow in exasperation. What was the matter with her tonight? She hadn't thought about the man for months on end, now she couldn't get him out of her mind. When she forced Scott from her thoughts, they turned to her job, and she found herself dreading going into the office the next morning and beginning another workweek. The vague dissatisfaction that had been present for the last several months was increasingly insistent; the daily corporate struggle between professionalism and one-upmanship to a growing frustration with the bustle of city life. Perhaps it was the long hours, perhaps the fact that she was no longer as driven to climb the corporate ladder that she'd been ascending for the last thirteen years. It all seemed superfluous somehow. When it came right down to it, what comprised her role at SBBB but to enable often irresponsible people to become yet more irresponsible?

She wasn't sure what, exactly, she was looking for with regard to her career, but she was becoming increasingly certain that it wasn't this job, even if it meant foregoing the opportunity to achieve partnership in the firm. After spending a couple of days at home with Scott and the kids, she was reminded anew how fleeting life can be and of the things that are truly important. Not earning a six-figure salary or driving a sports car, not striving endlessly to boost her investment portfolio or building up her earthly wealth, and not wearing herself out to the point that she was physically too tired to care about her family. What *was* important was that family and her willingness to step into their lives and help in any way she could. When Celeste thought about her niece and the difficult issues that she struggled with each day, her own life seemed remote, even superficial, in comparison.

What mattered most was turning everything over to the Lord; her ambivalence about her job and her concerns about Tawnya and Ty, even her desire for marriage and children of her own. It wasn't easy. She was a take-charge sort of person who was at her best during a challenge, always seeking a direction and resolution for problems that crept up. *But that's exactly when we're called to step out in faith,* she mused, *especially people like me, who like to believe they're in control. Sometimes God has to send a little wake-up call, a reminder that I'm meant to trust in Him and lean not upon my own understanding.*

"Father, help me. I'm becoming more and more aware that my life is no longer bringing me fulfillment. Is it You at work in me, challenging me to look at life differently, to trust You more? Help me to really hear You, Lord. Guide me, direct my path. Thank you, Lord. Amen."

Tomorrow was Monday and she'd get busy coordinating Ty and Tawnya's dental appointments and making arrangements with Connie to do some light housekeeping and meal-prep. This much she could do, even though it still didn't quite feel like it was enough. But it was a start, and she felt better for having an executable plan to move on.

As far as work was concerned, there would be plenty to do. She'd put her best efforts in and continue to pray for guidance, then make every attempt to do that which was one of her most difficult challenges; to wait on the Lord, His will, in His time.

By Wednesday, she'd spent a good hour and a half on the phone, setting up dental appointments, orthodontist, and dermatology consultations, and had made plans with Analiese to borrow Tori for a couple of afternoons and evenings while Tawnya was visiting. All that remained was to make the actual telephone call to her brother-in-law to bring him into the loop. For no reason she could put a finger on, she was feeling strangely shy and self-conscious about having even the most casual interaction with Scott and had put off making the telephone call until she knew she could delay no longer. She'd spoken to Tawnya and knew that she and Ty had made their dental appointments, had had their teeth cleaned, and that her niece had an appointment for fillings that would take place after the orthodontist had decided which teeth would come out in preparation for the braces.

Now, on a hot and muggy Wednesday night that carried the promise of a thunderstorm, she carried her cordless phone out to the balcony, seated herself on an Adirondack chair and, after inhaling a deep breath, dialed the number.

A young voice answered, "Hello?"

"Hey, sweetie, it's Celeste."

"Hi, Aunt Celeste. I'm all ready to come, I can't wait. Do you think we could go to the Aquarium while I'm there? I've always wanted to see it."

"Sure, we can do that, Tawn. So, I'll be at Grandma's around eight Friday night and see you Saturday morning, how's that?"

"Great. Do you want to talk to my dad?"

"Yeah, guess I'd better. I'll see you Saturday, kiddo. Looking forward to it."

"Me too. Okay, here's Daddy. Bye."

Muffled voices, whispered instructions, then, "Hello, Celeste."

Throat suddenly dry, she swallowed quickly. "Hi, Scott. Well, we're all set here, and I'll be over for her this weekend."

"I think she's already packed. I haven't seen her this excited about anything for a long time."

"I'm looking forward to it too. We're going to have a great time."

Silence fell, while both felt keen self-consciousness. As surely as if prerehearsed, they spoke simultaneously, both demurring, "No, really, go ahead…" "No, after you."

"Connie's been out already, made Tawnya go ride her horse, wouldn't let her in the kitchen or the laundry room once she'd gotten the lay of the land."

"Good for her."

"Yeah. The woman makes a killer meatloaf. Had that with scalloped potatoes and green beans tonight. There's some other stuff made up too. I have to really thank you, Celeste, it was good of you to think of this. I appreciate it."

"I'm so glad it's working out. Connie's happy to have the extra money, and I really wanted to take some of the pressure off of Tawnya."

"Hold on, okay?" Muffled voices once again, then the sound of a door closing. "I'm back. I had to bring my phone outside, it's quieter out here."

"Where are you?"

"On the porch swing. What about you?"

Picturing him lounging alone on the swing, Celeste replied, "I'm out on my deck, looking at the lake and the lights across the other side."

"I've never seen your place. It sounds nice."

"It is nice, but sometimes I wish it were a little quieter. I'd like to be able to walk along the beach without all the condos and sunbathers, without all the traffic noise."

"I think you picked the wrong lake, then."

"I'm beginning to think so too."

A short silence fell between them, then his voice returned, "Are you thinking about selling, then? Where would you go? I guess there's Lake Sammamish, but I was thinking it's every bit as developed as Lake Washington."

"Oh, it is, for sure. I don't know, Scott. I've just kind of been, well, it may sound crazy, but I guess I've been waiting for instructions, as far as what comes next in my life."

"Instructions? From whom?"

She replied simply, "From God."

"From God? What, are you expecting to be told to sell all your worldly possessions and be a missionary in Africa or something?"

"No, nothing that extreme. I guess I've just been feeling like I'm missing out on something, you know? That maybe everything I thought was important really isn't what I'm supposed to be doing with my life. The problem is, I don't know what I'd do instead."

There was silence for a few seconds, then he replied, "It's funny, isn't it? You have a good job, plenty of money, and don't want for anything and you're thinking about walking away from it. All I ever wanted was to farm, didn't much care about money as long as I could support Rachel and the kids, and now there's nothing left of the farm, and I can't even pay the bills on time. I'm not trying to make you feel guilty or sound like I'm having a pity-party or anything. I guess I just wish I had your problems for awhile."

"I can't even imagine having your problems. Money's one thing, but everything else you've had to deal with...I wish I could do more to help you."

He laughed, a bitter chuckle that carried no amusement. "How about a miracle? Short of that, I can't think of a thing anyone could do to help at this point."

Celeste raised her eyes to the stars that were beginning to sprinkle the night sky. Beyond lay God's domain, to whom she'd entrusted her future, her life and, ultimately, her soul. Wasn't Scott in desperate need of hope and the promise of His love and peace? Hadn't he believed, once, in God's goodness and love? Even through his pain and anger, Celeste recognized his need to be reminded of that goodness and love.

"I believe in miracles, and I believe it's okay to ask God for them. But I also believe that sometimes it isn't His will that our prayers are answered the way we'd like. But, Scott, regardless of Rach's situation, don't forget that He loves you and cares about your pain."

"If He cared so much, He'd bring her out of that bed and make her well. If He really cared, He wouldn't be putting the kids through this, watching their mother die by inches. Yet I'm supposed to believe He cares about us? Why should I?"

Praying for the right words, she approached him gently. "What happened to your faith, Scott? Because I know you did believe. When did that disappear from your heart?"

He snorted. "Well, I guess it was about the time Rachel got sick, Celeste. I mean, come on, do the math; it's what you do, isn't it? And *I* didn't abandon Him so much as He abandoned *me*. And the kids. Especially Rachel."

"Did Rachel believe He'd abandoned her?"

"No, but then it's been quite awhile since she could tell me what she thinks, hasn't it? Maybe she did give up on Him. Wouldn't blame her if she had."

"Have You told Him how you feel?"

"What, tell God I'm mad at Him, that I think He's cruel and heartless? Probably get struck by lightening or something. Of course, that's if He cares, anyway, which I doubt."

"But He does, Scott. He never abandons us. He wants us to talk to Him, even when we're hurting, *especially* when we're hurting! Think of it this way. Suppose one of the kids came to you with an issue they were upset about, that they were accusing you of something that you may or may not have done. Would you rather they kept it inside where it would just grow and fester and have them act out in other ways? Would you be angry with them for having the courage to confront you honestly, or would you hear them out and try to work things out with them?"

"Well, obviously I'd like to think they could talk to me about anything, but I guess I'm not up for Father of the Year this time."

"There's no such thing as a perfect father, Scott, except for our Heavenly Father. He's never too busy to hear our prayers, even the ones that are hard for us to pray and that you may think are not easy for Him to hear. But He promised that He *would* hear, Scott, and promised that we could come to Him with all of our hurts, even our anger. He wants us to turn to Him. That's the bottom line."

"And then what? Everything's all better? He turns back time to when Rach was healthy? Like I said, it's too late. There's no point."

So much pain. Such hopelessness and such fear.

It was difficult to speak to Scott in the face of these debilitating emotions, and she felt tears burn her eyes. How did pastoral staff, even fellow believers, share Christ's love with someone in such a state of devastation? Where were the words that could ease pain and bring comfort?

Pray with him. Share his pain. Do your part, then step back and allow Me to do Mine.

Peace flooded her, and new tears stung her eyes. "Thank You, Lord." She drew a deep breath. "Scott? May I pray with you?"

"Whatever. I'm not praying, though."

"That's okay. He knows your heart, regardless."

She sat silently for a moment, then began, "Lord, I come before you tonight with a friend in crisis. I know that You see every tear we cry and know our every thought. You know our pain, Lord. I know that You love Scott deeply, just as You love Rachel and the kids too. You know their struggles and have never left their side. I know it's sometimes hard for us to really see You, especially when we're hurting. Lord, Scott is hurting and desperately needs Your comfort and compassion. I pray that You will be very real to him, Lord, and allow him to experience Your grace and Your peace. Please be very close to him, Lord, and comfort him. I ask this in the precious name of Jesus. Thank You, Father. Amen."

There was silence on the other end, then, "Is that it?"

"Yes."

"I need to get going. See you Saturday." With a click, he was gone.

She sighed, turned her phone off and lay it on the table next to her. She shifted in the chair, then rose and crossed to the edge of the deck, watching the lights flickering across the water.

His pain was a palpable, living entity, and she felt it to the depths of her soul. If she were to put herself in Scott's position, how would she endure the loss of her life-mate, the one she'd had every expectation of growing old with? How would she parent the children they shared single-handedly, in the depths of her own pain? She shook her head, unable to envision the spiritual and emotional devastation that would struggle to dominate her spirit. It was difficult enough to accept the loss of her sister; the loss that Scott and the kids faced was an even greater sorrow than her own, perhaps even greater than Catherine's.

Scripture counsels believers to bear one another's burdens, Celeste reminded herself. *Never an easy task, and especially difficult when we're unable to really appreciate the full breadth and scope of those burdens. Perhaps the reason for this is two-fold; by sharing another's pain and uplifting that person in prayer, we not only allow God the opportunity to demonstrate His grace, it also serves to remind us of the blessings in our own life and gives us a little nudge to remind us to praise and thank Him for those blessings.*

Was it somehow more difficult to uphold someone in prayer when that person was resistant, embittered and angry at life in general and God in particular? It was somehow easier to bear the other person's burdens when he or she held fast to God's promise and believed that in Him all things are possible. To whom was God more inclined to demonstrate His grace and mercy, the one who trusted Him in all things, or the one who no longer had faith in everything? Each had special needs, for all that they may be in different places in their journeys of faith. Did the needs of one take priority over those of the other?

She believed that God was an equal-opportunity hearer of prayer; that no matter from whose heart the prayer originated, He listened and knew that heart intimately. Scott's heart had been broken and was mending in a jagged and disorderly fashion. Sometimes bones that had been broken reconstituted themselves in a way that wasn't adequate to support the weight they were intended to bear, making it necessary to return to the site of injury, take a good look at the damage, and make adjustments to that bone, so that it could serve its purpose in a stronger, healthier manner.

Wasn't that exactly what God did with hearts when a hurting person cried out for the touch of His healing hand? Didn't He come in, lay His hand on the brokenness, and make it whole once more?

"Lord, lay your Hand on Scott's heart tonight. Be very near to him and help him to feel Your presence in his life. Help him to feel Your grace and Your love."

She prayed for Tawnya, and for Ty, for her mother, and for Rachel, holding them up to the Lord, then thanked Him for the work He would do in their lives and in her own.

Tomorrow was Thursday, and Friday she'd return to Shuksan. Her family was there, and she was eager to see them again.

She was eager to see Scott. Her fear had dissipated, and in its place a new gentleness had taken over.

"Help me to be Your hands and feet, Lord. Help me to be a living witness to Your love and grace. Amen."

Chapter 10

The next two days passed quickly, and Saturday found Scott at home, awaiting Celeste's arrival. He'd had worked a few hours in the morning, then returned home at noon in order to be able to see his daughter off and to see his sister-in-law. Of course, that wasn't the primary motivation, even though scarcely an hour had passed in the intervening days since she had prayed for him that she hadn't been in his thoughts. Probably too much in his thoughts. His thoughts were also filled with the words she'd spoken to him of God's love and faithfulness. Friday night he'd even pulled Rachel's Bible from her nightstand drawer. He'd turned to Philippians and read Paul's exhortations to turn to the Lord in prayer.

> Do not be anxious about anything, but in everything, by prayer and petition, with thanksgiving, present your requests to God. And the peace of God, which transcends all understanding, will guard your hearts and your minds in Christ Jesus.
>
> Philippians 4:6–8, NIV

To not be anxious or worried about anything was a tall order. Could God really expect a person to not worry about one thing or another in his or her life? Another piece of the passage said to take everything to God in prayer. *Everything.* He remembered what Celeste had said about prayer, about talking to God about his feelings, and his remark about being punished for calling God's attention to his anger and bitterness. But maybe she was right; after all, everything was *everything,* wasn't it? Even the darkest and most painful thoughts and doubts. If this was true, and he could really bring all of these things to God, then perhaps the rest of the promise was true as well, the part about experiencing God's peace, even when it didn't seem possible. If he even deserved such peace, which, given his distance from God over the past several years, didn't seem likely.

But it had given him something to think about. He wasn't quite ready to approach God directly. Not yet. After all, one didn't just show up unannounced at the door of someone he hadn't been on good terms with, especially if there were hard feelings involved. There had to be some careful planning, the timing had to be just right, otherwise a guy could end up just making things worse. The other person might slam the door in his face or say things he didn't want to hear. Call it making amends, call it reconciliation, call it whatever you want, but it usually involved a degree of repentance and apologies. And if a guy wasn't really all that sorry for his part in the falling-out and was simply going through the motions, what was the point? Unless the other person didn't know him well, wouldn't he be able to sense the lack of sincerity?

If the other party involved was God, then there could be no doubt that He would know exactly what was going on in a guy's heart, his level of sincerity, and honesty. There would be no half-measures here, no lukewarm apologies or just saying the right things for the sake of smoothing things over.

He wasn't ready for that kind of reconciliation yet. To tell God of his anger and pain would imply willingness to lay those things at His feet and allow Him to move and act in his life. To walk away from those things would imply that he was willing to leave them behind, and that was the sticking point. The anger and fear had dominated his life for such a long time that he didn't really know how he'd function without them.

Rather than replace the Bible in the nightstand, he'd left it on top. Perhaps he'd read another passage or two in a day or so. He wasn't ready to take the next step and actually pray yet, but perhaps one of these days, as long as God didn't expect too much of him. For someone who didn't have anything left to give, maybe even approaching God smacked of hypocrisy; it wasn't exactly acting in good faith to ask for help when you weren't willing to reciprocate when called upon to do so, whether it was God or a friend.

It had been a long time since he'd had someone he could really consider a friend. Sure, he had his old high school buddies, but he'd pretty much let his outside friendships slide. Rach had been his best friend, confidant, sounding board, and advisor. She'd been the rock upon which he'd leaned, and their relationship had been the one constant in his life that he could depend upon. When she'd retreated into that dark place within herself, a large part of him had followed, but it was his own darkness in which he existed. Rach's dark place had room only for herself.

How could he admit to God that he was angry at his wife for abandoning him? To admit this to God would mean really admitting it to himself in the process. And what kind of person could be angry at his wife for contracting a terminal illness, anyway? Did he really think she'd made a conscious choice to take this path? Of course not, it was ridiculous, which made his anger toward Rach unreasonable and petty and painted an unflattering portrait of his own character in the process.

Perhaps he deserved this isolation, this estrangement from God. A good portion of the time he didn't like the person he'd become, and if he had these feelings about himself, there was a good chance that God felt the same way.

Forgiveness. Reconciliation. Those were the words he'd associated with approaching an estranged friend after a long period of time. Suppose he was willing to approach God? What if He did slam the door in his face? What if He said, "Sorry, buddy, you're too far gone. You're on your own"? It was difficult to apologize to someone, even when you knew you'd blown it.

When it came right down to it, why would God even care whether or not Scott Parnell came to Him and tried to wipe the slate clean? There were plenty of other people more deserving of forgiveness. What would God ask of him in return? How would he even prove he was worthy of a relationship with God at this point? What if he continued to make mistakes? Would God eventually throw in the towel and say, "You've had plenty of chances, Scott, and I've had it with you!'

What if he was *never* quite good enough?

> For it is by grace you have been saved, through faith—and
> this not from yourselves, it is the gift of God, not by works—
> so that no one can boast.
>
> Ephesians 2:8–9, NIV

The Scripture came unexpectedly to his mind, set free from deep inside his memory, speaking directly to his heart. Saved by grace, through faith, not through anything I may or may not have done. *Through faith.*

"Is it You, God? Are You speaking to me?"

The peace that flooded his spirit brought tears to his eyes, and he was aware of an easing of the pressure in his chest. Could this be the peace that went beyond explanation that he'd questioned earlier? It certainly seemed as though it was; he hadn't experienced this feeling for longer than he could remember. Perhaps he'd take a few minutes and read another passage now, before Celeste arrived. He reached for the Bible and opened it randomly, the pages falling open to Jeremiah, and he read the words as though they'd been written specifically for himself.

> For I know the plans I have for you, plans to prosper you and
> not to harm you, plans to give you hope and a future. Then
> you will call upon Me and come and pray to Me and I will
> listen to you. You will seek Me and find Me when you seek
> Me with all your heart.
>
> Jeremiah 29:11–13, NIV

The promise was that when he sought the Lord with all his heart, He would be there, that His plan was to provide hope for the future. Of all of the things he'd lost in the last few years, perhaps the most devastating had been the loss of hope.

He held the Bible tightly in his hand and claimed the promise, and for the first time in years, opened his heart in prayer as tears blurred his vision.

"God, I suppose I've always known that You're there and that You care. I guess I've been so angry with You for so long that it was easier

to just ignore You. I'm sorry for that, Lord. I've got a lot of problems, but I guess You already know that. So, I'm kind of starting from scratch here; I'm pretty rusty when it comes to You, when it comes to praying, especially when it comes to trusting You. So, help me here, Lord, because I'm about at the end of everything, hope, especially. Please help me. And forgive me for holding You responsible for Rach's illness, Lord. Help me to let go of these feelings. Thank You, Lord. Amen."

He rose to his feet, replaced the Bible on the nightstand, and pressed his eyes to his shirtsleeves to dry the tears that had come as unexpectedly as a desert rainstorm. Outside, Skip had kicked up a ruckus, barking as ferociously as though he had a mean bone in his body. Tawnya's voice carried up the stairs. "Daddy, Celeste's here."

"Be right there, hon."

He lay his hand on the Bible one last time, whispered, "Thank You," then went to greet the person who'd been the first to touch his heart in years. Thanks to her, the icecap that had held his heart prisoner had been breached. He hoped to be able to find the words to share with her what her words of God's love had set into motion in his spirit.

She stood at the screen door, tucking her sunglasses into her collar, and raised her gaze to meet his as he clattered down the stairs.

"Hey."

Reaching for the door, he held it open, "Come in. How was the drive?"

"Good. Isn't it a beautiful morning! How are you?"

"Good. Really good. In a hurry to get on the road?"

"Not especially, why?"

He smiled. "Want to go for a walk? I have something to tell you."

Chapter 11

*T*awnya's week in Seattle passed in a blur of late nights watching videos from her aunt's amazing collection, sleeping late in the mornings, and bustling about in the afternoons, visiting the orthodontist and dermatologist, then going to dinner or returning to the condo, where Celeste prepared light summertime meals that they ate out on the balcony. They'd enjoyed the hot tub as well, and Tawnya had reveled in what she considered to be a life of luxury; the light, airy condo overlooking the blue expanse of lake, with Seattle and all it offered lying basically at her feet, hers for the taking. Now, Friday afternoon, she was going to meet a girl named Tori, the daughter of one of Aunt Celeste's friends. Nearly immobilized with anticipation yet with a grinding dread lodging in her stomach, Tawnya rode alongside her aunt as they struggled through the downtown traffic, making their way to the Seattle waterfront. They were meeting Tori and her mother in front of the Aquarium and after the tour, they would eat dinner at Ivar's, the world-famous seafood restaurant on the pier and, according to her aunt, one of Seattle's must-do experiences. After securing a parking place, they crossed the street caught up in a great wave of humanity, Tawnya's eyes wide as she attempted to take everything in at once. People of every race, culture, and ethnic background thronged the crowded streets, voices mixed in a cacophony of sound. She saw both women and men with heads wrapped in turbans, watched graceful women in colorful robes, and avoided darting children clutching dripping ice cream cones or multi-colored cones of cotton candy in sticky hands.

Celeste's voice broke her awed reverie, "There they are," pointing to a great pillar rising from the water below, holding one side of the pier steady. A woman and young girl waved in return, making their way toward them. Mouth dry as cotton, heart thumping, Tawnya watched as they approached. The mother was a beautiful woman with kind, chocolate-colored eyes that softened as she spoke. The daughter, Tori, was about her height, but looked older. Fairer of skin than her mother, Tori had striking green eyes and curly brown hair with lighter tips, caught up in a hot pink scrunchie. Tawyna's heart did a swan dive of nerves as the introductions were performed. Standing quietly to one side, she watched as the other three women interacted among themselves, feeling self-conscious and out of place. As if she understood exactly how Tawnya was feeling, Tori addressed her, "We already have tickets for the tour, there's twenty minutes until the next one starts. Want to walk around the pier and look at the shops for a little while?"

Shyly, Tawnya nodded, glancing at her aunt.

"It's okay, hon, go ahead. There're all kinds of fun shops. You won't have a chance to see much, but they're open late and we can look around after dinner. Have fun."

As the girls walked away, Celeste murmured, "She's so nervous, Ana, I could feel it rolling off her in the car. I hope they hit it off."

Knowing Tawnya's situation and having heard a brief synopsis of her social struggles, Analiese nodded reassuringly. "They'll be fine, Auntie. Between Tori and the carnival atmosphere down here, she'll start to loosen up. If she thinks you're worried about her, it'll just be that much harder for her to relax."

Recognizing the truth in this, Celeste glanced at her watch. "Want to just hang out here and keep a place in line?"

"Might as well. So, do you mind a little shop talk while we're waiting?"

"Not at all. What have you heard?"

"Word is Charlotte's looking to jump ship. She's going to head up her own firm, over in Bellevue."

This was news. Charlotte was one of the partners and was a powerhouse of new client recruitment. She networked like no one Celeste had ever known and spent most meals power-dining, stroking potential clients along, and most of the time, successfully luring them away from their previous firms and delivering them, wrapped neatly, complete with portfolios, to the auspices of Biddle, Barton, Sutton & Swales. That Charlotte would set up shop on her own was a possibility they'd never considered, and one that Celeste knew would be in her own thoughts a great deal over the next weeks.

The girls, having reached the end of the pier, hung over the railing and peered at the oily water below. A gull, crying raucously, swooped down in a rapid arc of motion, beating wings missing Tawnya's head by inches. With a cry, she jumped aside, bumping the other girl in her sudden flight.

Mortified, she apologized, "Sorry."

"It's cool. Stupid seagulls, always looking for somebody to feed them. So, you're gonna be in eighth grade, huh?"

"Yeah. What about you?"

"Ninth."

"Is that high school here?"

"No, still junior high. Which is cool, I mean, my school's not too far from my house, but next year I'll have to take the bus to Garfield, which will really stink. Unless we move, but I doubt it unless Mama gets a promotion and some more money."

"What about your dad?"

Shaking her head, lightened curls bobbing in the breeze, Tori replied, "Don't have one. I mean, I do somewhere, but I never see him. It's just Mama and me, always has been. Oh-oh, look at the time! We've gotta get back or we'll be late, and they don't let anybody in once the tour's started. Come on, we'll come back and hang out tonight."

The girls weaved their way through the human maze, arriving at the Aquarium's entrance in the nick of time. An hour later, blinking as they re-emerged into the brightness of the sun, three pair of hands dug in purses for sunglasses. Tawnya stood silently to the side; she had no sunglasses. Noting this, Celeste reminded herself to pick up a pair next time they were shopping.

"What's the plan, are we going to eat or wait a while?"

After a brief consultation, they decided that as it was only five o'clock, they could wait awhile to eat.

"We'll walk over and make reservations for six-thirty, how's that? You can meet us there."

"Sounds good. Come on, Tawnya, let's go look around. Mama, can we walk up to the market?"

"Pike Place? Oh, I don't know, Tori, it's getting late."

"We'll be fine, Mama. There're some major shops there. Please?"

"All right, but don't lose track of time."

"We won't."

Celeste chimed in, "You girls be careful, now."

"We will, Aunt Celeste."

As they finally made their escape, Tori muttered, "You'd think we were going on a walking tour of Eritrea or something."

Eritrea? It must be a place, but Tawnya had never heard of it. Loathe to expose her ignorance, she said only, "Why is it such a big deal to come up here?"

"It's not, except when it's getting late. It's not the Market itself, just the neighborhood."

With a stirring of alarm, Tawnya asked, "Is it dangerous?"

"No more than anywhere else, but there's a lot of street people and then later on, once it's dark, it won't be safe." Silence hung between the girls as they made the steep climb, the great Pike Place Market sign and clock directly ahead.

Tori nudged her arm. "Okay, we're here. Come on, there's a shop upstairs that has the coolest retro stuff, real seventies tat; Elton John sunglasses, black lights, and posters. There's the meanest pair of rattlesnake boots you ever laid eyes on, and a whole shelf-full of lava lamps."

Chattering companionably, the girls spent a delightful hour picking through the relics of the psychedelic era, sharing dubious glances as they displayed various items of clothing, giggling, and then replacing them on the racks.

Finally, each sporting new mood rings, they returned down the steep street to the waterfront, clutching their treasures tightly and keeping a sharp eye out for purse-snatchers. Arriving at Ivar's at six twenty, assuming innocent looks, they joined the adults.

With a resigned shake of her head, Analiese queried, "Good grief, child, what on earth did you buy?"

"Just stuff, Mama. Look, check out this belt." Silver-plated rings looped together with two larger rings at the ends, tied together with a leather thong rode Tori's hips.

"Uh huh. I'll keep an eye open for the fashion police, sugar, and when they show up, you make a break for it, okay?"

Sighing, with a great roll of her eyes, her daughter enlightened her, "Oh, Mama, it's retro! You know, like, way cool?"

"She's right, Ana." Amused, Celeste nodded. "You know how a person never saw a halter top in the eighties, like it would have been a real fashion gaffe? Well, they're back. A lot of the seventies stuff is coming back into style."

"You have a point," Analiese mused. "My older sisters lived in halter tops when I was a little kid, but by the time I got old enough to wear the ones they'd left behind, I wouldn't have been caught dead in them. I'd forgotten about that."

"And look at your bag, Tawnya. Did you buy the place out? I do like your sunglasses, by the way."

Interrupted by the hostess announcing that their table was ready, they followed dutifully to the back of the restaurant and onto the wide deck bathed in the rays of the lowering sun, the salty tang of Puget Sound pungent in the air. After ordering strawberry milkshakes all around, attention was returned to the contents of Tawnya's bag. Presenting her treasures proudly, she beamed as the older women exclaimed over the ropes of beads; turquoise, mauve, pink, blue, lavender, green, and clear crystals.

"I'm going to get Daddy to take my bedroom door off and hang them right in the doorway, just like a real hippie."

Celeste grinned, holding a handful of beads, letting them spill through her fingers like water. "These always bring to mind the "Midnight At The Oasis" thing, you know? Belly dancers and sitar music by firelight. The pasha lounging on his cushions, servant girls feeding him grapes."

"Incense, belly button jewels, and the Dance of the Seven Veils," Analiese interjected.

Dropping the beads into their plastic bag, Celeste chuckled, "I think you may have to hang these in your closet door rather than your main door, Tawn; they're great for atmosphere but don't provide much in the way of privacy."

Turning their attention to the menus, they each ordered the seafood platter. Cracking shells, listening to the music of the other voices, Tawnya let her gaze drift west, across the blue expanse of Puget Sound to the massive bulk of the Olympic Mountain range. Sudden happiness suffused her entire being; what an awesome day it had been. The prospect of a new friend, even though she didn't live close enough to visit very often, filled her with contentment. She shouldn't have been nervous at all; Analiese and Tori had accepted and embraced her for who she was, Celeste's niece. They didn't know what an outcast she was at home, but here, today, tonight, she was accepted.

Such are the things that heal a wounded spirit, Celeste mused, watching her niece, seeing for herself the ease in which Tawnya accepted the presence of these new friends. The girls had hit it off just fine and, with any luck, would build something from which each could learn from the other and grow in their world views.

After agreeing to keep track of the girls' bags, Celeste and Analiese turned them loose once again after dinner, following a lengthy set of instructions; to remain in the pier area, not to cross the street, and by no means whatsoever were they to speak to anyone.

Finally making their escape, the girls spent a cheerful hour examining the shops set along the piers, from exotic imported items to polished walrus tusks and agates. After purchasing enormous strawberry ice cream cones, they returned to a bench at the end of Pier 57, seating themselves as the first stars began to twinkle in the sky. A loud blast split the air, causing Tawnya to startle.

"Bainbridge Island ferry." Tori grinned at her companion's reaction.

"Have you ever been on it?"

"Couple of times. When it's sunny out, you can see Mount Rainier and miles of the Sound. It's really pretty, but we don't come down here very often. Mama's awfully busy with work, and I do volunteer work a couple of afternoons a week, so there's not a lot of time to do much."

"What kind of volunteer work do you do?"

"The kids in my church group help out at a teen shelter; sweep and mop the floors, help in the kitchen, wash bedding, stuff like that. And we also spend time talking to the kids, try to witness, share our faith. I like it, but it's not always easy."

Intrigued, Tawnya queried, "How old are the kids who stay there?"

"We've had some young as eleven, all the way up to seventeen or so. By the time they're eighteen, a lot of times they're either in jail or so deep into their habits that you just don't see them anymore."

"Habits?"

"Drugs, alcohol."

"So young?"

Shaking her head, Tori replied, "I forget you're a farm girl, not that I'm putting you down or anything. You come from a different world, that's all. These are runaways for the most part, Tawnya, they call them "throw-away kids." A lot of their parents are addicts and are abusive or have kicked them out, so they survive any way they can."

Unable to imagine herself alone on the city streets, Tawnya asked, "Like how?"

"Prostitution, running drugs, pick-pocketing, running scams. Mostly prostitution."

Silent, Tawnya stared at the darkening water, hearing the slap of the waves on the support tiers. She'd had no idea of the ugly sub-culture that eroded the beauty of the Emerald City. "I don't think I could do that, work there, I mean. It would be too hard."

Tori eyed her companion with a considering expression. "There're girls a lot like you there, every day, Tawnya."

At the disbelieving glance, Tori continued, "Kids lose a parent, can't deal with it. Pretty soon they're dropping acid or smoking bowls, maybe just some booze to get them through the day. They drop out of school, take off from home. If they're lucky, eventually they'll end up at the shelter."

"I think my brother drinks, and I'm pretty sure he smokes pot. Sometimes I worry about him, but he'd just tell me to get lost so I pretty much leave him alone. So what church do you go to?"

"We go to a nondenominational church, kind of like a commu-nity church. How about you? Do you go?"

"We're Lutheran. I used to go every Sunday, but I don't so much anymore, unless I spend the night with my Grandma Saturday night. I'm supposed to start confirmation classes this fall, but I don't know…My dad, well, before my mom got sick, we went every week, but that's been a long time ago. I think my dad's mad at God, 'cause of my mom, you know."

Tori nodded. "What about you? Are *you* mad at God, too?"

"I don't know. I don't think so. I guess I just feel like He has better things to do than worry about our family. I try not to think about it too much, otherwise I probably *would* be mad at Him. My mom never hurt anybody, so why does she have to go through all this? Why does our family have to go through it if He cares so much?"

"I get that question a lot. Sometimes I even feel that way myself, when things aren't going right in my own life. But I know He cares. I believe that everything happens according to God's will, even the stuff that isn't so great. I think that's how we learn to really trust Him with our problems. And that's the whole point, for us to turn to Him and believe that He's there and loves us. That, and we have to learn to make good choices so we don't bring a lot of problems onto ourselves."

Staring straight ahead at the expanse of water, Tawnya asked, "What about things you've tried to stop doing and can't?"

"You mean, like shoplifting or something like that?"

"Yeah. Something like that."

"Sure, those are the things that we really need God's help with, things that we do that we know aren't right. I know that for me, I can't do it on my own. I'm just not strong enough."

"So, what do you do?"

"I ask Him to help me, to give me strength. To help make me want to do the right things."

"Does it work?"

Tori chuckled, "Well, I'm not perfect, but then He doesn't expect me to be. I don't always do all the right things, none of us do. When I mess up, I know that all I have to do is ask for forgiveness and ask Him to help me do better next time."

"What if you just keep doing the same things over and over, when you know they're wrong?"

"Well, then I guess you have to ask yourself whether you really want to stop in the first place, whether you're really ready to let Him come into your life and help you make the changes. But the thing is, every time we sin, you know, do something we know is wrong, no matter how many times we do it, He promises to forgive us, if we're really seriously sorry. But He also wants us to make better choices." Checking her watch, "Oh, man, it's almost nine thirty, time to meet Mama and Celeste. We'd better go."

The girls walked back to the square in silence, each lost in their own thoughts. After meeting the older women, they said goodbye. Tori scribbled a phone number on one of her mother's business cards and handed it to Tawnya. "Let me know when you're in town next, Tawnya. We'll go kick it. And call me anytime if you want to talk."

"Okay. Thanks."

"Take care of yourself, girl. It was nice to meet you."

"You too. Maybe sometime you can come over with Aunt Celeste for the weekend. I have a horse and rabbits, and we could go swimming."

"Yeah, that sounds like fun."

"Bye, then."

"Take care, girl."

As she rode beside Aunt Celeste through downtown Seattle, which, even at ten at night, seemed to be a whirl of bright lights and activity, Tawnya savored the events of the evening and even more, the anticipation of more days like this one. A new friend, one who didn't treat her like she was a bad joke, but who treated her like an equal.

Satisfaction clear to her toes, she leaned her head against the seat and enjoyed the cool air coming through the sunroof. Eyes snapping wide open, she exclaimed, "What is that place, Aunt Celeste?" pointing to a large building bright with neon lights, The Deja Vu billboard sign pronouncing, "SEVEN GORGEOUS GIRLS AND ONE UGLY ONE."

"Strip club, why?"

"I found a book of matches with that name in Tyler's room when I was getting his dirty clothes once. Do you think he's really gone in there?"

Brows raised, Celeste replied, "If he's been in there, he must have false ID because you have to be eighteen. I don't know, anything's possible, Tawn."

They rode in silence until they were out of the downtown area, Space Needle piercing the night sky behind them. Tawnya spoke again, "I wish I didn't have to go home tomorrow. I mean, I miss Daddy, but I've had so much fun this week."

"I'm glad, hon. It'll only be two weeks and then you'll be back for your braces, and we'll go hog-wild school shopping then, okay?"

"Okay."

They rode in silence for a distance, then Tawnya spoke, thankful for the darkness. "Do you believe in miracles, Aunt Celeste?"

Oh, sweetie. Choosing her words carefully, she replied, "You have to know that I would give anything for your mom to be well again, Tawnya. And there are new treatments being discovered for diseases every day. Yes, I do believe in miracles; absolutely. I think it's good to pray for a miracle, but remember that the other part of that is to realize that there are some things in God's plans that we're not meant to understand."

"I know." As Celeste turned the car into her parking space, Tawnya spoke quietly, "I don't think she's going to get well, Aunt Celeste. Does that make me bad?"

Removing the keys from the ignition, Celeste relaxed her shoulders against the seat and sighed. "No, it doesn't make you bad, hon. I think it makes you a realist. Like I said, there's nothing any of us wouldn't do if we could somehow bring your mom back to the way she was, but that's not in our hands. I think that what we need to do is keep her in our prayers and try to accept what is. Your mom wouldn't want you spending your life holding onto something that wasn't going to happen. She'd want to know you were living your life, growing up to be a well-adjusted and happy person, Tawnya. She'd want you to know it's okay for you to do that with no guilt."

Meeting Celeste's compassionate gaze, Tawnya nodded, "I know there's nothing I can do for Mom." Tears welled in her eyes. "Sometimes I wish God would just take her so she wouldn't have to lay there every day. She doesn't know who any of us are anymore, she can't even breathe by herself! Why doesn't He just take her to heaven so she doesn't have to suffer anymore?"

With a deep ache in her heart, Celeste murmured, "Come here, sweetie," wrapping the girl in a tender embrace. "It's okay, hon, you go on and cry."

Her niece had been needing this for a long time, Celeste realized; needing the unspoken acceptance to face this painful issue head-on and begin the inevitable grieving process for the mother she'd lost as a little girl and yet who was still an integral part of her life.

"But I'm here, hon. And I'll be here whenever you need me."

Tears finally slowing, Tawnya drew away, face awash with tears. Pulling a tissue from the box under the console, she blew her nose, then wiped her face dry. Eyes averted, she said, "I'm sorry."

"Tawnya."

"Yeah?"

"Never apologize for your genuine emotions. But do take them to the Lord, lay them at His feet. Promise?"

"Okay."

Finally exiting the car, Celeste activated the lock/anti-theft system. "Are you tired?"

"A little."

Sliding her key into the lock, she swung the door open, then locked it behind them. "Well, let's get to bed so we can get out of here by nine, okay?"

"Okay. Are you spending the night with Grandma?"

"No, I think I'll just come on home tomorrow evening. I have some work to catch up on, so I'd better get started on it."

"Okay. Can I use the bathroom a minute?"

"Sure. Take your time."

Tawnya entered the bathroom and locked the door behind her. It had been a long time since supper, probably too long, but she had to try. Dropping to her knees, she performed the ritual that would induce vomiting, bring up the food she'd eaten and get rid of it before it could add calories and pounds. Milkshake and ice cream. Crab and melted butter, sourdough bread. If it was especially painful tonight, she had no one to blame but herself; she'd eaten like a pig and had enjoyed each and every bite.

Given the length of time that had passed, it was difficult, and tears streaked her face as she flushed the toilet and settled her back against the tub. She hated this; hated the rolling of her stomach and the foul taste in her mouth, hated the necessity of her actions, and hated the way her body looked. But if she wanted to get into the new clothes Celeste had bought for her this week, the ones she'd told her aunt had fit when they were actually a couple of sizes too small, then this was the price she'd have to pay.

After a few minutes, she rose wearily to her feet, brushed her teeth, and washed her face. She flipped off the light, called good-night to her aunt, and went into the guest room. She lay in the dark, replaying her conversation with her new friend in her mind. Tori had said that God would help her with her problems if she really wanted help. But what did God know about weighing one hundred seventy pounds in the seventh grade? What did He know about how it felt to be a fat girl with pimples who existed at her school only as a target for the other kids to tease and bully?

No, God had plenty to worry about with people like Mama, people who were *good*. He had His hands full with the popular kids like Ariel, whose family went to church every Sunday and put a lot of money into the offering plate. Girls like herself didn't count, regardless of what Tori said. Tori was beautiful and thin, and her mom was, too, and they both really believed in Him. Surely God would give priority to the ones who He knew already believed in Him, and why should He care about her anyway?

Her stomach cramped and she rolled to her side, pressing her hands to her belly as tears dampened the pillow beneath her cheek. Fat was a lonely place to be, and the pain she experienced every night hurt so much more than just her stomach, but also reinforced her deficiencies, her inability to control her bingeing and purging, and her fear that she'd never be as good as everyone else.

The cramps finally passed and her stomach was calm once more. She flipped the pillow to the dry side and willed herself to relax. Tomorrow she'd be home. She'd see Daddy, and Ty, although he never said much to her when he was around. She'd have Daddy take off her closet door and hang the hippie beads, and then put her new clothes on hangers and be able to see them and visualize herself thinner. By the time school started, she'd be wearing them, even if she had to starve herself.

Whatever it took.

Chapter 12

*W*hen the Beamer pulled into the yard, the screen door opened, and Scott stepped onto the porch.

"Daddy!" Tawnya dropped her bags on the gravel and ran to meet her father as he descended the porch steps. "What are you doing here?"

"Hey, baby." Folding her in a warm embrace, he met Celeste's eyes over Tawnya's shoulder. "Done with haying for second cutting, so I have a few days off to get everything ready for harvest. Been changing oil in the thrasher and checking connections in the combine, that kind of thing."

Walking toward the car, arm around his daughter's shoulder, he greeted the silent woman standing at the open drivers' door. "Celeste."

"Daddy, I have to go back in two weeks to get my braces. Oh, and I met the coolest girl, she's Aunt Celeste's friend's daughter. Her name's Tori, and she's thirteen and she's really nice, isn't she, Aunt Celeste?"

"She's a sweetheart, for sure."

Hefting the bags sitting on the ground, Scott tipped his head toward the house. "Come in for a little bit, Celeste."

"Just for a few minutes. I'm driving back this afternoon, and I still have to stop in at Mother's."

Surprised, and more than a little disappointed, Scott queried, "Going back today? And miss out on Catherine's Sunday dinner special?"

"She has to make up some work, Daddy, that's why she has to leave early." his daughter informed him.

"Well, come in and have a glass of tea, at least."

"Okay, for a few minutes, but then I really do have to get going."

"After you." Scott swept an arm before him, suitcase swinging and detracting slightly from his grand gesture.

Once in the house, Celeste was gratified to see that things weren't a total disaster; either Connie had just cleaned in the last day or so, or Scott and Ty had done a creditable job of mucking the place out.

"Here you go." Scott presented a tall glass of ice tea, ice crackling in the cold liquid. His voice interrupted her musings and, jumpy as a cat, she startled. Turning at the sound of his voice, she came up short; he was standing close enough that she could count his eyelashes.

"Thanks." Aware that his eyes followed her every movement, she moved away, setting the glass on the coffee table.

Tawnya had taken her bags upstairs and from below, they heard her footsteps crossing her bedroom floor, hearing her stereo begin abruptly. Alone, steeped in self-consciousness, they cast about for conversation. Finally inspired, Scott asked, "Want to walk down to the pasture? I need to change the water. If you don't want to, you can just hang out here; I just thought you might like to stretch your legs before you head back."

"That sounds good."

"Just a sec." Moving to the foot of the stairs, he raised his voice to compete with the stereo. "Celeste and I are gonna go down and change the water. Be back in half an hour or so."

"Okay."

Holding the screen door open, he queried, "Ready?"

"Lead the way."

They set off from the house, shielding their eyes against the sun's brightness. Walking in silence, their shoes kicking up dust on the road, they avoided the leaping grasshoppers that lunged without warning from the weeds at the side of the road.

"How did the week go?"

"Fine, busy. She's all set at the orthodontist's, two weeks from Monday. She saw the dermatologist and he prescribed some antibiotic ointment to apply twice a day, she'll show you, I'm sure. Other than that, we played a little bit, and I think she just kind of enjoyed hanging out, a different routine, you know?"

"Yeah. Thanks again, Celeste, for everything you're doing for her."

"It's no great hardship; believe me. I've enjoyed it."

After a few moments, he remarked, "Sure hot here, how about in Seattle?"

"It's been beautiful; makes November through March seem worth the wait for the rest of the year."

He looked sidelong at her. "Are we really talking about the weather?"

She laughed, and he caught her gaze and grinned. "Okay, so what should we talk about?"

"How 'bout what you've been up to, other than playing auntie?"

"Oh, just work, you know. It's just getting harder and harder to go in there everyday and do the same things for the same clients. Even the new clients are the same, they just have different names. I guess I'm really struggling with my *purpose,* you know? I read somewhere that when you start feeling like what you're doing isn't satisfying you and you don't feel like you're contributing something, that maybe it means it's time to move on, that the Lord has something else in mind for you. I guess that's where I'm at; I'm feeling like I need to make a change, but I don't know what, exactly. And it's tough, because I've always thought I knew my path, where I'd eventually end up. Now I'm just kind of putting in my time until I figure out what I need to be doing instead. But you're not really listening to me, are you? Sorry, I tend to get so wrapped up in myself that I don't realize when I'm talking too much."

He sighed, eyes turned toward the mountain range to the west. Coming to a stop before the irrigation pump, they stood silently for a long moment. Moving to the side, Celeste watched as he knelt on one knee and turned the valve counter-clockwise until the jets of water spraying the second section of trees lost pressure and dwindled to nothing. Following as he strode to the last pump valve, she stood opposite the pump as he settled the valve on the head.

Scott straightened, exhaled deeply, then said, "Let's sit down,

Celeste." He waited until she'd settled herself on the ground, then sat across from her.

"I want to talk to you. I haven't talked to anyone besides my attorney, and I think it's time to…bring you into the loop. The thing is, I'm financially tapped out. I don't have any more land to sell, and I'm just about at the end of my rope. I've got a couple of hard choices to make and not much time left to make them."

Unable to stay seated, he rose to his feet and turned to face the mountains. "This isn't easy for me, Celeste; in fact, I've done my best to ignore the situation for so long that just dealing with it's tough for me. I haven't talked to anyone about this, except Rach, and I guess that doesn't count anymore, does it? Except that it does count, and that's where it gets tough. Do you know what a living will is?"

"Sure." She nodded. "Advanced directive, Do Not Resuscitate, no artificial means of sustaining life."

He could sense the moment it connected in her mind, even the silence was charged.

"How long, Scott?" she asked, mind whirling. "How long ago did she sign it?"

He sat down heavily once more and spoke quietly, as if by doing so he was releasing a heavy weight, "Four years ago. She wanted me to promise that I wouldn't let her be put on the respirator or hooked up to a feeding tube. She signed the form at the doctor's office, and I told her what she wanted to hear, then took the paper home and put it in my desk and ignored it. I figured I'd deal with it when the time came; I guess I was in enough denial that maybe I figured the time wouldn't ever actually come. And when it did, I couldn't honor her wishes. She'd been having trouble eating for quite awhile because she kept aspirating food into her lungs, getting pneumonia, so I gave consent for the feeding tube, and then a few weeks later, watched them intubate her, put her on the vent, and I still wasn't strong enough to say, 'No, we're not doing this.'"

He rose to his feet again, began pacing, and continued, "I've been thinking about this ever since she went on the vent, that she trusted me to respect her wishes and how she'd hate living like this. I know this, Celeste, and it's been eating me alive. I remember what she said to me the night she signed the form, and it was basically 'just let me go.' But I was caught up in this guilt thing, you know; how do I tell the kids I'm going to have the life support withdrawn, that I've made the decision to let her die? To say nothing of Catherine."

"Do the kids know about the DNR?"

"No. Her doctor knows, and he's been at me about it, which I understand, but I can't just say, 'Okay, kids, Mom's gonna die on Halloween because I can't afford to keep her alive any longer.' But I don't have any more magic rabbits to pull out of my hat. So, I talked with Peter Ralston, remember him? He's a lawyer now, practicing in Wenatchee. Anyway, he recommended that I divorce Rach, let the state take over her care. But I'm really struggling with that too. It just doesn't seem right, you know? I mean, marriage is for better and worse, financially and health-wise. It seems like it would be taking the easy way out, if there is such a thing."

He turned to face her, searching her face for signs of censure or anger. Finding none, he returned to sit near her. "Talk to me, Celeste. I honestly don't know what to do here. It seems like I only have two choices, and I don't much care for either one."

Celeste sat silently for a long moment. "I can't tell you what to do, Scott, even if I were presumptuous enough to think I knew what the right thing was. It has to be your decision, knowing what Rachel would have wanted. Since she'd signed the DNR, she obviously knew what she wanted for herself, right? I can't counsel you one way or the other. Have you prayed about it, asked God for guidance?"

"Not really. I mean, I've just now gotten to where I'm able to reach out to Him at all again, and I guess I'm out of practice at really trusting Him with anything. And maybe it's guilt because I know what Rachel would have wanted."

She sighed. "I guess all I can say is to turn it over, Scott, all of it. As hard as it is, you can trust God with this. You know what Rachel wanted. And you know she's not afraid of death. She's been ready to go home for a long time."

He nodded. "I know. And she absolutely trusted God, body and soul; so did I. Then everything I thought was important in my life started to slip away; Rach's health, having to sell off the ranch, watching the effect everything's had on the kids…I guess I just kind of figured He didn't deserve any more of me than I'd already given up. It's still hard to have that kind of trust."

"It is hard, because besides the fact that it's plain old human nature, we're culturally programmed to think we have to be strong and handle everything on our own, especially men. But I've found that when I finally do let it all go, I wonder why I hadn't done it weeks ago. Scott, would it be okay if I prayed for you?"

"Yeah. Yeah, that'd be good."

Celeste closed her eyes. "Lord, I know that You love us, that You love Scott, and the kids, and Rachel. I pray that You will be with Scott as he faces these decisions about Rachel's life, and that You will speak to his heart and grant him Your peace. Thank You, Lord. Amen."

She opened her eyes, surprised by the tears that had risen during her prayer. Seeing tears in Scott's eyes touched something deep in her heart, and she surrendered to her grief and allowed her own tears to spill over her cheeks. "I guess I didn't realize how much I've kept all of this bottled up inside myself. I think maybe I was afraid of how much it would hurt if I really let myself feel it, you know?"

"I know exactly. But I don't know any other way to feel it, Celeste; she was part of my life, the *bigges*t part of my life for so long, and now I'm having to face the fact that she's really not coming back. I think I'd sooner die myself than have to make these decisions."

"I know, but you don't have to make them alone. You'll know, Scott. Just let God speak to your heart."

"I'm going to try."

They rose to their feet and found themselves standing eye to eye as the evening shadows lengthened around them. The honesty between them, the simplicity of their quiet reaching out to God, had removed a barrier between them, and they were aware of a new closeness. Walking in silence, no words were necessary.

"Celeste?"

"Hmm?"

"Thanks."

"You don't have to thank me. I don't have all the answers, Scott; I don't even know what I'm going to do about my own life."

"But you cared enough to listen to me."

"I do. Probably more than I have a right to, and that scares me."

He slowed to a stop and turned to face her. "I thought maybe it was just me. I don't have the first clue of what to do about it, Celeste, or where it'll go. I don't have any right to care about you, and it scares me too."

"So, what are we doing?"

He shook his head. "I don't know. It's beyond me right now, and I can't see very far down the road at this point. But you're here, in my heart and in my thoughts."

She squeezed his hand and felt the answering pressure on her own. They entered the yard in silence and came to a stop beside her car.

"I'd better get going. Will you tell Tawnya I said goodbye?"

He nodded. "Call me when you get home?"

Slipping behind the wheel, she nodded. "I shouldn't, but I will."

"I'll miss you."

His quiet words hung heavily in the evening air until her own admission came quietly from inside the car. "I'll miss you too."

"Drive safe. And call when you get home."

"If it isn't too late."

He shook his head. "No matter how late it is. Please?"

She nodded, fired the ignition, and mouthed, "Bye."

"Bye."

He watched until he could not longer see her tail-lights, then sighed. His little girl waited inside, and he'd missed her. He wanted to hear about every moment she'd spent with her aunt, each new experience they'd shared. Perhaps one of these days they'd spend a weekend in Seattle and share some of those same experiences. Anticipation quickened his steps, and he bounded up the porch steps, suddenly eager to begin really living his life once again. His little girl was home.

Chapter 13

*I*t had been a week since Tawnya had returned home; in another week she would be returning to Seattle to spend another week with her aunt. He'd last spoken to Celeste when she'd arrived home after their shared prayer in the alfalfa field, although she was a frequent fixture in his thoughts. In the intervening days, he'd dug up some of Rachel's old tapes of various contemporary Christian artists, which he played as he circled the fields in the combine. It made him feel closer to Rach, knowing that she'd listened to these same songs in a healthier time, and he wondered if she'd been touched as deeply by them as he was upon hearing them now.

There was a new awareness of God's presence in Scott's heart, and he was learning anew the power of prayer, that God was easily accessible at all times, not just during that hour on Sunday mornings, seated in a pew in church that he'd always associated with prayer. Alone in the fields, he spoke frequently with God, praying for guidance as he struggled with his pending decisions with respect to Rachel, and also found himself thanking the Creator for the beauty of the world around him and acknowledging the blessings in his life. The bitterness he'd nursed for the past several years was quietly dissipating, and in its place, a new and welcome sense of openness of heart and newness of spirit.

On a blistering hot Tuesday afternoon, running the combine on Tucker's northeast section of winter wheat, Scott mused that in the ninety-degree heat, the mere words "winter wheat" made him long for chilly mornings and the sight of fog blanketing the mountainside. Keeping an eye out for the truck that awaited another load before being taken to the grain elevator to be weighed in and unloaded, Scott mentally calculated their progress. At this pace, with hot, sunny days and barring equipment breakdowns, another four days or so should be plenty to finish up here.

On this afternoon, high in the air-conditioned cab of his John Deere combine, he reached to the floor for his water jug, drank deeply, and belched loudly, excused himself, then grinned. Funny thing, manners; his mother would be pleased to know that something had sunk in all those years before, even something as banal as excusing yourself for burping when there was no one within earshot. Mom had been a perfect prototype of the proper ranch wife and had been nearly oblivious to the changing trends in clothing styles through the passing years. Of course, the ranch had been a pretty good place to insulate a person from the outside world.

A fastidious housekeeper and consummate gardener, Mom had lived to serve the men of her small kingdom and had put in nearly as long hours as her husband. She'd been a dab hand at everything she'd put her hand to, and from his earliest childhood, their home had been a quiet and peaceful refuge from the world outside. It was perhaps not surprising that Scott had, early on, associated femininity with a woman who prepared hearty meals in her snug kitchen, canned and froze vegetables from her garden, and greeted her husband with a welcoming kiss at the end of his workday. Someone like Mom.

As a young man, he'd come to his own marriage naïve in many ways, and he and Rachel had mucked about until they achieved their collective rhythm and had built their life together in a comfortable manner. And he'd been happy, happier than perhaps he'd had a right to be. Rachel had been happy, as well, he thought now, for she'd wanted only to be a wife and mother. She'd had no other shining, elusive dreams hanging in the balance.

If Huntington's hadn't stricken his wife, their lives would have continued on in the same quiet pattern in which it had begun, only the change of the seasons dictating fluctuation in their daily routines.

He noted that Ty had returned to the frontage road, ready to pick up another load. Casting a quick eye at the capacity gauge, he calculated that he'd be able to make one more pass before emptying the combine's cargo. Reaching for the two-way radio clipped to the visor, he instructed Ty to meet him at the turn, then returned to his thoughts.

If Rachel hadn't gotten sick, they'd have lived their lives out together, strengthening the bonds that intimacy and parenthood fostered in a committed marriage, but this hadn't been God's greater plan for their lives. What *was* His plan for the rest of Scott's life? Was he meant to live out his days alone, or did God have something else in mind for him?

He'd prayed for God's will in this, as well. He was confused and baffled that after so many years of complete devotion to his wife, he was feeling something more than he should be feeling for his sister-in-law. Was it just coincidence that he and Celeste were drawn to each other, or was it something more? And if it was more than just coincidence, why, then, were they experiencing these feelings now, when he had no legal or moral right to do so?

Moving slowly down the field, he watched as the combine devoured the rustling amber wheat, leaving a coarse, mowed stubble in its wake. Shifting the blade mechanism into idle, Scott wheeled the harvester around and pulled alongside the waiting truck.

After double-checking his position, he pulled the lever that would send the grain from the collection bin through the pipe and down into the waiting truck. After releasing the load, he threw the combine door open and stepped down into the ninety-degree heat, heading around the back of the combine to meet Tyler. His son looked as hot as he himself felt, Scott thought, eyeing the sweat-soaked T-shirt and baseball cap.

"Truck's just about full. I'm gonna head over to the scales."

"Right." Glancing over the fields, he asked, "What do you think, three days yet?"

"I make it four, but I hope I'm wrong."

Silence fell, then, with a deep sigh, Scott said, "Well, you'd better get a move on, then. Let's see…It's four-thirty, we aren't going to get another load in tonight, so after you unload, why don't you call it a day."

"Serious?"

"Yeah, go ahead. I should be able to keep cutting for another couple of hours, anyway. I'll see you at home."

"Okay."

Watching as the truck pulled out onto the main road, tasting the dust that hung heavy in the summer afternoon, Scott ran an arm across his brow, eyeing the dampness on his shirt sleeve. Climbing back into the harvester, he reached behind the seat for the water bottle, unscrewed the cap, and drank deeply. Blowing out a deep breath, he sat silently for a moment, then gunned the engine once again. Moving back to the spot where he'd left off a while ago, he lowered the blade and began moving down the field again.

Thoughts drifting, he imagined himself in Seattle, bombarded by city noise, smelling the exhaust, and seeing the ceaseless wave of humanity moving along the busy streets. Celeste worked downtown in one of those fifty-story buildings, and he tried to picture her in her professional environment. He'd have liked to tell himself that he couldn't see her there, but he had no trouble whatsoever. He could see her all too clearly, dressed in a business suit, that sun-bright hair pulled back in a professional style. He tried to imagine her workday; client meetings, hours spent in the firm's resource library, researching state codes and other regulations. He didn't know anything about the people she worked with, but he figured that at least a few had to be men. And if there were men, they'd be putting the move on her, Scott thought glumly, jaw tightening until he could feel his teeth grinding. Helpless to prevent his imagination from taking the obvious step, he winced at the picture his mind's eye presented him; nattily-dressed men in the latest fashions, down to their leather loafers, probably even color-coded socks.

He didn't own any fancy suits, much less matching socks; he was lucky if he had three pair that had both mates!

These guys probably smelled like they just climbed out of the shower. All day. He had no illusions about his own personal aura; after a day in the field, he stank like Bill Harlan's goat, and had as much an appetite for the forbidden as the goat had had.

You're jealous.

Oh, spare me. I'm just...

Jealous.

The fact that he had no business being jealous did nothing to improve his mood.

Slowing to make the turn at the east end of the field, Scott squinted against the brightness of the sun as it slid down the sky to hang suspended at the top of Karkeek Ridge. He never tired of the glory of the countryside in this place he called home. How anyone could leave the beauty of the mountains, the freedom of the open space for the city and all of the attendant hassles was truly a puzzle. How had Celeste managed to complete such a thorough transition? But not everyone felt about the land as he did, Scott reminded himself abruptly, feeling a sharp pang at the thought of the lost acres of the Parnell homestead, gone forever.

For the first time, he wondered whether he'd made the right decision. A purely rhetorical question, of course, because what was done was done. When faced with the choice of Rachel's care and well-being over what was basically just dirt and trees when broken down into the simplest equation, there had been no question of which had been the correct, the only possible decision.

As the sun finally slipped behind Karkeek, he lifted the blade once more and killed the engine, swung down from the cab, and walked across the field to his pickup, suddenly weary. Four more days here, then on to Jamison's. That would be the end of wheat harvest for this year, but then third cutting of hay would be starting right about the same time as school. Another six weeks of solid field work and he'd be able to call it good for another season, Scott thought with relief. For some reason, this year seemed rougher; the heat was a little harder to take and the nights seemed to be shorter too. He hadn't had a good night's sleep in weeks. Must be the heat.

Of course it was the heat. It couldn't have anything to do with his torment regarding his growing feelings for Celeste and in return, the other saner part of himself reminding him abruptly that he still wore the ring that another woman had given him. Looking at that ring now, the field dust did nothing to dim the wink of gold in the waning daylight. Sighing heavily, Scott flipped the key, settling himself into position as the engine roared to life. Shifting into gear, he moved out onto the county road. Lost in thought, he found himself at the outskirts of Shuksan, passing Fircrest. On impulse, he pulled over to the curb and looked across at the window to the room where his wife lay in uncomprehending silence.

Oh, Rach.

Two young boys veered down the street on skateboards, voices carrying through the near-darkness.

"…hate Brussels sprouts, my mom makes them all the time even though my dad and me hate 'em."

"Nasty."

Laughter, then the voices faded into the night.

What am I going to do, Lord? I'm listening, please help me to know Your will.

He sat, eyes on the window, as if the new pane of glass held the answers to the most painful struggle of his life, but there was only the silence of the quiet dusk, crickets in full concert, and the occasional sound of a passing car.

Perhaps, like Abraham, he was being called to embark upon the ultimate walk in faith, to be willing to give Rach's life over to God, much as Abraham had ascended the mountain with his beloved son, knowing what awaited at the summit. Perhaps this, then, was his own mountain, and God awaited there to demonstrate His grace once more. What a testament to Abraham's love of the Lord, of his faith; his unquestioning willingness to sacrifice the child for whom he'd waited so long, loved so dearly.

Hadn't God understood Abraham's pain perfectly? Had He not sent His own Son as the ultimate sacrifice for humanity? Could there be any question that He knew Scott's pain, sympathized with his own resistance now, two thousand years later?

Surprised by the dampness on his cheeks, he brushed at the tears, then closed his eyes, drew in a shuddering breath, and prayed. *"It's me, Lord. You know how hard this is for me, how hard I've tried to hold it all together. But I know I'm just kidding myself, because it's all falling apart. I don't have anything left, Lord. I've spent it all and still come up short on everything; money, time, energy, even availability to the kids. And I'm so tired, Lord. Forgive me. Take all of it, Lord, 'cause I can't do it anymore. Help me, God. Help me do what needs to be done for Rach. God, I put her in Your hands too. Just please help me, 'cause I'm at the end of the line here."*

The boys on skateboards skimmed past him again, eyeing him with curiosity, the old guy sitting in front of the nursing home, bawling like a baby. He ignored them and continued to pray, as peace suffused his spirit and he felt a Presence in his heart.

"Trust in My love for Rachel. Release her body and allow her to come Home to Me."

Head bowed, he prayed, "Help me, Lord. Give me the strength to let her go."

He turned the truck toward home, toward his children, and prayed anew for strength and guidance in the days and weeks to come, as they faced the most difficult challenge of their lives.

Chapter 14

awnya examined her teeth in the mirror once more, the light from the bathroom fixture glinting off of the shiny hardware. She'd sat in the orthodontist's office the better part of the morning and had emerged with what felt and looked like barbed wire snagged between her teeth; the ones that were left, at any rate. Last week, she'd spent a miserable afternoon having six teeth pulled, had eaten all the soup and scrambled eggs she could stomach and had felt too lousy to regurgitate them afterward. But all of the misery would be worth it in the end. Now, with the braces safely on, she couldn't get her fill of the sight of the metal bands. It was like a miracle. Suddenly, it was safe to imagine how nice her smile would be in a couple of years, when she wouldn't have to be self-conscious any longer. And when she was thin, too, just imagine how happy she'd be!

Her skin was clearing up a little bit; she'd been using the medicine the dermatologist had prescribed faithfully, washing her face with hot water and glycerin soap morning and night and practically swimming in Sea Breeze. It was working. There hadn't been as many new pimples, and some of the old blackheads and whiteheads were disappearing too.

Picking up her brush from where it lay on the vanity, she ran the bristles through her newly shorn brown locks, then shook her head from side to side, watching her hair fell neatly into place. After lunch, Aunt Celeste had taken her to her own hairstylist, and after a lengthy consultation, the stylist had suggested a shorter, layered cut that would accentuate Tawnya's natural wave and remove a lot of the thick, heavy hair that hung at the sides of her face. She'd sat nervously in the hydraulic chair, hearing the sound of the scissors and seeing snips of hair fall to the floor. Hands clenching the arm rests tightly, Tawnya allowed herself to be turned toward the mirror after the stylist had produced her hair dryer and had stared, stunned, at her appearance. She looked at least a year older, she was certain. And it was so much cooler too; she hadn't realized how long it had been since she'd had anything done to her hair except when Grandma trimmed her bangs.

Now, if she just had her ears pierced, that would be all she could ask for. Shaking her newly styled hair back from her face, she fingered an earlobe wistfully. She'd seen girls with as many as seven earrings in one ear. Of course, that was probably a bit of overkill, for Shuksan, anyway.

Switching off the light, Tawnya left the bathroom and walked through the condo to the sliding glass door that led to the balcony. Lowering herself into a patio chair, she looked out across the broad expanse of Lake Washington to the lights dotting the hillside across the way. Enjoying the moment, she thought again how lucky Aunt Celeste was to live here, right on the lake. The sound of the slider opening interrupted her thoughts, and she turned to see her aunt approaching.

"Here you are. How're you feeling by now?"

"My mouth's sore."

"Did you take some ibuprofen?"

"Yeah, but it still hurts."

Seating herself in the other chair, Celeste inquired, "Regrets?"

"About the braces? No way. I still can't believe I have them. I've hated my teeth for so long. I never thought I'd get to do this."

"Well, the worst part's over now, you just have to have them tightened every few weeks, but that won't be as bad as this first part. So. Have you thought about what you want to do tomorrow?"

"Do you think I could talk to Tori?"

"Oh, didn't I tell you? We're going to meet Ana and Tori at Northgate Mall tomorrow night. We can do some shopping and then have dinner. I've invited Tori to spend the night, does that work?"

"Yeah, cool. Oh, have you talked to Daddy?"

"No, but give him a call, if you'd like."

"Do you want to talk to him?"

"When you're done, I'll just say hi real quick."

As Tawnya picked up the cordless phone, she rose to her feet. "I'm heading to bed, kiddo. Just knock on my door when you're done. See you in the morning, okay?"

"Okay. 'Night. Hi, Daddy, it's me…"

As she prepared for bed, she debated the wisdom of another conversation with her brother-in-law. They hadn't spoken since Saturday, but he'd been in her thoughts a great deal, and she was struggling with her feelings with regard to the connection that they had begun to experience. Somewhere along the line, her feelings had jumped the track from the concern a sister-in-law has for her sister's husband to something more personal, something deeper. And it frightened her.

The knock sounded at her door, and Tawnya said, "I'm done, Aunt Celeste."

She drew in a deep breath, called a quick thanks to her niece, then slowly lifted the phone from her nightstand and waited until she heard the click as Tawnya hung up the other line.

"You there, Celeste?"

"I'm here."

"How's it going? How'd the braces go?"

"Well, she's a little uncomfortable, but she's a trooper. This will probably sound weird, but sometimes I feel like…oh, I don't know."

Prompting her, "You feel like ?"

Self-conscious now, she admitted, "Like she's mine, Scott, and we're just caught up in all this fun mom and daughter stuff. Except she's not mine, which is probably why we're able to have so much fun. If she were mine, we probably wouldn't be on speaking terms."

"Yeah, I hear you; that's how Ty and I relate most of the time these days."

"I guess it comes with the territory."

"Yeah, I remember giving my dad a hard time on occasion."

Tongue in cheek, Celeste couldn't resist teasing him, "Oh, surely not."

"Oh, yeah. I could tell you a story or two, but that was back in the days of my wastrel youth, before Rachel straightened me out."

"And how did she manage that?"

"You know, I'm not exactly sure, but I seem to recall her not having to say much of anything, it was more that I could tell when I'd crossed the line. I think she used the same tactics on Ty before she got sick. I sure wish I knew how she pulled it off 'cause I feel like I'm flying blind these days with him."

"I can imagine. It can't be easy."

"It isn't."

There was a moment of silence, then she asked, "How's everything else going?"

"Good, but it sure is hot. It's not cooling down much at night, but I guess that's what you have to expect in August."

"It's been hot here too."

Silence buzzed through the line and he said, "We're doing it again."

"What?"

"Talkin' about the weather."

She chuckled, breaking the tension. "Sure enough. So, what should we talk about this time?"

"Nothing in particular, it's just good to hear your voice."

"Yours too."

They sat in silence, then he asked, "Are you staying over Saturday night?"

"Hadn't planned on it. Why?"

"The fair's on this weekend. I just wondered if you were gonna stick around."

She hadn't been home for the fair since she'd gone off to college, hadn't given their local county fair much thought since graduating high school, but was surprised to find that it actually sounded like fun. Why not? "Sure, I guess so. Maybe I can bring Tawnya's friend Tori along, give them a chance to live life on Tawnya's turf for a change."

"Sure, bring her along. I was wondering..."

"What?"

"Well, Saturday night's the fair dance and pretty much the whole town's either at the fair or the dance, my kids included. I was wondering if you wanted to have supper someplace, just us."

She sat, mind running in hyper-drive, torn between longing and her better judgment. "I don't know. I mean, well…"

Embarrassed, Scott backpedaled, "Never mind, forget I said anything. It probably isn't such a good idea."

"Wait. How about…well, maybe I could cook supper for you, out at the farm."

"That'd be great, but I didn't mean for you to have to do the cooking yourself."

"I know, but it'd probably be better this way, don't you think?"

He sighed. "Yeah, you're probably right. What'll you say to Catherine, though?"

"I'll think of something."

"Well, then, thank you. I'm looking forward to it."

"Me, too." she admitted, stifling a yawn which managed to travel through the line. Picking up on the cue, Scott said, "Well, I've probably got a twenty dollar phone bill going here, so I'm going to let you go. And I'll see you sometime Saturday."

"We should be there around noon."

"Sounds good. Well, good night, Celeste."

Silence.

"Celeste?"

"Hmm?"

"Thanks again, for everything you've done for Tawnya."

"Don't thank me; I haven't had this much fun since the time we vandalized the scarecrow."

"What? Whose scarecrow?"

"Oh, I'll tell you about it sometime. It's a good Rachel story. And it occurs to me that we need to tell each other some Rachel stories, Scott, because it isn't healthy to have this 'respectful silence' about her. You know?"

"Yeah, I do. But let's wait awhile, Celeste, okay? Just for a little while."

"Okay, Scott. For a little while."

"I'm gonna let you go for tonight. Take care of my baby."

"I will. See you Saturday."

She replaced the phone on the nightstand, then lay back on the pillows, thinking about Scott and considering what she would prepare for their dinner Saturday night. It was hot, so something summery. Fish, maybe, or chicken. Did he have a barbecue?

She was beginning to doze when the sound of illness reached her through the closed door. Concerned, she knocked lightly on the bathroom door. "Are you okay, Tawn?"

"Yeah."

"You sure?"

"Yeah. I'm fine."

"Do you want some Seven-Up? It might help settle your stomach."

"No, I'm fine."

"Well, if you change your mind, let me know, okay?"

"I will. "

Celeste stood before the locked door for a moment before returning to her room. Something didn't seem right, but she couldn't quite put a finger on it. Suddenly it came to her; Tawnya had been sick when she'd been here two weeks ago too. She'd brushed away Celeste's concern and, indeed, seemed to be feeling fine the next morning. Celeste had chalked it up to the heat and too much excitement but wasn't willing to dismiss it so readily this time. She didn't have a lot of experience to draw from, other than asking herself if she would have downplayed a stomach upset enough to result in vomiting at Tawnya's age. Not a chance. If she'd been sick to her stomach, someone was going to know about it, especially if was something that was happening fairly frequently.

So why would a twelve-year-old keep this to herself? Celeste discounted her first notion, that her niece was too embarrassed to confess that she was ill or shy enough to not want to bother her aunt with an upset stomach. She certainly hoped that wasn't the case. The other possibility, also one she dismissed, was that Tawnya was afraid she'd have to go home early if Celeste thought she was catching flu. This was even less likely, as few things were more miserable than traveling while smitten with flu, and if this were the case, a person would certainly want to lay low and not migrate too far from the bathroom.

The only other possibility that jumped to mind was too disturbing to dwell upon, but which her mind kept returning to. An eating disorder. Purging, bulimia.

Did twelve-year-olds struggle with body image to the point of developing such extreme quick-fixes to their weight issues?

Had Tawnya been caught up in this self-destructive vice of desperation and secrecy?

Fear for her niece battled with her own natural reluctance to appear intrusive, and she wavered. What would Rach do? For that matter, what would *she* do if it were her own daughter in question? The answer was clear and immediate; she would intervene. Tawnya's mother was unable to step in, and she couldn't, *wouldn't* put her blinders on. Not about this.

"I'm way out of my league here, Lord. Help me find the right words."

She knocked on the bedroom door, then peeked in. It was dark, but she suspected her niece was awake. "Tawnya? Are you awake?"

"No."

Nice try. Undeterred, she persisted. "Can we talk for a minute?"

A rustling of blankets accompanied a grumpy voice, "What's wrong?"

Celeste crossed to the bed and asked, "Can I sit here and talk to you?"

With a wary tone to her voice, the girl replied, "I guess."

Celeste sat on the edge of the bed, praying mightily. "Tawn, I want to ask you something. And please be honest with me, it's important."

"What?"

"What's going on with your stomach?"

The wariness was full-on. "Nothing. Why?"

Celeste sighed. "Sweetie, I'm gonna spell it out for you, okay? I know you were sick tonight. You were sick last time you were here too. I guess I'm concerned that something's going on. Do I have a reason to be concerned?"

"What do you mean?"

"I mean, is this vomiting something other than an upset stomach? Because I don't think you have the flu. Can you tell me what's going on?"

"I'm fine! Can't you just leave me alone?"

She sighed. "No, I can't do that, Tawn. I know you well enough by now to know that you aren't usually this defensive when I talk to you. And I'll be honest, I don't know how to dance around the subject; I don't have any practice with kids of my own, so all I know how to do is just be upfront and tell you how I feel. And this is the bottom line, kiddo; if your mom wasn't sick, she'd be having this talk with you, which she isn't able to. But I am, and I'm not going to pretend everything's fine because I care too much about you. So, I'm going to ask you again, and please be honest with me. Is this about your weight?"

Even a spinster aunt could recognize obstinacy and resistance, and she knew that her niece would remain silent. She debated with herself a moment, then rose to her feet. "Okay, Tawn, have it your way. I guess we both know what's going on here, and at this point, I don't have any choice but to let your dad know about this."

The girl jumped as though fired from a cannon, rising to her knees. "No! You can't tell Daddy! I promise I'll stop, just promise you won't tell him."

Celeste flipped on the night light and eyed her niece. "Not gonna fly, babe. He has a right to know. He's your dad, Tawn. Do you think your mom would keep this from him? I can tell you that she wouldn't, and I'm not going to, either."

"Please, Celeste. He's got enough to worry about already."

"That's a dad's job, to worry about his kids. Don't you think he'd be a lot more worried if you end up in the hospital one of these nights and didn't even know what was going on? How do you think he'd feel if he knew I'd kept this from him? You have to look at this from our perspective, Tawn. It's our job to worry about you."

"I told you, I'll be fine. Why can't you just trust me?"

Celeste brushed a tear from her niece's cheek. "Tawnya, do you realize that people die from eating disorders?"

"I'm not gonna die."

"Maybe not right away, but one of these times, Tawn, you're going to do some damage to your stomach, and then what? There are healthy ways to take off weight, hon, and I'm more than happy to help you get on track, but you have to stop this. If you can't, then we need to get you some help. That's it. That's the bottom line."

Desperation tinged the girl's voice. "I said I'll stop. I promise!"

Celeste searched her niece's eyes intently, then nodded. "Okay, Tawn. We'll try this your way, against my better judgment, but know that I'm going to be on your case about it. I'm not going to just let it go. You have to promise me that, for your part, you'll be completely honest with me, and if I get the feeling you aren't, then the deal's off and your dad comes into the picture. Fair enough?"

"Yeah, but I promise I won't do it anymore."

"Sometimes it's hard to stop doing things we know are bad for us. Remember that when you're really struggling with temptation, to turn it over to the Lord, Tawn, and ask Him to be your strength at that moment. Remember that He never allows us more temptation than we can bear. Will you do that?"

"Yeah."

She rose from the bed, leaned over, and kissed her niece on the forehead. "I'll be praying for you, hon. I'm always here, whenever you need me. Okay?"

"Okay."

"Good night, then."

"Night."

She crossed to her own room, closed the door behind her, and leaned against it in a moment of mental exhaustion. Had she handled the situation the right way? Had she done the right thing, agreeing to withhold this from Scott? What if Tawnya continued the purging, regardless of her promise to stop? Worry assaulted her from every angle, and she dropped to her knees beside her bed.

"Lord, I don't know if I did the right thing or not. I'm so concerned about her, Lord. Please stay very close to Tawnya and help her to feel Your presence. And give me wisdom and guidance, that I can impact Tawnya's life in a positive way, Lord. Thank You, Father. And, Lord, please bless Scott and Rach. And Mother and Ty. Keep them safe in Your care. Amen."

In two days, Tawnya would return home and the guest room would again become unoccupied. This time, there was no denying the loneliness that would be her sole companion once the girl had gone.

She was suddenly filled with an inexplicable sorrow and, blinking the tears from her eyes, presented her pain to the Lord.

"What am I doing here all by myself? Is this really Your path for me, Lord? Why am I feeling all of this dissatisfaction with my life? Why am I suddenly so lonely, Father? Lord, I don't want to be alone anymore. Please show me what You would have me do with my life. Walk with me, guide me. Help me to see my life through Your eyes. Thank You, Lord. Amen."

Chapter 15

The next evening, Scott drove home after another blistering hot day in the swather, intent on only one thing, rummaging through his closet in the dismal hope of finding something decent to wear Saturday night. He couldn't remember the last time he'd dressed up, the last time he'd cared about his appearance. He was nearly as shaggy around the ears as Skip and made a mental note to get into the barbershop for a trim.

He was barely through the front door before the aroma of pasta caused his stomach to rumble loudly. Entering the kitchen, he greeted his son, already seated at the table with a plateful of spaghetti, tossed salad, and toasted garlic bread. Washing his hands thoroughly, he opened the oven door and removed the lasagna, reached into the cupboard to the right of the sink, and retrieved a dinner plate.

Carrying his plate to the table, he joined his son, who continued his meal in silence. Finished, Ty rose, carried his plate to the sink, rinsed and loaded it into the dishwasher. Leaning against the counter, he asked, "You have anything going on tonight, Dad?"

"Just some bookwork. And I need to figure out if I have anything decent to wear Saturday night."

At his son's quizzical glance, he explained that Celeste was going to come out to cook dinner. "You know you're welcome to eat with us, right?"

A look of distaste crossed Ty's face. "No, thanks. Why does she suddenly give a rip anyway?"

"I think Celeste's regretting not being around all the years before Mom got so sick. She wants to help do things for your sister and for you as well."

Resentment coloring each word, Ty retorted, "She can keep her stupid nose out of things as far as I'm concerned. We're doing just fine by ourselves."

"We're not the only ones who've lost Mom, remember. Celeste's lost her sister, and I think it's only recently started to really sink in."

Shaking his head, Ty retorted, "It's not my fault she never came around all these years. I'm sorry, but I think this is just an excuse for her to sashay into town and flash her money and fancy car around, impress everybody."

With an effort, Scott kept his temper on the leash. "You really don't know her if that's what you think, Tyler. At any rate, how your aunt chooses to spend her money is up to her, and it isn't any of your business one way or the other. She's trying to help, Ty, and I'm not going to listen to you badmouth her when she's stepping in to help your sister with all these things. I expect you to keep a civil tongue in your head when she's around, and even when she isn't. Are we clear?"

Pushing himself off the counter, Ty grunted. "Whatever."

"I mean it, Tyler."

"What do you get out of this, anyway; some special attention when Tawn and I are out of the house?"

Stunned, then furious, Scott moved to stand directly in front of his son. Nose to nose, he growled between clenched teeth, "I have never been unfaithful to your mother, Tyler. As long as she's alive, she's my wife, and I made a promise both to her and to God. I intend to honor that promise. If I ever hear that kind of filth from your mouth again, you're gonna lose your truck for a month. Got it?"

Finally dropping his eyes, Ty muttered, "Yeah."

After Ty left the kitchen, Scott yanked his chair away from the table, prepared to sit, changed his mind and, in exasperation, shoved the chair back into place. Were his growing feelings for Celeste obvious to everyone? Or was his son just lashing out in a manner predictable for a seventeen-year-old who resented another woman venturing into the space left vacant by his mother?

The kid was trying to drive him crazy, that's all there was to it. Today it felt like he just might succeed.

Ty's voice carried from the foyer. "I'm going out for a while."

In surprise, glancing at his watch, Scott asked, "Now? Isn't it kinda late?"

"It's not that late, Dad, and I won't be gone too long. I just need to run over to Dwight's. I'll be in by midnight."

"Well, can't you just call on the phone?"

Taking the defensive, Ty exclaimed, "Come on, Dad, you'd think I was seven years old instead of almost eighteen! I've worked my tail off all summer for minimum wage, and school's gonna start in another week and a half! It's not like I'm asking to go into Wenatchee, for cryin' out loud!"

Lifting his hands in surrender, Scott sighed. "Fine, go. But just remember that six o'clock comes awfully early."

"I know."

"Drive carefully, Tyler."

The screen door pounded against the porch wall. A moment later, the Dodge roared to life and after a flash of headlights, the yard was still once again.

With silence all about, Scott cast a glance between his cooling plate of food, his pleasure in the food diminished. After transferring what remained of the spaghetti into a Tupperware and filling the casserole pan with water to soak, he switched off the kitchen light and carried the plate down the hallway into his office. Deciding that he may as well reconcile his bank statement with his financial documents stored on computer documents, he booted the PC, bringing up his spreadsheet file.

The contents of the spreadsheet seemed to swim before his eyes, and the sight of the bills stacked to the left of the computer only served to produce an uncomfortable knot in his belly. With a muttered exclamation of exasperation, he pulled the phone toward himself and before he could lose nerve, punched the now-familiar number. When her voice came over the line, the tension faded and the tightness in his stomach eased. They spoke of nothing in particular, just shared in their tenuous connection, until he confessed, "I've been pretty jealous of the guys you work with," feeling his cheeks flame as if he were a fourteen-year-old confessing to a crush on the head cheerleader.

"Jealous? Why?"

"Oh, I don't know. I suppose because I can picture you with somebody dressed to the nines, who plays the game better than this old farmer."

Touched, Celeste replied, "Just remember that I prefer the "old farmer," not that I'm agreeing with your choice of words! If you saw some of these guys, you'd know exactly what I mean; they're soft, you know? Maybe some of them grew up having to mow the lawn and help their dad change tires on the car, but for the most part, they're useless around the house. Get this—one guy actually had to hire somebody to change a washer in his bathroom faucet. He didn't have a clue!"

As their laughter died, Scott pointed out, "Don't forget, though, that they can afford to hire stuff done. If you can't, you end up learning how to do it yourself or it doesn't get done. But when it comes to education, they've got me whipped by a mile."

"Oh, come on! It amazes me to think about all of the things that you need to know to operate your business; machinery repair, weather patterns, crop disease, and all of the other day-to-day things that creep up. Don't ever measure yourself by somebody else's yardstick."

Pleased and a bit embarrassed at her praise, he responded, "I'm gonna have to start calling every night just so you can give me compliments!"

"You can call anytime you'd like. I never get tired of talking to you."

"Same goes. I suppose I should let you go, though. Is Tawnya handy?"

She chuckled, "No, she's out in the hot tub; she's been out there all night. She's going to look like a prune when she finally drags herself out of there."

"Yeah, that's quite a love affair she's got going with that spa. Well, tell her I send my love."

"Sure."

After several more minutes of forbidden long-distance billing and cooing, Tawnya emerged from the hot tub and Celeste bid him goodnight. The moment the receiver hit the cradle, he was lonelier than he'd been before their conversation. Staring at the computer monitor, he conceded the fact that working on his financial spread-sheet held about as much appeal as tackling the dirty spaghetti pan soaking in the sink. Unfortunately, both tasks beckoned, but given his present state of mind, kitchen duty was about as much of a challenge that he was up for. He logged off of the computer and left the office, wandered down the hall toward the kitchen, stopping to view the family portraits in which Celeste was captured for all time.

Wondering how he was supposed to survive until Saturday night, he continued into the kitchen and tackled the mess with the fervor of a manic-depressive in full manic mode, scrubbing the casserole dish with an SOS pad. Up to his elbows in soapy water, he chided himself for not having had the presence of mind to insist that Ty clean the kitchen before he left. Wiping his damp forehead with the back of an arm, he had to admit that his mind had been on other things at that point, primarily the contents of his closet.

With the kitchen finally restored to some semblance of order, he switched off the light and climbed the stairs in the darkness. It had to be eleven o'clock, and still no sign of Ty. School started again in two weeks; that would definitely put an end to the late nights. Maybe. In the meantime, daylight still came around pretty early, and it was becoming tougher by the day to rouse the kid in the mornings. *So, put some restrictions on the kid—it doesn't take a rocket scientist to figure this one out,* he told himself wearily. Unfortunately, he seemed to be stuck between frustration at Ty's growing irresponsibility and his own guilt for working the kid like a dog all summer. At least he was earning some money, Scott reminded himself; when he was in high school, he made twenty bucks a month allowance for his work around the place. Of course, that was back in the Dark Ages, when twenty bucks went a whole lot farther. Although his parents gave new meaning to the word frugal, their finances were nowhere near to being stretched as tightly as his own were right now.

His thoughts turned to his next paycheck. At this pace, with hot sunny days and barring equipment breakdowns, another three days or so should be plenty to finish up at the Heinemann farm.

Unless the storm brewing with his son broke in the meantime. They were riding an uneasy see-saw of hostility on Tyler's part and frustration on his own, and to Scott's way of looking at the situation, there didn't seem to be any sort of balancing point in sight.

He was certain there had been situations of tension and poor communication between he and his father, even remembered one in particular. He'd gone out tomcatting with Jim once when he and Rachel had had a spat, had decided to spend the night camping out on Eagle Creek, just he, Jim, and a half-case of Schlitz malt liquor. They'd had themselves quite a toot; had drank every last can of beer, made short shrift of the junk food they'd packed in, and told stories until the campfire had burned low. Morning had dawned both too bright and too early for his liking. He'd helped break camp, thoroughly extinguished the campfire, and after dropping Jim by his house, had returned home to face the discordant music that waited in the form of his father. The old man had eyed him impassively, saying only, "You get rid of all your sick, boy?"

Wishing to prove his manhood to his father, he'd boasted something along the lines of being able to handle his booze. His father had regarded him from under bushy brows, steely gaze lighting with something Scott couldn't identify, and had directed him to start cleaning the barn in preparation for the hay that would soon be arriving in from the fields for winter storage. Pitchfork in hand, swatting ineffectually at the flies that swarmed in delight at the aroma of manure being disturbed by the machinations of his pitchfork, he'd managed to fill a wheelbarrow full of manure and straw, wheel it over to Mom's garden compost pile before his stomach pitched in revolt. In an instant, he'd dropped to his knees and proceeded to eat the cocky words he'd flung at his father. He'd lingered there on the grass for several minutes until he was relatively certain his legs would bear his weight. As he struggled to his feet, pale of countenance and humble of spirit, his father's hand caught him under the elbow and lifted him the rest of the way to his feet before his stomach had pitched and dove once again, and he experienced firsthand the misery of that phenomenon known as the dry heaves. His father had stood silently, and when Scott had again regained his feet, had simply remarked, "Day's wasting, boy. Get a move on and you might finish by lunch."

They'd never again discussed the events of that morning or those of the preceding night. Dad had been the stereotypical strong, silent type and was a firm believer in the old adage of actions speaking louder than words. Scott had taken away pieces of that parenting philosophy to apply to his own fathering; most of the time, life lessons could be illustrated, indeed, applied far more effectively by a child's negative experiences than by the incessant nattering of a parent's voice drilling into a kid's tuned-out consciousness.

Except it didn't seem to be working with Ty. Most days, Scott doubted his son paid much attention to him one way or the other when it came to something other than collecting his paycheck.

The question had to be asked; whose fault was that? Certainly not Ty's. No, the responsibility lay directly at his own doorstep, a father who'd been lost in his sorrow and anger for the majority of his son's ascent into adolescence. Remembering his own father, Scott was struck anew by a sense of inadequacy, and shame.

I'm not half the father the old man was.

"*I'm doing my best,*" he defended himself. "*This kid isn't exactly receptive to my trying to become involved in his life.*"

Maybe you haven't been trying hard enough.

Recognizing the truth, he had no ready argument to present to his conscience.

He undressed in the dark, dropping wearily to the mattress. Gazing out the window, his gaze caught the three-quarter moon shining brightly among its backdrop of stars. He silently wondered if perhaps Celeste was looking at the moon at this moment as well, from her balcony overlooking Lake Washington.

His last thought before sleep was that by the time the moon was full, he'd be with her again, wishing fiercely that the days would pass quickly until the weekend. Closing his eyes, he prayed, thanking God for the day's production and the fact that there had been no issues with the machinery. He prayed for his children, and for Rachel. Finally, he prayed again for wisdom and guidance as the relationship between he and Celeste grew ever closer.

He slept deeply, bathed in the silvery light of the moon, not waking even as Ty's truck labored into the yard.

Chapter 16

"*I* tell you, he's killing me, man. Summer's over and all I've got to show for it is sore muscles."

Dwight took a deep swig from the bottle before passing it to Tyler. "You get paid, don't you?"

"Yeah, minimum wage, and then he makes sure I bank part of it."

"Least you've got a job. Good thing you do, too, otherwise we wouldn't have any money for the good stuff." Extracting a Marlboro from a crumpled pack lying on the dash, his friend dug through his pockets in search of a lighter, cigarette bobbing between his lips.

Tyler watched his friend light his cigarette, mood taking another sour turn at the reminder of how, as the only one of the guys with a job, he ended up footing the bill for the good times. It was starting to bother him, the fact that while they were pretty good about thanking him for his generosity, nobody else coughed up any money for the occasional bottle of Velvet or whatever fit the ticket for the evening. And gas money, for that matter. The truck had a prodigious appetite, gas gauge sending a dismal message every few days. That was another thing; you'd think Dad would reimburse him for gas once in awhile, since most days he drove to the job sites. But, no, all he'd received in response to what seemed to be a perfectly reasonable request had been, "It's your own choice to drive, Tyler. You're more than welcome to ride with me." As if. Most days the old man stayed in the field until daylight was gone, and he wasn't up for that kind of schedule, no way. *He* happened to have a life, unlike others he could mention.

Dwight was speaking again, and dragging his attention back to the present, Ty heard him say, "It's about time for a trip to Seattle, isn't it? Do the Déjà Vu? How 'bout it?"

Yeah, Ty thought resentfully, cover charge for four, courtesy of himself. "This time somebody else is gonna kick in some bucks 'cause I'm not fronting the whole thing. Does anybody ever think about how many hours I work to earn that kind of dough?"

"Never really thought about it."

"Well, start thinking about it. For that matter, why don't you get a job yourself? Surely they'd hire you to flip burgers at Alpine."

Dwight rolled his eyes. "Man, you're depressing me. If you aren't gonna drink, pass the bottle over here." Complying, Ty watched his friend hammer down a good swig and wipe his mouth. "Agghhh."

Turning in the passenger seat, Dwight fumbled under the seat, triumphantly producing a can of WD-40.

Heart sinking, Tyler made a grab for the can. "Come on, man, don't do that tonight."

Holding the can away from Ty's reach, Dwight settled on a compromise, rolling the passenger window down.

"Don't do it, Dwight. You're gonna hurt yourself one of these times, man."

"Shut up, Parnell," a rough affection in his voice. "You kill brain cells your way, I'll kill 'em my way." Opening his mouth over the spray nozzle, Dwight depressed the plunger and inhaled deeply, sputtered and coughed for a moment; the can dropped, forgotten, to the floor of the cab.

"You all right, man?" He hated it when Dwight did this huffing. Nasty, and even worse, toxic. Dangerous. "Dwight?"

Head laying against the back of the seat, Dwight slowly rolled his neck around toward Ty, dilated pupils making the blue eyes appear nearly black. With slow, jerking motions, he patted the seat on either side of his body. "I can't find the can."

Shaking his head, Ty reached down and retrieved the can from under Dwight's shoes, placing it firmly behind his own seat. "Enough, Dwight. Come on, I'm taking you home."

"Home…yeah…old lady's probably passed out by now…safe."

Driving into town, Ty decided that the only thing worse than having a mother more dead than alive was to have one who used her kids as physical and psychological punching bags. Twice divorced, embittered with life's disappointments, and seemingly unbothered by the fact that she was considered to be the biggest shrew in Shuksan, Dora Phillips was a hard-boiled, sharp-tongued woman with bleached blonde hair and thin, pinched features who worked as a checker at Harvest Foods. He'd been best friends with Dwight since kindergarten and had lived in fear of the woman since the first time he'd spent the night at their house.

With conversation lagging, Tyler's thoughts returned to their last trip to Seattle, in particular, the trip home. There had just been the three of them; he, Dwight and Curtis. They'd been pretty messed up, and he'd known he wouldn't be able to make the drive home, so after they'd left North Bend and climbed the pass into the mountains, he'd pulled off onto a logging road. The other guys were sleeping, or passed out, and he'd applied the emergency brake and fallen asleep. They'd awakened to a late spring snowstorm, not a huge surprise, but not something he'd been prepared to deal with. No chains, no shovel, no way to dig out. They'd struggled on foot back to the highway and hitched a ride down the mountain into North Bend and, not knowing what else to do, had called Dad. The old man hadn't exactly been thrilled, but he'd come and picked them up at the gas station, taken them downtown for breakfast, then pulled Ty's truck out of the snowdrift and followed them home.

"Not your smartest move, Tyler, but one I expect you to learn a lesson from."

That was Dad, all right; *"Life's all about lessons; it's up to us whether we learn from them or end up with tougher lessons down the road."*

Life hadn't dished Dad up a very tasty dish as far as Ty was concerned; pretty much losing his wife in his thirties, left with two kids and a ranch to run, although there wasn't much of the ranch left at this point. And Mom, laying there at Fircrest, taking up pretty much every penny Dad brought in. How did the old man hold onto his sanity?

Not for the first time, Ty wondered where it would all end; Dad, Mom, himself, Tawnya. Dad was the only one who didn't have the axe of Huntington's poised over his neck, and with a flash of insight, realized that this was a key component of his resentment of his father.

He'd been driving as if by rote and was surprised to find that they'd arrived at Dwight's house. Shifting into park, he shook his friend's shoulder. "Hey, man, wake up. You're home." As Dwight shifted and groaned, Ty saw the front door open and Dora appeared on the porch with bare feet, wearing a ratty blue chenille bathrobe. Seeing the truck, she gathered the robe about herself, marched down the steps and down the sidewalk, throwing the passenger door open.

"Hi, Mrs. Phillips."

Ignoring him, the woman planted her fists on her hips, drew in a deep breath, and began to harangue her son. "Get out of that truck, you no-good little punk. Where the devil have you been? I'm out of cigarettes."

Gathering himself, Dwight reached for the pack riding on the dash and handed it to his mother. "Here."

"What's this? There're only three cigarettes in this pack, what good is it? You're about worthless, you know that? You and that Parnell kid, both a couple of stone losers."

Stomach clenching, Ty said, "See you later, man."

"Yeah, later, man." Dwight closed the door, walking up the sidewalk with his mother, who threw what looked to be a pretty good punch to the middle of his back as they started up the steps.

Ty sat silently in the cab for several minutes after the front door had closed and the porch light extinguished.

"You no-good little punk. You're about worthless, you know that?"

Dwight was eighteen years old and his mother still beat him, with fists and words. Ty guessed that, all told, the fists were probably the better of the two. Bruises healed, words had a nasty way of staying with a person.

As he drove home, his mind drew comparisons between his father's dropping everything on his schedule to make the two-hour drive to dig him out of a snowbank and the scene he'd just witnessed at Dwight's house. How did he deal with it? Sure, he was a party freak, could out-drink guys twenty years older, but it didn't ever seem to be enough. Now he was into huffing, and it scared Ty, though it wouldn't be cool to say so. Instead, he just tried to keep his eye on the situation and usually made sure he didn't have any aerosols in the truck, but he'd forgotten the WD-40; Dad had sent him into the house for it yesterday because one of the pumps was sticking. He hadn't wanted to go back to the house afterward and had stashed it under the seat. He'd just have to be more careful next time, that's all.

They'd have to do the Seattle thing pretty soon; Dwight could probably use some cheering up.

Ty reminded himself once again all things considered, he had the better of the two mother scenarios going.

But it's not fair. Mom was a good person, not an abusive witch like Mrs. Phillips, yet she's the one in diapers—the one who'd loved her husband and kids. It just isn't fair.

Yeah, they'd definitely have to "do" the Déjà Vu soon; Dwight wasn't the only one who needed a change of scenery. Maybe Dave down at the Golden Harvest could get them some Southern Comfort. Wasn't there an old saying, something about taking comfort wherever you can find it? Seek and ye shall find. Pulling to a stop next to Dad's truck, Tyler determined that he'd search as long and hard as it took. Anything that helped take the edge off was fine by him. Except huffing. Memory jogged, he reached behind the seat and removed the WD-40, replaced the Velvet under the seat, and closed the driver's door quietly. In the quiet moonlight, he lifted the can to his nose, lowering it in disgust. The stuff smelled like, well, *chemicals.* He was really going to have to talk to Dwight one of these days. As soon as he found a time that they were both sober. Probably not this weekend, though, because of the fair. But there'd be a chance one of these days. Maybe after school started. No point in getting Dwight upset right at the end of summer.

Feeling better now that he'd committed to a plan of action, he spoke quietly to Skip, let himself into the darkened house, and climbed the stairs to the welcome sound of his father's snoring.

Eyeing the digital clock glowing on his nightstand, he groaned; one o'clock already. The old man would be in to rattle his cage by five-thirty and wouldn't be sympathetic to the fact that his indentured servant had only had four hours of sleep, no, indeed.

Reminded once again of how much he hated farming, he punched his pillow into submission and turned his face toward the brightness of the moon. *Almost full,* he noted dreamily, then slipped into oblivion.

Chapter 17

*S*aturday afternoon was hot with clear blue skies, perfect weather for the fair and rodeo. Celeste lay on her old bed and allowed herself some quiet time to think about the evening to come. She'd be with Scott tonight. For the last few weeks, she'd vacillated between enjoyment of their increasing closeness and unease and discomfort because of that enjoyment. What was the protocol for dealing with attraction between a single woman and the husband of her only sister, when that sister was terminally ill and unlikely to recover? In her more rational moments, she told herself that the situation was insane and promised herself that she'd pull back from Scott, let the phone ring at night instead of running like a child to answer; basically put some distance between them. But for all of her good intentions, her thoughts turned to him frequently, and her feelings were growing stronger with each passing day, with each telephone conversation. She upheld the situation in prayer daily, asking for guidance and questioning the rightness of her growing feelings for the one man she shouldn't even be thinking about in this way.

It would be irony in the extreme if the one the Lord had in mind for her was already a member of her family. It smacked a bit of "kissing cousins," but she reminded herself that they weren't relatives, that even her family connection to Ty and Tawnya was more of emotional rather than blood ties. Still, a part of her was just the slightest bit unnerved by the unconventionality of the situation.

Wouldn't it be easier, less complicated, God, if the man you've chosen for me was someone new to my life, someone with whom I could build a fresh relationship, without all the baggage, without the family complications that are sure to come eventually?

Maybe she was putting the cart before the horse, anyway. Even if he felt for her the same things she felt for him, he was in no position to act on those feelings, much less make any sort of commitment. And then there were the kids, who were a huge part of his life, and they had significant issues of their own. So, the package was the full-meal-deal, so to speak; there would be no starting from scratch and finding their way together, the road was already paved and well-traveled. She would be the one to learn to navigate the twists and turns of that road and all of its attendant hazards, times of poor visibility, and probable countless rough potholes along the way.

When she really stopped and thought about all of the ramifications of a lasting relationship with Scott, she sometimes quailed from the prospect. These were the times she determined to let the relationship cool, but her resolve never held. Somehow she continued to arrive at a place of peace in her heart after all of the prayers she'd prayed. In another situation, she'd have taken this to mean that she was experiencing the Lord's peace and continue along the path, but how could she do that in this situation? Scott was already married.

Last night, she'd finally spoken honestly to Ana, had shared the story of her growing relationship with her brother-in-law, all the while watching her friend closely for signs of disgust or condemnation and found none. Ana was pragmatic and blessed with a simple and somehow old-fashioned common sense and often provided amazing insights born of her strong belief in God. At Bible study a couple of years before, the topic had centered around heaven, and whether a Christian, at the time of death, immediately ascended to his/her heavenly home, or whether they would sleep in peace until the Lord returned and then be taken unto Him on the day of the rapture. There had been some animated debate among the group, various opinions offered, until Ana had snorted and announced, "I can't be worrying about that; that's God's business. If He says I'll spend eternity with Him, that's good enough for me. I can't be worrying about what time the bus leaves!"

There had been a moment of silence, then laughter broke out and heads nodded all around.

Ana definitely had a way of cutting through the fluff to get to the crux of the issues. If anyone could give her a straight opinion about the situation with Scott, it would be Analiese.

So, after the girls had left the table, she'd spoken truthfully, holding nothing back. She spoke of her fear of her mother's reaction, if and when the time came that they would make their relationship known. She shared her concern about stepping into the kids' world in the role of stepmother, when her role as aunt hadn't been an especially close one until recently.

Finally, her deepest and most secret fear. What if the Lord *did* lay His hand of healing on Rachel? What if, after all this time, Rach arose from her sick-bed, eager to re-enter her husband and children's lives?

What on earth would they do in such a situation? She knew in her deepest heart Scott's response to such a scenario; he would welcome his wife back, even though it may cause him pain. The question that she tortured herself with was whether, and how, she would survive such an experience. She very much feared that she wouldn't, or at least wouldn't want to.

Ana listened quietly, then leaned back in her chair and cocked an eyebrow at her friend. "So this is what happens when you start going home for the weekend, hmm? Looks like I can't let you out of my sight for a minute, *gurfrin*. You know I'm just pullin' your leg, don't you? I guess I'm just surprised, is all; I would've never guessed you had someone in your life. You've kept it all together pretty well up to this point, but I'm glad you finally felt you could talk to me about it."

Feeling a blush stain her cheeks, Celeste replied, "Oh, Ana, it's not that I wanted to keep it from you, it's just that I…well, I don't know. I guess I've just been sort of pretending that it wasn't real, and as long as I didn't talk about it, it was just kind of this *thing* that Scott and I were feeling. As soon as I talk to you about something, it becomes real. I guess I just wasn't ready until now. But now I really need some advice, some words of wisdom. So, am I crazy? Have I lost my last marble?"

"I think sometimes we can't help who we love." A shadow passed over her friend's face as she spoke, and Celeste knew she was thinking about her own failed marriage, the death of hopes and dreams she'd held so dear. "I guess I'd just ask you straight up if you feel the Lord's hand in this, Cellie? What about Scott? Has he been praying too? Yes? Well, that's good, and it's good that the two of you talk about your faith together. I think that's the most important thing, that you share a commitment to Christ first."

Celeste nodded. "It's been such an amazing transition, Scott's journey back to the Lord. He's an incredibly strong person, Ana, and I just have so much respect for him, for holding strong all these years. He and Rachel had an amazing marriage, and I guess that's part of what scares me too; if we do take this thing to the next level, what if I can't live up to her standards? I mean, I have no experience in *anything* involved with marriage."

"Are we talking about sex?"

Feeling her face color, Celeste nodded. "Well, sure, but everything, Ana. I hate gardening, I'm plenty happy buying canned fruit and veggies at the grocery store. I'm not a seamstress. I'm not likely to make my own curtains or spend mornings quilting with the ladies, and I'm certainly not experienced at dealing with teenagers, especially ones that have the issues these kids have. The whole thing just seems overwhelming, but then I just end up back at the basics, my feelings for Scott, and everything else just kind of fades away until I start reminding myself of what I'd be taking on. Add to that the fact that Rachel's alive and Scott's still her husband, and I wonder what on earth I'm doing."

Ana shook her head. "It sounds like you're worried about measuring up in Scott's eyes?" At Celeste's nod, she continued, "That's a road that leads to nowhere, girl. You aren't going to fill Rachel's shoes, Celeste, because the Lord created you to wear your *own* shoes. I'm not saying there wouldn't be adjustment issues, but the fact is that you're *not* Rachel, and Scott knows that. He wouldn't expect you to be Rachel, Celeste, if he loves *you*."

A group of giggling teenage girls passed the table, and Celeste took a moment to process Ana's words. As she'd expected, Ana had helped to bring clarity to her thoughts, and she drew a deep breath and asked the final question that had been frequently in her mind. "Remember all the Friday nights we've had supper, then sat Tori down in front of a video and prayed together?" At Ana's nod, she

continued. "For years, we've prayed that the Lord would bring someone into both of our lives, right? You know how long I've waited for
'the one' to come into my life, how much I've longed for a husband
and family. Now I'm afraid that I've wanted it so badly that I'm
projecting my ideals onto Scott, because he's become involved in my
life. What if I'm just so desperate for a husband that I'm fixated on
him? I mean, he's vulnerable now, and lonely. What if we're both settling for each other just because we're tired of being alone?"

Ana chuckled. "Yeah, the old Mr. Right versus Mr. Right Now
thing. Come on, Celeste. Are you trying to tell me that you're so
desperate for a man that you have to put the move on your brother-
in-law? I understand what you're saying, and I know I'd be asking
myself the same thing, but I think you need to just stop all of this
and really listen to what the Lord is trying to say to you. Yes, we've
spent a lot of time in prayer, asking the Lord to send someone into
your life. And yes, I know how much you want this. So, this is my
advice, Celeste. If you and Scott are both asking that the Lord's will
be done in both of your lives, and you're really falling in love, then
trust that He knows what He's doing and stop fighting it. Did you
ever stop to think that maybe the reason you've been waiting all
these years is because the Lord was planning to bring the two of you
together? Scott and his kids need you now. God's timing is always
perfect, even when it doesn't make sense to us. That's what I think,
Celeste. You do what you think is right. Just keep the prayer chan-
nels open. And pray with Scott, both of you together. Build this
thing on the Rock and then walk in faith."

Tears filled Celeste's eyes. Bless Ana, she made it all so clear. "You
make it sound so easy, Ana."

"No, I never said it would be easy, girl. I'm just saying that if the
Lord is giving you your heart's desire, then take His gift and trust
Him to carry you through the rough spots. 'Be still and know that I
am God,' right?

"I have a hard time with the 'be still' part."

"Don't we all, *gurfrin?* Don't we all?"

She'd come away from her conversation with Ana with a lightened heart and renewed hope. And tonight she'd see Scott. Friday

had dragged on interminably, and with each mile traveled east on I-90, her heart had reached out to him.

Now, as the sun rode the crest of the mountains to the west of town, country music, punctuated by the muffled giggles of two young girls, wafted down the hallway from Rach's old room. With the dance that evening, they'd figured it would be easier for the girls to get dressed at Catherine's, then spend the night in town. From the sounds of it, they were really getting into the whole fair dance mode, right down to the country music that was blasting from behind the closed door.

She slipped into a narrow denim skirt that fell to mid-calf, then reached for the sweater she'd agonized over, finally deciding it wasn't too dressy for a dinner date, even one in which she'd be manning the stove. A delicate pink with a scoop neckline, the style accentuated her curves and narrowed her waist to nothing. Standing before the mirror, she examined herself with a critical eye. She'd dressed for plenty of dates over the years, but somehow she was more nervous on this evening than she could remember having ever been before. Was she overdressed? Should she just keep it casual and wear shorts? What if she did, and Scott showed up wearing something dressier? Did he even *have* anything dressy in his closet anymore? What if he showed up wearing overalls and work boots? What if he wasn't really the person she thought he was, and she came away from the evening disappointed, all of her growing dreams crushed? What if she was totally misreading the signals and all he wanted was a home-cooked meal?

Drawing in a deep breath, she forced herself to relax. *Remember that you've put your trust in the Lord, and that He's brought you to this moment, in faith, believing that you're right where you're supposed to be.*

Slipping a gold chain with a small diamond over her neck, she added a pair of tiny gold hoops to her lobes, applied her makeup carefully, then touched her pressure points with a delicate perfume. Stepping into a pair of low-heeled shoes, she noted with a sudden fluttering in her stomach that as she'd prepared for the evening, dusk had fallen.

At a knock at the door, she turned from the mirror. Chattering a mile a minute, the girls entered the room, making a bee-line for the mirror. Grateful for the distraction from her own thoughts, Celeste leaned against the wall. "Goodness, look at you! Oh, yeah. You guys are major league heartbreakers, especially for this town!"

A pleased blush staining her cheeks, Tawnya brushed self-consciously at her jeans, adjusted her new blouse, and leaned into the mirror to examine her mascara. Aunt Celeste had taken her to a makeup clinic at Macys; no one was going to laugh at her again. Satisfied with her appearance, she queried, "Doesn't Tori look beautiful?"

Celeste replied, "Yes, she does; you both look great. Tori, girlfriend, looking like you do, if your mother were here, I'd be hard-pressed to keep her from locking you in your room 'til you were twenty-five or so." As the girls basked in their glory, Celeste asked, "Are you sure you don't mind spending the night?"

"No, it's good, because this way we can just walk home later. We'll be fine."

"Okay. If I'm not back when you get home, call your house and let your dad know you're home safe."

"We will."

As if on cue, the doorbell rang and Celeste straightened, reached for her small tote, and said, "Guess this is it, guys. Tell your dad I'll be right down, Tawn."

As the girls pounded down the stairs, Celeste gazed into the mirror once again. This was it. After running a brush through her hair one last time, she freshened her lip gloss, snapped off the light, and closed the door behind herself. Standing at the top of the stairs, she took a deep breath, then descended the steps. As she reached the landing, her gaze fell upon Scott standing with her mother. As if by instinct, his eyes lifted to meet hers and for an instant everything faded to insignificance except the woman in the pink sweater.

Scott felt the heat rush to his cheeks and, feeling Catherine's eyes upon him, made an effort to speak casually, "Hi, Celeste."

His words may have been nonchalant but the warmth in his eyes gave him away. Suddenly, her nervousness fled and she knew everything would be okay. Feeling her trepidation wash away, ever aware of mother's assessing gaze, Celeste descended the stairs, warmth flooding through her.

"Hi, yourself. You look really nice." And he did. He was wearing a crisp new pair of Wranglers, a pair of highly polished western boots, and a sleek button-down shirt of a deep hunter green, sleeves rolled to the elbows. She suspected he'd made a run into Ellensburg or Wenatchee; she didn't remember seeing anything like this at Rumleys the month before. The fact that he'd taken the time to do so during his busiest, longest days, touched her deeply.

Turning to her mother, she said, "I don't know what time we'll all be home, Mom, but don't wait up, okay?"

Not bothering to respond to her words, Catherine addressed her son-in-law, "I don't think the girls should go to this dance, Scott. There's bound to be alcohol, and they're too young to be out late at night."

"Now, Catherine, we've been over this. They'll be fine; nobody's going to give them any trouble."

Frustrated that she was unable to control the situation, the older woman volleyed her parting shot, "Are you stopping by Fircrest tonight?"

Voice steady, Scott replied, "No, not tonight, Catherine. I'm looking awfully forward to finding out what Seattle women eat. And speaking of which, are we ready?"

"The ice chest is on the front porch."

Nodding, he said, "Well, Catherine, good night. Thanks for letting the girls stay over."

"I'll see you in the morning, Mom." Celeste gave her mother a quick kiss on the cheek, then followed Scott and the girls out into the summer night.

Eyeing Scott's truck, Celeste had an idea. Rummaging in her purse, she retrieved her keys, then tossed them to Scott. "Let's take mine, Scott. The girls shouldn't have to ride in the back of a pickup tonight, don't you think?"

Flashing her a grin, Scott caught the keys, preceded his ladies to the Beamer, and made a show of opening the passenger door, ushering the girls into the backseat and making sure Celeste was settled into the passenger seat before closing the door softly. Sliding into the driver's seat, he marveled at the luxury surrounding him; leather soft as butter, more bells and whistles than the space shuttle, and a sound system to die for.

"Sure rides a lot closer to the ground than my old truck," he remarked, sliding into gear, appreciating the purr of the engine. "I could get used to this."

Looking straight ahead, Celeste blurted, "I'm sorry about Mom, Scott. I should've known she'd have to get a couple of digs in tonight."

With a shrug, he dismissed her concerns. "Oh, that's just the way she is, Celeste. I think something's on her radar, but there isn't anything she can prove, so she's just trying to keep control of the situation. I thought about asking if she wanted to ride over to the fairgrounds, but then I chickened out."

"Yes, and thank goodness for that. Can you just imagine her sitting there, glaring at everyone, scolding everybody's kids and just being miserable in general?"

"Well, like I said, I *thought* about it. All told, I think she'll be happier at home." With an admiring glance, he queried, "Did I happen to mention that you look great?"

"Yes, you did, thank you. And you look really nice, too, Scott." Her gaze fell onto his muscular arms, tanned a deep golden brown, and moved to his hands where they held the steering wheel. The sight of his wedding ring reminded her that even something as innocent as cooking supper, alone together in the rambling kitchen, might constitute an intimacy that perhaps crossed a line or two.

It seemed only moments until they arrived at the fairgrounds, Tawnya pulling Tori's arm. "Come on, Tori, I need to check my lipstick."

Shaking his head, Scott cast a bemused glance at Celeste. "What have you done to my little girl, anyway? I hardly recognize her these days; makeup, new hairstyle, new friend. She seems so grown-up all of a sudden."

Celeste smiled. "We just polished the surface a little, but the biggest change is really her self-confidence. And I've loved it. I've enjoyed getting to know her."

The ride to the farm passed quickly, and soon Scott pulled up in front of the house, exited the car, came around to the passenger side, and opened the door for Celeste.

"Thank you, sir."

"My pleasure, ma'am. I'll grab the ice chest. Hope you've got enough to feed an army, I'm starving."

"If not, I can always whip up some fish-heads and rice."

"Think I'll settle for a tuna sandwich, if it's all the same to you."

"You'll have to, because the butcher kept the salmon's head when he wrapped it up."

"Oh, sure, *he* gets to have the fish-heads and rice."

"Gotta be some perks to a job where you're always risking chopping a finger off."

Shifting the ice chest to his other hand, he held the screen door open and allowed her to pass before him.

"Ty? You home?"

Silence.

"Well, that's interesting," Scott drawled. "Now that he's gotten used to eating Connie's home-cooked meals the last few weeks, he doesn't usually miss a meal. Not that I'm disappointed, of course."

"Well, this is Shuksan's big night. He's probably at Alpine Burger, choking down about seven cheeseburgers and three orders of onion rings."

"I remember those days."

"Great days, weren't they?"

Having emptied the contents of the ice chest onto the counter, Celeste cast a gaze about the kitchen. "If you'll just let me putter around in here, I'll see if I can't get this meal going."

"I'll put on some music."

"Great."

After he'd left the room, she took a slow turn around the kitchen, familiarizing herself with the location of various pots and pans, dishes, and stemware. She set the table for two, bypassing Rachel's wedding china and crystal for the Mikasa stoneware, which she'd finally discovered in the dishwasher, thankfully clean. Quickly setting the table, she stood for a moment, inspecting her handiwork. Looked kind of bare, but she hadn't had access to flowers except for her mother's own beds, and she'd known better to even pose the question. She'd waffled back and forth about a candle, finally deciding against it; she didn't want to appear to be working too hard to put a romantic spin to the evening.

She broadened her search until she happened across the tin foil, readied the salmon and dressed it with garlic, onion, and lemon wedges, then slid it under the broiler. Wondering what had happened to her dinner companion, she prepared the pasta, transferred the green salad she'd assembled earlier into a matching stoneware serving bowl, and raided the fridge for salad dressing. She was just setting the plate of sliced sourdough bread on the table when the screen door banged shut and Scott reappeared, an enormous armful of flowers in tow.

Her eyes widened. "My goodness! They're gorgeous."

"I think we have a vase around here somewhere." He rummaged through the cupboards until spotting the tall crystal vase, added water, and unceremoniously stuffed the flowers into its mouth. He wasn't sure why he should feel vaguely guilty for raiding his own flowerbeds, except for the fact that, truth be told, it was more Catherine's flower garden than his own, and he quailed at the prospect of her discovery of his pilfering. If she put two and two together and figured he'd picked them for Celeste, well, it didn't bear thinking of.

"Here, let me work on this a little." Celeste rescued the vase, removed the flowers from the vase, trimmed some ends, and rearranged the blooms in the vase in casual symmetry, then placed it in a place of honor on the table, centered on a lace doily.

"So I'm not a florist, what can I say?"

Celeste waved a regal hand, dipping into a tiny curtsy. "The master gardener need say nothing. He has done his part in producing the raw materials."

"So, if I told you your mother was the master gardener..."

She grinned. "Then I'd say you'd better hope she doesn't roll on out here and do a formal inspection. 'Specially if the evidence is still here in the vase!"

"I shudder to even think about it."

"Then let's not. Let's eat salad. And thank you, they're beautiful. Snapdragons, roses, what else am I seeing here?"

"Beats me, but whatever they are, they sure have an appetite for Green Thumb plant food and bone meal."

"Aren't you glad you have more palatable meal prospects then the flowers?"

"Oh, yeah. Looks great, smells wonderful. Come on, have a seat."

As they settled themselves, Scott asked, "Did you ever hear about Rachel's roses the year after we were married?"

At the shake of her head, he continued, "Well, we had this stupid mutt that just showed up one day, and we didn't have the heart to run him off. Money was tight, but Rachel had her heart set on roses, so she went in to the Grange Supply and bought a dozen bare-root roses, which were the cheapest they had. They were in pretty bad shape, but she was bound and determined that they were going to survive, and she babied those roses, I can't even tell you. Well, one morning she went out with the hose to put some water on them and every last rose bush had been dug up, just totally trashed. And there was that rotten mutt, laying right next to the last one, muzzle full of bone meal."

"You mean…"

"Yep. Smelled that bone meal and dug down 'til he found it and made himself quite a meal. Of course, besides the bone meal, he probably got quite a belly-full of other stuff that wasn't as good for his digestion, 'cause he was one sick pup for about three days. I don't think I've ever seen Rachel as mad as she was that morning, and I don't think I'll ever forget the sight of her throwing the rake at that dog's hind end. She stomped around those roses for about ten minutes and then sat smack down in the dirt and cried. That dog *knew* he was in way over his head, but I figured I'd get the rake myself if I so much as cracked a smile, so I made myself scarce 'til she'd calmed down, oh, about a week or so later, as I recall!"

Clutching her stomach, laughing helplessly, Celeste managed, "You didn't even stick around to help re-plant the roses and comfort your wife?"

"Nope, the old self-preservation thing kicked in and I just got out of there. But Rach re-planted the roses, and I could hear her all the way to the barn, hollering at that dog and threatening him with mortal injury every time he even *looked* like he wanted to set a paw onto the flower bed."

"So, did the roses survive the trauma?"

Scott gestured to the vase. "You tell me."

"These are the same roses?"

"The very ones."

She fell silent, examining the flowers, then lifted her eyes to Scott's. "That is a fantastic story. Thank you for sharing it with me. So, what happened to the dog?

"Oh, he survived another few years. When he died, I thought Rach was going to take to her bed; she'd really grown to love that old dog. You know that yellow rosebush on the side of the house? That's his grave marker. The next spring, she ordered it directly from Jackson-Perkins and planted it on his grave, even put an extra helping of bone meal in the ground as a special tribute."

Celeste speared a tomato wedge, suddenly pensive. Her sister had had depths that she hadn't been aware of. The fit of temper that must have erupted through Rach's tiny body was as alien a thought as the prospect of her sister donning a space suit and hitching a ride on the next space shuttle to Mars; she couldn't quite picture it. But...

"Was she by any chance pregnant with Tyler when this happened?"

"Yeah, about three months."

"Well, that makes it a little easier to imagine, then. Ana's always telling me stories about her various tantrums and rants during her pregnancy with Tori."

"Yeah, she definitely had her moments. But what about you? Have you ever thought about having kids?"

Pain and longing shafted through her heart, and in that moment, even the act of chewing seemed difficult. If he only knew how a husband and family of her own had filled her dreams for many long years, and how the longing for these things had become a living, tangible thing.

Scott's voice brought her back to reality, "You're awfully quiet. Did I say something wrong?"

Forcing a smile, she shook her head. "No, of course not. And yes, I would love to have a family some day. I guess I'm just trying to come to terms with the fact that maybe it isn't part of God's plan for me." Pushing her chair away from the table, she lay her napkin next to her plate and said, "I think the salmon should be done. Excuse me for a second."

He'd obviously inadvertently stumbled onto a tender spot. Unsure how to proceed, Scott rose, "Let me do that, it's hot."

"Thank you."

"Celeste…If I said something to upset you, I really apologize."

Embarrassed now, she pinned on her best smile. "Oh, you didn't upset me, I just…never mind. Come on, let's eat while it's hot."

Dinner officially served, they returned to the table, gave thanks, and made an effort to lighten the conversation. Finally waving his napkin in surrender, he groaned, "I don't think I'll eat again for a week. Everything was great, Celeste. Thank you."

"You're welcome. But I should have warned you to save room for dessert."

"Ohh…well, maybe we can take a few turns around the yard or something, get things tamped down a bit. I'd hate to miss dessert. What is it?"

"You'll have to wait and see, Mr. Parnell. The cook doesn't divulge her secrets that easily."

"You have a hard heart, Celeste."

"Well, for that, you can forget about dessert. I'll feed it to the dog. Oh, that's right, they aren't supposed to have chocolate, are they?"

"Chocolate? I promise I'll be good, I absolutely guarantee it. Don't make threats like that, woman!"

"Or you'll do what?"

Their banter had brought them nose to nose, and before he knew what had happened, she was in his arms and his lips were touching hers. A long moment, perhaps five long moments, passed before she disengaged from the embrace, took an unsteady step backward, then turned and addressed the dishes with a vengeance. Scott groaned mentally; he'd gone and rushed his fences and now she was as skittish as a yearling filly eyeing the saddle with trepidation, figuring out how to escape the corral.

Way to go, Parnell.

Running a hand over his face, he said, "Celeste? I'm sorry about that."

Standing before the sink, back ramrod straight, she was silent for two beats, then turned to face him. "Don't be sorry. I'm not sorry, though I should be, and that makes me one sorry sister, doesn't it?"

He crossed the room to join her. "No. It doesn't have anything to do with what kind of a sister you are. What it *does* have to do with has gone way beyond sisterhood, beyond everything in a normal brother-in-law, sister-in-law relationship. Because if you want to look at blame or responsibility, then put it on me, because I'm the one wearing the ring." Raising his hand, he wiggled his fingers where the ring in question rode his third finger, but she'd already turned to stare blindly out of the window about the sink to where the vegetables lined the garden in even rows and where the specter of Rachel was suddenly and vividly present.

Hands on her shoulders, turning her to face him, he continued, "If we're talking responsibility here, or *ir*responsibility, then you've gotta let me take my share of it. But somehow, for whatever reason, I'm just not feeling it like I should be. And I've prayed about it, Celeste, a lot. Seems like it's all I do lately. I've asked that He take these feelings from me, if this is wrong, but that hasn't happened. I don't know, maybe I'm just rationalizing the situation, but I think that there's a reason we're both feeling this way, and maybe it isn't so wrong, after all. That's assuming that you're feeling the same things I'm feeling."

"I'm pretty sure I am. I've been praying as well, and the more I try to get beyond these feelings, they just seem to grow stronger. But how do we know that these feelings are coming from God and not from Satan? Because I know that all temptation is from him and I've never struggled with temptation like this in my life. That's what I'm really struggling with; how do we know?"

Scott sighed deeply and thought for a moment before replying. "I think there's a Bible verse that says all good things come from the Lord. And I believe this *is* a good thing, Celeste. I believe that if we're both praying for guidance and asking the Lord that His will be done, then we just have to trust Him to show us the way."

She nodded. "That's what I keep telling myself, but I just want to be sure that this is from Him and not just my own wants and desires coming to the forefront."

They stood silently for several moments, then Celeste remarked, "Well, I guess we did find out tonight that we can talk about Rachel without being too self-conscious. And I'm glad, because I think it's important that we never try to diminish the life you shared with her."

"I know you're right. And you know what else? It came really naturally, talking about her and that old dog. I expected it to be a lot harder, and maybe it will be sometimes, but I think it's a good thing. The last few years have been so tough, coping with the way she is now that I forget all of the good years."

"And there were a lot of them, way back from high school."

"Yeah. Oh, we had some great times together. I guess for a long time I tried really hard not to remember because it just made me sad and bitter. It was easier just to try to put all of that behind me, but now I realize that it's all part of the process of letting go, that I have to come to terms with the past before I can look to the future."

Celeste smiled. "She loved you so much. No matter what the future brings, don't ever forget that."

"I won't. I loved her so much that I thought I wasn't going to survive it when we got the diagnosis and her prognosis. I just couldn't believe that I'd ever be happy again or ever be at a point where I wasn't totally devastated. It's been a slow process, but now I'm just thankful for the time we had together."

Celeste nodded. "Have you talked to the kids yet, about your decision to remove life support?"

"Not yet. Soon. I figure I'll let them get into the swing of school for a few weeks first. We have some time yet. I think about the middle of September I'll sit them down, show them the DNR, and explain that it was their mom wanted. That'll give them a month or so to process the situation and say their goodbyes. Or do you think I shouldn't wait?"

"I can't tell you that, because you have a better idea of how they'll react to the news. And as such, you have to make the judgment call on when to tell them. I guess I'm wondering when you're going to tell Mother?"

He shook his head. "I don't know. I honestly don't know how I'm going to tell her; she's going to take it hard."

"Just remember that this is Rachel's choice. Show her the DNR, just like you will the kids. Let her know you've sought guidance about this decision and that you've received the Lord's peace. She's naturally going to be devastated, but I think that when she really thinks about it, she'll accept it. Do you want me to talk to her with you? It might be easier, not that it's going to be easy either way."

"I hate to ask it of you. I guess I'm concerned that she'll think we're 'ganging up' on her. On the other hand, she's your mom, and Rach is your sister, and you have every right to be involved in this process."

"Let me know. If you want me, I'll be there."

They worked side by side, clearing the table and loading the dishwasher, then took a walk around the yard. The night air was soft, the heat of the day diminished, with the full moon hanging pale in the dimming light. Scott glanced at Celeste's feet, then said, "I need to run down to the pasture, turn the irrigation off. I'd ask if you wanted to come, but I don't think you want to be wearing those shoes. Want to wait here, and I'll be back in a few minutes?"

She shook her head. "I'd like to go with you. Does Tawnya maybe have a pair of tennis shoes I could borrow?"

"Let's look."

A few minutes later, Celeste's feet safely ensconced in a pair of hot-pink running shoes, they walked to the pasture. After he'd dealt with the pump, they sat under the trees in the same spot they'd sat before when they'd first spoken about the DNR. Crickets and frogs were tuning up for their nightly concert, otherwise there was silence.

She sighed and stretched her legs out full-length. "It's so beautiful here, so quiet. I can see why you love it so much.

He let his eyes wander across the meadow to where he knew the mountain range lay in the darkness. "Yeah. I do love it. I can't imagine ever wanting to live anywhere else." He was silent for a few moments, then turned to meet her gaze. "Could *you* live here?"

She went still, weighing his words. Was this a rhetorical question or something more directed? She finally settled on an ambiguous answer in a question of her own. "Do you mean Shuksan, in general?"

"Well, yeah. I mean, would you ever give up your condo on the lake and be happy back here in the sticks?"

"I guess it would depend on what was going on in my life. I've told you that I'm kind of in flux right now, as far as my job and my direction. Actually, I have been thinking about something that Connie told me last week. I guess Bill Koch is looking to retire, has his practice for sale but hasn't had any takers."

"That would be quite a change for you, wouldn't it? Dealing with farmers instead of businessmen? Trading the city for a two stop-light town. Are you really considering it?"

"Well, yes, I guess I am. It's been on my mind quite a bit. I've been feeling like I've outgrown my life, like it's a pair of shoes that don't quite fit anymore. And I think my focus has changed too. My life just isn't meeting my needs anymore, and when that happens, it's time to take a good hard look at what isn't working and try to figure out a new direction."

"Yeah. I know exactly what you mean."

With a smile, "Yes, I believe you do. If anyone could understand, it would be you."

They sat in silence for a while longer, then Scott sighed and rose to his feet, groaning as his knees protested his movements. Celeste remarked, "Sounds like that hurts."

"Nope, just my knees' way of letting me know I'm getting to be an old geezer. They've been doing this since I was thirty. Rach always called them Rice Krispy knees; you know, snap, crackle, and pop? I always told her that I was short a knee, that I had snap and crackle covered, but didn't have anywhere for pop, but now I think my right elbow's claiming it." She laughed, then took the hand he held out to her and accepted his help in pulling her to her feet.

"Ready to head back?"

She nodded. "I suppose we'd better."

They walked in silence, bathed in moonlight, hearing the song of a night-bird late to seek its nest. Celeste was struck anew by the quiet peacefulness of this place. It seemed so pristine, so untouched by civilization. She drew in a deep breath just to enjoy the freshness of the air; no tinges of exhaust or rotting garbage from dumpsters out here, just the scent of pine and earth, of pasture and irrigation. To Scott, she remarked, "I just realized that for all that I grew up here, I'm still a town kid. I never really realized how different life is just a few miles outside of city limits."

"Different in a good way?"

"Oh, for sure. I can't remember the last time I've felt so relaxed, just being in the trees, seeing the mountains. Did Rachel have this kind of epiphany when she moved out here from Mom's house after you were married?"

"I'm not sure that she ever said anything one way or the other. Rach wasn't one for taking walks like this. She wasn't much of an outdoorsy person. Her comfort zone was basically the house and yard. I would've liked to pack a picnic lunch and do a trail ride up to one of the lakes, maybe take the sleeping bags and camp for a couple of days, but that was never something she felt comfortable with. I remember being disappointed for the first couple of summers that I couldn't share those experiences with her, but then Ty came and I guess I just kind of forgot about it. Until now, anyway."

She was instantly chagrined. "I'm sorry if I stepped over the line by asking. I guess I need to learn where the boundaries are. I didn't mean to pry into your marriage, Scott."

He squeezed her hand in reassurance. "You didn't, Celeste. This is just one of the things that we have to expect, you and me. I didn't live in a vacuum for all these years, and it's only natural that you're curious about the life Rach and I shared. Ask anything you like."

They'd reached the perimeter of the yard and the house beckoned. They crossed the yard and ascended the steps to the front porch. Half a dozen moths danced about the glow of the porch light, scattering momentarily as Scott pulled the screen door open. "After you."

"Ready for dessert?"

"Chocolate? Are you kidding? Bring it on!"

He sat at the table, watching as she served up thick wedges of a decadent-appearing chocolate cake, smiling with appreciation as she placed a plate in front of him. "Thanks. Man, this looks fantastic!"

"Let's cross our fingers. It's my friend Ana's recipe and I love it, but this is the first time I've actually baked it myself."

He filled his fork and lifted it to his mouth, then with an exaggerated show of pure bliss, nodded his approval. "This is the best cake I've ever eaten, even better than Rach's, and that's saying something. What are you doing crunching numbers for a living? You should be in an apron, up to your elbows in flour, if you can bake like this."

She grinned. "Thanks for the compliment, but watch it or you might get a clout with a rolling pin. I'm not exactly the reigning Kitchen Queen, in case you didn't know."

"I'd have never known, not if tonight's meal was any indication. You're a great cook. You know what this means, don't you?"

For delicacy's sake, having just taken a bite of cake, she raised an eyebrow in query.

"I think you've just put Connie Ripley out of a job."

Successfully swallowing the mouthful of cake, she wiped her mouth with a napkin, then said, "Oh, you think so, do you? Two hours is a bit of a drive to cook supper for you every night, don't you think?"

The teasing light disappeared from his eyes and he replied in a serious tone, "Yeah, I definitely think so, but it might be easier if you were here. You know I'm just kidding about cooking supper every night, right? I guess I was just wondering how serious you are about checking into Bill's firm being for sale? I mean, do you really want to give up your job, the chance to make six figures, and come home and work on farmers' taxes? Pretty tame stuff compared to what you're doing now."

Feeling somewhat deflated, laying her napkin on the table next to her plate, she remarked, "You sound like you're trying to discourage me."

Shaking his head, he countered, "No, not at all; I'm just trying to process what you're telling me. I mean, this is a fairly huge step for you, Celeste. I just want you to be sure you know what you're getting yourself into."

Celeste rose abruptly, taking her plate to the sink. "Oh, I know exactly what I'm getting myself into, and out of, for that matter. For the last five years, all I've been able to see is making partner; working sixty hours a week, wooing clients away from other accounting firms. I've only just realized how much I really dislike what my job's turned into, Scott. It seems like the only people we service at our firm are rich and irresponsible, and the richer they become, the more irresponsible they become; it just becomes this unending cycle. Then we have to clean up the mess, give advice they don't pay any attention to, and then clean up the next mess, and the one after that. And for what? So they can try to cheat on their taxes just to prove they can? It's like a game to them; how close to the line can they go without actually breaking the law? I'm just not into it anymore. I went into accounting because I'm good at putting things together, figuring out what's the best way to deal with the financial end of it head-on; that's what I want to be doing, and for someone who needs somebody like me to help them. Honest clients, people who actually work for their money. That's what I want, Scott. Do you understand?"

"When you put it that way, yeah, sure I understand. It sounds like you've put a lot of thought into this."

"I have, yes."

"Well, then, I guess I just have to ask—where would you live? Move back in with Catherine?"

She sighed. "That's the one fly in the ointment. It wouldn't be my first choice, although it may come to that for awhile."

"Long-term, though?"

"Long-term, I can see myself buying some land out on the lake, putting in a log house. That's a big draw to coming back home, the chance to live on a lake that isn't overrun with people and speedboats."

"You know it's being developed out there, though, mostly Wet-Siders putting in vacation homes. One of these days it'll probably be just as bad as your lake."

She grinned at the reference to the Western Washington, Seattle area residents, "West-Siders." Eastern Washington residents, blessed with sunny skies, often used the term "Wet-Siders" when referring to the weekenders who came east across the mountains for a chance at some sun and warm weather. "Hopefully the county has lot-size restrictions and ordinances about condos."

He nodded. "Yeah, at this point lots have to be at least two acres. The county commissioners figured that would keep people from building right on top of each other; help keep more of a rural feeling out there. As far as I know, there isn't zoning for multiple-residence; I think a lot of people would put up a stink if some outfit came in and wanted to build condos, although I know the local businesses wouldn't mind the extra revenue it would bring in."

Good point, and it strengthened her resolve. "I'm thinking that this is a good time to tie up some land out there, before the word gets out to the rest of the 'Wet-Siders.' Being only two hours from Seattle, I have a feeling a lot of people are going to be interested in our little lake."

"I'm surprised it hasn't happened sooner, to tell the truth, though I'm sorry to see all the development out there."

"Does that include me?"

"No. Far as I'm concerned, you're a local. But..." Shaking his head, he left the sentence unfinished.

"But what?"

He eyed her for a moment, then shrugged. "I guess I just wondered..."

Celeste felt like shaking him. "Come on, Scott. Spit it out!"

He inhaled deeply, then sighed. "I don't have a right to have an opinion either way. I know that. It's just that, well, I guess I was just wondering where this leaves us down the road. If there is a down-the-road. I hope there will be. I'm not trying to pressure you, Celeste...Forget I said anything. If you want to live out on Carrot, then go for it. Do what makes you happy. That's really all I want."

She thought she understood what he was getting at, and the knowing warmed her through to the core. "Thanks, Scott, I appreciate that. But I want to make sure I understand what you're *really* saying. Are you thinking about that if I do build out on the lake, and we *do* end up together, then where would we live? Is that it?"

Feeling like an idiot, and a presumptuous one to boot, he threw his arms into the air. "Yeah, I guess so. It's ridiculous, and I know it, so just forget it. I have no business influencing your decisions one way or the other."

She glanced away for a moment, then met his eyes again, and replied, "Funny, it feels like you *do*."

They stood silently, sharing a gaze that spoke more than words could, then he moved to hold her once again. Standing in his embrace, she felt the steady beating of his heart and knew to her toes that the steadiness she sensed extended far deeper than merely his heart. This man was *solid*, a man she could lean upon, depend on, and yet who wouldn't hold her so tightly that she would seek to break free.

"Scott?"

"Hmm?"

She drew back a fraction, in order to look into his face. "Let's walk in faith on this, too, okay? It feels so right, being with you, holding you, and I could stay here forever. But it's not the right time. When the right time comes, if it comes, then that'll be the time to worry about houses. For now, let's just...*be*. I can't ask anything more of you right now, and I'm fine with that. You'll have to let me follow my own path in the meantime."

He loosened his embrace, dropped his hands to her shoulders, and gave her a squeeze. "How'd you get to be so smart, city girl?"

She rolled her eyes. "Must be the school of hard knocks, if you want to know the truth. Bumpkin."

With a mock-scowl, he pretended to rub his knuckles into her scalp. "Bumpkin? *Bumpkin?*"

Giggling, she twisted away with a shriek. "Well, as they say, if the shoe fits..."

"You're a fine one to talk about shoes fitting; I've been watching you prance around in those pink tennis shoes all night!"

Pirouetting, she held a foot up for his inspection, adopting a haughty mien. "A gentleman wouldn't cast aspersions on a lady's footwear."

"Yeah, and a lady wouldn't call the *gentleman* a bumpkin." Stepping close to her again, he brushed a tendril of hair from her forehead. "Much as I hate to, I'd better get you home. Your mom'll be wanting to have my hide."

They made the return drive to town, connected yet silent. When they'd reached Catherine's, Scott carried the ice chest to the front door, returned Celeste's keys, and said, "Thanks again for dinner. It was great."

"I'm glad. I really enjoyed myself too."

Not knowing whether Catherine was awake or sleeping kept the two of them at arms' length. Finally, he sighed, "Well…"

"Yeah…"

"Goodnight, then."

"Goodnight, Scott."

She watched as he strode down the sidewalk, watched until his truck had turned the corner and disappeared from sight, then sighed deeply and heaved the ice chest into the kitchen. All was silent; *the girls aren't home yet and Mother must be sleeping. So much for worrying about beating "curfew!"*

She set about tidying the kitchen, set the ice chest upside-down on the back porch to dry overnight, then sat next to it, heedless of the moisture seeping into the back of her skirt. It was only then that she realized she still wore Tawnya's pink running shoes. Nudging her feet out of the shoes, she replayed the events of the evening, the words that had passed between them, and the shared kiss, her cheeks growing warm with the memory. It hadn't been her first kiss, she'd had a few with which to make comparison, yet knew that none came close, nor, she suspected, would ever come close to the feelings she'd experienced in Scott's arms that night.

The shrill ringing of the telephone cut through the quiet, and she rose quickly to answer before it could disturb Mother. Expecting to hear Tawnya's voice, her pulse danced a quick beat when the now-familiar male voice danced through the line.

A long moment of silence hung between them, then he spoke. "I just wanted to say goodnight. One more time."

She smiled into the darkness. "I'm glad you called."

"I'm glad. I thought maybe I was coming on a little too strong tonight. I don't mean to, Cel. I guess, under the circumstances, maybe I'm not sure exactly how I'm *supposed* to act."

"Same goes, believe me. And no, you didn't come on too strong. It just seems that things are so intense between us. It's kind of like that feeling in the air before a storm breaks, you know? Where you feel it coming but you're not sure exactly when it's going to hit. Does that make sense?"

"Yeah, that's a pretty accurate description. You aren't gonna mind if I tell you I'm glad it's not just me feeling it?"

Funny how his words affected her deep in her stomach. Glad for the darkness, she whispered, "No, it isn't just you, Scott. But it scares me, you know? I keep expecting to wake up and find that none of it's real, that Rachel's bustling away in the kitchen and this has all been a dream."

She heard his sigh through the telephone. "This is one dream that none of us are gonna wake up from, Cel. It doesn't get any realer than this."

Silence hung in the air for a long moment, then he sighed. "I'm going to miss you so much. You're leaving tomorrow?"

"Yes, after church. Will you come?"

"I'll be there."

They sat in silence, content simply being connected in this tentative manner, then she yawned deeply and Scott said, "I'd better let you get some rest. I just wanted to tell you again how much I enjoyed the evening. Great supper. Thank you."

"You're welcome. It was fun cooking for you."

A moment of silence, then, "Well..."

"Yeah..."

"Goodnight, Celeste. See you tomorrow."

"Night, Scott."

He replaced the receiver in the cradle, then rose to cross to the dim hallway where the family portraits hung. Two sisters; one had shaped his past and the other would play a significant role in shaping his future.

Would you understand, Rach, if you knew that I've fallen in love with your sister? Would you believe I didn't go looking for this to happen, but it has, and I can't take it back. Don't want to take it back.

He extinguished the light and ascended the stairs. Tomorrow was another day, and he'd see Celeste again.

He slept harder and deeper than he had for months.

In her childhood bed, Celeste lay in the quiet darkness, listening to the night sounds and remembering the years she'd lived in this house with her older sister. Christmas Eves and Christmas mornings, Easter baskets and hunting for eggs. Arguing about whose turn it was to set the table or mow the lawn. Days that had seemed endless and static, and which, as a young girl, she'd thought would drag on into infinity.

The next few weeks would be difficult for all of them, and she quietly prayed for each member of the family, Rachel's children, her husband, and for Catherine. Finally, she prayed for strength and wisdom for herself, that the Holy Spirit would guide her words and spirit as the steps that would bring the end of Rachel's life were put into motion.

Heavenly Father, help me to be patient with Mother, because I know that this is going to be terribly painful for her. Help me to do what You would have me do, Lord. In Jesus' name. Amen.

Chapter 18

They arrived in Seattle about seven-thirty on a gray Saturday evening, dense forest giving way to shopping malls, park-and-rides, and busy five-lane freeways. Against the backdrop of the approaching September night, neon lights cast a garish glow that reflected on the faces of the old Chevy's passengers. Arguing good-naturedly among themselves, they made their way downtown, buoyed with anticipation of the evening ahead, and well-lubricated from the beers they'd downed on their trip through the mountains.

"Check it out." Tyler slipped a fifth of Black Velvet from beneath his jacket, brandishing the bottle discreetly.

"Well, hand that bad boy up here, Parnell, whaddya holding back for?" Dwight extended an arm in Tyler's general direction, the car jerking as he hurriedly corrected with his free hand.

"No way, man, you're already toasted. Just keep your eyes on the road, will ya?"

"Oh, spare me! I've never had a single ticket, in case you forget."

"You've been lucky, dude, that's all."

Catching Darrell's glance, Ty shook his head in exasperation, secreting the bottle safely into his jacket once more. *I should've driven; if the truck would've held all of us, I would have.*

Problem was, Dwight was out of control, and not just tonight, either. Since school had started, he'd been hitting it hard, booze, pot, huffing; whatever he could get his hands on. He'd come to class totally freaked last Wednesday, wired for sound, glassy-eyed, and trembling; No-Doz and a half-dozen Chlor-Trimeton as a chaser. He'd always been a heavy experimenter, but some indelible line had been crossed somewhere. The guy couldn't *not* be on something all the time now.

Putting his worry aside, Ty shrugged in irritation; this wasn't the night for one of those lame "interventions" that the school's idiot drug/alcohol counselor talked about, dropping ten-dollar words like "code-pendency," "twelve-step program," and "recovery." Bunch of garbage. As if anybody were going to get screwed up enough in high school to have to deal with all of that adult baloney that none of the adults bought into anyway. Resentfully, he told himself, *Everybody's parents drink, even my old man's been known to toss a few back once in awhile.*

That was the trouble with parents; everything was a double standard.

Tonight was for some laughs with the guys. Period.

They stopped at a greasy spoon and ordered burgers and fries, parked in the darkest corner of the parking lot, and washed them down with beer stealthily distributed from the ice chest in the trunk.

"What time is it?"

"Little past nine."

"Well, they're open—what are we waiting for?"

Driving the few blocks under the bright city lights, insulated by booze and brotherhood, Tyler relaxed, enjoying his friends' banter. The Velvet had burned down to a nice mellow flame in his gut, and he luxuriated in the smoothness of his buzz. If it weren't for Dwight driving like a freakin' madman, the night would be just about perfect.

"I'm driving home, I don't care what he says," Ty decided. "It'd be awful nice to get home alive!"

Even if they had to pull over somewhere like last time, spend the night in the car. At least there wasn't snow on the ground. No worries.

The night beckoned, full of promise.

Throwing his door open, Ty exclaimed, "Let's do it!"

They could hear the music from across the parking lot, thumping bass, muffled percussion beat. Pausing outside the entrance, Ty asked, "Ready?" then opened the door, the driving beat of the music flooding their senses, even as their eyes adjusted to the dimness within.

"Gentlemen."

The doorman waited, nattily dressed in a black tux jacket, white dress shirt, and jeans. "ID?"

Four young men retrieved their wallets with varying degrees of steadiness, only Dwight producing a legitimate Washington State drivers license proclaiming him to be eighteen years of age. John, Darrell, and Tyler produced the fake IDs they'd ordered over the internet. For a moment, all four held their collective breath as the bouncer cursorily examined the cards, then returned them with a smirk.

"You know the drill? Fifteen bucks to get in, drinks are five bucks each, and you pay for the first one with your cover. Twenty bucks each. Enjoy the show."

Following the dim hallway to the stage, Darrell crowed, "He didn't even look at my ID!"

John retorted, "Well, he looked at mine, and I could tell he knew it was fake."

Ty shook his head. "All he cares is that we have ID; he's covered in case of a bust."

The music was loud, bass thumping and vibrating into the lush carpet as they followed the dimly lit corridor to the stage room. No doubt about it, Tyler mused, glancing about the room, they were definitely the youngest members of the audience. With the cover charge here, he imagined the regulars earned significantly more than minimum wage. Of course, who *didn't* earn more than minimum wage these days, other than himself? Shaking off his mood, he tried to concentrate on the show; a sleek brunette slithering across the tile floor. Sliding a glance across the table at his companions, he noted that John and Darrell were goggling wide-eyed at the show. Dwight was off somewhere in an alternate reality; slack-jawed and glassy-eyed. His hands were trembling, Tyler noted, and he looked like he was wired to about fifty thousand volts. He didn't care for Dwight's color, either; he didn't *look* right, pale but dotted with perspiration. Feeling his buzz fading, he promised himself that when they got home, he'd absolutely talk to his friend about getting some help.

The pleasure had gone out of the evening.

It seemed like hours before he was able to convince John and Darrell that they needed to get going; they had a two-hour drive ahead. When nudged, Dwight peered at the rest of the group blindly and allowed himself to be led out of the building. The smell of rain was in the air, and they broke into a run across the parking lot, Tyler cursing as he fumbled for his keys before remembering he hadn't driven.

"Dwight, man, come on, it's gonna rain any second!" he hollered in exasperation at his friend, standing still and silent in the middle of the lot.

"Oh, man, he's totally tweaked," Darrell volunteered.

"I should've known this was gonna happen. You guys wait here, I'll get him moving." Moving toward his friend, Tyler called, "Come on, man, let me have the keys."

Dwight stood rooted in place, a fine tremor shaking his entire body. Tyler crossed the distance between them at a jog. "What is your problem, man?" Reaching Dwight's side, he took him by the arm, immediately felt the trembling, as if he were touching a high-tensile wire. "Hey...Dwight, you okay?" With a strangled sound, Dwight reached to clutch Tyler's shirt, hand convulsing, then pitched forward hard, pulling Tyler to the ground along with himself.

"What the...Dwight?" realizing that his friend was too still. "Dwight!"

Shaking his friend's shoulders, Ty called his name repeatedly with a growing sense of panic that it was already too late, even as he screamed for the other guys to get inside, call 911, get an ambulance. Hardly aware of his words, he continued talking to Dwight, trying to hold the panic at bay just until the ambulance arrived. Everything would be fine, then. Everybody knew paramedics saved lives every day. At a sound, Tyler looked up to see John and Darrell standing silently, shock imprinted over their faces.

"Tyler, man, get the keys and let's get out of here," Darrell spoke finally, unable to take his eyes from Dwight's white face.

"No! We're not leaving him here!"

"He's dead, man! There's nothing we can do for him now."

"Come on, Parnell," John pleaded with a trembling voice. "At least let us get our coats out of the car and ditch the booze before the cops get here."

Probably a good idea, Tyler thought numbly, searching his friend's pockets, pulling the key ring free and tossing it into the air. He was vaguely aware of the fact that he and Dwight were alone once again, heard the sound of running feet on asphalt, then heard the shotgun blast sound of the engine turning over, the squeal of tires and brakes, then the shrill howl of approaching sirens.

Déjà Vu wasn't just a strip club, he thought dully, remembering a night in June in front of Fircrest when his friends had ditched him when things got hot.

As the flashing lights of the emergency vehicles illuminated the parking lot, he knelt beside his best friend, a cold rain mingling with the tears that streaked his face. Reality hit him like a ton of bricks; in a moment the cops would be here. There was nothing he could do for Dwight, but he himself was a minor in consumption, not to mention in possession of an illegal fake ID. The decision was made in a split second. Reaching again into Dwight's pocket, he pulled his friend's drivers license from his wallet and laid it on his chest.

"I'm sorry, man, I gotta split."

He swung a look around the parking lot, dodged the paramedics now running toward Dwight's body, and slipped between the Déjà Vu and the mini-mart next door, then onto the sidewalk. Casting a glance behind to assure himself that he wasn't being followed, he took a deep breath and melted into the crowd. He wasn't sure exactly where he was, didn't have a clue where he was going but, at the moment, couldn't find it in himself to care.

His friend was dead.

Shaking his head, as if by clearing his thoughts the reality of the situation would disappear, Ty walked on through the rain, trying to figure out where everything had gone so wrong. Images of Dwight and he through the years, playing street hockey in elementary school, skinny-dipping out at the lake in junior high, Dwight confessing one drunken evening that he wished it was *his* mother who was in a coma. The tears came on again, hot and burning, and Ty stood on the sidewalk, stomach clenching, and knew that he was going to be sick. Glancing wildly about, he noted that he was in front of a car dealership, barely making it into the lot before he lost control. Wracked with dry heaves, soaked to the skin, and emotionally distraught, it occurred to him that he was wandering downtown Seattle in the middle of a Saturday night along with the dealers, working girls, and heaven only knew who else, and had nowhere to go. Inadvertently splashing through a large puddle, he shivered, knowing that he needed to get off the streets.

And realized that he did, after all, have somewhere to go.

Chapter 19

*I*t had been nearly weeks since the weekend of the fair, two weeks since Tori had returned home to Seattle, and Tawnya was lonely. Friday night and Saturday with her friend had been awesome, and her eyes had been truly opened to what it meant to have a friend with whom to giggle about nothing in particular, someone with whom to share secrets. And there had, in the end, been a secret that had been unearthed, due entirely to Tori's relentless chiseling away at the truth. *The* secret. There had been a midnight confrontation, a discussion held in hushed voices, tears on Tawnya's part, and unbending implacability on Tori's.

"If you don't think I'm serious about waking Cellie up, Tawnya, then you don't know me as well as you think you do. I'm *serious,* girl!"

The problem had started at the fair, because she'd gone hog-wild on corndogs and elephant ears. The dance had been a bust; there were mostly adults there, except for some high school kids, as well as Ariel and her crowd, who kept making passes by where Tawnya stood with Tori, whispering and looking back over their shoulders. The silvery tinkle of Ariel's laughter still cut like a blade, and the ugly words that had drifted back to them.

When, steeped in desperation and impotent rage, she'd asked Tori if she wanted to check out the rides, she'd almost burned a trail to the door, such was her relief to finally escape from her beautiful tormenter.

In true form, she'd fed her pain and embarrassment with food, blowing through her allowance on treat after treat until her wallet was empty and her stomach close to exploding. Even as she devoured the food, she was unable to enjoy it, images of the commode and recognition of the misery that lay ahead etched her thoughts like an engraver's pen.

The food did help to erase the scorn and belittlement she'd read in Ariel's eyes. It always did, at least for awhile. And so, awash in misery, she'd succumbed once more to her addiction.

Once they'd arrived home, after nudging Celeste awake to let her know they were back, she'd left Tori to change into her pajamas and went into the bathroom to face her ordeal. The problem was, it was virtually impossible to hide some of the noises a person's body made, and no way to take a radio into the bathroom and crank up the volume with Grandma sound asleep across the hall.

Long story short, Tori had overheard, much as her aunt had a month before. Unconvinced by Tawnya's well-planned cover story that the rides had made her sick to her stomach, Tori had battered away at her resistance until the truth hung in the silence that rang in her mother's old bedroom.

"If you don't think I'm serious about waking Cellie up, Tawnya, then you don't know me as well as you think you do. I'm serious, girl!"

She was ashamed of the way she'd turned ugly, rude and belligerent to the only friend she could claim and had lashed out at her.

"You don't know anything about it, Miss Tori Perfection! I'm not one of your...broken street kids that you have to preach to, so just leave me alone!"

Tori had gazed at her for a long moment, then climbed onto the bed, braced her back against the wall, and drew her knees to her chest. "There's all kinds of ways to be broken, girl. Doesn't just take drugs and alcohol."

At Tawnya's stony silence, she'd waited a couple of beats, then said, "Come on up here, Tawnya. Sit by me. Please?"

She'd complied, averting her eyes, sitting as stiffly as the old mattress would allow. Tori continued, "Do you remember the night we first met, when I told you that God's the only One who can help you, or me, or anybody stop doing things they know are wrong? You remember? Well, it's true, girl. That's why He went to the cross, because He knew that none of us can do it alone. But He loves you, Tawnya, and He knows everything about you."

At Tawnya's disbelieving gaze, she nodded. "That's right, *every-thing*. Every time you bend over that miserable toilet, He knows about it. He's right there with you, girl, just waiting for you to turn it all over to Him. I wish I could make you understand how much He loves you. And His love is worth any amount of persecution that little blonde hotsy can dish out. Yeah, I have a good idea what you've been goin' through, Tawn. And you may not be able to do anything to change *her* attitude, but you aren't alone." As Tawnya began to weep quietly, she repeated, "You're never alone, girl. Give it over. Lay it all down at His feet. Let Him have all of it, all the pain. Everything. Let Him heal You."

The night was silent except for the sound of her soft weeping, the sound of two voices lifted in prayer, and the unmistakable Presence of peace.

It was a moment of grace, and of perfection, and Tawnya knew she would carry the awesome power of that moment with her every day for the rest of her life. She'd never felt such lightness of spirit, such an unexplained joy, even in the fleeting moments of bliss she experienced polishing off a package of Oreos.

No, this had been something else entirely, awesome in its power and, to her eyes, the Hand of God laid upon her heart. She'd been so filled with His presence that she didn't believe she'd be able to sleep at all, but she had. And the next afternoon, after church, with Daddy standing close to Celeste on the street and Grandma standing sentinel on the front porch, Tori had lugged her suitcase down Grandma's cracked, bumpy sidewalk, struggling with a particularly large corner of concrete that her suitcase had hung up on. Tawnya stood by as her friend loaded her suitcase into Celeste's car, then with tears in her eyes, met the other girl in a quick hug. They stepped apart and smiled, sharing between them an experience shared by few, and linked together in faith and friendship.

There was so much to say, so little time to say any of it, and, struggling to maintain a steady voice, all she could manage at that moment was, "Bye, Tori."

Tori had plopped into the passenger seat and held out her palm in a high-five. "Bye, girl. You-all sure know how to party up here!"

Everyone broke into laughter, not believing for a minute that their little county fair had done anything to impress the city girl. Tori flashed a quick smile, and as the car pulled away from the curb, looked Tawnya in the eye and said, "Keep your finger outta your mouth, girl, hear?" She'd nodded back at her friend, knowing that she'd never spend another moment with her 'finger in her mouth,' so to speak. She was done with it. Absolutely no more. Ever.

And yet here she was, two weeks after her promise to Tori, two weeks after the powerful moment of surrender to God in Mama's old bedroom. Here she was, hunched over the toilet, intense pain doubling her over onto the floor before she'd even gotten started.

That wasn't entirely true. The whole cycle had begun again this afternoon in gym class, during the usual "Tormenting of Tawnya-Time," and she'd let it get to her, though she'd promised herself, and Tori, that she wouldn't. But she'd been so lonely since Tori had gone back to Seattle, and even though she prayed daily and every night that the Lord would help her ignore the taunts and ugly words cast by the other girls, it had once again started to wear her down.

"See ya, Ton-ya tubba lard, wouldn't wanna be ya!"

While doing her homework after supper, she'd come across her dictionary in her backpack and held it silently in her hand. So many words, so many ways to create sentences. So many ways to string words together to express one's feelings. Funny that by themselves, the words had little power to wound, but that joined selectively they could become near-deadly weapons.

The aching inside became so deep that, knowing what she would do, hating herself for her weakness, she entered the bathroom, knelt by the toilet, and prepared to rid herself of the pain. Maybe when her stomach was empty, the ugly words would leave her memory, and the place that stored pain in her heart would be empty as well.

But it wasn't working tonight. The pain was razor-sharp and stabbing, and when she was finally successful in her mission, she was appalled to see the blood that had come from inside herself. Fear caused her pulse to race, and genuine nausea to grip her abdomen. What had she done? She'd finally proved Aunt Celeste and Tori right; she'd hurt herself inside somehow, and now what?

Tears spilled down her cheeks as pain drove her flat to the floor, clutching her stomach and weeping silently. Curled up as tightly as she could get herself, she wept with genuine fear, with shame for her weakness, for breaking her promise, for failing God. With all the clarity a twelve-year-old could know in her heart of hearts, at that moment she understood that her very life hung in the balance.

Look at all that blood…Aunt Celeste was right. If I can't stop doing this, I'll die.

Then, lying on the cold tile floor, her last defenses ruptured, she remembered her friend's words.

"He knows everything about you. Every time you bend over that miserable toilet, He knows about it. He's right there with you, girl, just waiting for you to turn it all over to Him."

"Jesus, she wept, *help me! Take it away, Lord. Please, God, I can't do this by myself!"*

Slowly, she felt the pressure inside ease, and she rolled to a sit, leaning against the tub in exhaustion. With trepidation, she peered into the toilet, closing her eyes at the sight of the blood, then drew a deep breath and flushed it away.

She rose slowly to her feet, crossed to the sink, and met her eyes in the mirror, then heard the words that would forever change her life.

Tawnya, you are My child, and I love you. The day you were born, I smiled because I knew the plans I have for you, and you were finally here, to carry out the work I have laid out for you. You were created as part of My perfect plan, and you are beautiful in My eyes.

The floodgates to her heart burst open, and the tears she wept washed away all of the pain, all of the hurt and uncertainty, and filled the secret yearning for the unconditional love she'd sought and believed she'd never find. She knew that she would never lie on this floor, on *any* floor again, seeking to rid herself of the pain that lie hidden deep inside.

A miracle had occurred tonight, and the life of a twelve-year-old girl would be forever changed.

Thank You, Lord. Your mercy endures forever.

Chapter 20

Celeste had been deep into a dream; she was back in high school and was helping her mother and Rachel can green beans.

"There's the timer, Celeste, turn the valve off on the pressure cooker." She turned the valve, but the timer continued to buzz, then began to vibrate on the stove top, rocking back and forth, a loud thumping accompanying the noise of the timer.

"Celeste!"

"Huh? What..." She awoke all at once, the racket at the front door displacing the remnants of the dream. Alarmed, she pulled on her robe, slid her feet into slippers, and switched on every light she passed on her way to the door. Peering through the peephole, she was thunderstruck to recognize her nephew. She allowed herself a moment for a deep, fortifying breath before she unlocked and opened the door.

"Tyler."

They faced each other silently for a moment, then Tyler spoke in a trembling voice, "I didn't have anywhere else to go. It's raining and...I don't have anywhere else to go."

He was soaked to the bone, Celeste noted, hair plastered to his head, with rivulets leaking down his neck into his shirt collar. His clothes were drenched and reeked of beer and vomit. Moving to the side of the door, she said, "Come in, Ty."

Still standing in the same spot, he looked at her without speaking long enough that she began to question her good judgment into offering him shelter, when he blurted, "He's dead. He's dead, and I just left him there!"

Alarmed, Celeste questioned, "Who's dead? What's going on, Tyler?"

"Dwight! He's dead!"

He was white as a sheet and looked as though his knees were going to buckle at any second. Without another thought, Celeste stepped onto the welcome mat, took his arm, and spoke soothingly, "Come inside, Ty, and we'll talk. You're wet, and it's warm inside. Okay? Come in and then take your shoes and socks off and let's get you warmed up." As she spoke, she guided him inside, speaking calmly as he leaned against the closed door and mutely removed his shoes and socks, leaving them to lay where they fell.

Leading the way down the hall, Celeste spoke over her shoulder, "Come on, Ty, let me show you where the bathroom is. I want you to take a hot shower. I'll bring you something dry to wear and when you've warmed up, you can tell me what's going on."

Removing a clean towel from the cupboard, she said, "If you'll just put your wet clothes outside the door, I'll run them through the wash for you, okay?"

"That'd be great."

"Okay, get in the shower before you catch pneumonia. I'll put something for you to wear outside the door."

"Aunt Celeste?"

"Hmm?"

"I'm sorry I just showed up like this."

"It's all right, Ty. Go on, take your shower and I'll see you in a little bit."

She checked to make sure she'd re-locked the front door, then returned down the hall, gathered the wet, malodorous clothing and took it into the utility room, dumping the faded Ozzy Osborne shirt, black jeans, socks, and underwear into the washer after removing the heavy chain attached to Ty's wallet from a belt loop. Adding detergent, she closed the lid, turned, and leaned against the washer, still coming to grasp with the fact that her nephew had shown up unexpectedly at her doorstep at one in the morning.

His friend was dead.

How did a childless person comfort a kid who'd just lost a friend?

"Lord, help me to talk to Ty. Help me to find the right words."

She dug out a pair of old sweatpants and a "Jazz On The Pier" tee-shirt from her dresser and lay them before the closed bathroom door. It was fortunate that she was tall; the clothes would work until Ty's soiled clothing dried. Creature comforts were what were needed here, at least for a start. Those needs, anyway, could be met. She entered the kitchen, rummaged in the cupboard for a can of tomato soup, added milk, and placed the pan on the stove to heat. Mind working in overdrive, she put the soup on to heat and prepared a grilled cheese sandwich. Comfort food, and if there had ever been a better time for such things, she certainly couldn't bring it to mind.

She pulled another saucepan from the cupboard and heated water for cocoa, dug desperately in the back of the cupboard and triumphantly produced a bag of petrified miniature marshmallows; she'd had good intentions of making rice crispy treats for Tawnya and Tori last summer but hadn't quite gotten around to it. She supposed the marshmallows would soften up in the cocoa.

The bag of marshmallows also reminded her of Scott's crackling knees and Rach's likening them to the sound of Rice Krispies in milk. Would it always be this way? Would there forever be reminders of him popping up as she went about her daily routines?

Busy with her prep work, she jumped about three feet when Tyler appeared silently to the left of the stove. The sweats were only a little short on him, the sweatshirt a pretty good fit, and the thick Argyle socks snug on his long feet, but he was warm and dry.

"Thanks for the clothes."

"You're welcome. I'm glad you're not any taller, though, or that I'm not shorter. Anyway, are you hungry?"

The kitchen was filled with comforting homey smells, and he realized that he actually was hungry.

"Yeah, thanks."

"Go ahead and have a seat, and I'll get you set up here."

He sat at the table, examined his feet in the unfamiliar socks, pulled the sweatshirt away from his body, and eyed the jaunty saxophone spewing quarter notes from its bell, looking up when Celeste appeared laden with food.

He took inventory of the offerings, feeling oddly shy. "I love tomato soup. And grilled cheese. Thanks."

"You're welcome. I made some cocoa, although I won't absolutely vouch for the marshmallows."

"It's all cool."

She busied herself washing the pans, drying them, and replacing them in the cupboards. Calling from the kitchen, "I have some chocolate cookies. Want a couple?"

"Sure."

She filled a plate with cookies and placed it on the table, then sat in a neighboring chair and selected one for herself. "My one vice."

"Not such a bad vice."

"True. And you can't go too far wrong as long as it's chocolate, right?"

"For sure."

They sat in silence as he finished his meal, then Celeste rose to gather the dishes, pleasantly surprised when Tyler indicated that he'd carry them into the kitchen.

"Where do you want them?"

"Sink's fine, thanks. There's more cocoa, help yourself."

He refilled his cup, added a handful of shriveled marshmallows, then said, "I don't remember ever seeing your place before."

"I don't think you've been here."

"Tawnya said it was really nice. It *is* really nice."

"Thanks."

Cocoa mug in hand, he wandered into the living room, stopping to peer through the slider into the darkness beyond. "Is this your deck?"

"Um hum."

He wandered the living room slowly, deciding that he liked the neutral colors, accentuated with splashes of bright color; the sapphire blue throw pillows and emerald green chenille throws on the black leather sofa and love seat, the deep ruby Oriental rug under the glass coffee table. The walls were largely bare, only a large oil painting hanging over the mantle; a seascape in muted blues and greens. There was a fire burning in the fireplace, and he stood before the glass front for a moment, hands clenching the mantle, until his aunt spoke quietly.

"Do you want to tell me about it?"

He turned, gazed at Celeste where she sat curled on the loveseat, feet tucked under her bathrobe, and realized in some amazement that he *did* want to share the events of the night with this woman who had reappeared in their lives recently.

He settled himself on the sofa, silently asked and received permission to pull the chenille throw over himself. He noticed now that Celeste had turned off the lights; only the flickering flames cast their soft glow into the dimness.

He gathered his thoughts, then began to speak. The words came slowly at first, then poured from him as a river tumbles over the rocks under its surface. The drive from Shuksan, Dwight's erratic driving, his concern about Dwight's escalating drug and alcohol use over the last few months, his reluctance to upset the apple cart as far as trying to get help for his friend, and finally, in a voice choked with tears, the evening at the Déjà Vu, Dwight's collapse in the parking lot, John and Darrell's disappearing act, his own panic, the shock and pain of his friend lying dead in the falling rain in the parking lot of a strip club.

And his own overwhelming, gut-wrenching guilt.

"He's dead, Aunt Celeste. He was my best friend, since we were little kids." Tyler choked out, bent over at the waist, hands covering his face.

Tears burning her own eyes, pity and compassion battling for supremacy, Celeste moved to sit next to him. Putting an arm around his side, she felt the deep, shuddering sobs wracking his body. Tightening her embrace, she sat silently, allowing him to grieve.

"I killed him."

"No, Ty. You didn't kill him. It's not your fault. There wasn't anything you could have done to change what happened tonight."

"I could have told somebody a long time ago, the school counselor or, I don't know, *somebody!* If I had, maybe he'd be alive now."

"You don't know that, Ty. I don't know a lot about addiction, but I do know that you can't wish somebody clean or sober if they don't want to be. And you can't take responsibility for someone else's choices."

He nodded silently. They sat for some minutes without speaking, then Ty rubbed his eyes, gathered his composure, and said, "I'd probably better call Dad. He's gonna kill me dead over this."

Celeste hesitated, then asked, "Would you like me to call him?"

"What time is it?"

"Two-thirty."

Rubbing his hands over his face, Ty groaned, "Oh, man, he's gonna kill me for sure."

Celeste rose to her feet and said, "Come on. Let me show you where the guest room is. I'll call your Dad, and it'll be the truth when I tell him you're sleeping. How's that?"

"Yeah, okay." Tyler rose with the slow, aching movements of an old man, realizing he was bone-weary, physically and emotionally.

Opening the door just past the bathroom, Celeste switched on the bedside lamp, pulled the bedspread down, and plumped the pillows. "Make yourself at home, Ty. Anything you need, let me know, okay?"

"Thanks. I appreciate you letting me stay here, especially when I haven't exactly been nice to you."

"It's okay, Ty. I just want you to remember that I love you and Tawnya both."

Catching and holding her glance, he murmured, "And my Dad too?"

Forcing her voice to remain steady even as she felt her cheeks flush, Celeste chose the age-old option of evasion, "I love all of you, Ty. Now I'm going to let you get some sleep. Sleep as late as you want. Let me know if you need anything."

"Good night."

She stepped out into the hall, pulled the door shut behind herself, and stood for a moment, wondering if she'd done the right thing by deliberately sidestepping Ty's question, or had it been more of an observation? A person could go stark-raving mad second-guessing themselves all the time when it came to dealing with kids!

After transferring Ty's clothes from the washer to the dryer and flipping the switch that would turn the gas fireplace off, she made one last check of the locks, then went into her room. Curling herself into the blankets, she picked up the phone, hesitated, then speed-dialed Scott's number.

"Hello?" His voice was gruff with sleep and had never sounded more appealing.

"Scott? It's me. I'm really sorry to wake you."

A deep groan emanated through the receiver, then, "Celeste?"

"Yes, it's me. I'm sorry for waking you, but I wanted to let you know that Tyler's here."

Scott fumbled for the alarm clock, squinted at the face; two-fifty a.m. "Ty's there? At your place? What's he doing there? Let me talk to him."

"Well, he's finally sleeping. The thing is, Scott, something happened tonight. Ty's okay, don't worry about that, but his friend Dwight is dead."

"*What?*"

"Yes. They'd come over with John and Darrell and had gotten into a strip club downtown with false IDs. Apparently, Dwight's been having some drug problems, and he evidently collapsed in the parking lot on their way out. Sounds like cardiac arrest from how Ty described it. There wasn't anything anyone could do, it happened pretty fast."

Scott was already struggling into his jeans, receiver pinned between his shoulder and ear. "Does Dwight's mother know?"

"I don't know, Scott; all I know is that Ty panicked and ran. The other boys took off in Dwight's car and ditched Ty because he didn't want to leave Dwight alone. He waited until the ambulance pulled up, then took off; he was afraid he'd get in trouble for having the fake ID."

"I'll talk to Jim Clark, he's a friend of mine, and he can follow up with Seattle and notify Dora if he needs to. I'm leaving now, Celeste; I'll be there in a couple of hours."

"Okay. Scott, physically he's fine, he was soaked to the bone when he showed up here about one o'clock, but he took a hot shower and had some soup and a sandwich and then we talked and he's finally sleeping. So don't worry about Ty, just drive safely, okay?"

"I will, and Celeste? Thanks."

"You're welcome. Drive safe."

"See you soon." Scott replaced the phone in its cradle, grabbed a pair of socks from the dresser, and pulled a clean shirt from the closet. He made a quick dash into the bathroom, brushed his teeth, and ran a comb through his hair. Making his way down the stairs, he remembered Tawnya, asleep in her bed, and slowed mid-step, mind working feverishly. Moving quickly, he entered the kitchen, tore the top sheet from the notepad used for grocery lists, and wrote a quick note explaining the situation and that he'd call from Celeste's in a few hours to check in. He laid the note in the middle of the table where she'd be sure to see it first thing. He stopped at the porch, pulled on his boots, spoke quietly to Skip, quietly to Skip, then moved across the yard to his truck. After a quick check of the gas gauge, he gunned the engine and pulled out of the barnyard.

Once in town, he stopped by the jail, explained the situation as he knew it to the deputy on duty, and mentioned that Dwight's car had probably been dropped off in front of his house by now. Finally, at three-thirty, he turned onto the freeway on-ramp and gained access to Interstate-90, lightly traveled at this hour. As he headed west in the darkness, the thoughts that had been keeping him awake nights began their unending cycle through his mind. Although deeply saddened by the news of Dwight's death, he was filled with keen anticipation at the prospect of seeing Celeste again. This would be the first time they'd be together since fair weekend, although they'd racked up plenty of hours on the phone at night, but it wasn't enough, wasn't nearly enough.

He missed her. That was all there was to it.

Lost in thought, he was surprised to note that he'd left the empty freeway behind and was entering Issaquah with only about half-an-hour's drive into Seattle, and he mentally reviewed the directions Celeste had given him over the phone. Rain was sluicing over his windshield such that his wipers were having trouble keeping up, even on high-speed. He hunched over the wheel, squinting against the watery glare of the street lights and white-knuckled his way into the city; already a steady stream of traffic on Interstate-5 at six o'clock on a Sunday morning. To his great relief, he drove straight to the condo, pulled in behind Celeste's Beamer, and killed the engine.

Ducking out of the truck, he trotted to the front door and, hesitating to ring the doorbell, knocked softly. A couple of moments later, there was the patter of footsteps and then the sound of locks being thrown, and there she stood before him, sleepy-eyed, dressed in a pair of pink sweats and an oversized Casting Crowns sweatshirt. There was a fleeting moment of hesitation, then they were in each other's arms, locked in a desperate embrace, and Scott got the feeling that if she only could, she'd crawl into his skin right along with him. Finally pulling back enough so that she could see his face, Celeste said, "Hi."

"Good morning."

"Look at you, you're soaked! Come in, Scott. Let me have your jacket."

Complying, kicking off his boots, Scott murmured, "So this is your place."

"Yes, this is it. Want the two-bit tour?"

"Later. Ty still sleeping?"

"Yes. He was pretty torn up."

"How long do you suppose he'll sleep?"

"No idea. I don't have much experience in teenagers, in case you've forgotten. Come on in, let's sit down. Would you like some coffee?"

"Love some, if it's made."

"Coming right up."

Celeste flipped on the fireplace switch, then stopped at the stereo and selected a Rebecca St. James disc and slipped it into the CD drive.

"How about some breakfast?"

Turning from where he'd been standing in front of the slider, Scott followed her into the kitchen. "Don't go to a lot of work, Celeste. We can just run out and grab a bite after Ty's up."

After grinding the beans, she dumped the coffee into the filter, then slid it back under the coffeemaker. "It's no trouble; besides, I'm hungry now. It'll just take me a few minutes. You can sit at the snack bar and keep me company though."

Complying, he settled himself onto a padded bar stool, smiling his thanks as she brought a cup of steaming coffee to him. She moved about the kitchen, putting together a batch of blueberry muffins. Once they were in the oven, she whisked eggs into a pain, added milk and cheese, and scrambled them in short order. Finally, she made a couple of trips back and forth between the cupboards and dining room table, preparing three place settings. She was comfortable in her kitchen, he realized with some surprise; somehow it hadn't fit with his perception of Celeste that she'd enjoy making breakfast on a rainy Sunday morning. Rising, he went to stand again at the slider, hands in his pockets, looking out over the gunmetal gray water and low clouds obliterating the hills on the opposite bank. Lost in his own thoughts, he was interrupted by Celeste's voice, "Ready to eat?"

They sat across from each other, helped themselves to scrambled eggs and muffins, and poured orange juice from a cut-glass pitcher.

"Everything okay? Need a refill on the coffee?"

Shaking his head, he patted his stomach and groaned. "I'm good; everything's great. Thanks."

They finished breakfast, just enjoying each other's company. Finally, Celeste rose and began gathering plates, and Scott joined her in clearing the table. After piling everything into the sink, they sat on the loveseat, curled up under a quilt, and watched the flames licking the gas logs.

Engrossed in conversation, neither heard Ty until he spoke in a gravelly voice, "Morning."

Turning to see him standing behind the loveseat, dressed in his own clothes, they both returned the greeting, then Scott rose and stood without speaking. For what seemed an eternity but was only a couple of seconds, Ty faced the floor, shuffled his feet, then spoke, "I'm sorry about this, that you had to come over and pick me up."

Oh, kid, I can't even imagine what kind of pain you're in right now.

"It's all right, son. I'm sorry about Dwight, so sorry. How about you, are you okay?"

Shrugging, not meeting his father's eyes, he said, "Yeah. Where do you think he is now? I mean, does his mom know yet?"

"I stopped by and let Deputy Stinson know what was going

on. He was going to talk to Seattle PD and then notify Dwight's mom."

Shaking his head in misery, he blurted, "Oh, man. I just can't believe it's real."

Scott hesitated, then asked bluntly, "Were you using too?"

Ty's head shot up and he met his father's implacable eyes. He considered denial, then opted for honesty. After all, what was done was done. Maybe Dad would ground him from his truck, but at that moment, with Dwight's death at the forefront, losing the truck seemed pretty trivial by comparison.

"Not tweak. Had some drinks, yeah, but Dwight was the only one who did both."

"How long has this been going on?"

"What, Dwight or me?"

"Both. You now, especially."

Ty shot his father a defensive glare. "I don't know. Come on, Dad, I know you partied in high school. Don't go getting all righteous on me."

Feeling the usual frustration that accompanied most conversations with his son, Scott concentrated on keeping his voice even and replied, "What I did or didn't do in high school isn't the issue at the moment. What *is* the issue is whether or not we need to look into treatment for you."

"No way, Dad!" Ty exploded, voice reverberating through the room. "I'm no different than anybody else; so I party on weekends, what's the big deal? I don't go to school drunk or stoned." With resentment coloring his voice, "Why do have to talk about this right now, anyway?" with a nod of his head, indicating Celeste, still sitting on the loveseat.

"Anything we have to say can be said in front of your aunt," Scott retorted.

"It's okay, Scott," Celeste attempted to interject, uncomfortable for all of their sakes.

"No, it isn't okay, Celeste. Ty brought you smack dab into the middle of this by showing up here in the middle of the night. It's a little bit late now for him to be bashful about your being part of the conversation."

Celeste directed her attention to Ty. "I'm glad, really glad, that you did come here last night, Ty. I do care about you, so please don't feel that you can't speak freely in front of me. Are you hungry? Want some breakfast?" casting Scott a telling glance. "Come on, kiddo. Scrambled eggs and blueberry muffins do anything for you? Some more hot chocolate? No? I promise you don't have to have marsh-mallow rocks this time."

As Ty followed her into the kitchen, Scott ran his hands through his hair, heaved a huge sigh, then dropped onto the loveseat. What was it about the kid that any time he tried to have a conversation with him, they just ended up butting heads? Rather like the mountain goats that lived in the high country, which he'd witnessed during mating season, battling over females, rushing head-to-head with skull-battering force over and over until the stronger emerged victorious and the loser backed down or died from the injuries sustained in the battle.

Of course, their own head-butting didn't have anything to do with territorial issues or fighting over the same female, but it suddenly occurred to him that perhaps there was a similar parallel here. Eventually, at some point, the younger combatant would best the older; such was nature's way of bringing maturity and self-confidence to the individual animals and fresh blood into the herd as a unit. But what about the younger, immature animal who, with the single-mindedness of youth combined with insufficient life experience, challenged life's often cruel and unforgiving adversaries, perhaps not even fully realizing the long-term consequences of the challenge into which they rushed to engage? They'd slink away, in defeat, to grow and mature in order to live to fight another day, or they died from the injuries sustained in battle.

The mental picture of Ty and him, in the tradition of the mountain goats, squaring off to engage in battle had him shuddering despite the warmth of the flickering fire. For a while Ty would no doubt prove a capable opponent in this battle for control and independence, Scott had no doubt that he, with his own strength of will and healthy store of stubbornness, would win the day, but at what cost?

What of the animals who fought to the death; what indefinable something in their personalities drove them to the point where they would allow themselves to be destroyed rather than choosing retreat and survival? Did they become so caught up in the battle that by the time they realized the danger, it was too late to back off? Did they also fall into the animal equivalent of the human trap of denial, thinking that, for themselves, there would always be another chance? Or was it simply that the struggle during the battle for life became so intense and exhausting that they could no longer sustain the energy to fight?

Was this what had happened with Dwight? Sickened, Scott dropped his head into his hands, tears stinging his eyes. It'd been no great secret in Shuksan that Dora Phillips was a bitter and angry woman by day and a mean drunk by night. Dora had, by her attitude and behavior, isolated herself and her son from those who were concerned, and eventually everyone pretty much left them alone, even as the whispers about the obvious verbal and physical abuse in the Phillips house continued about town. Sure, every so often Jim Clark would appear in his official car and knock on the door, even locked her up a couple of times when Dwight was younger, but once Dwight turned fourteen or so, the general consensus was that he was finally big enough, physically, to defend himself, and that it would serve Dora right if he popped her back one of these times. Looking back, Scott conceded that the legal system and the entire community had failed Dwight; somehow everyone had basically *accepted* the situation and essentially turned a blind eye to the abuse and neglect. The child had survived, after all; sure, he was kind of a loser and didn't have a lot of ambition, but what could you expect with a mother like Dora? He'd survived, and that was what was important.

Except that he hadn't survived. Scott couldn't shake the image of the goats and the quiet conviction that Dwight's death hadn't been entirely accidental.

There wasn't anything he could do for Dwight, but perhaps there was something positive to be taken from this tragedy; a reminder that kids often suffered in relative silence, masking their fear and anger with chemicals, riding life's angry seas in a fragile life-raft of false bravado.

Dwight had had problems, no doubt about it, and hadn't had

the inner strength to ride the raft to secure ground. How, then, was Ty faring in his own struggles, facing the prospect of a debilitating illness that took no prisoners in its relentless battle for healthy young lives? In truth, he didn't have a clue as to Ty's feelings about the situation; the kid would sooner yank his own toenails out with pliers than speak honestly of his feelings, and Scott realized that he had been willing, even relieved, to avoid a lot of dialogue about Ty's situation. Hadn't he recently learned that reluctance to acknowledge unpleasant issues didn't make them any less real?

There was already a name for this particular demon, and that name was Huntington's. If the demon traveled with a sidekick, its name would be denial. A pair of dirty scoundrels to be sure, a pair that could no longer be ignored, Scott knew, because to disregard one would be to diminish the potential impact of the other, and that wasn't fair to Ty. Reality, even a lousy reality, still had to be faced eventually, and Scott acknowledged that he'd been so deeply burrowed in his own cave of denial about Ty's situation that he'd set the worst example he possibly could have, avoidance. As if by pretending it wasn't happening, the whole thing was just going to magically disappear.

No more, he decided, *starting today. I may not have any idea how to talk to my son, but I'm gonna have to figure it out.*

Feeling better, having resolved to break the code of silence that had existed for such a long time, Scott rose and went to join the ones he loved.

Chapter 21

The events of the next few days had defined the very essence of the word "stress," and Celeste had been waffling between alternating states of fatigue and euphoria. This business of getting her ducks in a row regarding the monumental decision to return to Shuksan had produced a psychological exhaustion that she rarely experienced, even during the busy months between the beginning of February and April 15. When she really thought about the situation, the fact that she was preparing to pull the plug on life as she knew it and take on the responsibility of her own practice, she vacillated between keen excitement and the fear that she was way off her rocker. One of her first concerns was that the local clients, loyal to the retiring accountant who'd been in practice for close to fifty years, would be reluctant to give their business to "that little Malloy girl." Scott had reassured her, reminding her that Bill was the only game in town and that while it may take people a while to get used to the idea, they'd eventually come around. He was especially confident in his feeling that Analiese's legal expertise would be a welcome addition to Shuksan, the nearest attorney being in Ellensburg.

She, Ty, and Scott had spent most of Sunday together. Ty had been surprisingly perceptive and made himself scarce for a couple of hours before they'd returned home, giving Celeste and Scott some quiet time together. They'd sat together on the couch, spoke of Scott's growing awareness of the inadequacies of the relationship between his son and he, and of his determination to peel back the layers of resistance until they found a middle ground on which they could begin to communicate about so many of the issues that had gone unspoken for too long.

They'd spoken about Celeste's returning to Shuksan and how

they'd handle their own relationship, when the eyes of the town, and Catherine, especially, were focused on their every movement. He'd spoken honestly about his concerns regarding Tyler and Tawnya, and their reactions to hearing that their mother would be removed from life support in less than a month.

Thoughts of Scott, kids and of her mother filled her mind constantly. She was also knee-deep in preparations for the changes that were coming in her own life; organizing the new practice, the sale of the condo, and the working out of the seemingly hundreds of details involved in a lifestyle change of this magnitude. She'd arranged to take a vacation day Monday morning and had made a quick trip home to meet with Mr. Koch, working out the minutia of the sale, and had been greatly relieved that her calculations had been pretty close; the sale of her condo would not only purchase the practice, but also the two-story brick building in which the offices occupied the bottom floor and a two-bedroom apartment on the second floor, with plenty to spare for renovations as well as to provide a several-month cushion to survive on while she got her feet underneath her financially.

Bill had had enough snowy winters and was planning to retire to Arizona. His wife had passed away several years ago, his children and grandchildren lived in various locations, and there was nothing to hold him in Shuksan. He'd been ecstatic to make a deal for the entire building, which had been more than he'd hoped for. For Celeste, it was a great opportunity, not only a tax write-off, but a home for Ana and Tori for as long as they needed it, something to "sweeten the pot" when she pitched her idea to Ana.

She'd asked Ana to the condo for dinner two nights later, when the earnest money had been wired, the contract signed, and the die cast. Over a relaxed dinner of chicken fettuccini, sautéed zucchini, and garlic bread, she'd presented her proposal and turned Ana's world on its ear in one fell swoop. After a thousand and one questions, Ana had asked for a couple of days to prayerfully consider the opportunity and discuss it with Tori, because she wouldn't make a career move of this caliber for herself without her daughter's input. "This is going to rock her world, Celeste; more than mine, 'cause we both know I don't *have* a life outside BBSS and Tori."

They'd left it at that for the night, and the next afternoon Ana stopped by Celeste's office and simply said, "We want to do it." They'd danced around the office for a couple of minutes, laughing and hooting from sheer nerves, then had gotten down to brass tacks and decided they'd both give a one-month notice the next day, Friday.

Ana had correctly predicted, "This is going to blindside the partners, Celeste; here they've been grooming you for partnership and they're not only losing their golden girl, but she's going back to Podunk, Washington, to calculate bushels to the acre for a bunch of ranchers. They're gonna be *appalled.* How *naïve* of you!"

Celeste assumed a haughty mien. "In the first place, it's Shuksan, Counselor, not Podunk, and in the second place, I'm going back there to calculate bushels to the acre for farmers, not ranchers, the difference being that farmers farm and ranchers ranch. Got it?"

"They can call themselves whatever they want as long as they don't expect me to be out counting hay bales or some such nonsense come summer."

"No, my dear, you're forgetting that you're going there to practice law. *I'll* probably be the one out counting hay bales."

With a delicious shiver, Ana repeated, "I'm going there to practice law. Pinch me and tell me it's for real, Celeste, because I still can't believe it!"

"It'll seem real enough when you're up to your ears in probate cases and DUIs."

"Yeah, the scourge of a small-town attorney."

"Don't start whining already, or I'll make sure I save a couple of fields for you to go out and count cattle. In your new Ferragamos."

"Keep it up, *gurfrin,* and I'll bring you some nice ripe cow chips for your desk."

Celeste laughed. "You don't scare me, Counselor. Somehow I can't see you out there scooping up cow-pies."

"Seriously, Cellie, have I thanked you yet?"

"For what?"

"For the opportunity, girl! If you only knew how much I've hated this job for the last couple of years. If I never see another Washington State Accounting Code/Regulation manual, it'll be too soon."

"I didn't know you were so unhappy here, Ana. Why have you stuck with it if you hated it so much?"

Ana shrugged. "Security, I guess. If it were just me, I'd probably have taken my chances somewhere else, but there's been Tori to consider too. I could've even gotten myself into something worse. I guess I just wasn't ready to take that risk."

"But you're ready now? And Tori's up for this?"

"We're ready. We've both prayed a lot, and we feel that this is the Lord's direction for us. She's the one who told me I'd be an idiot to let this pass by. She said, 'Mama, you're doing it, that's all there is to it!' Crazy kid, can you believe she's already packing?"

Celeste had a sudden thought, turning a troubled face to her friend. "I didn't really stop to think about the fact that Shuksan's, well, you know…"

"White? Yeah, I kinda figured that one out on my own. That's not such a big thing to us; people are people wherever you go. There'll always be some who you don't click with, but I'm not worried about it. And Tori, that girl is a born social butterfly. She'll do just fine."

They'd both given notice, and Celeste began the task of preparing her clients for reassignment to other accountants within the firm. She'd been surprised and gratified that a number of her clients wished to continue with her services, even given the fact that her office would be a two-hour drive from Seattle. Considering that the majority of Celeste's work was done independently, they could rely on modern technology for all but the touchiest aspects of client services. This was a great relief and would help keep the wolf from the door while she established relationships with Mr. Koch's former clients. As she'd told Ana, "And here I figured that with my luck, the only person who'd want to follow me would be that idiot, Spence Beckwith," to which Ana had snorted, "He'll probably be in jail by then." Spoiled Spence had opted to remain with the Seattle firm and Celeste washed her hands of him and his ongoing problems. SSBB could keep him with her blessing!

The condo had sold in three days, and she'd engaged in a flurry of packing, depositing those things that would eventually make the journey over the mountains when she had her own place into a storage unit, and ruthlessly culling a great deal of the rest. The last big item on her to-do list had been trading in her Beamer for a sturdy Ford Expedition; she had no intention of negotiating those mountain winter roads in a sports car.

The Expedition was packed to the gills with her clothing, stereo, TV, and collection of CDs and DVDs, as well as her personal computer. The final papers for the condo's sale had been signed, and the final papers for the purchase of the building and new practice were drawn up in preparation for signing the next day. Ana, in her first official role as Shuksan's new attorney, would be present for the signing; she and Tori waited outside as Celeste walked through her condo a final time. She stood at the slider for a long moment, looking out at the expanse of lake, and felt no regret, only anticipation for the future. A smile playing on her lips, she once again appreciated the irony of the situation; her ambitions had led her from Shuksan all those years ago, and now maturity was leading her home once more. Her life was coming full-circle. She recalled standing on the balcony only a few short months ago, convincing herself that she was happy, accepting a lonely spirit of independence in place of genuine fulfillment, and feeling superior in her loneliness, because to admit she'd become a victim of career burnout and longed for a simpler life would have been to accept weakness in herself.

Perhaps it was a sign of personal growth that she could admit these things to herself at last, although there were some who'd sneer and opine that she just hadn't held up under the pressure; this seemed to be the prevailing attitude at Barton, Biddle, Sutton & Swales. They could think whatever they wanted, she'd told herself resolutely; there had to be a generous serving of sour grapes on the menu at SSBB, what with losing several of their established clients to the fledgling accounting firm being established "out in the sticks somewhere."

People had a hard time accepting and understanding that circumstances, perspectives, and entire world views can change; perhaps witnessing someone else "switch horses midstream" made them nervous because they realized that they, too, could suddenly find themselves looking for a new horse. It wasn't an easy feat to make a career change, or other major life change, when one had all of the attendant baggage that accompanied the average life; spouse, children, schools, mortgage, and on and on. She and Ana were lucky,

Celeste knew; they both were relatively unfettered, and it was easier for them to up-stakes and start over than for most, because only in unique situations would a woman's career or life choice supercede her spouse's. In this way, she and Ana had a distinct advantage, although Ana had Tori to consider. The flip side of the coin was that there was no safety net below, no spouse's salary to cushion a fall, and no built-in support system waiting at home. Although it didn't always necessarily follow that a spouse would automatically be the support system a woman might need from time to time. Celeste had known plenty of women whose husbands or boyfriends habitually took without giving back and, in her personal opinion, simply made the whole situation worse. Sometimes it was truly better to be on your own, depend only on yourself, and be answerable to no one else. This had been her credo for her entire adult life, and it hadn't failed her yet. But, then, there hadn't been anyone worthy of the risk.

Until now.

Sometimes she still shook her head in disbelief that the person with whom she'd finally fallen in love was not only the last person in the world she'd have expected, but was already a member of her family.

It was time to go. She closed her eyes and prayed.

Lord, I believe You're leading me home, and that You have Your reasons. Please help me to serve You as I start over in Shuksan. Guide my path, Heavenly Father. Amen.

She whispered, "Goodbye" to nothing and everything and let herself out the front door for the last time.

Chapter 22

They'd survived the move and all of the accompanying miseries. Ana and Tori were tucked into the upstairs apartment, and Celeste had ensconced herself into her old bedroom at her mother's house. She was finding out in pretty short order that a weekend at home every few months was a whole lot different than officially moving back home. Catherine, never a particularly gracious hostess, had taken off that particular hat and "buried it out in the yard somewhere," Celeste muttered to Ana one morning over coffee and muffins.

"I'm about ready to invade you and crash on your couch," Celeste warned, pulling a dead split-leaf philodendron from a wobbly shelf in the office reception area. "This place is a disgrace, Ana! Wouldn't you think a man in his seventies would have figured out that you have to actually *water* plants if you want them to survive? And what about this carpet, and the paint, and everything else?"

"Yeah, the bathroom, for starters."

"That's a scary sight, for sure. So, what do we tackle first?"

Ana straightened, stretching her spine, hands on her hips as she surveyed the possibilities. "I'd personally vote for painting first, and then ripping this musty old carpet out. I don't think it's been replaced for forty years, and it stinks besides!"

They'd made the trip to Wenatchee, selected carpet and pad and arranged for installation, then tracked down paint and all of the necessary accoutrements; brushes, rollers, pans, and turpentine. Celeste had negotiated a deal with Ty and Tawnya, who'd spent the next Saturday painting, along with Tori, Ana, Celeste, and Scott. The new carpet had been installed the following Tuesday, and Celeste was relieved that the painting had been completed before the carpet was laid.

They'd also located an office-supply store. Two new desks, three computers, chairs, and end tables for the reception area, three new telephones, and a mountain of office supplies later, Celeste had staggered to the Expedition, exhausted and considerably lighter in the pocketbook than she'd been a few hours earlier. She was undertaking the expense to set the office up and had known it would be spendy but was unwilling to settle for lesser quality, as she believed that appearances did count. Their new clients would be evaluating every aspect of their professionalism, including the office setting, long before they developed a truly comfortable relationship with their new accountant or attorney, and Celeste was determined not to be found lacking.

Besides puttering around the office, tossing out dead plants, and cleaning out years of dusty accounting publications, many still in their original plastic mailing sleeves, she'd taken some time for some personal business. She'd had a pretty good idea of what she wanted, and after the third night in her mother's house, had she'd gone over her bank balance with a fine-tooth comb, calculated the remaining start-up expenses, penciled in estimated taxes, and finally sat back in the creaky chair that had housed a former receptionist, satisfied that she'd neither starve nor be forced to take a weekend job down at Alpine Burger in order to survive until some revenue started rolling in.

The fact that it had taken only three days to come to the point where she'd felt she needed to take some sort of positive action, for the sake of her sanity, didn't bode well for a long-term living arrangement under Catherine's roof. There weren't a lot of other options; she couldn't horn in on Ana and Tori, no matter how much she threatened to. Renting a motel room didn't fit into the financial master plan, and there wasn't a lot of rental property in Shuksan.

Mother was driving her stark-raving mad, and it was happening a lot sooner than she'd expected. She'd coped thus far by making sure she didn't spend a lot of time at the house and, in truth, there was enough to do at the office to keep her busy and provide an excuse Catherine would believe.

The memory of the property for sale out at Carrot Lake had lingered in her mind over the last few months, and she'd taken a drive out to the lake that afternoon, parked the Expedition, and walked along the quiet beach. Late-season Mallard ducks and Canadian geese glided silently on the choppy surface, and behind her, the tops of the pines swayed in the breeze.

Not a jet ski in sight.

She'd driven back to town, directly to the local real estate office. She examined the County covenants regarding the property's septic tank, drain-field requirements, and results of perk testing. She also reviewed well-depth estimates and the distance new construction must be from waterfront.

The property already had power to it, which was a huge relief; electricity was expensive if a person had to pay for installation to a building site from the county road. The parcel consisted of ten acres, but Celeste wanted only five. She'd correctly ascertained that the listing agent was the "seller's agent" and didn't want to show her hand by giving too much information. She'd returned to the office, tracked Ana down in the apartment where she was unpacking boxes, and laid out the situation for her.

Ana drew up papers for an offer for five acres. The seller wanted thirty thousand dollars for the ten-acre parcel, and Celeste offered fifteen thousand for five acres, figuring the seller would still be getting asking price; he'd just have more than one buyer involved.

The next morning, Ana appeared in full attorney regalia; navy business suit with matching pumps and ivory blouse with a sapphire lapel brooch completing the ensemble, briefcase polished to a glossy shine, and descended on the listing agent. She'd returned to the office a short time later, where she and Celeste had pretended to set up the filing system, jumpy as a couple of fleas on a dog with a new flea collar. When the telephone finally rang, both women froze, eyes locked, then Celeste pleaded, "Answer it, Ana. I can't do it!"

Ana took a deep breath and picked up the receiver, "Good morning, Malloy & Claiborne, may I help you? Oh, yes Mr. Stutzman. I see. Yes, I'll come over and pick it up right now. Thank you."

Ana replaced the receiver. "The seller countered twenty thousand for the full ten acres."

"What am I going to do with ten acres, Ana?" Dropping into a chair, Celeste ran a distracted hand through her hair. "What do you think I should do?"

Eyes narrowed, Ana replied, "Well, this property's been on the market awhile, right? And he hasn't had any luck selling the whole parcel; my guess is that he's waiting to see whether you come back with a counter-offer. He doesn't want to lose the sale, not after sitting on the market this long. Have you thought about buying the whole ten as an investment and then selling it yourself down the road?"

"Yes, I thought about it. I guess I just didn't want to pay more than fifteen thousand right now, and I don't really want to be stuck with having to try to sell the rest of it myself."

"You never know," Ana replied, arching a brow, "I might be interested in buying those five acres from you and living on the lake too."

"Really, Ana?" Celeste was delighted. "If that's what you want to do, we'll work it out. Okay, accept his offer. Once again, we walk in faith."

By the end of the day, the paperwork had been signed. They'd done a victory dance in the reception area, then gone over to the Hay Wagon and celebrated with prime rib dinners. Not ready to call it a night, they'd returned to the apartment after dinner to dream and make plans.

Finally, Celeste rose to her feet and gathered her purse. "I need to get out of here, let you guys get on with your evening. See you tomorrow."

Tori asked, "Hey, when can I come out to see the lake, check it out?"

"How about Saturday? We can take your mom and figure out where we want our houses."

"Sounds good. Can Tawnya come too? I haven't seen much of her."

Celeste nodded. "Sure, I'll check with her dad, but I can't imagine that it would be a problem. Night, ladies."

"Night."

She carefully descended the dark staircase, scolding herself for not having had the foresight to have left a light on earlier. Safely reaching the bottom of the steps, she tottered into her own office, dropped into her padded chair, and huffed out a huge sigh. The thought of going home to Catherine's was about as appealing as a side dish of pickled pigs feet at Thanksgiving. Suddenly needing to hear Scott's voice, she reached for the phone instead. He answered on the third ring and she simply said, "Can I see you tonight?"

"Umm, yeah. Give me half an hour. Are you at Catherine's?"

"No, at the office. Scott?"

"Hmm?"

"Hurry, 'kay?"

"Be there soon."

She met him out front as he pulled up in the truck, opened the passenger door, and climbed in. "Hi. Thanks for coming."

"No problem. It's good to see you."

"It's good to see you too. Wanna go for a drive?"

"Sure. Where're we going?"

"The lake, if you don't mind?"

"Not at all."

They'd driven through the darkness and spoken of the events of their lives since the last time they'd been together. Ty seemed to be settling down a little more and getting serious about school, something that hadn't been a priority for most of his high-school career. Tawnya was doing well in school, too, and had gained a sense of self-confidence that was coloring the way she was relating to the other kids; she was actually getting phone calls these days. In Scott's mind, they owed it all to Celeste, and to Celeste's thinking, it had much more to do with Tori's acceptance and friendship. Whatever it was, it certainly was good to see her blossoming.

To Scott's surprise, Celeste directed him to the north end of the lake, down the Old Forest Service access road that led down to the waterfront. They usually used the south beach access road, although he'd been at his share of high-school keggers down at this end of the lake as well. Finally reaching the lake, he killed the engine and said, "Come here a minute."

She slid across the seat, into his arms, and felt that she'd come home.

They sat silently for several minutes, each feeling the other's heartbeat, then she drew away. "Let's take a walk. Oh, I should have thought, do you have a flashlight?"

Scott groaned. "Serious? In the dark?"

She patted his cheek. "I won't let the boogieman get you. Where's the flashlight?"

He opened the glove box, fished around for a minute, then produced the flashlight and handed it to her. "Okay, lead the way."

They walked hand in hand to the water's edge, the flashlight's beam bobbing a few feet ahead of them. There were a handful of houses spread out on the other side of the lake, lights visible through the trees.

"It's growing out here, population-wise," Celeste murmured.

"Yeah, I suppose eventually it'll be full of houses."

Celeste turned to face him in the darkness, barely able to make out his features. "I bought this land today, Scott. Ten acres."

He felt his eyebrows shoot upward toward his hairline and leaned back in surprise. "Serious?"

"Very serious. Well, what do you think?" she asked, swinging the flashlight in a circle to illuminate a sweep of trees and beach line. "I'm now officially a taxpayer in Kittitas County."

"It's great, Celeste; I've gotta say, though, you move fast, don't you?"

"Well, not when you consider that I've had my eye on this parcel, or five acres of it, anyway, since July, before I'd even decided to come home, but I had to make sure I had all of the business start-up expenses taken care before I could make an offer. I really didn't want ten acres, but Ana wants to buy five and put a house in next to mine. It's perfect! We'll each have one hundred and fifty feet of waterfront, so our houses won't be right on top of each other, and at least we'll have each other on one side and hope for good neighbors on the other."

He squinted into the darkness. "I can't see much right now, but if memory serves, you've got a great spot."

"Yes, it's a fantastic view. So, what do you think? Have I bitten off more than I can chew this time?"

"Not if I know you; you're the craziest woman I've ever seen for chasing a dream. I can see you out here, sitting on the dock, kicking your feet in the water. I can actually see you out here a lot better than I could on Lake Washington."

Celeste snorted. "That's because I never sat on a dock back in Seattle and kicked my feet in the water. The only public docks around that area are for moorage. I don't think I'll ever want a boat."

"Oh, maybe a paddleboat, that'd be fun."

She nodded. "Yeah, I could live with a paddleboat. Can't you just see Tawnya and Tori out there on a hot August afternoon?"

Rubbing his neck, he pretended to cringe. "Oh, yeah, I can see it. I can see them paddling clear down to Charlie's rock and then whining that they're too tired to paddle back."

"Then we'll just have to go down and paddle it back ourselves."

"We will?"

Celeste cast him a droll look.

"Well, last time I checked, paddleboats didn't have outboard motors."

Scott replied slowly, "No, I was referring to the 'we' part, as in you and me."

Understanding came then, and Celeste took his hand once more, reached up to kiss him, then spoke softly, "I want to live with you in my new house. Our new house. You, me, and the kids. Scott, I know it isn't the right time to be talking about this, but I don't know when it'll ever be the right time, so I'm just going to go ahead and say it. I don't know what your 'intentions' are, and I'm fine with that, because I know the situation. If the time does come that you want to be with me, then I'll be here, in my log house, waiting for you."

She paused for a deep breath, then continued, "Here I am, probably rushing into something that you're not ready to think about, and that's fine. You take whatever time you need, but I need to live my life, too, Scott, and this is where I want to sink down roots and come home to at night."

He sighed a deep, bone-weary sigh, then said, "Let's sit down, Celeste, unless you're chilly? No? Okay, here's a log, will this work?" They settled themselves, and he took her hand in his. They sat in silence as he struggled with himself, then finally said, "You honor me, Celeste. There's nothing I'd like more than to wake up with you beside me on a snowy winter morning, or sneak out for a swim at

midnight in the summer. Just the thought of it tears me up inside."
He turned to face her, then took both her hands in his own. "Celeste,
I..." breaking off mid-sentence, averting his face.

"Whatever it is, Scott, just tell me. I just bared my soul to you;
if you can't be honest with me after all this time, then I don't know
what we're doing together."

"You're right. Okay."

Turning to face her in the darkness, he admitted, "This thing
between us was the last thing I'd ever imagined happening, and once
it *was* happening, I had a whole new guilt to deal with; it was like an
ulterior motive, you know, taking Rach off support so that we could
be together. I've had to come to terms with that part of it too. I'm
not making excuses, Celeste, and I don't want to sound like I regret
our getting together, because I don't. If Rach wasn't where she is
now, it wouldn't have happened. But she isn't, and she never will be
again, and now here we are, the two of us. And Tyler and Tawnya.
And Catherine."

"Yes."

"There's one more issue though."

"What's that?"

He sighed deeply. "I haven't told the kids about Rach."

"I wondered. I didn't think so. My gosh, Scott, why not? There's
only a week left 'til Halloween. I thought you were going to talk to
them weeks ago!"

"I was. I had every intention of telling them a couple of weeks
after school started, but then the thing with Dwight happened, and
I just couldn't put any more on Ty right then. I mean, he's doing
so well! He's getting his homework done on time and keeping his
nose clean. He hasn't been out of the house at night even on the
weekends, and I think he's finally cut loose from the rest of the guys
he was partying with. I believe he's staying clean and sober, which is
so huge in itself. I've been watching the days pass and getting more
nervous, but I just can't, couldn't...well, upset the apple cart."

He cupped her face in his hands. "Are you awfully disappointed
with me? You have a right to be. I should have been talking to you
about this, especially now that we're almost out of time."

"No, I'm not upset with you; I can only imagine how you've

struggled with this, and I don't have the right to condemn you for doing what you thought was right, what you could live with at the time. I'm glad you were able to be honest with me, but I do think you need to talk to the kids, Scott, tomorrow night. Don't put it off another day, because you don't have all that many days left to prepare, yourself and the kids both, not if you're looking at next week."

He nodded. "Yeah."

They stood silently, hand in hand, looking out over the lake's dark surface, lost in their own thoughts about Rachel's situation, the people who loved her, and the grief that lay ahead. Finally, Scott exhaled deeply and said, "Tomorrow night, then.

"Do you want me to be there, for moral support?"

He shook his head slowly. "No. I mean, of course I would like to have you there, but this is something I need to do myself." He looked intensely into her face. "Do you understand? I'm thinking of the kids and the fact that I don't want them to associate you with the situation, you know? Have them target you with whatever negative stuff they're dealing with."

"No, you're right, I didn't think about that, but know I'll be with you in spirit. I wonder about Mother, though. She needs to know too."

"I know. I'll stop by the house the next day when you're at work, talk to her then." Shaking his head, he admitted, "I think I'm dreading talking to Catherine even more than I am the kids, isn't that crazy?"

"Not at all, but you have to remember that Rachel asked this of you, not Mother, because Mother would never honor her wishes. Show her the DNR form, Scott, and stand firm."

He shook his head. "It isn't going to be easy."

"No," Celeste agreed. "It's not going to be easy. None of it will be, and that's why things stand the way they do now. But you're doing the right thing, Scott."

They'd driven back to town and he dropped her by the office so she could retrieve the Expedition, shared a final kiss, and then continued on toward home. Two hours later, Scott sat at his desk, light extinguished, DNR form in his hand, and remembered. In the past few years, it had seemed that he'd lost the memories of the pre-Huntington's Rachel and could only see the woman the disease had shaped her into. Now that he had finally come to accept his role in her final exit from their lives, the memories came flooding back, and he saw clearly, once more, the girl he'd fallen in love with his junior year.

Of course, in a small town no one was a stranger, and he'd know Rachel Malloy, but she was a couple of years behind him and they'd moved in separate circles of friends. He remembered the first afternoon he'd really noticed her; the Home Economics class had prepared Baked Alaska, and Rach's group had failed the project; the dessert had exploded in the oven. He'd wandered into the Home Ec room for lack of anything better to do while waiting for one of his buddies to finish spooning with his girlfriend and had come across Rachel, scrubbing the oven, eyes puffy and face stained with tears.

"What's wrong, did somebody die of ptomaine?" he'd joked and had felt immediate regret when she burst into tears anew, scrubbing the inside of the oven with such vigor that he was sure whatever they'd used to coat the oven's interior was going to wipe right off.

"Come on, I was just kidding," he'd cajoled, but she'd ignored him and continued with her project. He'd stood there at a loss; he was an upper-classman, an attractive kid who'd always had good luck with the ladies and wasn't used to being snubbed, even when he deserved it, which he had. He'd finally given up and left her still on her knees in front of the oven but hadn't been able to stop thinking about the dark-eyed girl who'd scrubbed that oven with a tear-stained face.

Then, on a snowy Saturday just before Christmas, he and Jim were headed out to the lake to kill some time. They'd cruised past the Malloy house and there she'd been, out in the front yard, building a snowman with her little sister. He'd pulled over, opened the driver's door, stood up, and hollered, "Wanna come out to the lake and do some donuts?" He'd figured she'd refuse and was surprised when she'd hollered back, "Only if my sister can come along." He and Jim had exchanged shrugs and he'd said, "Sure, bring her along." She'd said something about telling her mother where they were going and disappeared into the house, while the younger sister clambered into the truck, chattering ninety miles an hour in a sixty-mile zone.

They'd sat there for what had seemed like half an hour and Scott had asked the kid whether she thought her sister had ditched them, but then Rach had appeared at the front door, armed with a huge thermos of cocoa and a foil package, which turned out to be homemade cookies, still warm from the oven. She'd sat between he and Jim and when they'd each wolfed down three cookies, remarked sweetly that he must not be too worried about ptomaine. Scott had choked on his last bite, and Jim had to grab the wheel to keep them on the road, as he'd collapsed in laughter. Rach had grinned at him; Scott's heart had done one big somersault in his chest, and he'd been a goner. The circles they'd spun out on the lake didn't touch the ones skittering around in his gut, and he could still remember the sound of her laughter, a musical scale of sheer delight, as they'd rev the truck up to about sixty, then crank the wheel hard, sending them careening crazily over the ice.

The only indication of her innate, unshakable responsibility was the fact that she absolutely forbade her sister to ride in the back of the truck while doing donuts, so she'd waited on the bank while sending Celeste on ahead for the first go-round, then took her own turn in the cab. Even then she'd watched out for her sister, which he'd thought was pretty cool; most girls her age wouldn't have been caught dead with their younger sister.

Their first official date was to a hometown basketball game; Shuksan was playing Cle Elum, and it was a huge grudge match as Cle Elum had cleaned their clock last year in the playoffs and Shuksan's honor was at stake. He'd picked her up at her house, met and tried his best to charm her mother, which left his palms damp and heart thumping in his chest. He renewed his acquaintance with the kid sister, Celeste, and had been rooked into a quick game of Twister on the living room floor. He'd had one hand on blue, right foot on yellow and left on green, and thought he'd never been tied up in such a knot, even when changing oil in the old John Deere tractor. He and Celeste had collapsed onto each other just as Rach had come down the stairs, and she'd burst into laughter. Any last shreds of reserve had melted away, and he'd fallen as hard as granite and as smooth as the silk she'd worn at his Junior Prom three months later. He'd told her he loved her that night, and she'd said that she loved him too, and that had been all she wrote. They were together with a commitment as solid as though they'd already taken wedding vows, though that wouldn't happen for another three years.

It probably wasn't realistic to say he'd loved everything about her, because in all honesty, who can really say such a thing and mean it, after the kids come and the sleep-deprived nights and financial worries that plague a marriage take their toll on the romance factor? So, no, he couldn't say he'd loved *everything* about Rach, but it had been too close to count, even if he'd been keeping score. But he hadn't, nor had she, even when it would have been easy to notch their respective buckles with points they could have scored off each other.

Their marriage had been solid, their commitment an open book, and the glue had held through the years, even when the binding had begun to crack and the pages delineating their lives had become devoid of new experiences, new memories. The old memories were the ones he lived tonight, his only companion the dampness of tears on his cheeks. Wedding anniversaries celebrated together, holding each other close after the kids were asleep, secure in the knowledge that many more anniversaries would follow. Thirteen short years of celebrating their own and the kids' birthdays, Christmases, Thanksgivings, and Easters.

Thirteen years to gather memories of the lifetime that had been denied them.

But tonight he'd been transported back to the early days and he re-lived each memory as they came, almost as though the memories had been Rach's gift to him; a precious gift of trust even as she prepared to leave this life behind.

"If you love me, Scott, you'll let me go."

And so this was where it would end, that first great love, nurtured from adolescence, tempered through marriage and parenthood, and finally given over to peace, all in the spirit and the memory of that same love.

He wiped his cheeks, lay the document on his desk, and called it a night.

Chapter 23

No two ways around it; homework certainly stunk, especially the weekly report due in Contemporary World Problems. Ty leaned back in the creaky chair that sat at the desk tucked under the eaves in his room, yawned hugely, and glowered at the blank sheet of paper before him. He could choose any current "problem" for his weekly report and typically followed the continued rebuilding of Iraq, the attacks on American soldiers, and the ongoing saga of Muslim hatred for America, but it was getting old. There had to be *something* else going on in the world, he mused, and decided he'd look for the newspaper Dad had brought home the other day, get a fresh idea. He made no bones about the fact that writing wasn't his strong suit, and his weekly reports skirted outright plagiarism by a word or three, but, hey, what did he care? Old Mr. Graham had one rheumy eye fixed on retirement and the other in the latest *Readers Digest,* and probably one foot in the grave, and even though students were required to cite source, author, and date of publication on each report, Ty figured Mr. Graham wouldn't be cross-referencing too closely. Besides, if he decided to crack down on offenders, he'd have to deal with pretty much the entire senior class, which wasn't likely to happen.

One foot in the grave. The phrase triggered immediate thoughts of Dwight. The funeral had been surreal; it had seemed that most of the town's population had attended the service at Grandma's church, but the crowd had leveled off quite a bit for the graveside service. Mrs. Phillips had appeared sober, but she'd nearly taken Ty apart at the cemetery; for some reason she'd decided Ty was responsible for her son's death and had attacked him verbally, even as her son's casket was being lowered into the damp ground. Transferring her own anger and guilt onto Ty, she'd raised a hand to strike his face but had been stayed by Scott's hand gripping her arm, saying, "That's enough, Dora. I understand you're hurting, but Ty's hurting too. You just back off, now, hear?" And she had, but Ty would remember those angry, haunted eyes as long as he lived and try to convince himself that he wasn't responsible. Everyone said so, but *everyone* hadn't been there and seen Dwight die, and they sure hadn't been around for the weeks and months leading up to that night, watching him huffing poison into his lungs and brain, killing himself by centimeters. The thing that bothered him most was the niggling suspicion that Dwight had wanted to die…addiction was one thing, and everyone knew the guy could pack away the booze and dope, but somehow this felt different. Looking back, Ty could put his finger on a dozen different incidents that had "felt wrong" at the time and was grimly certain he'd intentionally chosen not to see Dwight's pain.   But if Dwight had truly wanted to die, wasn't that his choice? A rotten choice, for sure, and one that Ty railed against each and every day. It was just such a selfish thing to do; lots of people had rotten things or people in their lives but stuck it out, why not Dwight? Didn't he realize how much his friends would miss him, how much Ty would miss him? Hadn't he cared? Or had the prospect of finally having a measure of peace been so alluring as to be its own addiction, so to speak? And for a kid who'd felt he hadn't much control over his own life, wasn't suicide, even one that appeared accidental, a definitive way to take back that control once and for all?

That was the trouble with suicide; the opportunity to get into the person's head and ask the important questions died right along with him or her. The only thing left was the grief and the underlying anger at the selfishness that precluded even looking at other options, and wouldn't any other option be preferable to suicide?

Battling the same hurt and anger he'd carried with him for weeks, Ty scooted his chair back and took a hard swipe at the tears filling his eyes. If anyone had a reason to consider pulling the cord, shouldn't it be him? With Mom forever lost to her family and his own uncertain medical prognosis, why wasn't he flirting with the same "solution?" Because underneath everything else, he had that most basic, vital, element that Dwight had lacked, the security of at least one loving parent? He knew Dad was solid, there was no question of that.

For the first time, Ty fully appreciated his father's strength of character to endure Mom's debilitating illness and keep moving on with his life, knowing she'd never get better. Did he ever wonder how long it would take her to die, or did he even allow himself to think about it at all? Now that Aunt Celeste was in the picture, especially having moved back to Shuksan, wouldn't that make it even tougher on Dad? He wasn't one to seek out female companionship; there had never been another woman, at least to Ty's knowledge, and the grapevine in a small town is a pretty accurate barometer of goings-on in the romantic arena. If there had been other women, he'd have heard about it. When the attraction between Dad and Aunt Celeste had come out of nowhere and blindsided him, he'd reacted out of a mixture of loyalty to his mother, which had astonished even himself with its unbidden and fierce intensity. He'd had time to process that, too, and over the ensuing weeks, especially since the time at Aunt Celeste's condo, seeing the two of them together, he'd been able to admit that they seemed to really care for each other. They'd spoken to each other with respect, really listened to what the other was saying, even their body language, everything, just seemed *right*. He'd come to accept the situation for what it was, and why not? It wasn't like Mom knew, or would ever know, for that matter. Ty figured he'd leave the matter of conscience to his father and aunt; as far as he was concerned, they were old enough to live their lives without his interference. Freakin' paper wasn't getting written this way though. Better get on downstairs and find the newspaper. He made his way down the darkened stairs and into the kitchen, where the paper usually ended up, but tonight it wasn't on the table, which meant Dad had either pitched it already or taken it into the office. Hoping for the latter, he walked down the hall, switched on the overhead light as he entered the office, and gave a quick glance around, relieved to see the newspaper folded up on the desk. As he rummaged for the front page, a single sheet of paper fluttered to the floor, and he bent automatically to retrieve it, glancing at the paper absently, then stiffened, bringing the sheet closer, reading intently.

Advanced Directive/Do Not Resuscitate Order

I hereby certify that I give my husband, Scott William Parnell, durable power of attorney in all medical decision-making, and do declare that I do not wish any heroic measures or artificial means of sustaining life, in the event that I am unable to make these decisions for myself.

Rachel Catherine Parnell
Signed November 21, 2002

As still as though he were carved from marble, Ty reread the document twice again and decided he understood it well enough. Mom had authorized Dad to make sure she wouldn't end up exactly the way she was now, had trusted him to make sure she *didn't*. The form was signed almost four years ago! That meant Dad had been hiding this piece of paper for a long time, way before Mom had gone to Fircrest, and certainly after she'd gone onto the machines.

After the initial shock came anger at his father for putting his mother, putting all of them, through the last few months, when he knew full well what Mom's wishes had been. He studied his mother's spidery signature, stomach knotting at the sight of her handwriting. How long had it been since he'd seen anything that possessed Mom's personal touch? Sometimes he actually had to go to the wall under the stairs and look at the family pictures to really remember her; what kind of a son forgets what his own mother looks like?

One who hasn't seen his mother for well over a year, a bitter voice of guilt hissed in unwelcome reply.

Dropping the form back onto the desk, he spun around and strode from the office, newspaper and homework assignment forgotten. He grabbed his denim jacket from where it hung from a hook on the back of the kitchen door and pulled it on as he went out the front door. He wrenched the door of his truck open, hauled himself up onto the seat and, leaning over, reached under the passenger seat for the bottle he kept stashed there. Tossing the cap onto the passenger seat, he tipped the bottle up and took a hefty swig, leaning his head against the back of the seat as the Velvet began to grind down the rough edges.

That's better.

He took another swig, then another, and finally brushed his mouth on the sleeve of his jacket, capped the bottle, and gunned the motor. When life turned bad, he'd always been able to talk to Dwight. Tonight was one of those nights, but Dwight was gone forever. Who was he supposed to talk to now?

Hating the tears that blurred his vision, he turned onto the county road, reaching blindly for the bottle and driving faster than the two-lane blacktop ought to be traveled. Big deal. Maybe he'd miss the big curve up ahead and all of his problems would be over for good. Goodbye to the specter of Huntington's that, like a pirate's parrot, seemed to perch on his shoulder, along for the ride every single day and night of his life. Goodbye to the loneliness of life without Dwight, and definitely goodbye and not farewell to the prospect of having to eek out a living cutting and baling other people's hay, harvesting their wheat, and pinching his pennies to survive.

Am I really thinking about killing myself?

In that instant, he understand how it felt to be without hope, to be completely alone, to know that nothing in life would ever be *good* again.

This was how Dwight had felt.

Ty shivered under his jacket, cranked the heat on full blast, then took another pull from the bottle, the burn of the whiskey so hot that he figured it must be burning clear into his soul.

My soul.

From the recesses of memory, a Scripture verse came to mind. "Now the Lord is the Spirit, and where the Spirit of the Lord is, there is freedom" (2 Corinthians 3:17).

Where had that come from? He really must be losing his mind. Well, if he was going down, he may as well go feelin' no pain. He drew deeply from the bottle once more, then capped it and dropped it to the floor, fumbling with his right hand for a CD. That's what was needed here, some music. Good, hard, head-banging rock, maybe some Nirvana. Now, *that* would be something fitting to listen to on his way out. If it was good enough for Cobain, then it was surely good enough for Tyler Parnell.

He selected the disk, popped out the disk currently in the player and tossed it onto the passenger seat, then inserted *Smells Like Teen*

Spirit and cleared his mind, waiting for the words of another suicidal man to accompany him to the abyss.

What was this? This wasn't Cobain. He must've grabbed the wrong disk, but even if he had, this wasn't anything he'd ever listened to. It sure wasn't *his*. Wait a minute....hadn't Celeste given him a CD on his way out the door the morning he and Dad had left her place? He hadn't so much as given it a moment's thought once he'd gotten home, had just thrown it into the truck with the rest of his tunes. Brow furrowed in concentration, the alcohol dancing a merry jig through his nervous system, he listened to the words of Casting Crowns as they played through his darkness. Words of desperation, of hopelessness, pain and brokenness, and finally of God's healing power.

He drove on, something deep inside himself responding, aware of something powerful at work within him. By the time the third song began to play, his heart was ready to hear the powerful lyrics and music that, in that moment, changed his life forever.

The song faded into silence, yet the message rang loudly in Ty's heart, and punching buttons on the dash, he brought the song up again.

He was peripherally aware that his foot had relaxed on the gas pedal, and as the song spun to a close the second time, he was nearly coasting. Probably a good thing, as the tears that had overtaken him like a summer storm had been nearly blinding in their intensity. He slowed further and pulled off the county road into a dirt road leading to an apple orchard, then killed the engine. He sat silently, trying to get an emotional grip. What had happened back there? Laying his head against the back of the seat, he gazed up at the stars, suddenly aware of his insignificance in the universe. In the grand scheme of things, who'd really even care that he was gone?

"I have come that you might have life, and have it more abundantly" (John 10:10, KJV).

He closed his eyes to the stars above and wondered how it was that his mind was unearthing all of these Scripture verses from the depths of memory tonight.

Is it You, God?

He couldn't think back to the last time he'd thought about God, remembered the early training he'd received both at home and at Sunday School, and later through Confirmation Class. He remembered standing before the congregation on a fine May Sunday morning three years ago, confirming his faith before all. Mom had been in the pew with Dad, Tawnya, and Grandma. It had been one of the last times she'd been able to attend church, but he remembered the joy shining in her dark eyes as Pastor Olson had presented the Confirmands to the congregation.

He seemed to remember that he'd actually believed the words he'd spoken that morning. What had happened in three years to bring him from that place to where he existed now, hollowed out and empty?

Suddenly, the connection linked in his mind, and he shivered in his heavy jacket. The song that had touched him so deeply could have been written about himself!

God, was it me who let the darkness in? I didn't really think I was doing anything wrong...nothing the rest of the guys weren't doing!

In the dark silence, he made an accounting of the ways in which sin had separated him from God and again felt the hot wetness of tears coursing down his cheeks as a verse from Psalm 32 melded with the words to the song that had touched him so. "Then I acknowledged my sin to You and You did not cover up my iniquity. I said, "I will confess my transgressions to the Lord," and You forgave the guilt of my sin" (Psalm 32:5, NIV).

On the heels of this verse came another. "If we confess our sins, He is faithful and just and will forgive us our sins and purify us from all unrighteousness" (1 John 1:9, NIV).

If I confess my sins...but there are so many, Lord...I don't even know where to start!

He shifted in the driver's seat and his foot came into contact with the bottle he'd dropped to the floor earlier. Suddenly, the bottle became a tangible symbol of everything that had gone wrong in his life; energized, he threw open the door, swung his legs out, and leaned to retrieve the bottle. He strode several feet away from the truck and, with as much strength as he could muster, hurled the bottle into the darkness, hearing the tinkle of glass shattering as it came into contact with whatever object had slowed its projection.

He sank to the ground, eyes opened finally to his sin, and took honest inventory of all of the ways he'd allowed Satan access to his soul.

"You will not misuse the name of the Lord your God" (Exodus 20:7, NIV).

Forgive me, Lord. I can't even begin to count the times I've offended You in this way.

"Honor your father and your mother, so that you may live long in the land the Lord your God is giving you" (Exodus 20:12, NIV).

Forgive me, Lord. I guess You know better than I do how many days I have left on earth, but I know that there'll be another one tomorrow, and I couldn't say that earlier tonight. I know I've given Dad a hard time. Forgive me. I guess maybe it was easier to push him away than depend on him too much. I mean, what if something happened to him too? It was just easier to tell myself I didn't love him, that he didn't love me. And Mom. God, it just hurts so much…I thought it would easier to just be mad at her, but it wasn't. I don't know how to honor her anymore, Lord. Please take her home. Please, Lord. She's been ready for a long time, and now maybe I'm ready to let her go too.

"Flee from sexual immorality; he who sins sexually sins against his own body" (1 Corinthians 6:18, NIV)

Forgive me, Lord. Purify me, make me new. Help me to remain strong when temptation presents itself, and it always does, God, it always will. Help me.

"Do not get drunk on wine, which leads to debauchery. Instead, be filled with the Spirit" (Ephesians 5:18, NIV). *Forgive me, Lord. Be my hope, Jesus, and fill me such that I don't feel this awful emptiness anymore. Take away the part of me that longs for the numbing forgetfulness that alcohol brings.*

Lying flat on his back, gazing at the stars high above with eyes awash with tears, he felt the pressure inside ease with each confession he laid at the feet of the Savior. Nearly giddy with the very lightness of his spirit, scarcely able to remember such a feeling of genuine peace before this moment, he wept again.

Thank You, God. Take it all away, Lord. I hate where I've been. I don't ever want to go back there again.

He became aware of the dampness seeping through his clothing and realized he'd lain on the cold ground for close to an hour, lost in his time of prayer and supplication. His limbs were stiff and he rose with difficulty, hopping on first one leg, then the other, as the pins-and-needles sensations gave way to restored feeling in his feet. He crossed to his truck, opened the door, and swung into the cab, wrinkling his nose at the stink of whiskey that still hung in the enclosed space. How could something that smelled so nasty and really didn't taste any better have pulled him into its deadly embrace so fully?

Thank You, Lord, for helping me see the truth, that You are my safe place, not alcohol. Keep me strong, God. I can't do this on my own.

The key hung in the ignition, and he stilled the hand that reached automatically to turn that key. He felt fine, felt amazing, actually, and didn't foresee any difficulties getting home, but he'd been drinking. He'd promised God that he'd make some pretty big changes in his life. Let it start right here, right now. A responsible person stayed off the roads when they'd been drinking, even when they didn't necessarily feel drunk.

He patted his jacket, dug in the pockets, and finally came up with his cell phone. Flipping it open, he spoke into the memory bank. "Home." He closed his eyes and waited for the connection he knew would occur. For the first time in a very long time, he knew with absolute certainty that a genuine connection with his father was not only possible, but something he desired to the deepest part of himself.

As the sound of his dad's groggy voice, he inhaled a deep breath, then said, "Dad? It's me. Yeah, I'm fine. Listen, I need you to come get me. Stimson's apple orchard, just off County Road 14. Yeah. No, there hasn't been an accident, everything's fine. I just need…I just need you." He cleared his throat and wiped the moisture in his eyes on the sleeve of his coat. "Okay, great. Thank you. All right. See you in a few."

He snapped the phone closed and returned it to his pocket, then punched the Play button on the CD player and settled back to listen to the songs his aunt had sent him one more time. Although he was the sole occupant of the truck, he knew without a doubt that he was not alone.

He'd never be alone again.

Chapter 24

The week that followed was one that marked a turning point in the Parnell family, a time of healing and
renewal. Scott had thrown his clothes on after Ty's midnight phone
call had come in and, heart filled with fear and trepidation, had
driven County Road 14 to Stimson's orchard, unaware of what he
would discover upon his arrival. Regardless of Ty's assurances that
he hadn't been involved in an accident, a father's mind automatically
jumps to worst-case scenario, and it was with intense relief that he'd
found that Ty had not been lying, that he was uninjured.

More than that, his son was *safe* in every sense of the word. An
amazing, life-altering "God-thing" had taken place in that orchard,
beginning with his son, and continuing on in the major remodel
that was taking place in their relationship. The foundation had been
shored up and improvements were in progress. The bricks and mortar being utilized in this process were those of the affirmation of the
love he was now able to openly display to Ty and the ongoing res-
toration of the existing structure solidly in the Hands of the Master
Architect.

As with any construction project, there were, and would continue
to be, times of uncertainty, of slow progress, and at those times they
would return to the blueprints, God's Word. The structure, once
complete, would be one of beauty and grace, and Scott knew that for
massive change to occur, whether in buildings or relationships, there
was an element of tear-down involved. Walls needed to be removed
in order to create a larger space in an existing structure and in hearts
as well.

He likened the rebuilding of his family to the battle of Jericho; once again, the walls were tumbling down.

For himself, the inability to love his children freely, without reservation, and to embrace God's awesome love as freely, had been the walls that had held his spirit prisoner for so long. Once again, he could relate to David's words in the Psalms; his cup was full to overflowing. His soul had been anointed with divine grace, and a new morning now held promise rather than low-level desperation and hopelessness.

For Tawnya, the walls that had been breached in her own personal Jericho had been ones of which he'd been completely unaware, and he'd held his little girl tightly in his arms, the top of her head anointed with his own tears, as he'd heard the stories of her struggles with her weight, with her self-image and, feeding her feelings of insecurity, her ongoing struggles with Ariel Reardan. At one time or another, every parent who's ever witnessed their child's pain at the hands of another has probably itched to paddle that other child's behind and itched to give the other parent a healthy portion of his or her mind.

In the end, though, that wasn't really the solution to the problem. As tempting as it may be to intervene in Tawnya's struggles with Ariel and her followers, after much prayer and consideration, he'd known that this wasn't the way to handle the situation. Rather, his role lay in uplifting his daughter in word and prayer, encouraging reliance in the Lord's strength, and in her own growing confidence in herself. Unknown to him, the words he'd said to her had echoed the words spoken by her friend, Tori, on a night in August that had begun the process of Tawnya's own surrender to God.

We can't change anyone's attitude but our own. That's God's job. Our job is to make sure we're where we need to be ourselves, in our own faith and convictions. Let your light shine, Tawn—be the light that shines in the lunchroom, in the locker room, wherever you experience the darkness. Lead by His example and leave the rest in His Hands.

His daughter had steel in her; he recognized this as Rach's gift to their daughter. The same unwavering strength that had carried Rachel through the dark years of her illness, that same desire to mirror Christ's life with her own, was evident in Tawnya, and

Scott was both humbled and inspired by his daughter's faith. She'd been involved with her Confirmation class since the beginning of September and was experiencing a time of spiritual growth that served to strengthen her resolve to grow in faith and serve the Lord.

Your mom would be so proud of you, baby. I'm so proud of you.

And then there was Tyler. The transformation in his son's life was an awesome display of God's work in progress, and in many ways, the young man who'd joined them at the supper table and bore little resemblance to the haunted, sullen person he'd been.

It came to Scott one evening at the supper table, as the three Parnells joined hands and gave thanks for their meal, that he knew the true interpretation of luxury, and that it was time. While to some people, the word may induce images of sparkling swimming pools and sumptuous hotel suites in a tropical location, he knew better. Luxury was having time to prepare for a difficult path that lay ahead, time to buffer a fragile family unit against yet more pain.

If he'd had the luxury to choose, he'd have chosen to have these new days of hope and unity in his family continue uninterrupted, days into weeks, weeks into months, so that the healing might continue uninterrupted, and the rebuilding progress on schedule. But that wasn't the way it was going to go down here, and in the week after Ty's midnight telephone call, Scott had spent many hours in prayer, asking for wisdom and guidance. The decision had been made, and he was finally at peace. Rach would finally be allowed to go home.

He'd spent a painful thirty minutes at Fircrest the afternoon before, and the T's were crossed and the I's dotted. On Sunday afternoon, the family would gather for a final time at the bedside, then with Rachel's physician present, life support would be removed.

All that remained was bringing Tawnya and Catherine into the loop, and he'd rarely dreaded anything more. During one of their heart-to-heart conversations, Ty had confessed that he'd stumbled across the DNR. They'd spent an intense hour talking about the situation, and Ty was in complete acceptance of what lie ahead. Ty's knowledge of the situation had removed some of the burden from Scott's heart, but he still wished for a bit more time; a few more months, a few more weeks.

When he was a child, his mother had a saying that his memory had recaptured and which provided a degree of comfort.

We make our plans but God makes the weather.

He'd understood that there was a deeper meaning here, that it wasn't just a clever way of saying that harvest might get rained out, but that our desires are temporal, that everything happens in God's time, down to the weather. While a farmer's wife certainly kept an eye on the sky, his mother had held firmly to the deeper meaning. Ecclesiastes said there was a time for everything, a time for laughter and for sorrow, a time to be born and a time to die.

And now it was Rach's time.

Lord, I believe You're here, guiding me along. I couldn't have gotten to this place without Your help. I know You never bring us more than we can bear. It's just that…well, I'm scared, Lord. I'm so scared of everything; talking to Tawnya, talking to Catherine. I don't know how I'm going to handle Sunday, even though I think I'm finally ready to let her go. How can I be strong for everyone else when I'm so weak, myself? What if this sends the kids back into their old patterns? I'm so scared, Lord, and I'm sorry. I trust that You've got everything in hand, but I'm still having a hard time letting go, turning it over. Help me, Lord. Walk with me, guide me. Thank You, Lord. Amen.

The time had come, and now the task lay behind him. He'd spoken to Tawnya on the Wednesday night prior to the scheduled disconnect, on the way home from Confirmation class. There had been tears on both their parts, but she'd accepted the reality of her mother's illness months before, and she'd admitted to her father that she'd been praying that God would take her mom home, that her suffering would cease.

And then Catherine. Celeste had met him at her mother's house on Thursday afternoon, and together they had explained the DNR, presented the document for Catherine's inspection, and, as tenderly as possible, had relayed Sunday's final gathering at the bedside. As he and Celeste had feared, the older woman hadn't taken the news well.

"Rachel's life is in God's hands, not yours. How dare you presume to know God's will?"

The fact that this was the ultimate wish of Rachel herself had done nothing to assuage Catherine's pain, nor her anger. Faced with a situation in which she had neither control nor legal standing, she'd lashed out in anger, and the words had stung as surely as if she'd used a bullwhip.

"Don't think I don't know what's really going on here. The two of you are having an affair and this is all your doing, Celeste, so you can marry him. All the men in Seattle and you have to come back home and steal your sister's husband right out from under her nose! You're no longer my daughter. You're dead to me. And you, Scott! I've never been more ashamed of anyone in my life. To kill my daughter so you can fornicate with this…woman. You're not the person I thought you were. Get out of my house. Both of you. Take your things and get out. After the funeral, I never want to see you again."

He'd been aghast at the bitter ugliness that had spilled from his mother-in-law's mouth and deeply saddened for Celeste. She'd flinched as though she'd been slapped, and though tears had filled her eyes and rolled down her pale cheeks, she'd not said a word in her own defense, only turned to ascend the stairs to her room and gather her clothing and personal items. Unable to stand by and do nothing, he'd joined her upstairs and made several trips down the stairs and out to his truck with boxes of childhood memorabilia. On his last trip up, he'd entered the room to find her staring blindly about herself, watching the last vestiges of her childhood slip away. She'd finally looked at him, and he'd been wounded anew at her vulnerability and pain.

"Are you ready?"

She'd nodded, taken a deep breath, and hoisted the last box into her arms, then, after a final glance about, had followed him down the stairs. Catherine still sat where they'd left her, bathed in stony silence. Celeste had paused next to her mother as if waiting for a word of any sort, but her mother refused to meet her eyes, and finally she'd exited through the screen door Scott held open for her.

He followed her to the street and waited as she deposited the last box into her car.

"I'm so sorry, Celeste. I can't believe the things she said to you."

"Or to you."

He shook his head. "I expected a tongue-lashing, but I wasn't expecting one for you. I'm so sorry I agreed that we should do this together. I might have been able to spare you the brunt of it if it'd just been me."

She swiped hard at the tears that continued to leak from her eyes, then gazed at the house from which her mother had banished her. "She's never loved me, Scott. I guess I always knew that. She told me once I was supposed to be a boy, for my dad. What a disappointment I've turned out to be, huh?"

The desire to go to her, cradle her in his arms, and kiss the hurt away was a physical pain, and only the fact that other eyes than Catherine's were upon them kept him where he stood.

Finally, she composed herself, and wiped her eyes dry, then drew a deep breath.

"I have to get out of here."

"Where will you go?"

She shrugged, "Crash Ana's place, sleep on the couch, I guess."

With a sudden burst of frustration, he exclaimed, "This is ridiculous, Celeste. Come out to the farm, we have an extra bedroom."

With a bitter laugh that held no humor, she shook her head. "And confirm all of her suspicions? I won't give her the satisfaction but thank you. No, I think I'll just take a couple of days to get my bearings. After the funeral, I'll make other arrangements, even if I have to pitch a tent out at the lake!"

He watched her closely and saw the pain that darkened her blue eyes. The color had returned to her cheeks; they were flushed with emotion. Anger swept through him; this was his doing, his responsibility, not hers. How could Catherine treat her daughter so callously?

Perhaps Celeste was right. Perhaps Catherine had lavished all of the love she had inside her upon Rachel. His heart broke just a little for the little girl who must have always felt just a little bit unwelcome in her own home.

Suddenly, careless of whoever may be watching through closed blinds, he closed the distance between them and took her hand in his. She raised her eyes to meet his, and they shared a silent moment of joining. He gave her hand a final squeeze, then backed away. "Call me, Cel. Anytime. You know you've got somewhere to go. Anytime. Okay?"

She nodded, then whispered, "Bye."

"Anytime, Celeste."

They'd parted then, and apart from a few phone calls, had no contact until Sunday morning, when they'd shared surreptitious glances from their respective pews on opposite sides of the church. Catherine sat alone, a solitary figure surrounded by families and friends sharing worship together. Celeste had considered approaching her mother, but the older woman had fixed her with a cold glare, and she moved to another pew, where she, too, sat alone.

She'd participated in the service fully, spoken the liturgy, sang along with the hymns, and received communion, all the while completely numb inside. She tested herself every so often, reminding herself that in just a few hours they would gather at Fircrest and bid farewell to her sister. Somehow the reality of the situation had been replaced with a sense of unreality, as though her mind understood the words but refused to truly process them.

She'd been in a similar state since the scene at her mother's on Thursday and had hidden away in Ana's apartment on Friday except to meet a new client. She thought she'd pulled it off pretty well, considering she had no memory of the consultation. Fortunately, she'd had the foresight to stash a tape recorder in a desk drawer and captured the entire conversation on tape. Maybe tomorrow or Tuesday she'd listen to the tape and get back on the page.

Or maybe after the funeral.

She shook her head, still grappling with the fact that there would *be* a funeral. She'd moved down the aisle after the benediction had been spoken, had returned greetings as she received them, eyes on the door, driven by one purpose only.

She needed Scott. He'd speak to her, she'd be able to look into his eyes and draw strength from him, and then she'd be able to *feel* again. He would restore her spirit and she'd be whole once again.

Had she prayed in the last few days? She couldn't keep her mind focused, but she thought maybe she hadn't. Maybe that was the reason for this state of disconnect she'd found herself in. Maybe she needed to spend some time alone with the Lord in prayer, allow Him to share her pain. *I will,* she promised herself, then, catching sight of Scott and the kids just leaving the building, abandoned her train of thought and focused on squeezing through the parishioners gathered in the foyer waiting to greet the pastor.

She burst through the open doors, casting a frantic gaze about her. There they were, standing at the edge of the parking lot, in conversation with Tawnya's teacher. His eyes met hers as she approached, and it was all she could do to keep from running to him, burrowing into his arms and crying, "Protect me." Instead, she kept a firm grip on her emotions, even as she felt her limbs trembling. Would the conversation never end?

Go home, Mrs. Abbott. Please. Go now.

Finally, the older woman took her leave, and the four of them were alone, together yet separate. None spoke of what was on each of their minds, of what lay before them, and Celeste was struck anew by the surrealism of the day.

Finally, Scott sighed. "I guess it's time to head over," knowing all present had no doubt of the planned destination. On this day, no other destination existed, there was only Fircrest, and the woman who would soon be released from her pain and physical bondage.

In unspoken accord, they rode together in Celeste's car, silence hanging heavily around them. In a few short minutes, they arrived and sat silently in the car, no one in a hurry to face what awaited them inside. Scott closed his eyes, then met Celeste's and then, in turn, his children's. "Can we join hands and pray together first, before…" His voice trailed off, and he brushed a hand over his face. When hands were joined, he began. "Heavenly Father, Lord Jesus, we come before You today.…I don't know how to pray, Lord; I don't have the words to describe how I'm feeling, but you know the hearts of everyone before You now, and You understand. We just ask that You will be with us now, as we prepare to let Rachel come home to You. And bless Rachel, Father. Bring her swiftly to Your side. Amen."

He drew in a deep breath, then said, "Are we ready?"

Three heads nodded, three voices murmured acquiescence, and they took the first steps on the sidewalk toward the glass doors that waited to glide open at their approach. They moved silently, each lost in thoughts and memories, uncertainty and fear of what was to come. They greeted the receptionist, then for the last time, walked down the hall to the room that housed the mortal shell of a woman loved by all present. The door was open, and a nurse waited within, recording readings from the monitors onto a clipboard. Quiet compassion was alive in her smile as she greeted them, laying a gentle hand on Rach's forehead. "Take as much time as you'd like. When you're ready, I'll page Dr. Schmick; he's in-house doing rounds. Just press the call button and we'll be in shortly." Then, clipboard in hand, she padded to the door on silent shoes, pulling the door closed behind her, leaving the visitors alone with her patient.

Rach.

Mom.

She lay motionless on the narrow bed, linked to the machines that emitted an electronic glow from the digital readings reported by the monitors attached to her body. A steady thump and hiss emanated from the ventilator, her chest rising and falling to its paced rhythm. A plastic intubation mask held the tube at her mouth in place, and the curly dark hair was but a sad memory of its former glory, having been cut short to make it more manageable for those who attended to her grooming. For Tyler, who hadn't seen his mother since she'd left home, it was Mom, and yet it wasn't. This shell of a woman who barely made a bump in the institutional bed and who was only a distant shadow of her former self wasn't Mom.

They stood at the bedside, each lost in memory, still not quite able to associate the woman in their memories with the one occupying the bed before them. Celeste sat next to her sister and took a hand curled and twisted by with muscular atrophy. "I love you, Rach. You were an awesome sister. I want you to know that I'm back home now. I don't want you to worry about Scott and the kids; I'm here for them. You've got a couple of great kids, Rach. You'd be so proud of them, and of Scott too. You know they'll always love you, don't worry that that will ever change." Tears thickening her voice, she leaned in to kiss her sister's cheek. "Rest now. Love you, Rach." Straightening, she rose from the bed, wiped tears from her cheeks, then went to stand near the door, allowing Scott and the kids free access to the bed. One by one, they seated themselves in the place next to Rachel, spoke words of love and farewell, then, their own faces ravaged with tears, stood and waited uncertainly.

As they struggled to compose themselves, Tawnya spoke hesitantly, "Isn't Grandma coming?"

Scott's eyes met Celeste's, and the shared memory of Catherine's reaction Thursday afternoon passed between them. "What do you think, Cel? Should we give her a call? I thought for sure she'd be here."

"I'd have thought so too. I just don't know if I can do it, but I will. She deserves that much." Pulling the door open, she glanced back into the room, hoping to draw strength from those within. "I'll be right back."

She traveled the distance to the reception desk on shaky legs, heart filled with dread. Her mother...why wasn't she here? What hurtful words would she say to the daughter she'd cast from her life?

All too soon, she stood at the desk, dialing the number she'd known for thirty years, scarcely able to breathe for the anxiety that filled her. Finally, her mother's voice came across the wire. "Hello."

She drew a deep breath. "Mom?"

Silence, then her mother's voice, cold as ice, inquired, "Who is this?"

Tears flooded her eyes, even as frustration at her mother's obstinacy coursed through her. "Mom, it's Celeste. We're at Fircrest. We wanted to know...are you coming?"

Hostility rampant in every syllable, Catherine spat, "No, I certainly am not going to be a party to this...murder...you're about to commit. I, for one, will be able to face my Rachel in heaven, not to mention God above, with a clear conscience."

Closing her eyes, Celeste prayed that the Lord would soften her mother's heart, ease her pain. "Mom...you really should come see her now, before...well, it's just that this will be the last chance, and I know you'll be sorry if you don't. Please, Mom. We'll step out and give you privacy with Rach, but please come."

"You know nothing about how I feel, and you certainly don't care. No. You'll perform this abomination without my blessing, and may God have mercy on your souls, if it's right that He should."

With a distinct click, the line went dead, and with a shaking hand, Celeste returned the phone to the receptionist, murmured, "Thanks," then, with great weariness, returned to Rach's room.

Three voices asked, "Is she coming?"

Celeste shook her head, holding trembling fingers to her eyes. "No...no, she's...not coming. I tried to convince her, but..."

Scott nodded. The kids were aware of Thursday's nightmare session with their grandmother, of the way she'd banished her younger daughter from her home and life. They'd spoken at length about the situation, and he felt comfortable speaking honestly in their presence in this hour. "It's her choice, we can't force her to come, and I'm sorry that her bitterness is keeping her from being here today." He sighed heavily. "Well, are we ready? Shall we let them know?"

His eyes met those of each of his children in turn, then sought Celeste's. She nodded silently, and the look they shared bespoke sorrow, regret, and yet a sense of peace, of acceptance. Nothing they could do would sway Catherine's view of what was about to happen, and they'd done what they could.

It was time.

Scott pressed the call button, then stood back, gazing at the woman who'd captured an arrogant teenaged heart, held it safely in her hands, and ultimately helped to create the family they'd been. He touched her cheek, then smoothed the short dark hair with a gentle hand, fresh tears burning his eyes. "Rach..."

There was a quiet knock on the door, then an older man with tired eyes, dressed in a white medical jacket over a Sunday suit, entered the room, Rach's nurse following, clipboard at the ready. "Scott, kids. And Celeste. Are we expecting Catherine?" As heads shook "no," he sighed. "Ah, Catherine. I was hoping...Well. I'm just going to explain what will happen now. When you're ready, I'll remove the ventilator tube from Rachel's mouth. This is the tube that delivers oxygen to her lungs. After I disconnect the vent, it'll take a couple of minutes, then you'll see these numbers here," indicating the monitor, "start to drop, heart rate and oxygen saturation. There won't be any numbers for respirations, because the machine's been doing her breathing for her. It will happen pretty fast, but I won't lie to you and say it'll happen fast enough. It'll probably seem like hours, but in reality, maybe two, three minutes."

He paused, then asked, "Questions?" As each person indicated "no" by shaking of the head or speaking quietly, he continued, "Whenever you're ready, then."

Celeste, followed by Tawnya, then Tyler, said a final farewell, placed a final kiss on the silent woman's cheek, then Scott took his wife's hand. "Rest now, Rach. You're finally going home. I'm sorry I didn't have the strength to let you go sooner. I loved you, Rach, you'll always be a part of me." He lifted his free arm to blot the tears from his eyes. "Sleep now, Rach. Rest in God's peace."

He laid her hand gently on the bed, straightened and met the doctor's eyes, and gave silent permission to proceed, then stepped back to flank his children, hands gripping their own. The doctor and nurse worked efficiently, communicating in medical language understood only by themselves.

"Sat?"

"Ninety-eight percent, twenty-one percent FIo_2, PEEP of six."

"Disconnecting vent."

She glanced at her watch, then recorded the time on the form that lay on the clipboard. "Thirteen forty-four. Heart rate sixty-seven, normal sinus."

The doctor took his place at the bedside, removed the tape that held the ventilator tube to Rach's cheek, then grasped the tube in his hand, deflated the pouch, and removed the tube and port from her mouth. There was silence for a space of seconds, then the nurse spoke in a quiet voice, "Sat ninety-two and falling. Heart rate forty, junctional rhythm."

Dr. Schmick inclined his head toward the family. "Her oxygen level and heart rate are dropping. This will continue for another few minutes." At the sound of a choked sob, he spoke in a comforting voice, "She isn't in pain. The sensory receptors in her brain are part of what's already been destroyed. What you're seeing is simply the body systems shutting down. Remember that Rachel herself has been gone for a long time now. Vitals?"

"Sat twenty-six, heart rate sixteen. BP forty over palp."

The doctor held Rach's hand in his own, fingers pressed to her wrist. "It won't be long now."

Four pair of eyes turned to the monitors, waiting for what seemed like an eternity, unsure what would happen next. They didn't have to wait long. The monitors that measured heart rate and respirations continued to emit data, indicating that the values were steadily falling; 40...25...10. An electronic line of neon green squiggled across the screen, then disappeared, only to return as a straight line. *Flat line.* The monitor emitted a shrill alarm, which the nurse silenced with a flip of a switch.

Dr. Schmick held Rachel's hand for a moment longer, fingers at her wrist, then returned her hand to her side. "Time of death thirteen forty-seven."

It was done.

The doctor paused to speak words of consolation to each family member, then, followed by the nurse, exited the room, leaving them to spend a few final moments with Rachel.

Scott held his children in his arms, his tears mingling with theirs, as Celeste stood silently to the side, feeling conspicuously out of place, as though she were intruding on their grief. She crossed to the door and, after one last glance at her sister's body, slipped through the door and walked rapidly toward the reception area, gaining momentum with each step. By the time she reached the entry doors, she was nearly at a jog. It was suddenly crucial that she escape this place of death and sorrow, and with a feeling of great relief, she drew fresh autumn air into her lungs.

Oh, Rach...Mother, how could you not come? How could you not be here now?

She reached her car, hands pressed to her stomach, nearly strangling on the tears that slid down her face and fell to the asphalt below. Alone, she allowed herself the luxury of tears, purging herself of the salty knot that seemed to lodge in her throat. After a time, the knot eased, her tears slowed and she drew a ragged breath. Scott and the kids were just leaving the building, and she hastily wiped her eyes and tried to steady herself. As they approached, she realized that she needn't have worried; hers were not the only eyes swollen by tears, her voice not the only voice thickened by emotion. They moved slowly, and Celeste's tears freshened anew at the sight of their grief. When they'd reached the car, they stood together, shared embraces all around, and murmured words of comfort. Finally, Scott cleared his throat. "Well…"

Celeste nodded. "Come on, I'll drop you off at the church. I'm sure all you want at this point is to get home."

They rode in silence, each lost in their memories, but Celeste felt once more like an outsider, an intruder in this family's time of mourning. With everything in her, she wished that Scott would say, "Come out to the farm, Cel. Spend the day with us, you don't want to be alone today," even though she recognized the need for he and the kids to spend this day together, alone, processing what they'd witnessed and upholding each other in love.

After she'd turned into the parking lot and pulled alongside Scott's truck, she put the engine in park and turned sideways in the driver's seat. Three pairs of red, swollen eyes met her own, then with murmured goodbyes, the kids exited the backseat and Scott paused for a moment. "You gonna be okay, Celeste?"

Feeling anything but okay, she nodded. "Sure. What about you? Can I do anything for you? Cook supper…anything?" breath held, hoping…hoping. But he shook his head. "No, I think we're just gonna go on home, maybe try to get some sleep…none of slept very well last night. Thanks, though."

She nodded, feeling an ache in her chest that went above and beyond that caused by Rachel's passing. At that moment, she felt she had no family left, that not only Mother but even Scott and the kids were blind to her own pain, had left her to deal with her grief alone.

She'd never felt as alone in her life.

After they'd gone, she sat in her car until the sun began to fade in the sky. Finally, with nowhere else to go, she started the engine and made her way back to the apartment above the office, where Analiese waited. She'd feel better after she'd spoken to Ana, then perhaps this feeling of abandonment, of utter emptiness, would dissipate.

Where are You, God? Don't You care that I'm hurting so badly?

Throwing the car door open, she clutched her purse and, with great weariness, set her feet on the pavement. A new brittleness marked her movements, and beneath the pain, a sense of isolation etched her spirit.

What am I supposed to do now?

Digging for her key, she let herself into the office, stood uncertainly for a moment, then climbed the stairs to the apartment above.

Thank goodness for Ana. No matter that everyone else had abandoned her, she'd always have Analiese.

At least *someone* understood the concept of faithfulness. If she could count on no one else, she could count on Ana.

If Ana wanted to pray with her, fine; He sure seemed to have gone off-line as far as Celeste's own seeking of Him.

Dashing new tears from her eyes, she composed herself, then moved resolutely to the stairs. Her friend waited upstairs, and if there had ever been a time she'd needed a friend, it was today. Her only friend, the only one who truly cared for her.

Chapter 25

The October afternoon was blinding in its perfection. It was three days before Halloween and around Shuksan, scarecrows, ghosts, and jack-o-lanterns had appeared in yards and windows, while the unseasonably warm weather brought mourners to St. John's Lutheran Church in shirtsleeves, remarking among themselves that it was nice that Indian summer had stuck around long enough to send Rachel Parnell off in style. The day's crisp beauty barely registered with Celeste, and as she overheard some of the comments among those not among the family members, she supposed it was possible for someone not personally touched by grief to be able to give more than two seconds' thought to such matters. Those closest to the deceased had no energy for such banal observations.

There were no scarecrows marring the pristine grounds of the church proper, of course, but directly across the street, in the Hundabee yard, a fine specimen stood sentry. There hadn't been many adventures she'd been able to persuade Rachel to participate in, so the memory of their unprecedented prank on Alice's hapless scarecrow was all the more enjoyable for its rarity.

Alice was a large-bodied, formidable woman who monitored her property with the single-mindedness of a border patrol agent, forever on the alert for kids littering her front yard with pop cans or ice cream wrappers. She'd made a point of manning the rocker on her front porch during the half hour or so after school let out in the afternoons in order to keep an eye on any possible offenders and, as usual, had been sitting there on that late October afternoon that Celeste and Rach had passed by on their way home.

"Look," Celeste had hissed to Rach from behind her hand, *"She's*

got her underwear on the line in the backyard. Have you ever seen such a huge bra in your life?"

The grinning scarecrow holding court in the middle of the front lawn was adorned in an uninspired pair of suspender overalls and well-laundered red kerchief, and Celeste had decided he needed some sprucing up. She'd instructed Rachel to go up onto the porch and keep Alice occupied for a few minutes, called a greeting to the woman before telling Rach she'd see her at home, and then inched around the side of the house, opened the gate gingerly, and bee-lined to the wash line. Gadzook! The woman had panties (if you could even *call* them panties) the size of pup tents! She'd pulled a pair of "bloomers" and one hefty brassiere from the clothespins, stuffed them in her lunch box with a grimace, reminding herself that they *were* clean, after all. She'd let herself out through the gate, sidled to the edge of the porch, gave Rach the "all-clear," then made tracks for home.

Late that night, they'd snuck out after Mother was asleep, clutching a flashlight and alternately giggling and shushing each other. Once at Hundabee's, with Rach holding the flashlight, nervously swinging the beam around in every direction and hissing at her sister to hurry, Celeste had adorned the scarecrow in Alice's bra, stuffing the double-E cups with cotton batting she'd swiped from Mother's quilting supplies. She'd dealt with the panties next. Having anticipated some difficulty with this part of the process, she'd whipped out a pair of scissors and a couple of safety pins and dealt with the issue in short order. Finished at last, she'd produced a large piece of cardboard with the words, "Omar The Tentmaker Was Here," in large block letters, and propped it up against the scarecrow's wooden post.

The old scarecrow had enjoyed one night and a couple hours of daylight in his cross-dressing mode, until Alice had caught sight of him, screamed loud enough to set the neighborhood dogs to barking, and descended her front porch in robe and slippers, frantically tearing her abused undergarments free and, as rumor had it, kicked the "Omar Was Here" sign into the street in a gust of fury, where it had landed smack dab on Pastor Olson's windshield as he slowed to pull into the church parking lot.

Poor Alice had never figured out who the culprit was, and from that day forward, eyed all of the kids with equal suspicion, except Rachel Malloy, of course, because everyone knew *Rachel* would never do such a thing. It had been about five years before Alice's embarrassment and suspicion had diminished sufficiently to risk her scarecrow's appearance at Halloween again.

Celeste wondered what Alice's reaction would be if she were to confide that Rach had indeed been involved in the scarecrow debacle; she'd probably be the only thirty-five-year-old in history to receive a spanking on the day of her sister's funeral.

She spent a few minutes in the parking lot, receiving greetings and condolences. Flanked by Ana and Tori, she ascended the steps to the church, joined her mother, Scott, and the kids in the foyer and, finally, walked to the front row with the rest of her family, where they seated themselves quietly. The casket lay at the foot of the alter, the white roses draped over the gleaming mahogany, filling the air with their fragrance.

The church bell tolled three times and the final stragglers filled the pews as the minister took his place at the front of the church, and the liturgy began.

"In the name of the Father, and of the Son, and of the Holy Spirit."

"Amen."

Celeste followed the service in the hymnal, still feeling the urge to pinch herself, to force herself to accept that these words were being spoken, these songs sung, for Rach. The last three days had passed in a state of phantasm.

Scott had turned into a silent, pale stranger; the warmth and tenderness seemingly having been washed right out of him. The times they'd spent together, the moments that she'd believed were laying the groundwork for a relationship between them might never have happened; he'd holed up inside himself like a badger in its den.

And the kids, how were they holding up? They sat flanking Scott, hymnals in hand, Ty's face carefully devoid of expression, Tawnya's eyes puffy from tears.

"We have come today to celebrate the life of Rachel Catherine Malloy Parnell…"

The minister gave the eulogy, a brief synopsis of the life of a woman gone too soon from those who loved her, now safe in the hands of a loving God, speaking words intended to comfort those who grieved. "And God shall wipe away all tears from their eyes, and there shall be no more death, neither sorrow, nor crying, neither shall there be any more pain, for the former things are passed away" (Revelation 21:4, KJV).

Scott sat stiffly, his children, *Rach's children,* on each side, and numbly listened to the minister's voice but seeing, instead of the casket, the day they'd stood in the exact same spot and received God's blessing on their marriage. It had been a day much like today, their wedding day, and their lives had seemed to stretch out before them into infinity, into eternity even. *Until death do us part.* Grief, so intense he thought his heart would be pierced through, washed over him and his shoulders trembled with the force of the tears he struggled to subdue. Feeling his hands being grasped, held by his children, he squeezed their hands in return and surrendered, allowing the tears to fall freely.

The congregation rose and sang "Softly And Tenderly," the minister gave the benediction, then, as the church bell tolled mournfully, made the sign of the cross.

"Into Your Hands, O merciful Savior, we commend your servant, Rachel. Grant that she be received into blessed rest, everlasting peace, and into Your glorious company."

It was finished.

The congregation was ushered out, row by row, and finally the pallbearers appeared, bearing the casket. The bright afternoon sun was a sharp contrast after the protection of the church, and those who had shed tears inside shielded sensitive eyes against its brightness. Those who planned to accompany the family to the cemetery returned to their cars and joined the stream of vehicles that passed through Shuksan, past Fircrest and out of city limits, then up the hill to the cemetery. The service was brief, a prayer for the departed and one for her family, then the minister gave his final benediction. Rachel's children lay flowers upon the casket, Scott placed a hand on the sun-warmed wood, gathered Ty and Tawnya on either side for one last farewell, then guided his children away from the grave, indicating with a nod to the undertaker that his crew could proceed with the final interment.

There was a potluck meal hosted by the ladies of the church where the needs of the living were tended to, more condolences passed along, and finally it was time to go home, back to the quiet homes where Rachel's presence could still be felt. Catherine was surrounded by ladies from her quilting circle, Scott and the kids had presumably returned home.

Celeste had driven home to Ana's apartment, changed from her dress into sweats and a sweatshirt, then collapsed on the couch. Ana and Tori had attended the service at the church but not the graveside service, and she assumed Ana was busy in the office below. Tori, too, was gone; the apartment was silent.

A wave of exhaustion rolled over her. She hadn't been sleeping well, partly due to the fact that the couch was too short for her long legs, but mostly due to stress and emotional overload. Pulling an afghan over herself, she slept, waking several hours later to the comforting aroma of something bubbling in the Dutch oven on the stove top.

Ana glanced up from her position in front of the stove, lay a spoon on the counter, and wiped her hands on a dish towel. Concern evident in voice and eyes, she came to sit next to Celeste. "How you doing, Cel?"

Shaking her head in a vain attempt to dislodge the cobwebs, Celeste yawned. "My gosh, I can't believe I slept like that. What time is it, anyway?"

"Six-thirty. You hungry?"

With surprise, she realized that for the first time in over a week, she actually did feel hungry. "Yeah, starving. Something smells good."

Ana nodded toward the stove. "Vegetable soup and tuna-melts. Come on, let's get something into your tummy."

Celeste moved toward the table, stretching cramped muscles. "Where's Tori?"

"Oh, she's downstairs on the computer, doing some research for homework. She'll be up shortly. Come on, now, eat while it's hot."

Celeste seated herself, leaned over the steaming bowl before her, and inhaled deeply. "This smells divine. Thank you, Ana. One of these nights I'm going to surprise you and actually cook."

"Lemme guess, oatmeal and cinnamon toast?"

Celeste snorted, feeling the beginnings of a smile tug at the corners of her mouth. "You're never going to let me live that down, are you? Come on, it was only once, and you have to admit it hit the spot, right?"

"That it did. Although it still cracks me up to be invited over for supper and be served up oatmeal!"

"What can I say? April fifteenth was three days away! You can't tell me you do a lot of cooking right before tax deadline?"

Ana chuckled. "No, I guess not. Seriously, though, when it comes to oatmeal, I don't think I've ever had any that tasted better. Ah, there we go!"

At Celeste's questioning gaze, Ana shrugged her shoulders. "You're smiling. That's what I wanted to see. How're you really feeling? Be honest, now."

"Oh, I don't know, Ana. I guess I'm feeling more grounded now, maybe the fact that it's actually over, the funeral, everything…I guess I'm still feeling like a cast-out, you know…like I've lost all the family I have and I'm totally alone."

Ana shook her head. "I can't get over your mama; all of that bitterness and anger."

"I think she's been carrying it around for a lot of years, Ana; she's one of those people who aren't happy unless there's something to be upset about. I mean, now she has Rach's death to add to her arsenal. I don't think she's ever going to be truly happy."

"Pray for her, Cel. Seriously. I know how much she hurt you, but I think you have to forgive her before you can ever move on."

Celeste laid her spoon beside her bowl, appetite suddenly gone. "I haven't done anything *wrong,* Ana! That's what hurts the most, the fact that she could say those things to me in the first place! I mean, I'm not Rach, but doesn't she care about me at all?"

Ana reached a hand to cover Celeste's. "Sure, she cares about you, Cellie. She's just not thinking straight right now. But hear me now—this is your chance to demonstrate God's grace to Catherine, forgive like *you've* been forgiven. I think she's so bitter she's just plain lost sight of Him."

"I don't think I can do it, Ana."

"Not by yourself, Cellie. That's why Jesus went to the cross, 'cause none of us can do it by ourselves."

They continued their meal in silence, then carried their bowls and plates to the sink. Ana transferred the remainder of the soup into a large plastic container and slid the Dutch oven into the sink, filling it with water. "So, what's on the agenda tonight?"

Celeste paused at the refrigerator and closed the door. "Nothing. I can't stop thinking about Scott and the kids, but I just don't feel like they want me around."

"Make you feel bad?"

"Like you wouldn't believe."

Ana slid a pair of rubber gloves onto her hands and began to scrub the soup pot.

"You could always call out there, see how everyone's doing."

"They have my cell number. If they want me, they know how to dial the phone."

Ana refrained from comment, peeled off her gloves and rinsed and dried her hands. "Well, I'm going to get off my feet. If that girl ever gets done down there, she can zap herself some soup. The kitchen's officially closed." Flipping off the light switch, she followed Celeste into the living room and dropped onto the sofa with a huge sigh, piling her feet onto the coffee table. "Girl? Would you be offended if I got into my comfies?"

"Are you kidding? Go for it."

As Ana's bedroom door closed behind her, Celeste sat alone, thoughts returning again to her sister's family alone in the old farmhouse. *What could it hurt to just take a quick run out there, check in on everybody, maybe hang out awhile?* After a few minutes of debating with herself, she grabbed a pair of jeans from where she'd stashed them behind the couch and skimmed out of her sweats and into the jeans. After sliding her feet into her favorite running shoes, she ran a brush through her hair and called it good. She wasn't worried about impressing anyone tonight.

She knocked lightly on Ana's door. "I'm going out to the farm. Be back later." Grabbing her purse and keys, she locked the door behind herself and made her escape.

The drive to the farm was a challenge. A thick fog had descended, and she had to slow to negotiate the winding road, peering intently over the Expedition's steering wheel into the murky night air. There were the mailboxes, she was almost there. She slowed further still, turned off the county road onto Scott's gravel access road, and followed it to the house.

The house was dark except for a small light in Ty's room; Tawnya's room was dark, as were all the downstairs rooms. Celeste shifted into park and turned off the engine, wondering what to do next. If everyone was in bed, she didn't want to barge in and wake them, but she couldn't imagine they'd be sleeping yet. Not on this night. As she debated, she saw a light in the barn. Could it be Scott, trying to find some busywork to keep his hands and mind occupied? If Ty was in his room, that ruled him out, and she couldn't imagine Tawnya being out there at this hour. Deciding to take her chances, she left the Expedition, picking her way carefully across the barnyard, through the damp fog that left droplets of moisture clinging to her hair and lashes. She'd nearly reached the barn when Scott's voice traveled through the darkness, "Celeste? That you?"

"It's me."

Leaning against the barn door without moving a muscle, he asked, "What brings you out in this fog?"

He certainly wasn't going out of his way to be welcoming. Deciding that he was probably just surprised that she'd shown up without calling first, she replied, "I just wanted to see how all of you were doing, and I guess I didn't want to be alone tonight either."

He stood silently for a moment, then shifted his weight off of the door and sighed. "Come on inside, it's not much warmer but at least it's dry."

He held the door and, after she passed through, followed her in and let the door close behind him. Leaving her standing near the door, he walked to the first stall and heaved himself up to sit on the ledge, legs dangling nearly to the floor. Celeste hugged herself and shivered. "Guess the weather's finally turning, huh?"

He was silent for a moment, then in a flat tone, he asked, "We aren't really going to discuss the weather, are we?"

For all of the times they'd used the weather as a segue into deeper conversations, recognized the ploy for what it was and been able to laugh about it, tonight there was no humor in the question. His eyes were dark and shadowed, his voice dull, and she thought she recognized the Scott he'd been months before when she'd re-entered his life. There had been such a transformation in his spirit, in his life, and on this night, she saw none of the inner light that had burned so brightly in him.

"Are you okay, Scott?"

She barely recognized his voice, shot through with sarcasm. "Oh, I'm in great shape, Celeste! Couldn't be better! Other than burying my wife today, it was just a typical Wednesday."

Unsure how to respond, she said nothing.

Scott lowered himself from his perch and leaned his back against the stall. "Why did you come, Celeste?"

Taken aback, she replied, "Well, I…I wanted to be with you; I've missed you. We haven't had a chance to talk since the other night. I've been concerned about you, how you're getting along, how the kids are doing. I'm getting I get the feeling you're mad at me. Are you?"

He shook his head. "Mad at you? No."

"Somehow I don't believe you. What is it, Scott? Can't you talk to me?"

He asked abruptly, "Are you sorry she's gone, or are you relieved?"

"Well, of course I'm sorry, but it's also a relief, too, knowing that she isn't suffering anymore."

He nodded. "That's what I figured you'd say. That's what *everybody* says." He pushed himself off the stall and began to move slowly through the barn, hands on his hips, then eyed her directly. "But are *you* sorry?"

The emotion lying so close to the surface bubbled over and she exclaimed, "Well, of course I'm sorry, Scott, what do you think? You're acting like Mother; like this was all *my* idea so I could put the move on you!"

The moment the words had left her mouth, she regretted them, but it was too late to call them back. They stood with rigid spines, then Scott rubbed his hands over his face. Not meeting her eyes, he crossed his arms over his chest. "Am I? I'm sorry you feel that way."

"I don't know who you are tonight."

With a mirthless smile, he raised his hands in the air, then let them fall to his side. "Just me, that's all I know to be."

"You're not anyone I know right now."

He turned his back to her, reached up to straighten a bridle hanging lopsided on a hook, then turned to face her again. "No, you're probably right about that. I don't know myself right now. But I do know that this…thing…between us isn't going anywhere. We're just fooling ourselves if we think otherwise." He wiped dusty hands on his jeans. "I'm sorry, Celeste. I guess I'm just not in the market for another woman right now."

In the market? As though she were a commodity that could be purchased or sold? The hurt spreading through her was cold and clear as shards of ice. Speaking past the painful lump in her throat, voice thick with tears, she said, "I thought you wanted to be with me as much as I wanted to be with you. That's part of the reason I came home, so we could be together."

He leveled a gaze at her. "I never asked you to come home, Celeste, that was your choice, your call. I never made any promises, any commitments to you."

She shook her head. "No, you didn't. But I thought…well, obviously I was wrong. Can't you see? I'm not trying to replace Rachel, Scott. I thought what we had together was our own, that it wasn't about Rachel."

"How can anything between us not be about Rachel? You think that every time I look at you, I don't see a bratty kid tagging along after her big sister? Now, I appreciate everything you've done for Tawnya, and for being there for me the last few months, but there is no us. Just isn't gonna happen."

He may as well have taken a dagger to her heart as say the words that hung heavily between them. How could she have misread the situation by such a margin? Would there ever be a time that this pain wouldn't dominate every cell in her body?

She drew in a shaky breath. "What did I do wrong? Just tell me! All I tried to do was care about you!"

"And I appreciate it. But now…Just go home, Celeste. Go on ahead with your life and let me get on with mine."

She nodded. "Home. That's an interesting thought. I don't have a home, Scott, or have you forgotten? My relationship with you destroyed the one I had with my mother, and now I realize there wasn't really anything between us anyway! Thanks, Scott. I wish I could say it's all been worth it!"

She turned to leave, then paused and met his eyes. "You aren't the only person who lost Rach, you know. You aren't the only person who's hurting."

Turning again toward the barn door, she spoke quietly. "Tell the kids they can call anytime."

She was halfway to the door when Scott spoke.

"Celeste…"

She paused without turning to face him.

He struggled for a moment, then said, "Nothing. For what it's worth, I'm sorry."

Without replying, she pulled open the barn door and slipped through, leaving the door open behind herself. A moment later, he heard her engine start up and watched from the open door as the Expedition rounded the barn and disappeared into the night.

That was that.

His conscience gave his heart a sharp jab. *You really are a piece of work, Parnell; did you see the look in her eyes?*

"Well, I'm sorry I hurt her, but I'm hurting, too!"

You're hurting because you ended up loving her more than Rachel in the end, and you were determined to punish her for it.

"That's baloney. I'm not punishing anybody."

Punishing Celeste for your own feelings and lying to yourself, to boot.

"Shut up! Just leave me alone and let me mourn my wife!"

Fine, go on and mourn Rachel, that's your privilege and your obligation. But at least be honest with yourself if you couldn't be honest with Celeste. She hasn't done anything wrong, remember? You're transferring your guilt onto her and making her the whipping boy!

The barn cats ranged around the stalls, peering at him in curiosity, and he realized he'd been shouting, battling with his conscience. His throat was raw but the pressure in his chest had eased just a little. He eyed the cats and muttered, "Whaddaya looking at?" He stalked to the barrel that held the dry cat food, filled the scoop that lay inside, and emptied it into their bowl. He replaced the scoop in the barrel, fastened the lid securely, then switched off the light and closed the barn door behind himself.

It was almost pitch-black outside, which suited his mood to a tee; he was feeling pretty dark inside. He walked to the house, intent on spending the night in his recliner, waiting for daylight to lighten the sky.

His solitary prayer was one of anguish and a spirit in turmoil.

Help me, Lord. I'm coming apart, here. I can't bring myself to thank You for anything tonight, God. Just please...help me.

But no peace was forthcoming this night, and in the bleakness of his pain, he wondered if it would ever come again.

Chapter 26

*S*he survived those first days following the funeral by shutting down emotionally, existing in a fog of self-preservation that matched the fog that blanketed the valley day and night for over a week. Ten days later, the autumn winds whistled down from the mountains, clearing the air and sending the last of the dead leaves dancing from the trees. As though the weather outside had signaled that it was time for Celeste, as well, to emerge from the lassitude in which she'd enveloped herself, she awoke one morning feeling that she might actually survive after all. It had been two weeks since Rach's funeral, two weeks since that final scene in the barn. She hadn't seen Scott, hadn't seen the kids. And she'd had her hands full with Mother. In the words of Agnes, one of Mother's long-time neighbors, she hadn't come around, *bounced back,* after the funeral, and the neighbors were concerned. It wasn't as though Mother was physically incapable of dressing herself and attending to her daily activities; she evidently just didn't care to be bothered. She hadn't even been to church, which was a pretty huge red flag.

Several of the ladies from Mother's quilting circle had tried to visit a few days after the funeral, but Mother had flatly refused to open the door, and the ladies had finally returned to their cars and departed.

But the social isolation wasn't the worst of it. Agnes had called again to report that Mother had decided that it was time to plant her garden and nothing she could say would dissuade her. Upon hearing this, Celeste had garnered her courage, left work, and driven to her mother's house. With great foreboding, she had watched her mother struggle with wheelbarrow and gardening tools, attempting to dig rows in the near-frozen earth, rows of dry cornstalks rustling in the wind as she labored.

She'd called Mother's long-time primary care doctor, who had come to the house and performed an extensive evaluation. After he completed his examination, he recommended that Catherine be hospitalized for neurological testing.

"I think we're seeing an acute situational depression, but I'm concerned about some component of dementia as well."

Mother had spent three days in the hospital, had MRI and CT scans of her brain, as well as a lumbar puncture and, in the end, had been diagnosed with a stress-induced dementia; none of the tests had shown anything organic—a medical explanation such as Alzheimer's or even a brain tumor—to explain her behavior. It had been the social worker's opinion that Mother needed full-time care, more care than Celeste could provide, and at their recommendation, Celeste had signed the paperwork at Fircrest and Mother was ensconced just three doors down the hall from where Rachel had lived out her last months.

She'd visited Mother every day, and yesterday had left in tears for her mother had laid in her bed and prayed aloud for death.

She'd left the building, walked to the Expedition under heavy gray clouds, feeling once more that she'd lost her mother.

There existed no medical therapy that could help someone who believed, simply and irrevocably, that her only hope of happiness lay in the next life. Her issue wasn't with Mother's unshakable faith in God's promise of eternal joy, but with the fact that she'd seemingly given up on life here on earth.

Now, with Mother incapacitated, it had fallen to Celeste to deal with the insurance business, fielding calls from clients, explaining to the home office in Spokane why deadlines weren't being met, and having no clue of what to do about the whole mess. The ringing of the telephone brought instantaneous panic, because chances were better than not that it was an insurance call, one that she was ill-equipped to deal with; certainly there were few enough calls that came in for Celeste personally.

With Mother at Fircrest, she'd returned to the house. If, when Mother was stronger and had regained clear thought processes, she still wished the estrangement to continue, Celeste would take a room at the Tall Pines Motel down on Main Street until something else came along. For now, she'd care for the house and try to come to some solution for the insurance business.

By Thanksgiving week, she was about as low emotionally as she'd ever imagined possible, and the slightest stressor sent her over the edge into tears. The practice was building up steam and more days than not she actually had an appointment with a client. This, at least, brought some relief. After the funeral, several of Bill's former clients had decided to trust her with their business, and she knew that her performance on behalf of these first of Shuksan's brave souls would make or break her in the eyes of those who were still undecided about whether to trust "Ed Malloy's girl" with their financial well-being.

The pressure was intense, both external and internal. It would have been stressful enough had it just been the practice she was dealing with, but worrying about Mother's situation, combined with dealing with insurance issues in addition to coming to terms with Rach's death, she felt as though she were stretched as thin as a piano wire. Scott's defection lay heavy on her heart when she allowed herself to think of that night in the barn.

In the dark hours of those chilly autumn nights, alone in her childhood bed, she struggled with her pain and alternated between prayers asking for strength and comfort in her moments of greatest pain to moments of anger at God.

Why hast Thou forsaken me?

Underlying everything else were thoughts of Scott, not the person she thought she'd come to know, but a stranger who'd blockaded himself from her in every way possible. He hadn't called, though she hadn't really expected him to. A glimmer of hope had remained, although it was dimming as the days, then weeks, passed without contact.

He didn't want her. End of story. It hurt like nothing had hurt before.

How could she have been so wrong about their relationship? And where, if the love that had seemingly grown between them had been of God, was He now?

Lord, it all hurts so badly. Please make Yourself known to me...I need You...

Outside, the wind whistled through the bare branches of the old sycamore tree. Tomorrow was Thanksgiving, and she'd be spending it with Ana and Tori here in her childhood home. They were going to do up a proper Thanksgiving feast with all the trimmings, and Celeste had debated whether to ask Tori if Tawnya had said anything about their own Thanksgiving plans. She'd decided it wasn't fair to put Tori on the spot, and, in the end, had said nothing.

It wasn't too late. She could always call and invite them for dinner, if only for the kids' sakes, but the memories were too fresh, the pain too close to the surface, and she dismissed the idea.

Tomorrow would be a good day, just the three of them, and in keeping with a Malloy family tradition, she would find five things that she was thankful for, write them down, and put the list on the refrigerator. Every time she passed by the fridge, she'd be reminded of those five blessings. She was coming to realize that even through the pain that had ripped her world apart, she was truly blessed in so many ways. How many families in the war-torn Middle East and parts of Africa had no roof over their heads this holiday season, no resources or jobs, and little hope for their future? Her mother had always counseled she and Rachel to remember that no matter how bad things seemed, there was always someone else whose troubles were greater.

Help me, Lord, to see through Your eyes, to not let me become so caught up in my own problems that I fail to recognize the pain of others.

Like a giant cedar felled in a windstorm, everything had just come crashing down around her, and she'd been overwhelmed. Instead of turning to God for comfort and guidance, she'd "leaned onto her own understanding," and that was where the train had jumped the track. Looking back on that few days leading up to Rachel's death, she understood that she'd been stricken with fear, the kind of fear that lives so deeply inside a person that it can't be elucidated, can't be shared aloud with others. She'd been overcome by fear so devastating that God seemed so distant that He'd become unapproachable.

The reality of Rach's coming death, compounded by her mother's emotional and physical abandonment, had created a hurt deeper than she could have imagined. Like a wounded animal, she had retreated into a dark corner, unwilling, even unable to reach out for help.

She'd surrendered to her pain and forgotten that her Heavenly Father waited patiently to share her tears, to listen, and to comfort. What did this say about her faith? Was she just one more person who believed in God as long as it was convenient to do so? Was her faith flimsy enough to be shaken as soon as trouble arrived?

Forgive me, Father. How could I have allowed myself to drift so far from You?

Her inner darkness hadn't completely given way to light, but she again had hope and renewed faith that Someone cared completely and was ever by her side.

She said a quick prayer of thanksgiving, then proceeded to record the remainder of this year's list of blessings; a growing, thriving business, a faithful friend, and the promise of her new home on the lake. Most importantly, the realization that true happiness lay in letting go of those things that were obviously not meant to be, trusting that God had paved a path for her, and that He held the compass. All that was required of her was to simply *trust* that He would guide her along that path.

Thank You, Lord. Help me to discover my purpose, the reason You've led me back to Shuksan. You've brought me this far; help me to trust You to finish what You've begun in my life. Amen.

Chapter 27

The worst thing about winter, in Scott's opinion, other than the weather itself, and aside from the fact that there was no income generated during those long months, had to be the boredom, the isolation. He typically spent November performing repairs on the combine, thrasher, and baler, and once the machinery had been tuned up, belts replaced, and any other problems dealt with, he could rest easy that his work was done for another season. This year, when the last wrench had been replaced in the tool box, instead of the quiet satisfaction he usually felt at the end of another year's labor, he felt only hollowness inside. He spent a few days cleaning the barn, removing the old straw and replacing it with new, the final words he'd exchanged with Celeste ringing in his ears. He'd shaken his head in frustration and worked harder yet, determined to forget their last exchange here in this very barn on that painful night.

But he missed her. The last weeks following Rach's death had been spent grieving, and not just for the loss of his wife. In the dark hours of night when he lay in bed and explored his innermost thoughts, he mourned the loss of his relationship with Celeste; yet another casualty, just one more thing that had died.

It didn't help to admit that if it was dead, it was because he had performed the kill.

Regrets were a dime a dozen, though, and sometimes it seemed as though he'd gone into hock for the next ten years spending those dimes; regret for his inability to deal with Rach's situation for so long, regret for the mistakes he'd made with the kids, of holding himself apart emotionally from them and, finally, regret for his treatment of Celeste.

Those dimes spilled through the coin-counter in his head, falling in perfect symmetry to form ever-growing stacks of heartache and feelings of inadequacy, of failure. The kids were hanging tough, and his relationship with them continued to grow and solidify, and he gave thanks daily for this. There were occasional setbacks, but those were to be expected; they were teenagers, after all.

He had no such excuse for his foul mood; the days of hormonal fluctuations were a good thirty years behind him. Still, most days he felt as though true happiness had bypassed him, or that perhaps he'd already lived those days when Rach was healthy and the biggest worries they had were keeping the bills paid and the kids in shoes.

At those times, he was reminded of those months during the summer and early fall, when his relationship with Celeste had blossomed, and he'd experienced a completeness and a promise of happiness he'd believed would never come again. At the end of the day, he wondered what the point had been, why he'd allowed himself to be drawn into something he had no business being a part of. But it had felt so right, and all of his prayers concerning his feelings for Celeste had brought such a sense of peace and rightness. What, then, had gone wrong?

In those days of early winter, one day passing quietly into the next, he had a great deal of time to reflect upon the situation, plenty of time to rake himself over the coals.

He hated this idleness and the cold weather that brought an end to the long, exhausting summer days, days in which physical fatigue led to nights of uninterrupted sleep. He'd come to *need* those physical demands over the past few years; it had become his pattern, and now, prevented from working himself into utter exhaustion, he felt displaced and unsettled.

Of course, there were other things contributing to this restlessness, and the knowledge that he was in way over his head only added to his tension. For the first time, he was truly on his own as far as the kids were concerned, for with Catherine out of the picture, everything had fallen to him. He'd appreciated her help, but in an abstract way; he'd never really realized all she'd done to help keep things on an even keel. Helping with grocery shopping, making sure the kids had new clothes when they needed them, even helping to raise the kids over the years, all of these things were glaringly apparent now that she wasn't there to help fill in the gaps any longer.

Another dime for the count; his sadness over Catherine's deteriorating mental status and the fact that he feared he'd never properly expressed his appreciation and heartfelt gratitude for her involvement in their lives over the years. Now she'd slipped into a place in which no one could reach her any longer, not himself, not the kids. They'd gone to Fircrest to visit, a painful irony after the months spent visiting Rachel in the same place, and had come away feeling that they'd lost yet another member of the family. Catherine had lost any will to survive, had simply given up, and in doing so, had pulled another brick from the already crumbling mortar of the kids' lives.

They'd experienced too much loss in too short a time, and he couldn't blame them for wondering if there was any stability left in their lives. He understood and accepted that there would be some stress, some acting out, while they came to terms with those losses and the changes they would represent in their lives. What he hadn't expected was that, for all appearances, he'd be the one with the greatest adjustment issues.

The kids were doing amazingly well, and he placed all credit for this squarely in the Lord's hands. They were both experiencing amazing "God-moments" in their lives, and he was both humbled and inspired by the strength of their faith and their unshakeable commitment to Him.

And then there was Celeste.

Of all of the issues he'd come to face in the last weeks, his feelings for her and the breakdown of their relationship were the ones left unresolved. He'd tried to put the whole situation out of his mind, but it seemed that she was always there with him. They'd created memories during their time together, and those were the images that appeared with annoying regularity, and he acknowledged that if it had only been a transitory thing, he wouldn't still be suffering like this.

He'd thought of calling her many times, just to hear her voice, just to say, "Hey, I've been wondering how you're doing," but when all was said and done, he was embarrassed by and ashamed of his behavior, of the things he'd said to her that night. If he was having a hard time forgiving himself, he could only imagine how much harder it must be Celeste, who'd done nothing to deserve his poor treatment of her.

But he missed her.

He'd hoped that she'd put the first foot forward at Thanksgiving, maybe invite he and the kids to dinner, and he'd practically camped by the phone up until Thanksgiving morning, when he finally accepted that she wasn't going to call. They hadn't had much of a Thanksgiving, and he felt bad about it, but deep down he'd thought that they'd end up having dinner with Celeste, Ana, and Tori, and so hadn't given much thought to their own meal.

Tuna sandwiches and tomato soup; how 'bout them apples? A Thanksgiving to remember, and one he'd prefer to forget. The kids had seemed to take it in stride, but the whole situation just served to remind him of how hopeless he was at the day-to-day business of parenting; planning meals, grocery shopping, all of it. These things had always been capably dealt with by other hands, first Catherine's, then later by Connie Ripley's, and it didn't escape him now that his role as father was again, still, evolving.

Well, he was doing his best, wasn't he? Who'd have thought that something that seemed as straightforward as laundry came with its own set of rules? What could be easier than dumping clothes in the washer, adding a scoop of detergent, and turning on the water? But no, it seemed there was more to it than met the eye. Whites with whites, colors with colors, and absolutely never greasy coveralls with the kids' school clothes. He could've sworn the chickens had gotten into the house that day; feathers had certainly flown and there had been some unmistakable squawking, but there had been a silver lining regardless; neither Ty nor Tawnya would let him touch their dirty clothes. So now he just took care of his own, and if his underwear was turning a dingy gray from being washed with blue jeans, so be it. He could live with that.

He had a healthy sense of the ridiculous and wasn't too stiff-necked to laugh at himself on occasion, and these were among the times he missed Celeste the most. She had a rather pithy sense of humor that had meshed well with his own. They'd been able to *laugh* together, and he missed their shared mirth; she'd brought the laughter back into his life.

One thing was sure, and that was that Celeste knew how to *live* her life, never hesitating to extract every last drop of marrow from the bare bones of her life with the courage and tenacity to take on new challenges, new risks. Leaving her job in Seattle to take over a small-town firm, knowing full well she'd never stand a chance to make the kind of money she was looking at as partner in her old firm. He didn't know of many men, or women, who'd consider it an even trade and walk away from that kind of financial security, regardless of how they felt about their job.

But that was Celeste; bold in action when led by what she believed was God's path for herself, willing to take risks when the payoff was something she deemed of value, and with a loyal and loving heart.

If there'd ever been a time that he'd counted on that heart being loyal enough, loving enough, to override her better judgment, it was now.

His failing, he knew now, had been fear of a future he'd only recently been able to contemplate; the fear that his feelings for her had been a betrayal of Rachel. Fear of financial ruin, fear for the kids and their unknown Huntington's status, and finally, fear that his feelings for Celeste would arm her with the power to ultimately hurt him when he feared the prospect of more emotional pain above all else.

He'd recognized a slow slide back into his state of estrangement from God and, tears slipping down his cheeks, had come to a moment of full surrender, alone on his knees in the barn on a snowy December afternoon.

He laid everything out before God; his feelings of guilt both on Rachel's behalf, as well as Celeste's, his fear that he'd cheated both women out of the commitment he'd shared with one, yet longed to offer the other.

Forgive me, Lord.

He confessed his inadequacies as a parent, the fear that had kept him immobile and distant from his children when they'd needed him so badly.

Forgive me, Lord. Guide me, show me how to be there for them now.

Finally, he lay his love for Celeste and his shame at his treatment of her at God's feet.

Father, what have I done? Is it too late for us? Lord, if it was Your Hand that brought us together, please help me to find the courage, the words, to make things right again. If it's even possible. I love her, Lord. I can finally admit it. I love her.

The words of Jeremiah came once again to him, and he held tightly to their promise. "For I know the plans I have for you, plans to prosper you and not to harm you, plans to give you hope and a future." *I have given you the promise of life eternal, Scott; now I grant you the peace to make a promise of your own. A new promise.*

The wind howled outside the wooden structure, and he remained on his knees, there among the cats and horses, until he felt renewal of spirit and of hope. Wincing at the discomfort in his knees, he rose to his feet and hobbled the few steps to the cat food bin, filled their bowl, then threw fresh hay to the horses. Wrestling the heavy barn door open, he pulled his collar tightly around his neck, then paused in the doorway, remembering the peace he'd been granted at the moment of surrender. There had been nothing in his life to compare with that moment of grace, and he knew deep in his heart that the Lord walked with him, whatever storms overtook him in this life.

Thank You, Lord. Create in me a clean heart, God. Make me a mirror of Your grace, and help me to be the man You would have me be.

He started toward the house to physical warmth and security knowing that today and for the rest of his life true security occurred at the moment of surrender. In that moment of admitting vulnerability came acceptance and promise of forgiveness and grace. It was a lesson he would carry with him the remainder of his days on earth, and one that would enable him to open the door that led to Celeste's heart.

Walk with me, Lord. Help me to find the right words, the words that will tell her how much I love her. Let Thy will be done. Amen.

Chapter 28

*C*hristmas Eve was bitterly cold, just one more day in a two-week stretch of unseasonably frigid weather for the Cascade Mountain Range in December. The Weather Channel and King-5 News out of Seattle inundated viewers with satellite images of the jet stream, sweeping arctic air into the Pacific Northwest from Alaska, informing their audience that these were the lowest recorded temperatures on record for the month of December since 1925. Dressed in her warmest sweats, curled up in the corner of her mother's couch, Celeste huddled under a heavy quilt and contemplated the Christmas Eve candlelight service she'd attended earlier. The prospect of going out into air so cold that it quite literally hurt to breathe had served to dim her resolve; the fact that she'd promised to drive Mother's car to church didn't inspire a lot of confidence in herself, or the car. A 1962 bottle-green Cadillac with the requisite fins gracing the rear panels, she and Rach had dubbed her the Batmobile in their childhood, and the Batmobile she remained to this day. For about the thousandth time, Celeste wondered why her mother had not only held onto the old relic all these years, but refused to replace it, gas hog that it was. Gas hog or not, the Caddy occupied the place of honor in the immaculate garage and, Celeste suspected, in Mother's heart, as well.

Whoever had said that beauty was in the eye of the beholder must have had Mother's long-standing love affair with the Batmobile in mind.

At any rate, the car hadn't been driven for two months, and no amount of coaxing had induced the engine to turn over. Mother had expressed concern about the car when Celeste had visited earlier that afternoon, and the fact that Mother had had the presence of mind to worry about her beloved Batmobile had heartened and encouraged Celeste. This was the first time Catherine had indicated any interest in the trappings of her life, and Celeste assured her mother that she'd drive the car that very night, if it would start. Surely this was a positive sign with the hope of more to follow; the insurance agent within the woman herself would want to make sure her car was being well-maintained. Celeste also promised that she'd get the car in for a tune-up after the first of the year, as well.

She'd have promised pretty much anything in that moment of hope and had come away from Fircrest with lighter spirits and, for the first time this year, a true sense of Christmas within her heart.

The weeks she'd spent alone in her childhood home had been a time of reflection, of looking at old photo albums, when Mother and Daddy had been the age she was now, continuing through she and Rach's formative years. She'd touched wistful fingertips to fading photographs of Halloween costumes, Easter dresses, and footy-pajama-clad Christmas mornings. She had rummaged through Mother's cedar chest and found other memorabilia from their childhood that must have been especially precious to Mother; bronzed baby shoes, Rach's and her own, tiny dresses of velvet and lace, and two plastic bags containing locks of baby hair from first haircuts—one corn-silk blonde, the other of satiny black curls. She'd held Mother's memories in her hands and recognized mother-love. In the days and weeks that followed, she'd come to believe in and accept the fact of her mother's love, as evidenced by this collecting of memories, and to reexamine her childhood with an open mind and open heart. At last, acceptance had come.

She'd been loved. *Was* loved. It wasn't, perhaps, the same love that Mother had shared with Rachel, but had been love nonetheless. She'd heard it said that a mother loves none of her children in exactly the same way, that each child is unique and the love is as well. She had a better understanding of this now, and with understanding came peace; with peace came an acceptance of her own value, her own *worth,* as a daughter and a sister.

With these things came forgiveness, of her mother for her hurtful words and, finally, forgiveness of Scott for his seemingly easy obliteration of her dreams for their future together.

This, perhaps, had been the hardest to relinquish, and the pain was still there when she allowed herself to think of him and what might have been. But in the end, what had he really done but love his wife? It was hard to fault him for that, much as it hurt to face it straight-on. When she'd asked herself whether she might have reacted differently had the wife involved been anyone but Rach, she'd had to admit that the first degree of separation, Rachel being that one degree, hadn't allowed her the distance to fully appreciate the natural process of grief that Scott had been experiencing. So that had been one more thing to forgive, and she was still working on this one; the forgiveness of herself for her resentment at Rachel's coming between she and Scott, even from the grave.

She'd been appalled, then disgusted, with the part of herself that would be angry at a dead woman for the fact that her husband still loved her.

As hard as some dreams died, and this one ranked right up there with the best of them, it was time to let him go too. She'd been working toward acceptance of this and had been making slow, steady progress, but tonight reality had smote her between the eyes and directly in the heart. She'd survived thirty-five years without him; surviving, even thriving, over the next however many years shouldn't be an impossible feat.

It was time to focus her attention and energies on those coming years, starting with the new year just around the corner; the new firm, her new house on the lake, and on acceptance of God's ultimate plan for her. Perhaps He would bring love into her life again, perhaps not. She had finally come to a place where she could accept His will in this, and the lonely longing that had been with her for so long had finally been quieted in her heart. Instead, she was filled with celebration of the birth of the Christ Child, who brought shining new hope to all who searched for that elusive *something* to make their lives complete.

There was no tree standing next to the fireplace this year, no freshly-baked goodies waiting to be consumed, and no turkey thawing in the refrigerator, but for Celeste, Christmas had come. New hope had come.

Tomorrow she'd visit Mother, then take a drive out to the lake and work on the site plan for the new house and decide where to install the dock. Come summer, there would be a paddleboat waiting for the girls. There would be starlit summer nights spent lying on the gently swaying dock. There would be crickets and frogs, the song of coyotes, and the sharp tang of pine in the air. And there would be peace in her life and in her heart.

She'd spend the afternoon with Ana and Tori, celebrating Christmas in their tiny apartment, gathered around their tree, enveloped in their love.

With these simple things, she would be content. For now, Christmas had come, and with it, peace. For Celeste, there could be no greater gift.

Chapter 29

They'd had a tree this year, and the kids had had several gifts each under that tree. There had even been a couple under the tree for Scott, and he'd gotten a good chuckle from the silly socks the kids had wrapped up for him. Plastic google-eyes above puffy yellow-balled noses and individual toes in a variety of hues, they were the craziest socks he'd ever seen. With the kids watching, he'd immediately stripped off the plain white socks he'd been wearing and donned the new ones, sending Tawnya into a paroxysm of giggles and prompting Ty to dare him to wear them to church Sunday. "*Not gonna happen, kid,*" he'd assured his son, but was secretly tossing the idea around. The kids, all of them, had had little enough laughter in their lives for too long, maybe he'd surprise them. He'd probably never live it down among the congregation; those socks would liven things up when he knelt at the alter for communion, but one of life's simple lessons that he felt he'd been remiss in teaching the kids was the ability to laugh at oneself.

Maybe he'd get a ration of teasing about the socks, he didn't particularly care. His children were overdue for some silliness and laughter in their lives, and this, as well as proper nutrition, adequate clothing, and a secure home, were things he would see to.

The gifts they'd shared this Christmas hadn't been expensive, weren't the latest and greatest, but it hadn't mattered in the least. Their family had been together in front of the lovingly-decorated tree, had eaten uninspired store-bought Christmas goodies washed down with scorched cocoa, and opened packages containing gift certificates for barnyard car-washes and for meals at Alpine Burger. Simple things. It had been the best Christmas in years.

Christmas dinner would be the highlight of the day. The memory of their humble Thanksgiving fare had prompted Scott to come up with a meal plan. It wasn't going to be fancy, but it sure wasn't going to be tomato soup and tuna.

Any idiot could bake a ham; that was the gist of the impression he'd gotten from the gal at the meat counter at Harvest Foods, and he'd desperately wanted to believe her. When, tongue in cheek, he's asked for the any-idiot-guarantee, she'd laughed and taken pity on him, helped him select a plump, pink ham, and suggested draping pineapple slices over the ham, hold them in place with whole cloves and basting frequently. She'd also suggested canned yams with marsh-mallows, scalloped potatoes and a vegetable as sides, maybe a Jell-O salad, with heat-and-serve dinner rolls, and had walked the aisles with him, helping him make his selections. He'd come out with a loaded shopping cart, complete with bakery-prepared pumpkin and apple pies, whipping cream, a gallon of eggnog and, with memories of childhood Christmases fueling his shopping frenzy, five pounds of assorted nuts and huge tubs of divinity and peanut brittle.

There was a feast befitting a king awaiting them; all that remained was the daunting process of rendering the contents of the assorted boxes and cans into something the king and his consorts could safely consume.

Celeste would know. She'd be able to walk into his mother's kitchen (he still, after all this time, tended to think of it as belonging in equal parts to his mom and Rachel) and make sense of the confu-sion that filled his refrigerator shelves and countertops. He could see her there, had had the picture in his mind for several weeks, and had been on the verge of calling her so many times he'd lost count. In the end, though, he hadn't been able to summon up the courage to make the call, and now Christmas morning had arrived and he still hadn't reached out to her.

The food was just the means to an end. While he couldn't deny that he would welcome her presence in the kitchen, he readily acknowledged that he could eat saltines with Cheez-Whiz and be happy about it as long as she was with them. Thus, the plan had been devised, and he was hopeful that she'd be sharing Christmas dinner with them later that afternoon. All he had to do was convince her that he was hopelessly inept and in imminent peril of subjecting his children to food poisoning. *Shouldn't be that hard to pull off,* Scott mused; someone who'd accidentally put buttermilk into instant tapioca pudding and then mistaken salt for sugar shouldn't be allowed within shouting range of the kitchen. Now, that had been a fiasco; even Skip had turned up his nose at the gelatinous mess, and Skip was renowned for his indiscriminating appetite. The dog who cheerfully consumed gophers and dead birds in quantities available (not to mention the occasional horse biscuit) had backed away from his dish, lip curled in disgust, and returned to his mat with the long-suffering mien of St. Stephen the Martyr.

Silly mutt had the memory of an elephant; he examined his food with a wary and distrustful eye to this day.

Skip could rest easy today; any table scraps coming his way would be safe. Ana and Tori were active participants in the plot and would be joining them for dinner, and dinner had been relegated, with great relief on Scott's part, to the capable hands of Ana and the two girls. All that remained was to do his level best to mend fences with Celeste, then convince her to join them for dinner.

Seeing that he'd done such a bang-up job of tearing down the fence in the first place, he had serious doubts about whether he possessed the tools and skills capable of rebuilding that fence. Sometimes the old boards became warped and the wire rusty, and the only thing you could do was junk the lot of it and start fresh with new. But you never knew, until you examined the material in question, what condition it was in. Quality accounted for a lot of it; if you'd started with something solid and true, more times than not it was sturdy enough to withstand the rigors of rebuilding. Sometimes you even ended up with a better fence than you'd had before.

Christmas Day. An odd time to be mending fences, but if he'd been a cattleman and had fence down and livestock at risk, it wouldn't matter what day it was, he'd have tended to the problem. He'd have gone in pursuit of the missing stock, regardless of temperature or conditions, returned them to security, and then made sure the repairs were done with care and dedication, making sure the fence would hold this time.

Christmas Day, and the most important rebuild of his life awaited.

"I'm out of here," he called in the general direction of the kitchen. Tawnya's voice rose above the clatter within, "Good luck, Daddy." Ty appeared at the top of the stairs, nodded in affirmation, and said, "Go get her, Dad."

He slid his feet into warm boots, shrugged into his winter coat, and donned the new gloves Santa had left for him. If he'd taken more care than usual with his morning routine, applied a liberal amount of the spicy new aftershave he'd found in his stocking, he just considered it a bit of old-fashioned Dutch courage. Of course, this particular Dutch courage came in a different sort of bottle than the traditional sort, but he had both bases covered; there was another bottle, filled with sparkling cider, chilling in the fridge. If all went well, if the boards were salvageable and the nails true, they'd be breaking out that other bottle this afternoon.

He cast a long glance around the warmth and comfort of the living room, sparkling tree, and garlands festooning the banister; perhaps this would be the last Christmas they'd spend in this old house. It was his hope that it would be.

He left the warmth of the house behind him and set out into the crisp morning. It would be colder yet at the lake, but with any luck they wouldn't be there long.

He gunned the engine and set out to bring home the one stray whose value was beyond measure. With the Lord's help, she'd enter the protection of the lovingly reconstructed enclosure of his heart willingly, believing in the builder's dedication and commitment to solidity.

If Ana was correct, Celeste would be at the lake about now, developing a mind's-eye picture of her future. With a little bit of luck, and a little help from above, that future would include him and two others who waited in the warmth of the home their father had grown up in. More than anything, certainly more than he deserved, he was counting on that loyal heart of hers to include them in the big picture. He whispered a prayer and left the situation in the hands of the One who knows the secret-most desires of our hearts; the rest would be up to himself.

Chapter 30

The arctic cold snap that had burst frozen pipes, left road surfaces treacherous with black ice and, Celeste guessed, had frozen the Batmobile's alternator, had also left Carrot Lake with a good eighteen inches or better of thick, air-bubbled ice, stretching the length and breadth of the lake. It was a rare sight, as there had been no snow during this bout of cold weather, another anomaly for December in the Cascades, but the lack of snow made it possible to walk well out onto the frozen surface of Carrot Lake and marvel at nature's immaculate winter blanket. The sun hadn't presented itself today, and the sky was a unique shade of winter-white. A snow sky. It would be nice to have snow on Christmas, perhaps make the day more festive, and certainly brighten Ana and Tori's overall experience away from the traditional Christmas rains of Seattle. Not that they'd particularly care today; they'd both come down with the flu sometime between Christmas Eve service and this morning, which meant Celeste's own social calendar had opened up. Under the circumstances, she was in no hurry to return to the quiet solitude of Mother's house.

Her visit to Mother had been encouragement in and of itself; Mother had asked right off the bat, immediately after Christmas greetings had been exchanged, about the Batmobile's well-being. She'd insisted that Scott would know what to do, would Celeste get him over to the house to look at it? With an ache in her heart as thick as the ice she now stood on, she'd made the promise. Having had some time to mull the situation over, she now realized that she had a perfectly viable excuse to call him. Perhaps Mother, and the Batmobile, had come up trumps.

Hands deep in the pockets of her coat, she took an experimental slide on the ice. Unencumbered by snow, conditions were perfect for ice skating, and she wondered where her old skates had ended up. The garage, probably. Maybe she'd take a look out there, see if she couldn't find them. Maybe she and Ana could get the girls together in a couple of days, bring them out skating; a thermos of hot chocolate and a log fire on the bank. Hot dogs and s'mores. A winter picnic. The first of many, hopefully.

Lost in her thoughts, she didn't see the truck approaching, and the sound of the door slamming shut carried through the icy air like a gunshot. She whirled around and he was there, at the edge of the lake, still as an ice statue. Heart pounding in her chest, mouth dry as the Mojave in mid-August, she stilled, unable to force movement into her feet, watching him pick his way over the ice toward her. Why was he here? Had something happened to Mother? No, she'd just left Fircrest herself; there hadn't been time to try to reach her and then remember the family connection and contact Scott. So why was he here? She pulled her disjointed thoughts together and resolved to remain as cool as the ice below her feet, let him do the talking.

But he was here now, and all of the longing of the days and nights since he'd sent her away returned in an avalanche of pain and longing. He must have come looking for her, tracked her down. But why, and why now, today?

He paused about ten feet from her, stood awkwardly for a moment, then found his voice, "Hi."

"Hi." So far so good. If she were lucky, he'd never know how her heart threatened to beat clear through the down parka she'd bundled into.

"Merry Christmas."

Celeste nodded. "Merry Christmas to you too."

Well, so much for the pleasantries. If he'd thought of it in time, he could have brought along the kitchen tongs; he hadn't figured on having to yank the words out of himself.

"So, how've you been?"

"I'm fine. And you? How are the kids?"

"Oh, we're all fine, thanks."

"That's good." This was ridiculous. Surely he hadn't come all the way out here to exchange the type of polite banter she'd expect from a nervous client, especially on Christmas Day. Suddenly, impatient with the whole situation, she asked, "Not to be rude, Scott, but what do you want? I mean, it's Christmas and this has got to be about the last place you'd want to be right now. Let's just cut to the chase and you can get back to your family."

So this is the way it's going to play out, he thought. She was about as chilly as the icicles hanging from the eaves on the farmhouse, and every bit as sharp. Well, okay, it's not like she doesn't have good reason, but it sure wasn't making it any easier for him to find the words. After a couple of false starts, exasperated and clammy with nerves, he said, "I came out here to invite you to dinner. No, that's not true. I mean, I did want you to come to dinner, I *do* want you to come, but…This isn't coming out right."

Celeste quirked an eyebrow. "Maybe just say it the way you practiced in the truck on the way over. That used to help me when I had to make a presentation at work."

Scott smiled, a mirthless smile that barely tipped the corners of his lips. "That might work for words you say to a bunch of people you don't really care about, but this is different. I'm afraid I won't find the right words or put them in right order. And maybe I'll say them and it won't matter anyway. That's what scares me the most."

"I've never known you to be afraid of anything."

"If that's true, I must be a pretty good actor, because it seems like that's all I've been lately. Scared. Scared about almost everything in my life. Scared to make a decision about Rachel, scared about how the kids were holding up. Scared that I've lost you, because I was too scared to admit how much I loved you. How much I do love you. I've been scared plenty, still am. Maybe it's too late to be saying this to you, Celeste, but I've come to realize that being scared and being a coward are two different things, and that if I didn't get past being scared and tell you how much I love you, how sorry I am, I wouldn't just be a coward, I'd be a fool."

Taking a deep breath, he continued, "How am I doing? The way this is coming out, all my rehearsals were a waste of time because this doesn't sound anything like what I'd planned to say."

Her voice was so soft he had to strain to hear her. "You're doing just fine."

Meeting her gaze straight-on, he said, "I'm sorry for the way I treated you that night in the barn. I want you to know that, Celeste, for what it's worth. I stood there listening to myself and couldn't believe those words were coming out of my mouth. It's taken awhile, but I think I finally have my head on straight, or as straight as it's gonna get. I know how badly I hurt you. I'm sorry, Celeste, so sorry I don't think there're words that can tell you how much, and not just because of the things I said. I guess I wanted to keep all the pain and grief and guilt for myself. I shut you out when you needed someone to mourn with, and I'm sorrier than I can say."

His words had come in a great rush, and when he fell silent, Celeste closed the distance between them. "It's okay, Scott. It was a bad night, just about the worst night on record, but it's over now. I've had a lot of time to think, too, and I owe you an apology for putting pressure on you."

"Pressure?"

"Expecting more than you could give. I sat at my sister's funeral and found myself wondering how her death would affect our relationship, how long until things got back to 'normal' between us. What does that say about me?"

Shaking his head, he advised, "Give it up, Celeste. The guilt, being angry with yourself, all of it. Let it go. It's the only way I was able to see things for what they are, that I'd come to love you harder, stronger, than I had a right to."

They stood silently, boot to boot and heart to heart, already with a lightening of the burden they'd each carried in the past weeks.

It was time. Scott took Celeste's mittened hands in his own, a hint of a smile in his eyes and said, "To risk hiding behind talking about the weather, I'm gonna say that it's way too cold to be standing out here much longer, Celeste, so I'm going to say my piece and then hopefully I can talk you into coming to dinner. Okay." The smile slipped from his face and he spoke in utter sincerity. "If you've ever believed a word I've said to you, believe that I love you very much. Believe that it's possible for lightning to strike pretty close to the same place twice. I loved Rach, and I love you, Celeste, and the fact that you were sisters is just a good indication that God has a sense of humor too.

"We stood over on that bank one night and you asked me and the kids to share your life. I'm asking you now to share our lives, if you'll have us. If you'll have *me*. I'm not going to promise that it's all gonna be sunshine and roses, 'cause we both know we'll have some obstacles to overcome. I came out here today to mend fences, so to speak, and I came to build a bridge as well; one that will take us from where we've been, with regard to Rachel, to a place that'll be just ours. If you'll have me."

The breath she hadn't realized she'd been holding escaped her lips and the tears she hadn't been aware were building slid down her cheeks. She blinked her eyes, focused on their joined hands while she steadied herself, then raised her eyes to his. "I'll have you, Scott Parnell, in every way possible. I'll have you whether there's sunshine and roses or whether it's fifty below. I'll have the kids running the hot water tank empty and running me ragged, because I love them too. I'll have all of you right over there," pointing to where their rigs were parked, "and I'll love all of you with every breath I take, for Rach's sake, and for my own."

He pulled her into his arms, and they rocked together, hot tears mingling on their cheeks. "I was so afraid you'd tell me what I could do with my fence *and* my bridge, and I wouldn't have blamed you if you had."

"And I was so afraid you hated me, that I'd have to live the rest of my life hoping to run into you in town and being afraid that I *would*."

They chuckled, then Celeste stilled for a moment, pulled away slightly, and lifted her face to the sky as tiny snowflakes swirled downward. "It's snowing, Scott! It's going to be a white Christmas after all."

"It's gonna be a great Christmas."

She moved into his embrace again, tipping her face up to his. "So, what's for dinner?"

"Oh, ham, sweet potatoes, a little bit of this and a little bit of that."

"I was supposed to have dinner with Ana and Tori, but they have the flu. Ana called earlier and sounded horrible."

"Well, uh, actually, they're not sick, in fact, they're probably out at the house by now."

"They aren't sick?"

"No, I just hedged my bets a little; I figured I had half a chance at getting you to come to dinner if your plans had fallen through, so I called and invited them too. Truth be told, I got down on bended knee and begged Ana to take over cooking dinner."

Celeste landed a teasing shove to Scott's shoulder. "You're horrible! Inviting somebody to your house for Christmas and saying, 'Oh, by the way, would you mind *cooking* dinner?' I can see I've got my work cut out for me, teaching you how to behave in civilized society!"

"Yeah, well, you can laugh; you didn't have the Thanksgiving we did. I wasn't taking any chances for Christmas dinner."

"What did you do for Thanksgiving? I wanted to invite you and the kids but just couldn't quite get up the nerve."

"We had a lovely meal of tomato soup and tuna sandwiches, with dill pickles as a side dish and tapioca pudding that even the dog wouldn't eat, for dessert. We didn't actually *have* it for dessert, but that was the plan. Long story. "

"I can see why you were willing to take a risk for Christmas. I'm sorry I didn't have the gumption to make the call on Thanksgiving."

"Me too. I sat by the phone for days up until that morning, when I finally figured out you weren't going to call."

"Next year," Celeste promised, "We'll have Thanksgiving right over there in our new house with turkey and all the trimmings."

"And one year from today, we'll look out our living room window to where we're standing and remember being out here in the cold, making a new start and freezing our noses off." He looped an arm around her shoulders. "Come on, let's head back. I want to kiss you something terrible and I'm afraid we'll end up frozen together out here. I suppose we'd better think about heading back to the house before they send out a search party."

Like a child, Celeste extended her tongue, capturing snowflakes on the tip. Closing her eyes, allowing Scott to guide her over the ice, it was as if the years had melted away and she was a child again; the wonder and anticipation of Christmas filling her heart, snowflakes gently pelting her face, and the sheer pleasure of knowing that she had another full week of freedom before school resumed. Instead of a week's vacation from school, though, today she had the promise of a lifetime with the man she loved. Joy brought a giddiness to her spirit and a gleam of mischief to her eyes, and with a sideways glance, she asked, "Do you remember the first time we met, Scott? "

With an exaggerated groan, he replied, "How could I forget? I wanted to impress Rachel with my wheels and macho-ness and ended up having to bring her little sister along for the ride. And you about talked my ear off, and Jim's, too! Some first date, huh?"

"Hey, I was ten years old; what did I know? I just remember thinking I was hot stuff, hanging out with a couple of high school guys. I remember we brought a bunch of cookies we'd just baked and Mother pitched a fit, but for once Rach just blew her off and told her that the two of us would bake some more later in the afternoon. And we did. It was a great day."

"Yeah, it was. You *did* manage to cramp my style, though. Here I was, trying to show Rach a good time and she ended up standing on the bank watching me take you out on the ice instead."

They shared a laugh at the memory, then Celeste met his eyes somewhat shyly. "Did you know that I told Rachel I was going to marry you when I grew up?"

"Serious? No, I never heard about that. When was this?

"The night of your prom. I waited up until she got home, I wanted to hear all about it. I'd never seen her look as beautiful as she did in her formal that night."

Scott nodded. "Yeah, she was. It was the night I told her I loved her for the first time."

With a sigh, Celeste adopted a mock pout and said, "She didn't tell me that. I would have been seriously jealous."

"So what did she say when you announced your intentions as far as marrying me?"

Celeste grinned. "She said, 'Get in line.'"

He grinned, then threw back his head and laughed. Struck by the humor, the improbability of the whole situation, she began to laugh as well. After laughing himself into a coughing jag, hand supporting a stomach that ached from mirth, Scott said, "Well, she sure called that one, didn't she? I'll bet she's up in heaven laughing right along with us."

Softly, Celeste replied, "Yeah, I'll bet you're right."

They shared a gaze filled with love and understanding, then he said, "Well, are you ready to head home?"

Celeste grinned. "If we have a few minutes, I'm having an appetite for donuts again, and I promise these won't spoil my appetite."

He opened the truck's passenger door with a flourish and said, "Buckle up."

They sat for a few minutes while the engine warmed, listening to holiday music on the radio and indulging themselves in the simple joy of being together. As the last chorus of "I'll Be Home For Christmas" faded away, Scott shifted into gear, paused, searched Celeste's eyes with his own, and asked, "Is Rach riding shotgun, Celeste?"

With a slow nod, Celeste replied, "She'll probably always ride shotgun, Scott; she's too much a part of our lives to expect that we can leave her on the bank all the time. I don't think we'd want to, anyway, you know? Especially for the kids' sakes. I think we'll have to learn to set boundaries with Rach, for our *own* sakes." She paused, smiled, and said, "Starting now. This ride is just for us."

He reached for her hand, gave it a squeeze, and said, "I love you."

"And I love you."

Popping the clutch, Scott set the truck into motion, descending onto the ice slowly, steadily, gaining distance from the frozen bank and increasing speed until they'd reached the middle of the lake. "Hang on." With a quick turn of the wheel, the truck spun to the left as if it had sprouted wings, Celeste's delighted shriek splitting the air. Around and around they spun, until their sides ached from laughter.

As if preordained, the jagged shards of Scott's life fell into immaculate precision. His love for Rach, and the children born of that love, conjoined now with the life they'd share with Celeste, all meshed seamlessly into a jigsaw puzzle in which the final two pieces completed the greater picture of the life that awaited them.

Christmas, the season of miracles. The season that brought renewed hope for peace on earth, one heart at a time.

Scott caught Celeste's hand in his. "Ready?"

She nodded. "Ready."

The old truck jolted to life, and they began the journey to the ones who waited in the old farmhouse, the first leg of the journey home. Snow fell gently onto the ground that would soon be broken for the new house; a blanket of white as pure as a new beginning, gathering in the boughs of the stately pines that would shelter them through the storms of life. Carried along on the north wind, perhaps on the wings of a prayer, came a song of peace that sighed through those same trees.

The land slept and dreamed under its mantle of white, waiting to fulfill the dreams of those who would come to send down new roots in its soil. There was stillness in the falling snow, a stillness born of peace in this tiny corner of the earth.

New hope and new beginnings; tiny blessings disguised as snowflakes falling from the sky. In a cozy farmhouse on the other side of town, these things were the cause of celebration.

And all around, the silent snow continued to fall.